I0659269

CHRISTOPHER MORLOCK's

F O U L
TERRITORY

FOUL TERRITORY

The Chronicle of Calvin Connor, Vol. 2.

CHRISTOPHER MORLOCK

The Foul Territory Publishing Co.
Pennsylvania, United States of America
www.foulterritory.com

Colophon

This text, the story, all characters and situations © 2024 Christopher M. Morlock. All rights reserved.

Cover image "Baseball, Fallen, Accessory" (CC0) 2015 Laila Juliana. To the extent possible under law, Laila Juliana has waived all copyright and related or neighboring rights to "Baseball, Fallen, Accessory."
https://www.pixabay.com/en/users/lailajuliana-536040/

Scripture texts in this work are taken from the *New American Bible, revised 2nd edition* © 1986, 1970 Confraternity of Christian Doctrine, Washington, D.C. and are used by permission of the copyright owner. All rights reserved.

No part of this book may be reproduced, exchanged, transmitted, or recorded in any form or by any electronic or mechanical means, whether extant or yet to be invented, including but not limited to information recording and retrieval systems and audio performances captured on recorded media or broadcast on streaming services, without permission in writing from the author, except by a critic who may quote brief passages in a critical analysis of the work.

Foul Territory is a work of fiction. Names, characters, places, histories, institutions, products, sports franchises, incidents, and other entities are the product of the author's imagination or have been used fictitiously, and any resemblance to actual persons (living or dead), locales, events, school districts, business concerns, happenings, and other points of reality is entirely coincidental.

NOTICE: do not attempt any stunts or activities portrayed in this novel. The author and publisher are not responsible for your actions or any resultant consequences of your actions.

Tip of the Axes' A cap to L.K.(S.)M.
Thanks for that original "bound" edition! It was totally meh.

3 4 5 6 7 8 9 10 11
First Foul Territory Publishing edition, February 2024.
ISBN-10: 099718082X
ISBN-13: 978-0997180824
e-book ISBN-10: 0997180838
e-book ISBN-13: 978-0997180831

For Dale.

Contents

Dramatis Personae

Axsubeen High School Students

The Suicide Kings
The Irish Raging Ape—Calvin Ciarán Connor III, 16.
Art—Arthur Aganju Maguire, 16.
Ryan—Ryan Daniel Phillips, 15.
Spazz/Liam—William Lloyd Watson, 17.

The Cable-Knit Cardi Girls
Kitty—Kathryn Amelia Howe, 16.
Abby—Abagail Jessica Malone, 16.
Sigourney—Cindy McKee, 15.
Roni—Veronica Lynn Vogel, 16.

The Scoundrels
the little wanker—Sean David Corgan, 16.
Davey—Brion Kenneth Davey, 18.
Reggie—DeReginold Raymond Roberts, 15.
Chicken—Cuauhtémoc Panos Ysderrhi, 17.

The Mall Chicks
Kare—Karen Marie McGillicutty, 16.
Stephanie—Stephanie Anne Millar, 17.
Jill—Jillian Jane Pedersen, 15.
Rayche—Rahel Marion Schultz, 16.
Jenny—Jennifer Lynn MacDonald, 16 (excommunicated).

Other teenagers
Val—Valerie Crenshaw, 17.
Saint Mark—Mark Duffy (of Bishop Guilfoyle High), 17.
Gus—Augustus Jacoby, 14.
Paddy—Padraig Millar, 18.
Jon—Jon Oldroyd, 16.
Shelley—Michelle Quince, 17.

Grown-ups & Family

The Connors
Da—Calvin Ciaran Connor II, 40.
Ma—Eileen Connor, née Eadaoin Ní Dubhthaigh, 38.
Robbie—Robert Críostóir Connor, 18.
Rose—Rosaleen Sorcha Connor, 17.

The Howes
Daddy—Eric Howe, 41.
Mom—Gudrun "Judy" Howe, née Schultz, 40.
Eddie—Edward Mark Howe, 18.

Baseball coaches
Lucky—Richard Louis Cheeseboro, 44.
Gym Teacher Man—Francis Paul Falcone, 35.
Skip/Sergeant Slaughter—Perry Phillips, 60.
Sheriff Steve—Stefan Schultz V, 40.

Other adults
the little man—Vincent Bachner, esq., 41.
Mr. Bown—Algernon Bown Jr., 57.
Doc—Claudius Jacoby, D.O. (Gus's dad), 43.
Mr. Maguire—Paul Maguire (Art's dad), 42.
Mrs. Maguire—Annie Maguire (Art's mom), 39.
Fartin' Martin—Principal Roger Martin, 52.
Kimmy—Kimberly McSween/Pedersen (Jill's momma), 35.
Father Sean—The Very Reverend Sean O'Coyle, S.S.P.X., 62.

(ages listed are as of Opening Day, March 16, 1989)

No A.I. was used in the creation of this novel.
It is, in its entirety, the product of a human being.

Chapter 1

WHAT IF FAY WRAY WASN'T HOME THAT DAY?
THURSDAY, JANUARY 26, 1989.

FOUL

A FIT FELLA WITH feathered hair and a fat flavor-saver ejaculated his safe sex platitude onto twenty young faces: "Only a fool fools around." The tenth-graders sat open-mouthed but none swallowed it. They were all, like, *Gag me!*

All but one. Calvin Connor was the very fool Mr. Falcone talked about. Young Calvin had fooled around. Three whole times. With two girls (not at the same time, sigh). Once, he even used a condom.

… not that time.

You know which time the chronicler means—*that* time, when the whole goddamn world saw Calvin and Jenny MacDonald beasting with two backs on Sean Corgan's front lawn during his Halloween party.

"Premarital sex isn't worth it," Mr. Falcone spurted. Spurted at Calvin, deliberately singling him out. Of all the kids in fourth period Health, Calvin was the only confirmed nonvirgin.

"Too right, Mr. Falcone," he spat, "premarital sex's a sin now."

A snigger from behind him. "Apes can't sin, they don't got souls."

"Miss Pedersen, that's enough," said Mr. Falcone.

Calvin silently thanked the man. Jill Pedersen was still upset that he'd dumped her in seventh grade (and, unlike her, was over it). He treated her less like a girl and more like one of the lads, a pal to prank. She treated him with public contempt. Her purple eye shadow did nothing to hide those psychotic hateful eyes.

It was Jill who'd christened Calvin "the Irish Raging Ape." The name stuck instantly, summing up his faults: ungainly foreignness, aggressive nature, hulking stature. He'd proudly defied the usual slate of *Breakfast Club* stereotypes—neither hunk, babe, nerd, jock, slut, prude, skater, dork, airhead, tomboy, nor tard Calvin be—so Jill Pedersen created a new category just for him.

Skaters were adroit, cool, had soulful brown eyes. Irish Raging Apes were clumsy dorks whose steel gray eyes crushed souls underfoot.

Chicks got awed when jocks did the crab pose, flexing big biceps and splitting the sleeves of their pastel Ocean Pacific T-shirts. Chicks got annoyed when the crabby brass clasp on an Irish Raging Ape's webbed Chess King belt failed to keep his Bugle Boys above the split of his butt-crack.

Hunks roamed Axsubeen High's halls charming girls and decking underclassmen. Irish Raging Apes harmed the walls by accidentally hip-checking girls into lockers like the blundering-ass men they were.

Yet the Irish Raging Ape—yes, *this* Irish Raging Ape—had gotten lucky. This Ape porked. He had boffed. He had had coition. Forsooth, ye olde Irish Raging Ape had e'en done the humpty hump. All the skaters, jocks, and hunks ever did was strike a pose and jerk the gherkin.

"Unprotected premarital sex is bad," said Mr. Falcone, brushing the embarrassment of teaching Sex. Ed. off his back-bacon mustache.

Listen to this shite, thought Calvin. *Can't take it anymore!*

Two and a half years left to graduation, then Calvin could tell Gym Teacher Man here to kiss his arse. And Principal Fartin' Martin, and Mr. Hussing with his Algebra tests, and the Scoundrels, a crew of jocks whose buzzcuts had hair-scrotums (scrotæ?) dangling pendulous over the backs of their necks.

The Scoundrels actually wore their hair like that. On purpose.

Screw Axsubeen. I am sooo outta here.

Future-Calvin would not stay here. He would *not* end up like his parents, with a boring job and boring cars and a boring house in a boring burg. Future-Calvin was miles away. Lookin' smooth, leaning on his red Lamborghini Countach. Lookin' hot at Muscle Beach, sculpted pecs rippling under a neon green crop-top mesh. Lookin' cool on *Club MTV* dancing under amber-gelled PARcans, his Ray-Bans kicking star-flares away like Luke Skywalker deflecting blaster bolts with his lightsaber.

Future-Calvin's gonna rule the world.

"Let's touch on the phallus," said Mr. Falcone. His hand, the blocky sort that could wear out a sinew-sharpening squeezy-spring thingy after a week, pumped the overhead projector's ON switch 'til a long erect lens sprayed a white vignette over the wall.

Fetching some transparencies, Gym Teacher Man made a wire-frame boner dance over the cinder blocks, setting off a dozen gag reflexes. "Settle down, class. Okay, this here's the urethra … and that there's the dartos … and this's the scrotum."

I'd give my prepuce to be anywhere else.

A different projector threw smoky red images on the ceiling mirror of the lad's libido. Real flesh, not Falcone's kielbasa cutaway. Bewbs. Muff. None of that NC-17 crap; this flick's rated X, baby.

Dream-Calvin whammed Lisa De Leeuw, bammed Madonna, then thank-you-ma'am'ed that babe from *Mischief.* All were rendered in 3-D: he saw their Skene's glands, he heard their heart hyperactivity, he felt their filliped lobules.

Real girls came next. A fun-size dyed-red girl on a lake shore, the clip in 4-D—he tasted the Camp Souviens reservoir lapping against the lass's left labium minus. Then a blonde bunny way out of his league on a McMansion lawn under a full moon. This one was 5-D—he smelt the mulched lawn clippings as they chafed his dartos.

Cut to a new memory, hours old: a fellow sophomore mounting the school bus. Actual-Calvin sat near the back but Editor-Calvin zoomed in as the girl bobbed down the aisle. With a twist of the FWD-REV knob, he made the girl's boobs bounce up and down under her cardigan. He added a hot sax cue and keyed in a new background, dark, private … like backstage at the auditorium. Sure. Him and the girl cozied up between those vertical ropes with the wooden throw-switches for the backdrops. Whatever they're called. The kids fit snuggly there. Very snuggly. Dream-Calvin borrowed the black Ray-Bans from Future Calvin's costume (though certain rich kids like Sean Corgan owned them, Present-Day-Calvin couldn't afford that shite). The Ray-Bans kept banging frames with the girl's cheap pink shades.

Editor-Calvin made her hot breath cinnamony. The Big Red jingle came to mind. The commercial interruption snapped his mental movie, the reel going 'round and around, a celluloid tail flapping his mug.

Another laugh from behind him. Calvin (and everyone else)

wheeled to glare. Jill Pedersen, the prissy prude in perpetual purple, popped a paw over her puss to prevent further peals.

"Miss Pedersen, how many times I gotta tell you?" Mr. Falcone said from his overhead projector. "The testes are no laughing matter."

The whole class roared at her, but Calvin made sure his booming guffaw bit hardest. He knew about Jill's mortal shyness regarding sex. That's why the Mall Chick never showed up in the lad's highlight reel: Miss Pedersen wasn't that kind of girl. *Waaay* too starchy for shtupping.

At the head of the classroom, the beefcake dude with the clitoral tickler fingered a new transparency into place, that of a crude cooch, then babbled dryly about the vagina's natural lubricating function.

"Jaysus," said Calvin. An unironic Catholic, he used the spectacles-testicles-wallet-watch gesture to slyly check his pits for B.O.

Jaysus would understand.

Both hands on Calvin's Swatch stood straight up; Health was nearly over. Time to meet that smiling, curvy cardigan lass who was on his bus this morning. The girl of his dreams (this month, anyway).

He had never spoken to her, not once in his whole life, despite sharing classes in prior years and seeing her on his bus every Thursday morning and attending the same 9 a.m. Sunday Mass at Saint Brigid. Considering Keillor's First Law of Small Town Dynamics—"everyone knows everyone else"—Calvin's chance with Kitty was handicapped. She'd have heard of him, of course, of his famous Raging Ape boner foibles. She might take his lifelong distance as a judgment and be like, "Suddenly you're interested? Now that I'm developing?"

Tough starting spot.

In baseball terms (which Calvin didn't know [yet] [still!]), it was like starting an at-bat already down 0–2.

"Labia," Falcone said, needing half an hour for all three syllables.

"Great flick," said jokestress Roni Vogel. *"Lawrence of My Labia!"*

Unlike some teen boys, Calvin wasn't afraid to try with girls, or try again. He struck out on most first contacts, sure, and now had tons of female "friends" asking to copy homework, except for his Algebra. But once, a first contact led to a girlfriend, twice. (It was complicated.)

First contacts succeeded with confidence, not nerves. Smoothness, not desperation. He had a rep to disprove: Calvin Connor III was not an Irish Raging Ape, but independent, rugged, awesome.

He did a full S.P.E.D. review:

(S)low. Speed brings clumsiness. Move slow. Talk slow.

(P)osture. Be loose. Only dweebs use two hands on books. One paw on the Trapper Keeper, the other tucked away. And no pocket hockey!

(E)yes. Eye contact's important. (Well. Some may argue it wasn't necessary this time, but it was. You never know who's watching.)

(D)eodorize. The big one. The Ape sweated a lot—and not sexily, like a buff dude working out in a Miller Lite ad. Calvin's sweating got him nervous of smelling unsexy, which made him sweat more ... an endless wheel of stank.

"When the man deposits sperm in the woman's vagina," splooged Gym Teacher Man, "it's called, 'in·SEMM'·eh·NAY·shin.'"

"That's my favorite nation," cracked jokester Reggie Roberts.

The bell rang.

The Irish Raging Ape bullied out the classroom ahead of the other tenth-graders like King Kong busting through a line of Black Marias.* In the hallway, he forced himself to a saunter. Saunters drew fewer eyes, caused fewer collisions, and produced less sweat.

He reached the cafeteria but couldn't find Kitty Howe. *C'mon, she was on the bus just this morning!* He could've set his watch by Kitty's punctuality: she got in the lunch queue at 12:01 on the nose, every day.

Today of course, the day of first contact of course, she was late.

He checked his Swatch again. He wore the White Window model, which, as the name implied, was black. Every bit of it black: band, hands, everything ... *except* the day and date windows. Those were white, and the text inside the day one read THU.

Kitty normally took Axsubeen School District Bus No. 6 but on Thursdays she rode *his* bus, No. 10, cuz it made daily voyages in the mornings up State Rte. 666 to Altoona to ferry area kids to the Larsen Academy for Affluent Boys, Bishop Guilfoyle Catholic High, A.A. Vo-Tech, and, in Kitty's case, the Blair County Institute.

Where she attended classes every Thursday.

The Irish Ape got in the lunch queue and raged at himself.

---

* Police vans. Yanks, but not Calvin, call them *paddy wagons.*

Chapter 2

CHEESECAKE KILLS THE KHAKIS.
FRIDAY, JANUARY 27, 1989.

FOUL

BY HOMEROOM FRIDAY, EVERYONE knew.

Oh that's bollocks, most knew by the final bell Thursday. A phrase Calvin often heard at Art Maguire's weekly poker game was "tipping his hand." Yesterday, the lad had done just that. He'd stationed himself inside the cafeteria's door with a spiffy costume on and did all that watch-checking: waiting for a chick. Two hundred eyes saw him tip his hand. A hundred mouths below those eyes got to flappin'. Only the most hermitic won't have gotten wind by the time he got on the bus today.

Ma called his exact hole cards: K♥ Q♥. "Making yourself beautiful for some slut again?" she said, thumbing the wardrobe pre-arranged atop her son's messy desk: crisp khakis and a kelly green silk shirt.

"Bugger off, Ma!" Alone of the four bedroom doors, Calvin's had no lock (removed for past transgressions). Ma came in his room all the time, especially first thing. He hated getting up, hated having to stand, bathe, transition from dream-hazy rest to people's shrill shite.

Eileen Connor said, "Better not be that MacDonald wench again."

Calvin Connor rolled over in bed and aimed his arse at her to issue the flatulent equivalent of "Blow me."

Ma smacked his cheeky cheeks. "Get that arse up 'fore I put a wallopin' on it! Should've sent you to private school, laddy, Larsen Academy. You need discipline!"

In short order the teenager stood in the tub, arrayed in cold droplets, hating life. The Connors' Usonian had exciting and warm sun streaking through the common rooms' slab glass walls, exciting and warm rows of red wood on the ceilings and floors, and exciting and warm corridors winding tight around stanchions of red brick, but only the one fucking tub and a hot water heater whose tank was a very unexciting 25 gallons. Da got up first and got the loo first, and Rose needed to go next—needed to, mind you, she was a senior after all—so the youngest child's shower seldom featured hot water or dry towels.

Dressed to impress in his *Club MTV* clothes, limpen hair slicked back again with a dab of Rose's gel, Calvin went to the front door closet to fetch his winter coat and repulsive scarf of many colors.

A freestanding wall of glass block, which shielded the sitting room from the front door, showed dozens of tiny Rose Connors approaching. The girl gave him an up-and-down. "I like how the green turns silver when the shirt creases," she said, "but it gives your belly a *huuuuge* outline. Don't spill crap on it! I hadda go all the way to Elephant & Rhino to find your 9XL Ape-size. And quit stealin' my L.A. Looks!" She shook her head at him. "Yer whole look screams, 'please do me.'"

"Better than saying 'please do me' aloud," said Calvin, "like *you* say to every boy going by."

"Guys like *you* say it to every boy, cuz you're fags."*

Rose popped her bubblegum and laughed simultaneously, a Mall Chick superpower.

He gnashed his teeth. "Stand-up comedy suits you, Sis. Better than lying on your back." He tried to block the way out.

Rose was much smaller and bounced herself off the glass block wall to carom past him out into Axsubeen's weenie-shrinking winter winds. She didn't ride the bus like him ("That's for little kids!"). Sometimes she drove her VW Beetle. Sometimes she got rides from senior boys. In exchange, the rumors went, for riding said boys.

On Bus No. 10, Art Maguire flopped on the vinyl bench seat next to him. Art *was* that little kid, despite being older than Calvin. Art had a license but rode the bus since his parents couldn't afford a car for him. The kid filled what space there was betwixt his narrow butt and the Ape's wide one with his usual prattle. "Lookin' all fly, Irish, two days in

---

* You'll see a lot of this talk in the chronicle's early volumes, especially from the kids; social norms were different in 1989. (If that bothers you, go fuck yourself.) Also, back then no one called L.A. Looks or the other shit Rose put in her hair *product*. It was *hairspray, mousse,* or *gel,* and if used by old men, *Brylcreem*.

a row. Who ya hard for?"

Thinking it clever, Calvin said, "Oh, you'll *see* now."

"Wow, so it's Kitty Howe? That's cool, brother."

Calvin elbowed him and turned away.

At his locker, the lad surreptitiously applied fresh Right Guard. He felt too hunky for homeroom. The rowdier guys whistled catcalls. Slutty Bon Jovi girls in denim jackets and crispy Aqua Netted curls made obscene half-joking offers. A lass pinched Calvin's ass.

As one more cake than beef, Calvin was unused to such attention. He played up to it by giving the girls a small bow.

'Twas to be his downfall: the Trapper Keeper slipped from his grasp. Its chintzy plastic binder rings opened on impact. Papers exploded in an upside-down mushroom cloud along the doo-doo brown/pus orange checkerboard tiles. Several handouts and F-graded Algebra tests fluttered back up to waist height, far out of Calvin's reach, then calmly zigzagged back to earth.

The Irish Ape got on hands and knees and raged at his fellow sophomores. None helped. Some gave a standing O, some kicked his notes further afield, one "accidentally" kept a British Knight on some handout's corner so he couldn't retrieve it. Homeroom minder Mr. Browne had taken roll by the time Calvin surfaced, flopping in his desk with papers cradled in both arms. Immediately the lad was obliged to stand back up, angling one occupied hand over his heart, for the Pledge of Allegiance.

As Principal Fartin' Martin read announcements over the P.A., Calvin re-sorted five months of schooling in five minutes of homeroom.

Jill Pedersen, seated in front of him, turned to give the Irish Raging Ape two shit-eating schadenfreude eyes drowning in indigo shadow.

One beefy hand left his precarious packet of pedagogy to present Jill with a middle finger, and he nearly dropped the lot all over again.

"She's gonna say 'No,' whoever she is," said Jill. "Girls like a nice shirt but hate getting crushed by clumsy Irish Raging Apes."

Spittle from her "Apes" landed on his hand. He clenched it shut, annihilating an old Social Studies quiz. Jill's embarrassment shone through her cheeks' amethyst blush and she whipped forward to hide.

Art, seated to Calvin's right, pointed at Jill's back and cupped a hand to his mouth as if to whisper. The pantomime meant, *Be nice to the Mall Chick who I got the hots for, or I tell her who you got the hots for.*

Calvin pointed at Jill's back then made his hand into a V and tongued an imaginary twat. *You mean Jill, the girl I ate out that one time?*

Reminding the blackmailer that the blackmailee had once gone down on the blackmailer's crush wasn't the best idea. Behind Art's gray glasses, his icy blue eyes blinked Morse code: *Okay dude, I'm tellin' her it's Kitty you want. Jill'll have a field day shitting on your plans. I'll probably score a blowjob as a reward.* (Or some such bollocks.)

Calvin signed back, *Once I make first contact with Kitty, everyone'll know. No time for that blowjob.*

And no chance, either. Art didn't seem to realize how one-sided his feelings for Jill were. *Never mind the blowjob, he'd be lucky to score a pat on the shoulder from her.*

That didn't stop the ticking clock Calvin had just put on things. Again, he'd tipped his hand. Art reached over to tap Jill's shoulder. To tell her here, now, right in front of him.

Calvin thwapped him with a Trapper folder. Art leaned back with a laugh and did his Lando Calrissian smile, like *I won't talk, trust me.*

The Apc's steel gray eyes glared at him.

Then, down at some Biology notes found amidst his Social Studies handouts. He wasn't in Biology. The title ("1/17/89 Reproduction") was written in blue ballpoint and traced over in red, a psychedelic swirl. All the I's were lowercase, dotted with hearts.

He stuffed the page in the Trapper's shite slot in the back.

"Try-outs are Monday for Axes baseball and softball. Run the bases for the brown-and-orange," Fartin' Martin said over the public address, reading the copy like a grocery list. "See Mr. Falcone or Mrs. Geoffries for details. Please bring proper footwear."

Calvin triumphantly slammed his Trapper shut. The flap didn't dig the extra bulk from his hasty reorganization and sprang open. He parked a big elbow on it to pin it down; the Velcro squealed in disapproval.

"Even your Trapper Keeper's fat," joked Jill without turning.

"Your lip'll be fat if you don't—"

The bell went off.

FOUL

The White Window Swatch insisted it was FRI. No sign of Kitty Howe in the cafeteria. She was late, again, for the first time.

Calvin Connor III stood by the queue, waiting. He was three days from joining the school ball team and four years from his MLB debut. This position—all eyes on him, alone on the mound, getting heckled after a bad curve—begged for a Major Leaguer's poker face. The Ape wore an anti-poker face: snarling at all the staring pricks.

It hadda be this way, though. At no point in Calvin's normal travel pattern did he pass Kitty Howe in the hallway. Lunch was their only common class. He saw her at Mass every Sunday, true, but her parents and older brother never left her side until Bible Study, when she joined the girls' class. He saw her on his bus every Thursday morning, but her best friend Abby Malone raced to share the seat.

Art told Jill, and Jill told Kitty to scare her off, thought Calvin. *Jill ruins everything. Art needs a thumping.* He checked his Swatch: a minute past noon. *Don't panic!* Today of course, the (second) day of first contact of course, Kitty—

—oh there she is.

Kitty and Abby got in the queue. Calvin fell in behind them. He immediately addressed that third wheel: "Hello, Malone."

Abby swiveled 'round to snarl. She and Calvin shared body types (Rubenesque, shall we say) but never got along. Abby called him "ugly," and he called her "half-melted" cuz her face was slanted.

It'd been a while since he was this close to her. Had Abby's mug yawed *further* to starboard? Both her eyes'll end up on one side, like those bottom-dweller fish the mulchies pull from the Axsubewa Crick!

Abby's slabby hand waved at Calvin's sharp *Club MTV* kit. "What's this, makeup on a pig?"

He spread his arms. *You don't like my style?*

Abby fell for it, locking blue eyes on his green shirt with its shiny metallic creases. Her slanted sneer slewed to spew a wicked comeback.

The timing was perfect: the queue crept forward behind her, and Kitty moved to keep up. Calvin zoomed over to fill the gap beside Kitty, left open by Abby's flat feet.

"Hey!" said Abby, swiveling front to shove Calvin out of her spot.

The Irish Raging Ape glared back at Melty's grabby slabby hands. Fear caught Abby's breath and she froze. The onlookers' laughed, flushing her in embarrassment, and she shriveled back.

His plan worked. He was next to his dream girl. *Now's your chance!*

"Hello there," Calvin said to Kitty.

Yelped, more like.

The lad's voice had dropped to a buttery smooth baritone soon to feature in worldwide ads for Guinness Stout and local spots for Lucky Cheeseboro GM–Chevrolet in bun·YOO′·tee·full al·TOO′·nah!!, but anxiety over this long-rehearsed, once-delayed first contact had reanimated the zombie of pre-teen Calvin's crackly whine.

Clearing his throat, he recited his next line all manly and stuff: "I'm Calvin Connor. I don't think we've met."

"Hello, Calvin," the lass said. Her voice was steady, measured, and deep for a teenage girl. A purr, one might say. "No, we haven't met. But I've heard of you. I'm Kitty."

You've "heard of me," eh? Lemme guess: the white hair, the Binaca affair, me and Jenny on the lawn at Corgan's that one time …

He had never been so close to Kitty and soaked her in. What a babe! She had alluring wispy attire that he wanted to remove, an innocence about her demeanor that he wanted to sully, and curves taking shape all over her body that he wanted to explore.

She wore her hair rather like Calvin (usually) did: limp and loose, bereft of those '80s-defining cemented-down bangs and gravity-defying hairsprayed tufts. No spiky bits on one side or flappy scrotæ down the back. Just straight curtains. Kitty's russet tresses splayed off her thick shoulders and glistened in the caf's gross fluorescence. Her acne-free, freckle-free teenage face was all wide smiling cheeks, whether she was smiling or not. Hot pink glasses hid her eyes; in the dark lenses, Calvin Ciarán Connor III saw his horny-as-hell face.

He said, "Nice to meet you, Kitty."

She said, "Nice to meet you, too."

He recited the next line: "I like your cardi. Quite fetching, love."

He winced. "Love"—his *Alfie*-influenced pet name for girls—was definitely not in the script. Ad-libbing was a good way to crash the bloody Countach while it was still parked in the garage.

She didn't care about the "love," though. "Ugh, my cardi's ugly as sin!" she said. "What're you, blind?"

Abby Malone, stuck behind them and relegated to a mere witness, laughed her uncomely laugh. Calvin had never called Abby "love."

"My brother gets me the grubbiest clothes for Christmas," Kitty went on. "My mom makes me wear it. What's *his* sweater like?"

She said that last with no body cues to indicate she'd switched conversation partners: she didn't point a hand at Calvin or turn to direct the words over her shoulder.

Abby knew it was meant for her and didn't miss a beat. "The Irish Ragin' Ape's got a shirt on today, not a sweater. It's like a puke green."

"Neon green," Calvin sassed. "You'd hafta eat half a dozen Hi-Liters to puke up a green this bright, retard."

Sarcasm about vomitous hues made for fine japes with Art and the rest of the chaps in the Suicide Kings. During first contact with the girl of his dreams? Not the best spot. The lad's pits kicked on the taps to full hot and he prayed his Right Guard was up to the job.

"I like green," Kitty said, without any cue that she'd switched back to addressing Calvin. "Green's my favorite color, y'know."

Don't ask! Calvin ordered himself. *Everyone else would ask, and therefore you will not. You will be different from everyone else.*

His fat mouth opened to ask how Kitty could have a favorite color but she cut him off. "People think my favorite color's gotta be pink cuz I'm a girl," she said, "But green's awesome. I don't even need to ask what your favorite color is—you're Irish, so it's gotta be green."

Well.

She was right. And Calvin *was* Irish.

Not British, as a fair number of his stupid American classmates thought. Or worse—English. "Eh, it's all the same!" they dissed.

And Calvin's "Irish" meant "from Ireland," as in "born in County Kildare, moved to Pennsylvania aged ten," not "the great-grandson of some long dead immigrant and therefore automatically a Notre Dame fan." Axsubeen was riddled with such sham shamrocks, all these O'Ryans and Quinns and Conleys, who had never spent a coin with a harp on it, never watched *Anything Goes* on RTE 1, and never used the terms "shite" or "queue" or "boyo," not even ironically.

Calvin had done all that and gabbed constantly about it. It was a safe assumption on the lass's part that the lad was quite fond of green.

Yet some self-defense piston in Calvin's teenage nonconformity engine fired up to protest. "Why's it 'gotta be green?'" he said. "I'm half-American too. What if my favorite color's red, white, and blue?"

"Then your favorite color would be three colors," said Kitty.

"Would it surprise ya that Ugly here's flunkin' Math?" said Abby.

"Am not," said Calvin. "Don't make me flunk your face, Malone."

Realizing such ire wouldn't be attractive, he smiled at Kitty, all like *Only kidding, ha ha, I'd never flunk your best friend's already failing face!*

Realizing how stupid it was to communicate with Kitty by facial expression alone, he said aloud, "Only kidding, ha ha, I'd never—"

"—flunk Math?" Kitty supplied.

"Jaysus, I am NOT flunking math!" He crossed himself and ignored the girls' laughter. "My favorite color's green. Fine. I admit it. So what. And I'm actually not half-Irish but three-quarters."

"One-half, three-quarters," said Kitty. "Fractions are hard."

"Fractions equals math," said Abby. "Equals hard."

"My point was stereotypes now."

"Mine too," said Kitty. "We agree on that! I don't hafta automatically like pink just because I'm a girl."

"Hang on!" Calvin steered the Lambo off the pavement into the hedgerow of Ad-Lib Farms. "You hate that people stereotype you, but it's okay for you to stereotype me?"

"Is it a stereotype, or is it the truth?" Kathryn "Kitty" Howe stood encased in a shimmering yard-thick ray-shield of raw girl power. "Besides, double standards don't apply to girls. Duh!"

Simmering, the Ape fought a curious primal urge to curl down to match Kitty's eyeline, like he would when talking to a small child. He'd never done the like with his prior girlfriends, who, like Kitty, were all five-four-ish. (Calvin had a type.) "Well," he said, trying to sound cool with it all. "From now on I, uh, shall assume no standards apply to you."

"When you 'assume,' you make an arse out of you and me."

A second to digest that.

A single issuance of his booming guffaw.

It blasted across the caf like jovial thunder. Kitty had changed the cliché's American "ass" to his favored "arse," without ever previously suffering his pretentious British Isles idioms. And she did so without pointing out how clever she was about it, as Art would've. And she did it with ample boobage, as Art wouldn't've.

"We have a comedian here, I see," he teased.

Then gasped.

"You're a comedian too, I 'see,'" she said. Teasing. Warmth.

"I'm sorry," he said. "I can easily see other prick kids using words like that to make fun of—

"… er, I can easily *picture* other kids—

"… *envision* other kids—

"… *imagine* other kids doing that. You can 'imagine' without sight, right?"

"The word 'imagine' comes from 'image,'" she said.

"I'm sorry."

"It's okay. I appreciate that you noticed."

"You guys make me wanna ralph," Abby said behind them.

"Not on his shirt, it won't match," Kitty quipped.

"Shut up about my shirt," he said. "My shirt rules! I'd totally rock it on *Club MTV* now."

"You'd rock a hole in the dance floor, lard-butt," Abby said.

"Don't interrupt, young lady," said Kitty, using a strange character voice, a noble British snob. Behind them, Abby sighed out her nose.

"Can we drop it about my shirt?" he said. "Trust me, it's great."

"I don't trust boys, 'specially ones who watch *Club MTV!*" said Kitty. Her right hand shimmied free of the safety loop 'round her wrist. "Is your shirt long-sleeved? Gimme your arm, lemme check it out."

He plucked his free hand away from his slacks' pocket, wiped the wet palm on his khakied thigh, and stuck his arm across Kitty's personal space. Using both hands, the girl grabbed out, connecting with his ulna.

She's touching me. In front of the whole world!

Kitty's hands slid to his, crackly electrons leaping from one fingertip to another, signaling love or probably something else.

"Hold this."

If he'd said that, it'd be gross. Since she'd said it, it was startling.

Kitty Howe had surrendered her cane to Calvin Connor.

A buzz rolled through Axsubeen High's cafeteria like fans doing the wave during the middle innings. Kitty never let other kids touch her cane, never, never, *never,* no matter how much the dickheads begged or promised to give it back. Bullies who managed to steal the device faced automatic detentions of incremental duration; Principal Fartin' Martin tolerated no shite with his handicapped or disabled charges.

Yet here she was, forking over her precious cane after knowing Calvin for, like, two minutes. It was like King Arthur turning over Excalibur to some random wench loitering by Camelot's portcullis.

Not random wench—a foreign ape-wench of many famous rages.

Calvin saw all the O-faces and his inner child took over. He winked at them, like *You totally wish you were me!* He prepped answers for the inevitable questions: "It's surprisingly light. Not metal but plastic. Fiberglass I suppose. And it was cold where her hand hadn't been."

Then he heard Ma's shrill voice: *Show her some respect, boyo!* A rare honor had been bestowed. Face noble, Calvin held the cane aloft, a pose to make the Lady of the Lake wet were she not already naturally so.

In the midst of this asininery, Kitty ran her hands along the fabric of his right sleeve, "looking" at his shirt.

Abby watched the show; those further back in line got impatient, peered out to see a growing gap in front of Kitty, and hustled up to cut ahead … only to collide with each other as they skidded to a halt to gawk as the blind girl felt up the Irish kid's arm.

Young Miss Howe was the only non-elderly sightless person in Axsubeen. People always gaped at the girl's perpetual dark glasses, her guide dog, her probing hands, her cane. Kids were like, "Whoa, she actually uses a white cane like that woman on *Sesame Street* and shit."

This first contact couldn't have gone better: flirty talk, physical touch, and public trust.

Belay that last: "Why do you boys always say 'trust me?'"

He shrugged. "Probably cuz us boys lie a lot."

A laugh. "Honesty about lying? You're too much."

She made him feel so welcome with that warm laugh. Welcome enough to quote scripture: *"Truthful lips endure forever, Kitty."*

This caught her by surprise. *"The lying tongue, for only a moment,"* she finished with a certain delight.

Calvin slid his Trapper Keeper over his crotch; his other hand held a stiff white rod straight up.

Kitty's hands weren't soft like other girls' but sweaty and calloused like his own. Her fingertips traced through his shirt, finding two scars on his right elbow: a rough stipple in the crook and a sleek surgical ridge along the outside. "Huh," she said. "Is it tucked in?"

"Of course. And buttoned to the top."

She pulled a bit of the sleeve away from his goosebumpy skin. "Can't believe you wore silk to school."

"Believe it, love. Uh, people are skipping ahead."

"Yes, Calvin, I can hear them," she said, using his name! Kitty liked this game and wanted to keep playing … but he was right. Time's up. Her hand glided to his and took Excalibur back. Their fingertips touched again, magic static electricity, it's like Halloween, stop giving out this fucking hard-on candy!

Kitty faced front and tapped Excalibur's metal tip on the caf tile. She took two steps and stopped right behind the kid in line in front of her. She didn't get too close or strike the kid's shoe with the cane's tip.

Calvin stood aghast at this sight. It's like she used the Force.

Moussed blonde curls and a neon blue cardi flashed by. A slanted face smirked as it went past, all *'Nuff bullshit, Romeo!*

Calvin metaphorically threw inside to knock the batter back from the plate by physically grabbing Abby's thick arm and yanking, nearly casting the big girl to the tile. He retook his spot at Kitty's side.

When they reached the caf's food service alcove, he let Kitty go first then set up trays and forks for them both; a service Abby normally performed. "What's the verdict, love?" he said. "Is my shirt puke?"

"It's a nice shirt, so what," she said. "Stop with the 'love' stuff, Connor. You lay it on *waaay* too thick! I get it, you wanna impress me."

"And are you now?"

"Impressed? I dunno. Maybe. I don't even know you!"

"You do so know me! *And* you just learned a bit more."

"… like?"

"Like, you checked out my arm. Its size'll tell you my proportions. You know I'm taller cuz of where my voice comes from."

"Mmmm, your voice." Kitty all but moaned that. She turned to him and tilted up her head. The hot pink glasses made a perfect eyeline: the 5′ 4″ girl "looked" up at the 6′ 3″ boy.

He realigned his Trapper Keeper to cover his crotch. His taut flute couldn't hold any more blood.

"I smell food," she said to his face. "Read me the menu."

Before he could comply, the inhuman lunchlady at the hot food counter put her compulsorily cigarette-damaged voice to work: "We got turkey, stuffing, mash taters, and cream of broccoli, Kitty."

"She asked me to do it, Ms. Jonckheere," Calvin pissed.

Jonckheere's eyes, a couple of dice hammered into a tree trunk, blazed with irritation. "Holdin' up the works! What'll you have, dear?"

"I love cream of broccoli," Kitty said. "Just that, please."

The lunchlady ladled white-green goo in a bowl. The exposed flesh along Ms. Jonckheere's neck and forearms roiled as though wriggling fish were trapped under her skin. She set the bowl on the countertop.

Kitty reached out and intentionally grabbed the counter, then slid her hands together under the bowl. She set the soup on her tray next to the fork. The rising steam made it appear all the more heroic.

"Bravo," said Calvin.

"And for you, Casanova?" Ms. Jonckheere hacked.

Calvin found the woman revolting. And that "Ms." thing! Ms. was still new and noteworthy in 1989 and this heifer used it cuz no fella had married her. She didn't want to be "Miss Jonckheere" in her fifties. She might still be a virgin! A guy'd need to be drunk, desperate, or blind—

"Ugh. Gimme the turkey. So Kitty, w—"

"Stuffin'?"

"Please. So—"

"Gravy? Or is that too 'ugh' for you, too?"

Lunchladies are not members of the human race. Any high schooler will testify. "That'll be lovely, Ms. Jonckheere," Calvin oozed (audio) and snarled (video), "thanks a million."

Kitty slid her tray down to the self-serve cold food units, giggling the whole way. Calvin collected his lunch plate and hustled after her. "That woman is the Devil," he hissed.

"Let he who is without sin throw the first stone!" said Kitty, so happy

to openly quote the Bible.

It wasn't an exact *New American* 2nd Ed. quote. Calvin used his head and didn't correct her. *"I'm* not the Devil either," he said instead, "no matter what you've heard."

Kitty stopped at the cold food unit. Thinking. Other kids would've looked at the ceiling or held their chins. Kitty simply stood there.

Then, in bold defiance of her usual lack of body language, she waved a hand at the particular cold food unit she'd just so happened to have stopped in front of. "Tell me there's cheesecake in there!"

"There is cheesecake now. Want one? Cherries or plain?"

"Better make it plain," she said with a stage sigh. "Some of us need to watch our weight, you know."

With this one droll remark, his good slacks finally met their demise.

Back in her butterball pre-puberty stage, Kitty Howe had never been more than an extra in the cluttered epic of Calvin Connor's life. Recently, rapidly, and rakishly, the lass gained some height and began to fill out her cardigans with curves, to puff out her loose floral-print knee-length skirts with bouncy buns, to pull taut her perpetual white hold-ups with wide American thighs. Calvin had tried athletic girls and fun-size girls, and they were fine, but now the girl of his dreams had that Lisa De Leeuw earthiness.

Baby-fat girls aren't permitted on the stage at *Club MTV,* though. Her "watch our weight" joke acknowledged that. Soup alone for lunch, another teenage girl starving herself ...

... 'cept she asked for cheese-cake. Kitty didn't care about her weight. How could a blind girl be ashamed of her body when she can't readily compare it to others?

She was referring to *his* weight!

Squiiiiik!

January 27, 1989, specifically this lunch period, would live in infamy for all present. This particular moment wouldn't be the one everyone talked about for years (that was five minutes away) but it easily could've been. Later on, Calvin had to pat himself on the back for not casting his head upward and moaning as he came.

Instead he executed the greatest poker face of his life, staying frozen in sticky sangfroid, eyes open, pushing air in and out of his nostrils steadily, licking his lips to occupy them, keeping his Trapper Keeper against his trousers' crotch to hide the still-spewing carnage.

If Kitty noticed, she made no sign. He peeped back at Abby; the big girl was busy fetching an overflowing plate from Ms. Jonckheere.

Some fucker out in the cafeteria picked the worst random time to yell out, "Hey batter-batter-batter-*swiiing,* batter!"

Kitty loosed a jocular puff. "Getting me cheesecake or what?"

Calvin fumbled at the glass door on the chilled counter unit. "Naturellement," he said, hoping French would be distracting.

"Merci beaucoup!" she hooted. "Sans cerises, remember!"

"Sans cerises, oui." Half the plastic-wrapped cheesecakes were covered avec cerises. Half the lad was covered avec crème. He plucked out a plain slice for her.

And one for him. Fuck his weight. He needed it today.

Kitty slid towards the cash register leaving excited words in her wake. "I was *sooo* afraid of taking a foreign language but French is cool! I call it beautiful. Just rolls off your tongue."

I'll roll something off your tongue.

Oi! Stop that! Your cock'll re-engorge if you keep it up.

"Keep it up"—arrgh! *Listen up, vocabulary: fuck right off!*

"Hello, Kitty," said the register lunchlady.

"Hi, Mrs. Rieflin." Kitty picked up her tray and stepped back. The blind girl didn't have to pay for lunch: a taxpayer concession for the legally handicapped. Conscience-clearing for a tiny fee.

Neither Irishism, Ragehood, nor Apeness counted as encripplement so Calvin had to pay cash. Mrs. Rieflin rang up his meal. The woman was that rarest of beasts, a non-monster lunchlady, a retired kindergarten teacher. Calvin had seen her at Saint Brigid many times, with Mr. Rieflin and their kids and grandkids. No "Ms." she.

"$1.60 there," said Mrs. Rieflin.

Keeping the Trapper over his splattery pants with his left hand, Calvin used his right to retrieve his leather wallet. A fiver fell out and nearly landed on his hot turkey lunch. "If you'd be so kind?" he asked.

The lunchlady was so kind, fetching the five-spot and making change. She held the cash and coin at his much-occupied hands.

"On the tray, please," he directed sweetly.

Mrs. Rieflin's quaint kindergarten teacher's smile faded. Her blue eyes tilted down to his Trapper Keeper. "Calvin," she said, the very word a judgment. She dropped his change on his lunch tray.

How'd she know? His pose? An odor? He never noticed an odor, and he produced spunk and checked for stank in equal measures. He took a deep whiff to try and pick up any smoke trailing out his gun barrel (a Dirty Harry magnum, of course). All he got was turkey and gravy.

The lad shuffled his belongings between his hands and recollected them all at once, dazzling watchers when he slipped his momentarily free left hand under his lunch tray. The maneuver kept the crotch-splotch hidden and was cool besides.

Kitty still stood to one side, a big grin between wide pink cheeks. "Enjoy the cheesecake, love," Calvin said. "Nice meeting you."

"Sure, 'love,'" she said. "Catch you again tomorrow?"

"That'd be awesome, but tomorrow's Saturday."

"It could happen. Au revoir."

Not adieu—au revoir!

He replied in kind and beat feet.

Chapter 3

THE ORANGE HEARD 'ROUND THE WORLD.

⚾ CLUBHOUSE ⚾

SPAZZ WATSON HELD HIS fork like a microphone and did his best Howard Cosell. "Connor's getting her some cheesecake. A good sign. But what's this?! Is he weak in the knees?" The wild-child with the wild hair broke character to say "I think he pee-peed his jam-jammies!" in his usual three-ring circus vibrato.

Ryan Phillips, the Suicide King who wore the most black and spoke the least, suddenly cupped hands at his mouth. "Hey batter-batter-batter-*swiiing,* batter!" he called.

Art Maguire, he of the imperious opinions and sweet biracial fade, kept his face in his food. He was totally too busy eating to care about Calvin mackin' on the blind girl.

Spazz switched back to his Howard Cosell voice. "I think, I truly think, that Howe likes this Connor kid. One more run up the middle and he'll get in her endzone!"

"Yo," said Art, "is that an impression? Who's it s'posed to be?"

"Ain't it obvious, Artillery Shell? I'm doin' Howard Cosell here!"

"*Ewww,* yer 'doing' him? That's gross, bro."

Spazz snorted. "Says you, Na-Pole-leon Bone-ap-Art."

Ryan, from his seat between them, made his sharp face inquisitive. "What's gross about it?"

"Two dudes doin' it is unnatural!" said Art. "That's how diseases happen!"

"Two hairy dudes, arm in arm," persisted Ryan.

Spazz jumped in. "Two furry fellas flickin' each other's dicks."

"Stop," said Art, "you're makin' me *think* about it!"

"About what? Tasty hot meat in your mouth?" said Ryan. He

gobbled a hunk of gravy-slathered turkey. *"Mmmm!"*

"Speakin' of oral pleasure," said Spazz, digging in his acid-washed Wranglers for a balled-up single. "A buck says Connor-ect Four eats Titty-Committee-Kitty's muff on the first date. Dude's always chowin' down in Mufftown! And rotten pussy's why all them micks got rotten teeth." Spazz clicked his bright white choppers.

Art's blue eyes sparkled over the gray rims of his glasses. In his cold assassin's voice: "How many cavities *you* got?"

Spazz's choppers froze mid-click.

Art had zugzwanged him nicely. If Spazz answered "None!" he'd sound like a virgin with no chance to muff-dive. If he said "Lots!" he'd sound like a perv cuz only deviants dug dining on the bearded clam.

Vaginal sex was cool, like shooting your torpedoes down the Death Star exhaust port. Cunnilingus was gross, like some squishy ritual the Klingons did on *Star Trek: The Next Generation.*

Stuck in a no-win scenario, Spazz's long hair went all a-wobble in the follicle equivalent of Ralph Kramden going "Homina-homina."

Art slid in the dagger: "I got one cavity. From eating out yo momma."

"Ugh, yer sick in the head," said Spazz. "Y'ever *seen* my moms?"

Calvin Connor flopped into his throne at the Suicide Kings Table, dropping his lunch tray, Trapper, and Algebra text. A quarter from the loose change on his tray twirled away. Ryan deftly snared it.

Art lit up at his friend's arrival. "Behold!" he whooped, "the mighty warrior returns from the hunt!"

"The hunt for cunt!" said Spazz.

"'Behold?'" spat Calvin. He pulled his seat closer to the table, totally not shielding his trousers from view, just getting close to lunch.

"Awww," said Spazz, "did Señora Connora get all excited around Kitty-Kat's kitty and peece in his Polo pants?"

As so often was the case, the wild-child's blindly flung-out alliteration hit the bullseye.

"Leave 'im alone, guys," Art said, his assassin tone again. "Mr. Hussing's giving us a test next period and that makes me wee-wee my Polos, too."

"Jaysus!" said Calvin. "It's Friday—we got a test in Algebra!"

"Yep." Art pointed at Calvin's hidden lap. "So what's—"

Irish crushed African's pointing hand with all the force at his disposal. And the Raging Ape had *force*. Art's knuckles ground together, bringing tears. "Lemme go, butthead!"

"You're always 'prepared,' like emergency jeans in your locker," said Calvin. "Lemme borrow 'em. Even sweats'll do."

Art pried his hand free. "No way they'd fit you!"

Spazz swept aside paroxysmal swells of headbanger hair. "I got my sister's prom dress in my locker. Her corpse is still in it. I'll let ya practice muff-divin' on her for a buck!"

The jests and japes of the Suicide Kings carried on.

Presumably. Calvin didn't know. He erected walls and shut his ears; this was his concentration helmet. All thoughts about B.O., stains on pants, and the clammy congealing spunk stuck to his now-limp junk fell away. The lad made his entire being about Algebra.

Abby was wrong: Calvin wasn't flunking math. Yet. Tests were coming back graded D-. Cracking open his accursed text, he held it above his untouched turkey for some crisis cramming.

At once a shadow fell over the page. Calvin turned.

Behold! Brion Davey, paying a visit! Of all people, of all times!

Davey was one of the Scoundrels, the squad of douchebag jocks. Davey was a junior and so upperclassman to Calvin but with an asterisk: he'd flunked sixth grade or something and oughta be graduating this year. With his peach-fuzz 'stache, blasts of acne, and missing front tooth, Davey was the walking stereotype of a hillbilly. He was the first kid at Axsubeen High to wear the buzzcut with a nutsack of hair down the back of his neck. Locally, the hairstyle bore his name.*

Calvin Connor had rarely interacted with Brion Davey and had no idea why the guy was here now, standing behind his chair, snarling down at him. Davey was a growly goon, always grumpy, picking on other kids. His favorite curse word was "faggot."

---

* Use of the post-modern term "mullet" is anachronistic, a retroactive reference. The fashion had no contemporary name. "Mullet" is often erroneously employed towards any example of long, loose men's hair of the '80s. As for the Scoundrels' edition, they themselves called the 'do the "team haircut." The rest of Axsubeen High's student body called the style after its originator: it's the "Davey Dangle."

A donnybrook seemed inevitable.

Art Maguire would be useless. He'd hide under the Suicide Kings Table so his precious glasses wouldn't get broken.

Spazz Watson would be eager to brawl, all glory and trumpets, but the kid had Slinkies for arms and Nerf footballs for fists.

Ryan Phillips was a rock and would defend Calvin to the end, but fought like a gentleman in a top hat and monocle. Davey would spit in your eye, kick you in the nuts, go for the shins, and (if he lost) take a dump in your bookbag. If he won, that dump was going in your mouth.

Calvin suddenly missed Anthony Sandmiller. He'd stopped being friends with Sandy after Camp Souviens. The guy had extorted kisses off Cindy then took Inky's side vs. Calvin in the big fight at the campfire. Calvin couldn't stand to look at Sandy after that. The Sandmillers moved out of the area last summer, killing any shot at hatchet-burying … but goddamnit, Calvin wanted Sandy here now. Wanted his lying, cheating, alcohol-fueled assholic feistiness. Sandy would stand up and send his caf chair flying back, pointing a stubby finger at Davey's tooth-gap and hollering, "Are you shitting me with that shit?!"

"Strike last, strike fast, get hard," was their catchphrase.

Gripping his lunch tray with white knuckles, Davey bent at the waist over Calvin's left shoulder. "Kitty's mine, faggot!" he hissed, breath rotten and moist. "Don't even think—"

Calvin didn't think. Striking last would not do. He struck *first,* and fast, emptying both Davey's lunch tray and his own down onto his lap.

Davey jerked backwards and spilled himself onto his ass. What bits of Davey's lunch that hadn't ended up on Calvin's lap set sail in inertial confusion: cutlery clanged, empty milk carton and crumpled napkins splatted, and a peeled orange rolled.

Heads turned. Chatter halted. Lunch became theater.

Calvin got to his feet. Davey's plate and his own plate flew off his lap to shatter on the doo-doo brown/pus orange checkerboard tile.

The Irish Raging Ape stood over Davey and roared with a mighty voice, "See what you've done now!" He motioned at the sloppy gravy and stuffing sliding down his crotch.

Peeling a slice of turkey off himself, he flicked it at Davey's face.

Davey deflected it aside with his lunch tray. Discovering the peeled orange by his feet, the goon palmed it and fired.

Too many movements. Calvin backed up a step and caught the fruit with two hands. He made to send it right back when the lunch monitors showed up. Mrs. Barker, approaching from behind, jumped up to seize Calvin's throwing arm in mid-windup. Big Mr. Jourgensen stood over the kneeling Davey and made a human wall between the battlers.

Fifth period lunch groaned in disappointment.

The thin mopers in black Joy Division shirts over at the Alternative Arses Table moaned in disorder and confusion. The Drama Club Dames, rehearsing their overdone line-readings of *The Mikado,* wept with aspect stern and gloomy astride. Engines sputtered and stalled over at the Vo. Techies Table (Italian-Retards-Out-Cruisin' Division). At the Cable-Knit Cardi Table, where Kitty and Abby sat, their leader Roni Vogel booed like a Pittsburgh Penguins fan letting Andy Van Hellemond know, "There's no goddamn way that was holding!"

"Get some napkins," Mr. Jourgensen ordered Davey. "Let's clean up before we go to the Office."

Davey's beet-red face went white—*I am sooo dead.* He slogged his tall frame to the dish return counter and plucked napkins from a tin dispenser. He looked over his shoulder; Calvin still had his throwing arm back; Mrs. Barker, the dumpy lump of a Social Studies teacher, dangled off his wrist, trying to pry the orange away.

Calvin's gray eyes had never left Davey.

Davey mouthed, "Fuck you, faggot."

The chronicler estimates the distance between the Suicide Kings Table and the dish counter was—roughly—sixty feet, six inches.

⚾ **PRESS BOX** ⚾

Eighty-seven students and two adult chaperones witnessed Calvin Connor III's first pitch. The lunchladies and two kids missed it.

By the time he'd pitch in his first Major League game, everyone who was in the building will have witnessed the orange. By the time he started his first World Series game, every Axsubeen grad from '86 to '95 will've been in the caf. No radar gun was present of course but pitch speeds often accompanied the tales: "Irish threw that orange 70, 80, 90 miles an hour!" Fellas at the Biergarten on the corner of Railroad Street and Mueller Way swore that orange broke triple digits. Dr. Jacoby, one of the town's more exaggerative storytellers, delighted in saying young Calvin went over to the condiments station first to put a dollop of mustard on the orange.

If Calvin *had* thrown a citrus fruit 144 m.p.h., who would blame Davey for getting pegged? "He never had time to duck!" was a common comment. Yet the orange—that peeled, tossed, lost, thrown, and caught orange—never broke Sammy Hagar's 55.

And the target wasn't some glasses-wearing pimple-farm, some nerd covering his '80s buttoned-up top button under a goddamn necktie like he was Gordon Gecko, carrying an actual briefcase to class with a calculator and mechanical pencils and an *Unearthed Arcana* hardcover to peruse after finishing his tests early ... hell no, Brion Kenneth Davey was a jock. He didn't carry nothing with no handle 'cept a gym bag of stirrup socks and his cup *(size XL cuz I'm packin', and fuck you for askin', faggot!)*. He didn't wear no button-up shirts or ties 'cept when his asshole dad dragged him to Mass at Saint Brigid. Davey hit cleanup on the Varsity and took cans of corn to the fence.

He stood there and let that orange crush his gap-tooth mug.

Juice doused his eyes. Threads of pulp lodged up his sniffer. He crashed backwards off the dish return counter, all flailing arms and legs, and jostled the tin napkin dispenser. The second his body came to rest on the tile, that dispenser bonked him right atop his Davey Dangle 'do.

Finally getting the ending they were promised, those teenagers present who acknowledged their passions—otherwise known as "teenagers"—stood and cheered. The only disapproving faces were found at the Marching Band Mavens Table, the ultra-pious poopers at the Proverbs Patrol Table, and the repressed "young adults" at the Student Counciling (No Boobies Bouncing) Table.

Kids stumped for one side or the other in heated breakdowns. Anyone with an orange on their lunch agenda was beset by thieving thespians looking to re-enact the show. The more picked-upon kids had their antennae up full, ready to evade facially aimed fruit.

During the perp-walk out the caf, Calvin scanned 'round. At the Scoundrels Table, Reggie Roberts and Cuauhtémoc "Chicken"

Ysderrhi traded high-fives and laughed themselves silly. Scoundrels King Sean Corgan—whose rich dad owned Pizza Putt, and on whose McMansion lawn everyone saw Irish rage his mini-ape into Jenny Mac-Donald—Sean was gone. *Run off to bail out his pal Davey's arse?*

At the Cable-Knit Cardi Table, four largely large girls all had opinions: Cindy "Sigourney" McKee's sneer, Roni Vogel's sass, Abby Malone's jubilance, Kitty Howe's horror.

What the lad saw at the Mall Chicks Table made him trip over his own shoes. Karen McGillicutty, Queen of the Mall Chicks now that Jenny had transferred to Catholic school, was staring right at Calvin. Kare's eyes scowled, while her mouth hung open like hunger.

The very look his ex-girlfriend *Jill* usually gave him.

As they exited the caf, Davey and Calvin got a second round of applause. Thus ended one teenager's dignity and began another's life.

⚾ BLEACHERS ⚾

Jill Pedersen had had foreknowledge of this crisis ... and dismissed it.

"Wanna hear a secret?" said Art Maguire, sprinting to catch her after homeroom. Art stalked Jill, always drooling over her. Just like Brion Davey had been doing to Kitty Howe since grammar school.

"What secret?" said Jill. *It'll be lame.*

"Connor's gonna ask out Kitty at lunch."

See? Lame! "Why would he dress up for the blind piggy?" said Jill. "Get bent, Maguire! Mall Chick ≠ airhead!"

Art put on that retarded grin of his. He thought it made him spicy when it really made him dicey—especially as he dished dirt about his best friend. "It's the truth! Kitty is the Ape's new crush!"

"Go away, asshole," said Jill, quickening her pace. *You know a boy's weird when he makes me wanna get to class sooner.*

She put the whole thing out of her mind until lunch. Then she saw the Irish Raging Ape—a nickname of Jill's own devising that everyone used now—with cartoon hearts popping over his head.

Over a handicapped girl.

The only things that popped outta Calvin's fat head when Jill dated him were sarcastic insults. Other boys followed his lead, making snarky jokes right to Jill's face as if she was an ugly boy like Chicken or Leggers.

Right to my perfectly made-up face. They don't see my Mall Chick fashion, my cool hair. I got hips to die for. I got boobs! Not my momma's—no one's out-boobing Kimmy McSween—but I got more than most!

Didn't matter. Boys picked on her weight and farted on her when she had her face in a book in class and all sorts of awful shit.

Boys never did that to Valerie Crenshaw, the trailer trash with her natty clothes and a stick figure and filthy mouth and arrest record. Boys panted over her. None of them farted on Val! *It makes no sense.*

It's all my fault. In seventh grade, she thought Calvin's sarcasm and insults were the product of shyness, like he was attracted to her deep down but covered it up with insults. She'd developed such a crush on him based on this theory.

Momma encouraged it. She said he'd change once they got close.

Ha! Momma don't know shit. Calvin never changed. The hurtful jokes kept coming and wore down Jill's sweet face. Her carrot-on-a-stick coyness bored him and he pushed for more kisses, making out, rounding the bases, and actual sex.

"I'm not that kinda girl," she said. *Momma* was that kinda girl. With her boobs, Kimmy McSween the ex-Prom Queen could pick any man. But after she kicked Daddy out, Momma only picked losers.

Like Daddy.

Then Jill snapped and told Calvin, "No, and THAT'S FINAL!"

So he dumped her. And never looked back.

Lunch was agonizing. Everyone was pointing at Calvin and Kitty, even the other Mall Chicks—her friends—who *knew* that Jill didn't care about the Ape anymore. "Look Jill, she's caressing his arm!"

Kare McGillicutty, Steph Millar, and Rayche Schultz* enjoyed her distress. It was the same sorta treatment she got from the Ape.

Jill perked up when Davey went over to Calvin's table. *FINALLY,*

---

* To pronounce Rayche, take "Rachel" and chop off the L.

Mall Chicks traded under their given names' first syllable; hence "Kare" for Karen. But as a Schultz—the legacy family went back to the town's founding—young Rayche was given a proper hardcore Teutonic name: Rahel, pronounced "rah-HHCHEL," all phlegmy and dumb. Grown-ups constantly asked Rahel if she was Jewish, and why she didn't smile more.

my prayers get answered! Everyone knew Davey considered Kitty *his* and no other boy's. Davey was a barbarian. *Kill him, Davey! PLEASE!*

But that didn't happen. The Ape put the barbarian on his ass in what might've been the most embarrassing way possible.

Kare, Steph, and Rayche were hysterical. They laughed at Davey's demise, then went *"BWAAAAH-HA-HA!"* at Jill, a taunt like a fire truck's siren, hosing her in anxiety. The Mall Chicks had been forced to listen to Jill bitch about Calvin for years. They *loved* that the Ape won.

Jill moved some stuffing around with her fork. She'd never done a better job of keeping the feel of devastation inside her.

How come boys never hit on me out of the blue? Or try to defend me by punching out the Ape?

"You gotta move on!" Kare told her. Maybe last year, maybe now. *Was it live, or was it Memorex?* The Mall Chicks made such statements so often that time formed a singularity on the matter.

And whatever, Jill *tried* to move on. Really. She'd find a boy to hang out with, usually over summer vacation, until they asked about doing it or got too stalker-y. Until they ended up like Art, basically.

Meanwhile, Connor's always there, always with some other girl. Flirting with that horse Cindy "Sigourney" McKee ... dating Jill's ex-friend, the ex-Mall Chick Jenny MacDonald (ugh) ... screwing some punk girl at summer camp in Maine or wherever ... dating Jenny again (ugh ugh) before she left Axsubeen High ... snapping Kare's bra through her shirt last week ... and now, the blind girl—a Bible-thumper!

Kitty'll give it up. He always gets in our panties.

Jill could testify. Calvin got in her panties once. More accurately, he tore them panties off her like they were a stubborn snack pie wrapper.

I let it happen to see if he'd come back to me. I broke my own rules. And he murdered my magic panties.

That's right, those panties were magic. Calvin had even said so: the lilac-shaded "knickers," as he called them, appeared like "magic" one day at the mall. The only pair of post-puberty purple-colored underwear she'd ever owned. One wouldn't think purple undies were so rare, *especially* in the '80s!

Jillian Jane Pedersen adored purple. The color of kings and queens. *The greatest color—like, ever!*

Today she wore poofy mauve-and-white striped socks, a button-up shirt of the most intense fuchsia, some iris lip gloss, and a raspberry barrette. A standard canvas of neutral whites (charcoal gray bottom-layer shirt and white Jordache capri jeans) matched her skin and made the various purple bits pop. The capris and her lacquered-up auburn locks created the illusion of height and slimness; Jill stressed at being shorter and wider than other tenth-graders. Jordaches were her favorite denim; they gave her butt a nice curve without emphasizing her puffy thighs. Her brown eyes swam in indigo shadow.

Miss Pedersen looked at her wardrobe mirror this morning and saw the quintessential Mall Chick—the malliest Mall Chick ever. Purple did for Jill what it could only *dream* to do for Prince.

The Irish Raging Ape didn't notice.

Said nothing at the bus stop or homeroom. Oh he spoke to her, but not about her fashion. He never did. Not that she dressed this way to impress *him* … but it woulda been nice to get a reaction.

The Ape had only mentioned her fashion sense once, on a date at Logan Valley Mall back in seventh grade. Jill went all out: no neutrals. Purple head to toe. Eggplant OshKosh B'Gosh overalls, even.

The kids strolled the concourse and made fun of old people. They stopped at Gadzooks and she went inside to check out this tight orchid-color denim skirt on display.

Calvin stayed in the concourse, glaring at her through the partition glass and checking his Swatch (his old Swatch, the all-transparent one, not the cool black one Jenny bought him, not like Jill kept track).

When Jill came back out without the skirt cuz it was too big, Calvin's guffaw boomed through the mall. "Seeing you through that window, all purple and stuff, I kept thinking of a jar of grape jam!"

She ran away from him and burst into tears outside Wicks'n'Sticks.

A burst of applause serenaded Calvin as he left the caf. He was a hero, even with that turkey lunch all over his pants. Nothing beat the asshole down.

Mr. Jourgensen led Davey out to a chorus of heckling—he'd hear about this orange thing forever. The guy had a missing front tooth and the most retarded haircut … but Brion was tall. Older. Had big hands. Had a *spine*. Had gone to punish Calvin. That's how a man does it.

As much as she loved the color purple, Jill suddenly hated orange.

OFFICE OF THE COMMISSIONER

Vertical venetians covered the single narrow window in the Principal's office. Calvin had never seen those blinds open. The lad smelt the lubricant on the many filing cabinets and the turkey gravy on his pants. An oaken desk filled one side of the Principal's Office. It bore nothing besides a blotter and a brown paper grocery bag. Behind the desk sat Fartin' Martin. The colorful nickname—not unknown to him—stood in stark contrast to his monochrome manner. Mr. Martin had pale white skin, solemn silver hair, and black-framed '50s nerd spectacles.* While the rest of the world had embraced sweaters and '80s geometric flair and hot neon, Martin wore a suit of somber gray coat/slacks, white shirt, and pale blue tie at all times. Work. School plays. Mass. Civic functions. Calvin's family once bumped into Mr. & Mrs. Martin at My Friend's Diner up in Altoona; the Principal had been enjoying a Saturday afternoon hamburger and milkshake in a full fucking suit.

His speech lacked stall prefixes like "Well" and "So." Other adults walked about in a fog, half-listening to teens, but Mr. Martin heard every goddamned word you said. He could *detect lies* like a 30th level wizard. No innocent kid ever got an undeserved detention from him.

"Mr. Davey," he said, opening the testimony phase.

The goon studied his Nikes, damn near burning holes in them. His blond Davey Dangle tail curled down the left side of his red neck.

"Explain why you crossed the cafeteria," Martin bade. "Spare us the usual 'I was just walking past, minding my own business.'"

The crisp words nipped Davey's nose like frost. Said nose had recently been orange. Calvin laughed at the memory, then shut his trap.

Martin's iron eyes shifted between one unpadded interrogation chair to the other. "What's so funny, Mr. Connor?"

The lad wriggled in broiling anxiety, or maybe it was the icky slacks. "It was an accident, sir. The orange slipped outta my hand."

"I did not ask what happened. I asked what was so funny."

---

* As kids termed Wayfarers when they had clear lenses. When those same frames held *dark* lenses, they suddenly became cool: they were Ray-Bans.

"Uh, the orange was funny. Guess you hadda be there, sir."

Martin's glare hammered Calvin's soul like a mace. "The orange did not 'slip,' was no 'accident,' and would not have been 'funny' even given my attendance."

"I'm sorry."

"I doubt it. As myopic as ever, Mr. Connor. You act from primal instinct, nary a thought of the long-term."

Calvin chambered a tart reply at Martin's vocab-word pomposity but decided to be clever and not fire yet. *I'll show you "long-term!"*

"Employing vittles as missile weaponry is a violation of school policy," Martin stated, turning away. "Mr. Davey: out with it."

Davey reflexively rubbed his throat. He wouldn't get away without saying something. "Wasn't even my orange. It was Corgan's. He only eats the peel, y'know, to make weight. He put it on my tray."

"Possession is nine-tenths, and you did not answer my question."

"Why do ya *think* I went over, Mr. Martin? He insulted me."

"From a hundred feet off?"

"By talking to Kitty. Yeah."

Calvin looked over at him. "You fancy Kitty?"

"Where the hell you been, Irish?" Davey snapped. "I've liked her since elementary school! Who don't know that?!"

"Does *she* like *you?*" Calvin snapped back, fearing the answer.

"What greater insult is there than to be 'spoken to' or 'fancied' by the likes of either of you?" said Martin. "Miss Howe is the only victim."

Calvin and Davey had nothing to add, to Martin or each other.

"Mr. Davey," said the Principal. "Three days' Official Detention for classroom disturbance. Handle romantic competition like an adult or earn I.S.S. by the week. Depart."

Davey slinked out the door, a trail of steam hovering in his wake.

"Mr. Connor," said Martin, "you get five days' worth."

Calvin's jolt of disgust carried him out of his chair. "He came over and attacked me, and I get *twice* as much detention?!"

"Three twice is not five. Your Algebra 2 grades accurately reflect your competency. As for your crime, fracases occur and are forgotten but your flung fruit will mark this one. There will be copycats. I'll direct Ms. Jonckheere to remove oranges from the menu.

"Note the effect your actions have beyond immediate benefit."

"Well. Didn't you just yell at me for not looking long-term?"

"Now it's a grand conspiracy to make yourself a legend? Please." An iron finger aimed at Calvin's heart. "None of your actions were self-defense or to protect your precious dignity. You sought dominance."

Calvin gave up. Unlike other adults, Fartin' Martin could not be cowed or bargained with. Staying here only dug the hole deeper.

Time to fold this hand. "I …," he said, deliberately letting himself falter, a show of contrition before saying he was sorry.

He never got the chance. Principal Martin made his face into the equivalent of folded arms. "I believed your tears three years ago during the Binaca affair. Not now."

The lad was genuinely offended. "I wasn't going to cry!"

Martin fetched the brown shopping bag on his desk and drew out a pair of doo-doo brown Axsubeen High gym sweats. "These should fit. I'll not have you disrupting class by smelling strongly of gravy."

Chapter 4

YOU ARE A PUFF OF SMOKE.
SATURDAY, JANUARY 28, 1989.

FOUL

AS A SMALL BOY, Calvin C. Connor III walked everywhere. School, the shops, Our Lady's Nativity, the pitch ... it's how one got around in Leixlip. The States introduced him to car culture and overnight he pined to drive. If he missed the school bus, he'd still use shoeleather express to cover the two miles to Axsubeen High, but now it sucked.

He got why adults hiked for "fresh air," how a daily stroll "cleared the head." He also got why American kids said walking "blew heavily."

Calvin had his learner's permit; in a few weeks he'd turn sixteen and get his license. So close to four-wheeled autonomy! He still lacked wheels—the only sixteen-year-olds with their own cars were the rich kids who lived in Overlook Estates like Jon Oldroyd, Sean Corgan, and Jenny MacDonald—but three vehicles jammed the Connors' driveway at 34 Maple Street. Four, when Robbie was home from college. Calvin had many schemes to borrow, or "borrow," a family car at need.

Don't fret, by '92 the lad'll have his beloved Countach. Well, a used one; Lamborghini discontinued the model this very year, 1989.

For now, the young Ape was hoofin' it.

The so-called "tree roads" ran in columns off Rte. 666 (Main Street), cutting southern paths across the Axsubewa Basin. Maple Street ran astride the Mueller farm tract. The empty corn furrows, strewn with rock and slush, set many traps for Calvin's booted feet.

The Pennsylvania Railroad as a business entity was long gone but all four lines they'd set up through the township still saw use: two for diesel freight and two for electric passenger cars. The four sets of rails converged here, bisecting this band of crop fields. Catenary wires held aloft by endless steel gantries marked the incision from a distance. Calvin scrabbled up the thick ballast stone and crossed the tracks' wide hillock, leaving the Mueller farm tract and tumbling to the Millar tract. He wiped his slicked face with that ugly scarf of many colors.

He cut through a phalanx of firs to reach 41 Cherry Street's back yard. Calvin had made this cross-country voyage many hundreds of times; prior to the Maguires' purchase of this house, the Sandmiller family lived here.

He popped in the back door to give a courtesy "Good morning!" to a middle-aged black man and white woman, sitting red-eyed and blue at their green formica table, eating toasted brown wheat bread with orange juice.*

"Hello, Calvin," said Annie Maguire. She was a whale of a woman with wispy blonde hair and skin like Elmer's Glue. "I hear you're sweet on the blind girl!" she said, her wide smile showing both her approval of his wooing romance and her disapproval of regular dentist visits.

"Let's see how it goes," said Calvin, grimacing at the verb "see."

"No poker today," said Paul Maguire. The coffee mug in his hand motioned towards the connecting wall between the kitchen and the garage. "Art's in his lair though—you can probably hear."

Indeed, Calvin heard bass beats and emceeing. "Jungle music," his da called it, though Art said that was kinda racist. The lad popped back outside and over to the garage's side door. Axsubeen's ranchers, built along Elm, Maple, Cherry, Walnut, Pine, and Cedar Streets during a late '50s boom, had no interior doors connecting to the garages.

Young Art was hunched over his drawing board, ghetto blaster blaring from atop a tits-tall bookshelf. A small easel with the legend NOW PLAYING held a cassette case with *The Streets IV* down the spine and cover art of a trash can in front of a brownstone. Schoolly D *ascribed an august acronym to 1) acrimonious adversaries, 2) his adroit articulation in answer, and 3) an aptitude for amalgamating album-based amputations with automata-applied acoustics.*

"WHAT THE FUCK IS THIS NOISE?!"

---

* Got any ideas how to shoehorn in the remaining colors (yellow and purple), short of having Mr. Maguire eating his breakfast in a Lakers jersey? The chronicler's all ears.

Art jumped, then made it smooth like he was leaping up to greet his homeboy. "It's rap. Too black for you!" One gangly hand spun the boom box's VOLUME knob down while the other held out for five.

Calvin didn't return the five until it was safe to pry his mitts from his ears. "Your da said no poker," he said, then waved at how Art had set the lair up for such: extra seats 'round the drawing board, a bowl of Chex mix, and the camping pot of coffee perched on R5-D4, the white barrel-shape kerosene heater with red accent stripes.

"Spazz says he got called into work," said Art. "I think he's welching out on the five bucks he owes me."

"'Welshing.' Grape jelly has honor. People from Wales do not."

Art both ignored the correction and made a note of it. "I called you but you already left. Anyway, Ryan's dad said he's 'unavailable' too."

"Sergeant Slaughter grounded him?"

"Pro'bly. Caught him out doin' the Lord Low Almighty's dirty laundry again." Art glanced down at the report card on his drawing board and waggled his beloved mechanical pencil. "Can you, uh ... "

"I'll park it in the waiting room." Calvin poured himself a coffee, remembering to wrap his horrid scarf of many colors around his hand before gripping the tin pot's handle. Flopping onto his usual milkcrate stool, he warmed his hands. "Who you doing surgery for this time?"

"No one." With the coolness of a no-look pass, Art kept his face in his work and sent a free hand to the boom box, setting it to radio mode.

"—cold one out there with temps droppin' into the teens MAN! I'd love to drop into some teens *woof woof* OKAY! don't Phil Collins ever take a day off HEY! he's been on the charts since 1492 when Christopher Cross discovered your mom YIKES! ping pong it's half past a monkey's ass on Wacky 103's Bob-a-Slob Waaaaacky Weekend!"

"He said 'ass!'" Art said. "Bob-a-Slob gets away with murder!"

As Phil Collins *called on his cohort to correct the chaos by completing their contract,* Calvin plucked out a pocket New Testament and snapped the onion-skin pages. "Fuck Bob-a-Slob. And fuck Phil Collins too."

"No way, Phil Collins is the man!"

"Only on *Miami Vice.* His songs are all sappy love shite."

Art waved at his bookshelf. "We always got Maguire's Mixtape Medley. Just finished *Eclectic VIII.*"

In this pre-Walmart, pre-IKEA world, young Calvin had never seen a black bookshelf. Art had painted it himself, one of his billion black possessions. The shelf held hundreds of tapes, mostly dupes of other people's store-bought albums, all in clear plastic cases (no loosies) with spine labels written in black marker in Art's anally perfect handwriting, like they were stenciled. The cassettes were arranged in alphabetical order by artist then year of release. The "Curation Series" of home-made mixes had nine volumes of *The Streets,* fifteen of *Lazer Beemz,* and now eight of *Eclectic,* all with pretentious Roman numerals.

"Wacky 103 is fine," Calvin said firmly, never dreaming the sentiment would leave his mouth ... much less as the truth!

Art turned back to his drawing board, tapping his mechanical pencil in time with Phil Collins's drums. "You're the only one I know who hates Wacky 103. You don't even like Hyperspace Eddie Pace. Best morning show ever!" He raised his pencil like a petulant finger. "Did you know his real name's Ed DePace? 'Eddie Pace' is just a pun."

"Did you know no one cares? You got all this knowledge—music, firearms, science—but you apply it to two things: bomb squad shite, and *that.*" Calvin waved at the cassette bookcase. "*That* is Arthur Aganju Maguire to a fucking T. Show anyone that tape collection and they'll understand you. 'Cept no one sees it here in your secret lair."

"Would a mad scientist set up his secret lair at Wendy's? And people do *so* see it. You, and Ryan and Spazz. I got friends."

"That's all lads. No chicks."

"Yes-huh, you brought Jenny here that one time. Valerie tags along with Spazz. Oh and Spazz's sister. Not the dead one in his locker."

"You know what I'm getting at, African."

"Blow me. I talked to a chick on the phone last night."

"I don't believe you."

"'Course not. Yer just trying to piss me off, Irish. It's desperate."

Normally a thin-skinned priss, Art saw right through Calvin's needling. Just like he saw through Calvin's bluffs during poker. Maybe it was this setting. "She called about report card fixing?" said Calvin.

"*Errnt!*" said Art, the incorrect answer horn from *Family Feud.*

"Some school project. Physics, was it? With Mall Chick Kare."

"*Ding!* And it's Biology. But we talked about TV and junk. She's gonna tell me when Jill's ready to get asked out. Kare says Jill's going through somethin' serious. Can't be her mom kickin' out her dad, that was like a year ago. Maybe she's on her period?"

"She still wants me."

"No she don't, Calvin! She always looks at you like *Ugh*."

"Cuz she still wants me. She's disgusted with herself cuz she can't move on." Calvin broadened his shoulders. "And who can blame her?"

"But *you* don't want *her* no more. Right?"

"I do not. Once was enough."

"And she knows that?"

"I remind her constantly. She's still—dare I say it?—my friend, but I wouldn't date her if she was the last chick on earth."

Art frowned. "Yet, she still wants you. I don't get girls."

Correct, boyo, you don't. The lad dropped it and donned his concentration helmet to zero in on Bible Study. This week's passage was James, Chapter 4. A "do this/don't do that" list, Old Testament adultery and making the Devil flee, told in that delightful New Testament epistolic brevity. Verse 14 …

> *you have no idea what your life will be like tomorrow. You are a puff of smoke that appears briefly and then disappears.*

… made Calvin Ciarán Connor III reflect on his own life.

This, of course, was the purpose of Bible Study. The young man gazed off in deep thought. He took in the setting, the Sandmiller garage. Ha—the Maguire garage. *Did I really just forget who lives here?*

As Sandy's garage, all this room held was an '83 Buick Electra Estate wagon in gold firemist with woodgrain paneling, and cases of Rolling Rock and Pepsi cooling in a shady corner. The walls had been bare, the concrete floor oily, and the bug and spider population considerable.

The Maguire edition was packed: beer fridge, drawing board, plumbing supplies, Spuds MacKenzie posters, firefighter gear, footlockers of shotgun cartridges, a TV and Nintendo, folding chairs, R5-D4 glowing hot and making little *tick!*s … no room for the Bronco, much less Mr. Maguire's Econoline work van with PAUL'S PLUMB-

ING emblazoned in Pirates/Steelers/Penguins black-and-gold. The garage's roll-up door never got rolled up. The air stank of kerosene.

Six months ago Mrs. Sandmiller, a frustrated wife and homemaker, dumped Mr. Sandmiller, a failed husband and folk singer. Eight weeks later the whole family disappeared outta Axsubeen, like the *puff of smoke* James the Just pissed on about.

What'll vanish six months from now? This thing with Kitty? My garage? Ma and Da would never divorce ... would they?

Art had desired the post of Calvin's Best Friend ever since the lad turned his back on Sandy but Irish never warmed up to African's mix of antagonism and sycophancy, leaving the gangly kid stuck in the Near-Best Friendzone. *Will me and Art still be friends still in six months? Six years? I better have my own garage in six years, with a Lambo in it!*

God would be there, but free will determined things. He knew what he *didn't* wanna be—boring, like his da. Or dead. *Do I have a say in it?*

You have no idea what your life will be like tomorrow.

"What you wanna be when you grow up?" he asked.

"Alive," Art said. The joke had been sitting on his launchpad, engines primed, ready to blast off at a moment's notice.

"I'm serious, mate."

"You know already. I'm gonna be Black Bill Gates, making computers and programs for the common man."

"How can you be the 'black' anything? You're as black as fag ash."

"'Fag ash,' like cigarettes, that's good. And yer as white as them rice paper wraps on summer rolls."

Calvin hated that one cuz he had no idea what summer rolls were. Art's grin ate shit. "Someday you'll eat Vietnamese and get it."

"I'll never get Americans," said Calvin. "Your da went to 'Nam to kill people and came home with a new favorite cuisine."

"Spoils of war. What *you* wanna be when you finally grow up?"

"I'll open the world's first 'Nam/Irish joint. Green summer rolls."

"Guinness and gook food? Get real! C'mon, what ya wanna be?"

"Sexually spent."

"Y'all do that now, one-handed. In fact, you spend so much sexually yer gonna be in debt for fifty years!"

Calvin guffawed at Art's joke and mimed wanking. He stopped

when he saw the pocket New Testament still in his wanking hand.

"Looks like Hell is yer future," said Art. "After detention."

"Why you gotta bring that up? Wish I hadn't thrown that orange."

"Yo, it was worth five days of O.D.! Davey looked like such an asshole. Hell of a throw!" Art held up a hand for five and this time Calvin readily slapped it. "I ain't kiddin', Irish, you should play ball. I been playin' since little league and that orange woulda struck out fuckin' Reggie Jackson."

"Oh would it now. Who's Reggie Jackson?"

In his smooth Lando drawl: "The straw that stirs the drink."

Then Art switched to his Victim Industrial Complex® whine: "I mean, *I* coulda nailed that cracker from a mile off too, but that's before Cindy ripped my arm out its socket back at Camp SUE'·veenz."

He abandoned the report card surgery to rummage in a wooden chest, coming up with an old outfielder's glove and a scuffed ball. "If you made the team, we'd be together again. In a group. In uniforms."

Calvin snorted. "And two matches in, you'll bleach my hair?"

"'Games.' Baseball don't have 'matches.'" Art pointed at Calvin's Bible: "Look up 'forgive and forget,' bro."

"There's tons in here about *forgive,* but nothing about forget."

"Forget this." Art tugged his nuts. "Got a mitt? A baseball glove?"

"My brother does."

"He's a righty too, right? Like you."

"Uh. Me and Robbie are both right-handed now. So what?"

Art's ashen gray skin went pink in delight; he relished in moments when he could talk down to the big dumb foreigner. "You can't wear his glove if he's left-handed. Duh!"

"Sure I can. Just won't be able to throw. Duh!"

"And you can *throw,* bro. You'd fan all them fags at Larsen."

Calvin only partially understood that.

"'Fan' means strike out," said Art. "Larsen Academy's in our conference. Swanky joint in Altoona."

"Jon Oldroyd goes there so fuck it. You've actually been there?"

"Ain't no negros allowed on that campus." Art gave a grin. "'Cept during ball games, can't keep me out then. Let's see what ya got!"

Calvin flung his unsightly scarf of many colors around his neck.

"Shame to leave Phil Collins behind."

Art popped in the house to report his itinerary. Annie Maguire recited the usual bullshit list: be safe, don't bring your .410 into Calvin's home, etc. "We got chicken for supper," she said. "Be back by dark." As the boys slipped out to the back yard, Annie switched the porch light on and off a few times. She always did this when her only child left, even during daylight hours. Art had explained that it was something his grandmother would do back in Washington State. Calvin had replied that his da's parents were long dead—the lad had never met them—and his ma's parents back in Ireland were very grumpy and cold. They shut the porch light off the second guests were outside the door.

The boys slid through the back yard's border trees into the Millar farm fields. Calvin puffed on the arduous terrain; Art, shorter and much lighter, sprung from furrow to furrow. "Come back for chicken supper, Irish," said the latter. "We don't hafta serve it on a plate. We can dump it straight on your lap! Ha ha, I kill me!"

"Eat me, Maguire. And it was turkey, not chicken."

"All the same on your pants. You should start the first Irish/Soul joint. K.F.C.C.—Kentucky Fried Crotch-Chicken!"

"Belt up, boyo!"

"All right, fine. Sorry." Art gave the absolute minimum pause to convey contrition, then plucked a folded sheet of graph paper (his paper of choice) from his winter coat. "Came up with a new design for my arsenal." He offered the paper.

"Nice," said Calvin, not looking over.

Art used his pay-attention-to-me whine: "C'mon! If I hafta listen to ya yap about Kitty, the *least* you can do is—"

Calvin snapped up the paper and unfolded it. A detailed diagram done with that bloody mechanical pencil. Measurements and a scale and that little information box in the lower right-hand corner. The device pictured was a shotgun cartridge with a little casing or skirt along the firing plate.

African sidled up to Irish to wave a cinereous hand over the paper like Dian Parkinson showing off a canister of Ajax on *The Price is Right*. "The M.S.S.M.—Maguire Shotgun-Shell Mine."

"Your latest violation of the Geneva Convention," said Calvin.

"Home defense is the right of every American! Here's how it works: I make a casing with a thumbtack inside, pop in a shell, and bury it in the ground. Instant anti-personnel protection."

"Instantly killing-anyone-who-trespasses—"

"Yo, it ain't a friggin' Claymore! Taking a buckshot blast in the foot ain't killin' no one, unless they bleed out." Art's brow crinkled. "Although, if I can get flechette cartridges instead of buckshot …"

"Your *da* was in 'Nam, not you!" Calvin handed the paper back. "Why don't you figure out how to make, I dunno, solar energy work? Something useful."

Art pushed up his gray glasses. "Already did. The M.S.P.S., remember? Maguire Solar-Powered Switch? Thinkin' about rigging that to my Eat-at-Joe's bomb."

Calvin pictured the whole Maguire household going up in a fiery explosion after an errant shaft of sunlight poked in the garage door. "Good luck with that. I'll be over here."

Art laughed as his pal put some distance between them.

They scrambled over the railway's ballast hillock. When the Ape wiped his sweaty mug, Art ragged him: "How you stay so fat walking this much? Your diet's too rich in muff. Need some low-cal beaver."

"Quit bringing up the muff!"

"You're practically Mr. Muff-Diver: Cindy, Jill, Jenny, and next on the menu, Kitty."

"Don't talk about Kitty either."

"It's a free country, I'll talk about Kitty all I want. I talk *to* Kitty. Like in class and at church. She's my friend. Made her a mixtape once."

Calvin lowered a brow. Art never talked to girls, but suddenly Kitty's his friend? Made her a precious mixtape even? How long ago?

"Tell me what she did to make ya jisim," said Art, "and I'll never bring her up again." A lie, carrying a little sign which read **I AM A LIE**.

Art had seen the crotch-splotch. Calvin cycled through possible excuses for it. His poker face sucked the big one. He sucked at bluffing.

Whatever, cards on the table time. "She asked me to get her cheesecake. I go, 'Cherries or plain?' And she goes, 'Oh, plain. Some of us need to watch our weight.' And then it happened."

Art stopped. Looked down at his own crotch, then back up. "Don't do it for me. She meant *your* weight?" The kid put his big brain to work, disassembling the problem. "I saw her 'looking' at your gay-ass shirt."

"'Smooth-ass' shirt, you prick. Your ma's 'gay-ass' now."

"Yeah that makes sense, lots of gay mommas out there. Ooh—I got it! She felt your arm under the shirt and extrapolated how big ya are!"

"Very good, Sherlock."

"Wait up, so's you got off on the fact that she figured out you're fat? Heh. Yer into some *weeeird* shit!"

"She's no Mall Chick. She's got wit. And tits. She's my queen."

"She's Davey's queen, bro. He been shadowin' her since way before me or you moved to this cowpat burg. Hungry for another hour of makin' out. They did that back in fifth grade or some shit. She hates him but he don't take the hint." Art put up his pedantic finger again. "Wait 'til Fat Pig Abby tells Kitty about you creamin' yerself!"

"Fat Pig Abby don't know about it." The Irish Raging Ape ripped the mitt off his pal's left hand. "And if you tell her, this gets jammed down your throat. Shitting it out won't be easy!"

"Stop! If you drop a leather glove in the snow, you'll fuck it up!"

The boys reached the Maple Street back yards: Phillips, Schaefer, Connor, McSween/Pedersen. Calvin went in his house to fetch Robbie's glove and the two lads spread out on the snowy back yard to play catch. Calvin's Swatch got in the way of the mitt's wrist loop so he took it off. They got a rhythm down, firing the baseball back and forth.

In the cold, with snow gear on, working on flat ground, with a shitty pitching motion, Calvin still threw smoke. Art barely spoke. How come he never noticed this talent? How did *no one* notice it? Surely someone got hit from a mile away by a blazing snowball …

Chapter 5
THE RECRUITMENT(S).
SUNDAY, JANUARY 29, 1989.

FOUL

THE CONNORS WERE LATE to Mass. Ma's favorite dress had a hole way down the hem; no one would've noticed 'til her surgery on it turned it into a gaping fissure. Rose's shower took approximately three and a half days. Calvin the Third couldn't find his White Window Swatch; it was in his jeans' pocket from playing catch with Art.

No spots in Saint Brigid's lot. Calvin the Second had to street-park the Caddy past the graveyard to the very end of Cemetery Lane, in front of the Watsons' ramshackle home. Spazz loved living next to a necropolis. Calvin said it seemed more like Ryan's kinda thing.

The family sat in a rear pew. Their kids wanted to sit in the back cuz it was cooler, but as a town dish Eileen Connor desired a wide view to see who wasn't there, whose wife sat a little too far apart from her husband, who spared the rod when their brats misbehaved. Calvin the Second liked to leave the instant Mass ended. Sometimes to enjoy a quiet smoke in the Caddy, sometimes to head over to Schultz's Lumber Co. for an hour's paperwork. He'd return to collect Ma from Committee and the kids from Bible Study at 11:30 and take them to lunch at Pizza Putt in town or up Rte. 666 (Hollidaysburg Pike) to the Double D or the supper club.

Their distance at Mass was also spiritual. The Connors held the opinion that Yanks worshipped Jesus a little too fervently. In the Emerald Isle, church was what you did. Where you went. You lived life, and the Lord was with you. No biggie. Not less believing, but far less broadcasting. Americans didn't care how insane their faith came off! Putting the cross on their business cards. Wanting children to pray in school.

Calling an 800 number and sending God cash via some telly preacher. Loudly informing the checkout girl at Merk's Super-Merket of God's glory since He'd made sure they still had lowfat milk for sale in the panicky hours before a snowstorm.

Zeal to the point of spittle down the chin. Sitting in the rear of Saint Brigid got the Connors away from the droolers like Mrs. Snyder and those bloody Duffys.

Rosaleen checked out hunky boys in their suits. Calvin's gray eyes peeped over his hymnal at the Howes, about a dozen rows up in the right-hand section. Ma and Da Howe paid rapt attention to Father Sean's sermon. Kitty's older brother Eddie, a senior like Rose but no candidate for dates (way too fat and dorky), picked his nose. Kitty had her pink shades on. Excalibur rested against the pew. Abby Malone sat with her; the big girl lived with her divorced ma, who never showed up for services. Lord knows where Abby's da was.

Calvin planned to go up and say hi after Mass. Meet Kitty's family. He started writing a script in his head, then his radar pinged—Brion Davey, four rows up in the left-hand section, was blaring blue eyes back at him. His snarl exposed the missing front tooth. The tail of that silly Davey Dangle hairdo was tucked into his dress shirt collar.

Choking down his guffaw, Calvin mimed peeling an orange.

Brion's asshole dad Ralph punched the kid in the head, right where the topside buzzcut met the wave of long back strands. A full-on punch. Ralph Davey got his son sat proper, facing forward at the priest.

"What was that about?" Ma hissed at her son.

"I dunno," Calvin said. He peeked towards the Howes and saw Abby whispering in Kitty's ear. Had she seen it too?

After Father Sean dismissed the parish, Calvin stood but couldn't get out. Rose lingered on one side, his parents on the other. Even Da took his sweet time getting out of Dodge. The lad's beefy hands gripped the pew back in front of him, meaning to vault it.

He stopped when he saw Mark Duffy slide to Kitty's side. "Saint Mark," they called him, a senior at Bishop Guilfoyle Catholic High. One of those Yanks rubbing his crucifix in your face. His older brother, Matthew, was called "Father" by Troop 666.

Saint Mark did lots of tutoring. Was Kitty a tutee?

Calvin relaxed his vaulting posture. "Bollocks," he said.

"Strong language for the house of God, son." A man came up the row in front of the Connors, moving with the confidence of a leader, a coach, a killer. Perry Phillips was all those things. One time Calvin and Ryan were monkeying around at Ryan's house and Mr. Phillips barked an order at the Ape to double-time it home; Calvin nicknamed him Sergeant Slaughter after that. At sixty, Mr. Phillips was far older than any of the lad's other friends' fathers.

"He's just dying to get away from us and go sin," said Ma.

"Got four sons," said Phillips, "I know all about it."

"Pfft," said Rose, "that's why I am *never* having kids!"

"Ditto," said Calvin. "Imagine me taking care of another me."

"Perish the thought," said Ma. "But you'll have kids someday."

"And everything'll change," nodded Sergeant Slaughter.

Rose rolled her eyes. "Yeah, can't wait."

"Speaking of the future," said Calvin, "I'm off to Bible Study."

Sergeant Slaughter had none of it. "Let's talk about Davey first."

Calvin leaned a bit to see past the old man.

"Davey's already gone," Phillips told him. "His dad dragged him out. But I saw him starin' at you during Mass. Still sore from you beanin' him with that orange, I bet."

"You what now, boyo?" said Ma.

"At lunch Friday," Phillips told her. "From roughly sixty feet."

The lad's blood ran cold. He'd failed to inform Ma of the incident.

Calvin the Second stalked out to the vestibule. You'd think a man might stick around when the neighbor bloke came by with news of his son's ill-deeds at school, but no.

Calvin the Third parked his butt back in his pew. "Ryan told you?"

Sergeant Slaughter stayed standing at attention. "Sean Corgan told me."

"Corgan? The little wanker?"

"Called me right after school."

"Bloody tattle-tale."

"Nope, he was impressed. Said your throw was greased lightning."

Calvin shrugged, like *What's that mean?*

"A fast pitch. And yesterday I seen you and Art playin' catch in the back yard. I bet Artie put you up to it."

At all this boring sports talk, Rose split to go chat with fellow seniors Pete Hennessey and Matt Winowski. Ma sat down by her son. "I thought it was weird, you playing catch."

"So that makes two of my players who think you got hot stuff, son," said Phillips. "I do need new blood on the mound. Maybe you're a blue chip."

"I'm a what—a blue shit?"

Ma hit him across the lips.

Sergeant Slaughter's hard face betrayed no amusement. "Blue 'chip.' As in, a prospect. It ain't like Corgan to get all excited and call me up at home, soundin' like he's got a boner the size of Kentucky."

"Perry!" gasped Ma.

"The little wanker plays it all cool, like he's Mr. Unfazed," Calvin said, "but he gets excited sometimes. Like when he stole my girlfriend."

Now Sergeant Slaughter laughed. "He said you'd bring that up."

"Did he now. I bet he also said, 'Connor'll be bitter but Jenny left him for me. Cuz I rule.'"

"I'll be damned. That was precisely his side of it."

"Now he's inviting me to join baseball?"

"My ass," Sergeant Slaughter said with a jolt that jiggled his brown necktie. *"I'm* the manager. *I* decide who joins."

"Wait, so you're recruiting me?"

Phillips looked at Ma. "They're in their own world, aren't they?" To Calvin: "What've we been talking about, son? Spring's comin'. I'm doin' tryouts tomorrow after school. How about you stop by?"

"I, uh, got detention all next week." Calvin braced for another slap. Ma didn't disappoint. After the *thwap,* she said, "All week?!"

"Five days. Through Thursday."

"Consider yourself grounded!"

Calvin clicked his teeth. "Guess I can't come, Mr. Phillips."

"I'm sure your mother will make an exception. As for detention, I'll pull you out."

"With Davey right there?! Do us a favor, sir!"

The fact that Davey might be in the same detention room with Calvin hadn't occurred to Mr. Phillips. "Afterward then. I won't end tryouts 'til you show. It'll take half an hour." He turned to Ma. "I'll bring him home. Or, if he don't wanna ride with 'Sergeant Slaughter,' there's a late bus."

"There's two—one leaves at 4:00 and one at 5:30," Calvin said defensively, as if Mr. Phillips considered the lad way too much of a nerd to know about the late busses for student-athletes.

"Yep. Lucky Cheeseboro'll be there too."

"Really?" burped Ma, starlight in her eyes. Everyone knew Lucky Cheeseboro—he'd gone from pitching for the Axsubeen Axes to Penn State to the majors (Red Sox, Braves, Red Sox again, Twins) and came back to open a car dealership in Altoona with his big league money.

"Lucky's not an official coach," said Phillips, "but he comes by a couple times a year and helps me with pitchers."

"The guy from TV?" asked Calvin. Lucky's ads were local celebrity cheese, nakedly tacky, cowboy hats, booby gals, and low-mileage used half-ton sidesteps.

"Here's your chance to meet 'im." Deal-sweetening was out of character—Sergeant Slaughter was practically begging.

"Well." Calvin drew a breath. "I never played baseball before. And Davey ain't the only baseballer who'd love to fight me. Broke a guitar on Chicken's face once—*he* won't have a boner the size of Kentucky!"

"Good Lord," Ma said, crossing herself through a sigh.

"Rivalries keep the energy up," said Phillips. "Baseball's a team sport and it's one-on-one, batter versus pitcher. I think the other Axes, even the assholes, will appreciate you on the mound. I certainly will."

Calvin let the speech steep. *Quite a good one,* he thought. "Who says I need anyone's appreciation, Mr. Phillips?"

"You don't. Fuck 'em." Phillips waited for Ma to slap him, too. The woman clutched her rosary instead. "Prove it to yourself, though. That'll help your whole life. Need money for college? Get us to States and baseball'll put you in front of recruiters. Good players get full scholarships, paying for whatever degree, whatever college."

"Like Carlow?" asked Ma. "I hear that's a nice Jesuit college."

Sergeant Slaughter stifled a laugh. "It's a girls' college, Eileen."

"Oh. I thought there's boys there."

"Sure, two of them. Carlow won't have a baseball team."

"Hang on," Calvin smirked, "you're saying the male to female ratio at Carlow is, like, 3,720 to one?"

"Carlow's out," said Ma, "so it is. Too much temptation."

Phillips pitched alternatives: "Duquesne has a team if you got your heart set on a Catholic college. There's Pitt or Penn State."

The lad balked at Penn State. That's where his father went, and ended up with a boring degree and a boring job.

Sergeant Slaughter caught on. "The best kids get recruited west and south: Texas, Stanford, Miami."

Calvin perked up. *Miami Vice* was his favorite show. "Cool."

"Son, you got Bible Study and my mouth is starting to draw flies here. See you tomorrow?"

You are a puff of smoke that appears briefly and then—

"I'll be there."

"Great. Bring your arm and your heart. And some good sneakers."

FOUL

Next to his Countach poster with LAMBORGHINI in quartz calculator letters, Calvin had nailed up the gatefold cover for the Beach Boys LP *Endless Summer*. Bearded white men, swirling greenery, a bikini girl with a seagull on her belly. Summers past. The sun. The sea.

The snapshot in his hand brought back a specific summer. Not much sun. A gross lake. Two bearded men—make it three, but fuck the one who trimmed his like a chin-strap. Plenty swirling greenery.

And one girl. The highlight reel kicked on his cerebral Bellend Howl and his free hand fell below the desk. What a girl. No bikini for her. No seagull on her belly either, but something landed there the second time they'd ...

Calvin was too parched to wank. He hid the snapshot amongst his junk and hit the kitchen for water. Halfway back to his room, bells jingled from all three extensions. "I GOT IT!" he yelled, his girth twisting 'round, sending shockwaves to wobble the freestanding glass block wall. Ma's precious crystal things tinkled in fear on the sitting room shelves.

He slid across the kitchen tile, aiming one hip at the dining table to cancel any ricochet. He grabbed the handset off the wall and panted, "Hello, Connor residence, Calvin the Third speaking!"

"Hi … Calvin?"

Not only was the call for him, but it was Kitty! His heart went to hyperdrive. "Hi! How are you?"

"I'm good," she said. "How ar—"

"I got it!" he said, half at the air around him, half at the handset.

Rose's gum-smacking suddenly came over the line. "Fine," she spat. The sound of her gum went away quietly.

"Not the MUTE button trick, Sis—*hang it up!*"

Ma entered the kitchen from the basement stairs, wondering what all the thunder was about. Calvin hissed, "Make sure Rose's not eavesdropping on her phone."

"Who's on the line?" said Ma. "Not the MacDonald wench!"

"Bollocks, it's someone else! Now go stop Rose. Please?!"

Ma ground her teeth at all the aggravation her feckin' offspring gave her. She took the act on the road, heading towards the bedrooms.

Calvin inhaled triumphantly. "How about this weather?" he said.

Kitty got it. Banal talk until it was safe. "Pretty cold out."

Muffled from afar: a Ma shout.

Over the line: Rose's retort ("Jeez Mom, all ri—") and a loud click.

"Foiled again!" Calvin said, like William Dozier narrating *Batman*.

"Good," said Kitty. She sounded skittish. Nervous.

He licked his lips, the moisture making them crackle like Rice Krispies. And he'd just drank water. "How'd you get my number?"

"I got Abby to look it up in the parish directory."

"Well. Coulda called 555-1212."

"Ha!" A spritely tinkle of embarrassed mirth. "Guess I coulda."

"Surprised Abby didn't give you the wrong number on purpose."

"She wouldn't do that, she's my friend! But … I had to ask her like three times. She kept trying to talk me out of calling you."

"Everyone's got an opinion, Kitty."

"Oh, you have no idea! You were all everyone talked about. Abby and Roni and Cindy I mean. They're all like, 'he's hard-headed.'"

Calvin sat in his usual seat at the kitchen table, so he could squirm properly. This was like a police interrogation, reciting a Shakespeare soliloquy by heart, and burying his face in Lisa De Leeuw's tits all at the same time. "We Irish say 'bloody-minded.' And that's about right."

"Oh my—you admit it?"

"I won't lie to you. Didn't we cover trust at lunch?"

"We did, and I still don't trust boys, but … you're like, genuine. Boys like Sean Corgan are phony."

Abby Malone and Sean Corgan brought up in the first minute. Sweet Jaysus's dartos! "Oh you can trust Sean. To betray you."

"Sean is so fake. 'Such a nice boy,' Mom says, but he's not. He did the whole breath spray thing to you in seventh grade, right?"

Binaca Affair, check. *What's next—Art bleaching my hair, Sigourney rejecting me, or me and Jenny on Corgan's lawn that one time?*

"Sean was selling it at recess after the school banned it," said Calvin. "I was like, 'I'll try it, why not,' and Fartin' Martin caught us. First time I ever did anything like that. We got two weeks of I.S.S."

"Two weeks? Get out! It's not like cocaine or anything, you can buy it at Schoenberger's Pharmacy!"

Calvin stretched the curly-cue cable and hooked himself up with a fresh glass of water. The sounds of women arguing on the other side of the wall stopped. Ma had set Rose straight, or the other way 'round.

"Mademoiselle," he said, making his baritone brogue sugary sweet, "let's talk about something else, s'il vous plaît."

"Okay!" He heard her sit up. *She was lying down?* "Let's talk about Bible Study!" *In bed.* "Was it James 4 for the boys too?" *In the nude.*

A cold hand smacked the hot flush right outta Calvin's chops.

It also slapped the phone away. The taut curly-cue cable jerked the handset back to the wall cradle, nearly taking his glass of water with it.

"Christ our Lord!" he wailed, crossing himself with the hand holding the glass. Water sloshed onto his threadbare AquaZoo T-shirt.

Ma slammed Rose's pink clamshell phone on the table. "Take this back to your sister when you're done!" She stomped downstairs to berate Calvin Ciaran Connor II on his lack of direct parenting.

Calvin Ciarán Connor III gathered up the kitchen handset. Kitty's voice buzzed out, "—rything all right? Hello? Calvin, talk to me."

"I'm fine. My ma had to take Sis's phone away."

Again, sounds of Kitty moving. *Rolling onto her belly, mmmm.*

"Good! She can't eavesdrop on us and start rumors. Rumors suck."

"Speaking of—hang on, love!" He bustled to the junk drawer. Among the AA batteries, decks of Hoyle Jumbo, packs of Zippo flints, three-to-two-prong adapters, and dry pens from banks whose names had changed, Calvin found the kitchen copy of the *New American*. He flipped to the back. "Found it! *Who then are you to judge your neighbor?*"

"Yes, James 4!" said Kitty. "You had a bible just sitting there?"

"Ma keeps one in every room in the house."

"That's a lot of bibles! And the quote is perfect. My whole life I been searching for a biblical quote about not talking behind people's backs. Read the whole thing, please. I love hearing your voice."

He cleared his throat and recited,

> *Do not speak evil of one another, brothers. Whoever speaks evil of a brother or judges his brother speaks evil of the law and judges the law. If you judge the law, you are not a doer of the law but a judge. There is one lawgiver and judge who is able to save or to destroy. Who then are you to judge your neighbor?*

In Father Sean style, he sourced it: "The Letter of James, Chapter 4, verses 11 and 12."

Kitty said, "I am so tired of hearing about what 'they' say."

"I noticed something about 'they.' 'They' talk about us cuz we're different. You probably get that way more than me."

With rehearsed confidence: "I gotta live my life, Calvin."

"Same here, Kitty. We seem to have a lot in common now."

"Lots in common. We move to our own beat."

Boiling blood warmed his skin. "I like that."

"I like this," she said.

"I can't wait to see you again."

"Hmm," she said flatly.

"Oof, sorry. Or wait, no I'm not—since I can see, I get to say 'I can't wait to see you.'"

"True, but since I *can't,* maybe you'd respect that and change the word. That's all. Just one little word, Calvin."

"But 'I can't wait to "meet" you again' sounds so lame." Inspiration struck: "How about, I can't wait to 'behold' you again?"

"Ooh I like that! It's all Biblical and stuff."

"Let's go with that now," smiled Calvin.

"I can't wait to 'behold' you again too," said Kitty. "How come it took so long for us to behold each other? To be interested in each other? You in me, and me in you?"

A Serious Question, with a side of Unlikely Double Entendre. He gave the Risqué Answer: "Hell, love, I'm interested in 'me in you.'"

It took her a second. "Oh my!" she said in that noble British snob voice. "The compliment is taken but the young man needs subtlety!"

His heart thumped. *Was this love?* The Phil Collins songs said so.

"It's too fast," she said. Not complaining.

"I know. We just met," he said.

"Right. It's not based on anything."

"But it's there. I love it. I love this thing we have. So awesome."

"I like it too. It's really sweet. Whew, yes."

She's fanning herself. "Jaysus," he wept. The index finger on his right hand, hooped through the curly-cue phone cable, did a little mid-air cross in the same zip code as his chest.

"It's not like anything anyone's done to me before," she said. "I mean, done *for* me. Or cuz of me. Whatever. I'm trembling here!"

"Doing it myself." Sips of cool water turned his hot blood to steam. "I wish you were here so I could kiss you for the first time."

Kitty said nothing.

Calvin cursed himself. He'd gone too far.

"Yeah, I wish I was there, too," she breathed at last.

Whoosh! went Calvin's skin as it combusted. *Oh, the fire hurts!*

He looked down. His flute was rock-hard ... and he was rubbing it against the edge of the kitchen counter. "There was another bit in this chapter," he said, pinching the phone between his head and shoulder and grabbing his flute with both hands. "*You have no idea what life will be like tomorrow. You are a puff of smoke that appears, then disappears.* It's true. I didn't see this coming."

"Neither did I, Calvin."

It took a second. "Goddamnit! I never noticed how much I say things like that!"

"Yes, lots of common phrases are biased towards sight," she said.

"I hear that word a lot—*biased*. What is that?"

"It's not a vocab word, it's pretty common. If you prefer mustard and not ketchup on hot dogs, then you're biased against ketchup."

"Hot dogs are not meat," laughed Calvin, making vomit sounds. "What if I'm biased against hot dogs too?"

"Okay, my example is bad. It's not your likes and dislikes but when you *exclude* others that it's biased. Like if you made a law that hot dogs were illegal just cuz you didn't like them."

"Oh I see," said Calvin, then slapped himself. "Your point is, avoid using sight words."

"If you could," said Kitty. "I'd really appreciate it!"

"But even the Bible quote is, like, *appear*."

"That's different. Appear *can* mean, 'Now you see it, now you don't,' or it can be like, 'here today, gone tomorrow.'"

"God can *appear* in many ways," said Calvin.

"So can we. We're His children. By His will, we *appear* and *disappear*."

He thought about that.

"We've appeared," she said. "Me and you."

"Well," he said. "We have, but I need to disappear. If we talk too long, my sister'll rise from the dead. See you at lunch?"

She moaned in disappointment.

"I mean, *behold* you at lunch?"

"Demain? Non! J'ai un rendez-vous chez le médecin."

"Heh?"

"I thought you take French!"

"I take it for a ride but I don't bring it home."

That bombed. "What I *said* was, 'Tomorrow's no good, I got a doctor's appointment.' Conveniently during lunch, which sucks."

"How about we do homework together after school?"

"Bonne idée! Chez moi, 40 Liberty Road."

"Should I take your bus, or—"

"Après le dîner. Sept heures?"

All this French threatened to kill the Ape's hard-on. Too much like homework! "Oui. Now, just to recap: after dinner. Seven. Tomorrow.

40 Liberty Road."

"Au revoir!" she yelped, hanging up.

Calvin staggered to the wall cradle (charred legs were wobbly things) and hung up. He swept up the pink clamshell phone, made a sixty-second detour to the loo to play the pink flute in his 501 Blues until sweet white notes came, then—wiped and smiling—trudged to Rose's.

The young lady lay sprawled on her bed, back to the door, her cherry red Son of a Gun hair dryer cast to one side after failing to straighten her thick coarse mane once more. Rose leafed through a teen mag with Niki Taylor on the cover (as usual) and tapped her Parliament into a tiny tin ashtray stolen from McDonald's. The Connors' Usonian had wall-slab windows in the common rooms but the bedrooms had to make do with a single tight slice of glass high up on the wall. Rose's window was open; a chill nip tickled the torn edge of her favorite poster, the one with Springsteen's denim-clad butt.

BORN IN THE U.S.A., *ha, the irony.*

"Twenty-one degrees," purred a husky lady from Rose's boom box. "If the temperature was your big brother, he'd be old enough to buy you beer. Pinwheel Pippi on Wacky 103, gimme a spin sometime, Michael Hutchence." *The guy from* **INXS** *insisted all human inhabitants were inherently infested by the Imp.*

"O spymaster!" said Calvin over the noise. "Thou canst practice thy craft again anon!" He held out her pink phone.

"Bite me, Oscar Wilde!" Rose turned the magazine page so roughly she ripped it. Patrick Swayze's hunky face stuck to her finger.

Calvin set the phone on the bed by Sis's feet and positioned his shins out of its path, should it be angrily kicked. "We're doing fractions in Algebra," he said. "You've half of Wilde's wit, Sis, but twice his ego. If my math's right, that makes you four times as annoying."

"Fuckin' nerd! And you get laid sayin' that shit?!" Rose kicked the phone angrily and the lad *still* had to leap back to dodge it.

He hustled back to his room and shut the door. The winter wind beat a tree branch into his own high slice of window, an effect he enjoyed. He sat at his desk and glared at his Algebra text, still open from Saturday afternoon, when he gave up on homework and read *Restaurant at the End of the Universe* instead.

1.

$$\frac{2}{x} = \frac{4}{\frac{1}{2} \cdot 60}$$

Fractions *and* variables in the denominator?! Fuck you!

He lifted the text and ferreted from the junk underneath Wren's latest handwritten letter. It'd come with a snapshot: a teenage girl in a high school gym locker room. Not the pus orange lockers of Axsubeen High, but pale goldenrod with a purple accent stripe. The girl wore black hair; no more dyeing it Johnny Rotten-red. Stonewashed jeans instead of lime green shorts … but still that yummy fanny, *mmmm,* and thrusting it towards camera, *mmmm,* and pulling the waistband down slightly, *mmmm!*

Her pale face got washed out by the flash. She was slightly off-center and slightly out of focus. All the hallmarks of setting the camera on timer and racing back to pose.

Calvin put the letter and pic under a different pile of junk and attacked that Algebra, gleefully copying the answers for the odd-numbered questions out of the back of the textbook.

Chapter 6

ROCKET, PUT YER PICKLE IN MY POCKET.
MONDAY, JANUARY 30, 1989.

FOUL

GARFIELD GOT IT RIGHT: Mondays sucked moose cock.

Back at school. No Kitty at lunch. He got Friday's test back in Algebra and the red circle around the *59* was like a chalk outline. Mr. Hussing was having a good go at usurping the Devil's throne.

The capper was O.D.—Official Detention. This wasn't teacher's detention, held in the teacher's classroom and filled with extra work. When administrators banged the gavel, detention got capitalized and held in Room 101 across from the Office. Mr. Barnes taught Economics here but after the final bell, the desks were swiveled 180° and the felons were made to look at the blank back wall. No books or naps.

As punishment went, O.D. was cruel but oh so usual.

Mr. Walsh, O.D.'s warden, sat Calvin next to Davey. Teachers are so dumb. Davey spent the eighty minutes either making snarling grunts at Calvin or choking on his own breath trying to stay awake. Davey had avoided crossing paths with Calvin but only cuz he didn't want more punishment. From the school, and his asshole dad.

At 3:55 Walsh threw open the door. Calvin slogged over to the hallway entrance of the boys locker room. As set out in the *Axsubeen High School Student Handbook,* pupils maintained a separate Phys. Ed. locker with 1) school-issued white cotton short-shorts, 2) school-issued doo-doo brown T-shirt with 𝔄xsu𝔟een in pus orange blackletter, 3) calf socks, 4) athletic shoes, and 5) a towel. Calvin stowed his French text, coat, and scornworthy scarf of many colors and got in his Gym uniform.

Using the locker room's direct exit to the gymnasium, Calvin found none of the usual after-school crowd. No kids in the bleachers doing homework, shooting the shit, watching significant others practice for basketball or cheerleading. No wackos running laps on their own volition. The janitor had shut off every other row of lights to save power; the piss-sodium bulbs' stroby effect *increased* with only half of them on.

Four adults and eight teens were here. Calvin drew up short: half of them were female. Mrs. Susan Geoffries, a Science teacher disguised in track pants and an Axsubeen High doo-doo brown polo, chatted with three girls in softball kit. Among them was junior Valerie Crenshaw. Her boyish skater cut, lack of curves, and drawly contralto often led to gender confusion. Val was Spazz Watson's squeeze. "Can't squeeze her too hard or her red tip combusts!" was a line he used a lot.

One lass was in a catcher's armor and mask; that was Jill Pedersen. The Ape recognized those thick thighs anywhere. When Jill caught sight of Calvin strolling over in his short-shorts, she laughed cruelly.

He was cruel back: "You know you want me."

Steam hissed from between the tines of her catcher's mask.

Mrs. Geoffries ended her chat and led the softballers towards the girls locker room. That left only the males, three adults and five teens:

Mr. Fran Falcone, the chiseled Gym Teacher Man, wore a neon blue Adidas T-shirt and a wire-frame facemask. A foam chest protector the size of a car door dangled from loose shoulder thongs. Calvin had only seen umpires in the movies, played by old fat men with snarls. Seeing a fit fella in his 30s wearing the costume made the lad snicker.

Mr. Rick "Lucky" Cheeseboro's curly blond locks dripped from a perpetual navy ballcap, this one with a red B on the crown. Lanky, leathery arms stuck out a white polo with his dealership's logo.* This was Lucky's post-Major League uniform, worn at work and for personal

---

* Picture, if you will, a sedan viewed from the side. Make it a flattened oval, so the car now resembles a cheeseburger. The cabin roof/top bun is made from a word-art of LUCKY. The bottom bun is BORO, with the O's as the car's tires. The roadway beneath is GM/CHEVROLET in flat Copperplate. The burger itself is the word CHEESE, with the E's representing (in order) the right rear window, right passenger side window, and windshield.

   Up close, you can see hash strokes like a baseball's stitches through it all.

   From any appreciable distance, though, the logo looks like a nice fat titty.

   Lucky had commissioned it from a starving student at the Art Institute of Pittsburgh and got a great return from that $40 investment.

appearances. The man carried what Calvin knew from countless viewings of *Smokey and the Bandit Part 3* on cable as a radar gun.

Mr. Perry Phillips, a.k.a. Sergeant Slaughter, sat in the top row of bleachers at the far corner, a spot Art Maguire called the sniper's nest. In this setting the old man was known as "Skip."

Ryan Phillips sat in the bleachers too, many rows down, in school clothes: black shirt, jeans, Nike high-tops. Ryan didn't need to try out; his da was the manager. Teammates called him "Skipson" (SKIP′·sin, cf. "Simpson"). Ryan toyed with a bat, bored, stuck here.

Lastly we have the Scoundrels: Sean Corgan, Brion Davey, Reggie Roberts, and Chicken Ysderrhi. They wore last year's baseball uniforms: black cleats; doo-doo brown stirrup socks, belts, and pants; white polyester V-neck shirts, sweat-yellowed, stained with infield dirt, with 𝒜xes silk-screened in brown across the chest. Trucker hats with white foamy bills, doo-doo brown crowns, and pus orange 𝒜 logos covered the spiky top halves of their stupid hairdos. All four Scoundrels wore a Davey Dangle; Reggie's was the afro version.

The ironed-on back numerals had warped from sun and salt. Sean's shirt was different, base color pus orange, signifying a spot on the Varsity team last year. The edges of his number 2 had chafed loose against the straps of his chest protector. He wore his complete catcher garb: batting helmet (turned backwards), mask, shinpads—all doo-doo brown. Calvin thought he looked like a plastic dog poop. Even the hilarious oversized glove on Sean's left hand was the color of crap.

Davey saw Calvin and drew his Easton aluminum bat up like a knight brandishing his sword. Ryan Phillips hustled over to be Calvin's backup but needn't have bothered; Sean Corgan had stuck his catcher's mitt in Davey's belly to keep the goon in place.

"Glad you could make it," said Mr. Falcone, meaty hand out for a shake. He popped the umpire's mask up, mussing his frosted feathers.

"Thanks a million," said Calvin. He changed his mind on how Falcone looked in the umpire costume. Not silly at all. Like a man.

Lucky Cheeseboro didn't offer to shake. Didn't say shit. In person, he was older-looking, leather-ier.

Skip stayed in his sniper's nest, silent.

"I didn't know the Scoundrels would be here," Calvin hissed to

Ryan.

"You'll see lots of 'em if you make the team," said Falcone.

Lucky said, "Ain't gonna back out, are ya?"

Hard to believe that weary voice belonged to the same prick on TV and Wacky 103, screaming, "Get'cher buns to Lucky Cheeseboro GM Chevrolet, in bun·YOO'·tee·full al·TOO'·nah!!"

Mr. Falcone led the lad over to a one-foot stripe of white tape placed seemingly at random in the middle of the gym hardwood. "Let's see you in a uniform," he said, fussing with a pile of old shirts, plucking out an orange one with 43 on the back. "This one's XXL. That fit?"

"Hope it covers his panties," Lucky coughed, pointing at Calvin's white short-shorts. "Baseball ain't figure skatin', kid."

The Scoundrels, in their doo-doo brown polyester pants, laughed at Irish's pale thighs.

"I can go change—"

"It's fine for now," said Lucky, checking his watch.

Calvin gulped. He had to swap shirts here, in front of everyone. He'd gotten self-conscious about disrobing; previously he'd never given a fuck (e.g. his shameless public nudity in *Striking Out*). Future-Calvin's slim belly, chest hair, and arm muscles were a fantasy; Actual-Calvin had a pasty gut, sweat-slicked man-boobs, and triceps like lava lamp goo. The doo-doo brown Phys. Ed. T-shirt came off and the pus orange Varsity uniform shirt went on as fast as possible. The polyester stunk of old sweat and picked at his skin.

"Tuck it in," said Falcone. "Wear your uniform like a suit, properly, at all times. You're a righty?"

Apparently, this was a vital thing in baseball. "That's right, sir."

"'Sir?' What'm I, the Principal here? Call me 'Coach.'"

Calvin took the pitcher's mitt Falcone offered. Knowing his White Window would be in the way, he popped it off. Axsubeen's gym shorts had no pockets so he held the Swatch out for someone. Anyone.

Lucky Cheeseboro snatched the flimsy Swiss bauble and compared its time against that of his own watch.

His fucking Rolex.

"Warm up," Lucky ordered. "Ten easy throws."

Falcone hustled with Sean over to a home plate set up near the back wall. Calvin stood on the white strip of tape. Lucky fetched a dented aluminum farm pail of baseballs and flipped one to the lad. Calvin threw it to Sean, not a fastball, just a throw. Like when he played catch in his back yard with Art. The hilarious size of the catcher's mitt made sense now. The reactions of those present did not: lots of immature giggles.

"He throw gayer than four-dollar bill," said Chicken.

"Like a girl," laughed Reggie. "Ugliest girl I ever seen!"

From down at the plate, Sean hollered, "Yo Davey! You let Boy George here hit you in the face?"

Calvin could hear Davey's remaining teeth grinding.

"That's enough," announced Mr. Falcone.

Sean lobbed the ball back ... to Lucky, who snared it with a bare right hand. "I'll let ya catch 'em after you're warm, kid."

"How big is the home plate?" Calvin asked.

"Sixteen inches," everyone called out.

"And it's sixty feet, six inches away," said Reggie.

Calvin's next ball hit the hardwood before it reached the plate.

Reggie: "Ah crap, we broke him already!"

Chicken: "Psychological warfare," every syllable a chore. At the English language, and at shortstop, Cuauhtémoc Ysderrhi frequently bobbled routine flies.

"I used to bullseye womp rats in my T-16 back in Ireland," Calvin bragged. The next throw went wide, forcing Sean to stretch.

A distressed crease formed across Lucky's tanned forehead. "How well ya know baseball? Y'even know what the strike zone is?"

Calvin had to admit he did not.

"... shit. Okay. So, there's balls and strikes."

"That I know. Four balls is a walk and 'three strikes and yer out.'"

"Right. The strike zone goes edge-to-edge across the plate, and from the batter's knees to here." Lucky held a ball at his belt and slid it upward three times in ball-high increments. "'Bout yay-high. If the uni's got the team name across the tits, it's the bottom of that."

Calvin forced himself to concentrate on Lucky's tutelage and not marvel at how different the guy was in real life. That carnival-barking persona was nowhere to be found. The dude's polo shirt seemed shaggy compared to the rhinestone-covered Terminator jacket and silver lamé tricorn hat he wore on the tacky billboards.

"What if the batter's really tall?" the lad mused.

"Then the strike zone's tall too." The man rudely got on the white tape stripe, forcing the blue chip off it. "Ya throw like a fag but it ain't hopeless. First of all, ya gotta use yer whole body, not just yer arm. Follow through. Good pitchin' comes from the legs and the back. Keep yer body straight up and down, like this. Make yer back a boner, rock-hard. Lotsa kids lean back to get extra *oomph,* like Bugs Bunny—don't. Only causes trouble. Oh, and see how my back foot's on the rubber? This white bar here. Pitchin' is like safe sex, brother—always use the rubber."

When Lucky finally shut up, he handed over the radar gun.

Calvin drooled over the cool device. He saw a PROPERTY OF AXSUBEEN BOROUGH POLICE sticker on the side. "Bloody hell, did you steal this from Sheriff Steve?!"

"Pay attention, sweetheart." Rolling the baseball with the fingers of his left hand, Lucky stood erect, kicked his right leg out, and fired a four-seamer right over the plate. Sean Corgan caught it with ease.

Lucky vacated the white tape stripe and snapped up his radar gun before Calvin could break it. "Get on there and throw for real."

"This is a lot to take in," the lad whined.

"That's what she said." Lucky peeped his Rolex. "Chop-chop."

Calvin wanted some water. He adjusted his short-shorts' elastic waistband; the uniform shirt was tucked too far down. Sean took note after Calvin wiped his sweaty right palm on his belly and called out, "Show him about the rosin bag, Lucky!"

From the sniper's nest, Skip yelled, "Let 'im sweat for now."

"He'll chuck it to the moon drippin' like that!" Sean yelled back.

"Shut the hell up and catch, 2!" said Skip.

Calvin had no idea what that was about. Sean crouched back into the catcher's spot, slapping his big mitt to get Calvin's attention. Coach Falcone fixed the umpire mask over his face and went to one knee.

Remembering all forty-three points of Lucky's advice, Calvin kicked up his left leg and brought the ball around. His back was straight. He threw three-quarters style with the ball up and out from his shoulder. He fell down as he followed through but the ball came out straight and fast.

The sound of it slapping Sean's mitt echoed, but said mitt was a meter left of the plate. "Ball," Falcone called, his voice like a shrug.

Reggie Roberts asked, "How fast?"

Lucky had moved off to clock the pitch with his radar gun: 73.

Reggie went *whoa!*, Chicken clucked in spastic surprise, and Ryan went, "Nice!" Poor Davey shook his head like he'd lost a bet.

Calvin blinked. "Is that good now?"

"It's up there," said Lucky. "Let's get the ball in the same ZIP code as the plate. Yer usin' three fingers up on the runway. Ain't never seen that in my whole life, pardner. Three across the horseshoe for a change, sure … shit, what if that's yer slow pitch?!" A twinkle lit up in the leathery man's eye as he showed Calvin a proper fastball grip.

The next pitch came out hot. The lad released the ball late and it struck the floor. Sean leapt, barely snaring the ball before it could ricochet over his head.

"*Waaay* too much mustard," said Sean, lobbing the ball back to him. Short, on purpose. Calvin had to scoop it up. Using the pitcher's glove this way was weird. Chicken burped something about limp wrists.

The lad's next fastball was even wider.

"Yer tryin' too hard," said Lucky. "Emotions are the Devil. Don't act like some chick on the rag. Ya gotta be a monk. Poker face." The guy popped on a grin. "Like me."

Calvin's teenage sarcasm spat like a Sparkler. "Do us a favor—you got the worst poker face I ever seen. You keep lookin' at your watch!"

"Cuz yer wasting my time, sunshine. Get over there and pitch."

"Cunt," hissed Calvin, not caring if anyone heard. Inhale. Exhale. He envisioned making the perfect throw.

The ball went wide again, though less wide, and much straighter and faster. Sean loved it: "There's some lightning!"

Lucky checked his gun. "86," he called out.

"You are a vlákas," said Chicken. "You hold thing upside-down."

Lucky turned the radar gun over. The LED readout now said 98.

Chicken *cock-a-doodle-doo*'ed at his own imbecility.

"My main mick throwin' heat," Reggie laughed.

"Again," Lucky told Calvin. 87.

"One more, baby." 89.

"Come on, rocket, put your pickle in my pocket." 90.

Lucky's dry eyes drank Calvin in. The kid hit 90 without really using his legs or back. "He'll break a hundred," the man wheezed.

"Frozen rope, all miss plate," said Chicken. "As blind as Kitty."

Up in the sniper's nest, Skip yelled, "He needs a target. Hey, 89! You're up!"

Davey's long spine went from bent in sulk to upright in shock. "No way, Skip! That's how I ended up in detention in the firs—"

"I didn't *ask,* 89! Get your ass in the box or get it out the door!"

Skip's words boomed down, blowing Davey towards the plate.

This was inevitable, Calvin thought. He felt hot and sweaty and the damn ballcap they gave him was too tight with all his hair.

Seeing his pitcher's jitters, the catcher trotted over. The clackety-clack of Sean's cleats racked Calvin's nerves. The little wanker, as Calvin called him, was a foot shorter but built better and quite uncowed by the Irish Raging Ape's hulking girth. Sean's whole thing was ultimate confidence. Too cool for you. He was only two months older but treated Calvin like a thick younger cousin. The guy's compliments felt like insults in sheep's clothing, even when they weren't.

And yet ... Sean always invited the lad to his wild parties.

The little wanker came right up to the white tape-stripe acting as the pitcher's mound but cleverly stood to Calvin's left. He knew he was too small to block out the background (home plate, where Davey was), so he changed the background instead.

Once Calvin swiveled to face him, Sean inched close enough to kiss. They hadn't been this close since the famous Halloween party when Calvin took Jenny's virginity. And, presumably, Sean's lawn's virginity.

Moving the big mitt up to cover most of his wire-frame mask, the little wanker said, "You'll be driving soon. Some old junker. You ain't cool enough to roll in an IROC like me. Still, my dad pays four bucks an hour cash down at Pizza Putt. Easy work for gas and rubbers. Just stick to humpin' her on your own lawn."

Flummoxed, a recent vocab word in English 2, didn't begin to cover it. Calvin's mouth pried open and fell shut with gummy smacks.

"Deep breaths, yes," the little wanker said, keeping his voice low. "Once the Ragin' Ape calms down, he can throw strike one."

"I'm sorry, *this shite* you're doing is supposed to calm me—"

Sean grabbed Calvin's glove, forcing it up.

Suspecting the ol' lemme-punch-you-with-your-own-hand trick, Calvin jerked his glove-hand back.

Sean dropped his own mitt down. "IF YOU COVER YOUR MOUTH," he screamed, "THEY CAN'T SEE WHAT YOU'RE SAYING!"

Calvin put his glove over his face from the nose down, like Sean had done. "You're telling me these pricks can read my lips?"

Sean covered his own pug again. "Ballplayers read lips like your mommy sucks dick. They ain't blind like your new girlfriend, chief, so you gotta take away their ability to see you jabberin'."

From behind Calvin's glove came the sounds of seething.

"This is the game," said Sean. "A pitcher's all alone on the mound. People stare at you and call you names. Must be what it's like when you walk around school." Sean's emerald eyes defied the piss-sodium lights, shining out the shady catcher's mask like virescent stars. "Lucky's gonna talk pitch location and not to overdo it, but fuck that. Gimme the hottest heat you got. Mustard galore. Show 'em how big your dick is. I seen it. We all did—it's huge. Now show *them*." Sean clacked back to the plate.

"Don't," Lucky hissed. The man was suddenly at Calvin's side.

"Don't what?" Calvin hissed back through his glove.

"It's all over your mug. Told ya to stop that shit. Poker face."

Steel gray eyes burned the ex-Major Leaguer's tanned face.

"I'm sure he tol' ya to throw hard," said Lucky, "and ya got a 'clever' idea where to aim it. *I'm* telling ya now: don't."

Steel gray eyes opened wide, realizing Lucky was right.

He turned to the plate, flat eyes now. Expressionless.

Davey popped on a doo-doo brown helmet and took up position where the left-hand batter's box would be. Once Sean was behind the plate, Davey brought his bat up and stared Calvin down.

Both kids fell out of the gym and into a narrow, darkened battle arena. Just the two of them, pooled in personal spotlights, mano a mano. Far off, trumpets blared the fanfare of war—

—Calvin fired.

No windup. Flat-footed. Sean and Mr. Falcone weren't in their crouches yet. The ball came high and tight, aimed right at the gap in Davey's teeth, and sailed through the airspace where his baby blues had been. The goon had thrown himself to the hardwood just in time.

The ball rapped the gymnasium's back wall with a noise like thunder, leaving an imprint in the safety padding.

Everyone in the gymnasium moved towards Calvin.

"No fair!" said Chicken.

"That's my friend!" said Reggie, not laughing.

Seeing a red haze flooding the black kid's white eyes, Calvin flung off the mitt to make fists.

Lucky Cheeseboro inserted his lanky body in front of Reggie and Chicken. Ryan Phillips closed on the two Scoundrels from behind.

The only real violence happened at home plate. Sean dashed forward, then turned to stand arms akimbo over the prone Davey. The goon rose with his reddest face yet and tried to get around Sean.

The catcher re-blocked the path.

Coach Falcone corralled Davey by the shoulders but the goon wriggled away. When Sean moved to re-re-block the path towards Calvin, Davey's aluminum bat came down on his face.

The catcher's mask took the blow, flying aside to the hardwood. The catcher himself went back, a dozen skitters of staggerment, but stayed on his feet. And stayed positioned between pitcher and batter.

Falcone threw his finger into the sky. "Yer outta here, Davey!"

"He threw at my head!" said Davey. "What the f—"

"Suspended from practice for a week! Hit the showers!"

Davey hissed at him, at the cruel world. He ran to the locker room.

The air needed a minute to cool before Lucky could make his joke: "Finally got some location work outta you."

"Go and shite," Calvin told him.

"I warned you, bubba. I said, 'don't.'"

"The cunt deserved it. Attacked me without warning at lunch!"

Coach Falcone checked that Sean was okay, then made for Calvin, his fat mustache bristling with contempt. "Zip that lip, Connor! You can kill a batter with the baseball. It's happened. If you throw at someone's head deliberately, it's murder."

"*ffffff,*" the lad sighed, going from flushing to blushing. He wiped his hands on the pus orange polyester uniform, which didn't so much soak up the moisture as spread it about. He went whole days with fewer emotions. And now he needed to appear contrite for the grown-ups.

He could do that; he was Catholic, after all. "I'm sorry, Coach."

"Not me," said Falcone. "Apologize to Brion."

"Tomorrow, when he's cooled off," said Skip. In the commotion, the old man had left the sniper's nest, descended the bleachers, and crossed the floor without anyone noticing. "Clock on that one, Lucky?"

"9 1."

Skip raised an eyebrow erased by age.

"On a flat-footed throw," Lucky went on, no poker face here. "From a tenth-grader. Pitching for the first time. I think I'm in love!"

"Spectacular," said Skip. "Congrats, son. You made the team."

No one applauded or offered a high-five to the lad, not even Ryan. *Is this an honor or a death sentence?* Calvin popped off the ballcap and used both hands to push his wet mane back his scalp.

"Oh, I get it now," said Lucky, snaring Calvin's right arm and showing off the scars to everyone: a rough one in the lad's inner elbow, and a longer, cleaner one along the outside. Letting go, the ex-Big Leaguer pulled back the left sleeve of his car dealership polo. He had the same long, clean scar along the outside of his throwing elbow.

"So that's why he's Nolan Ryan right out of the wrapping paper," said Perry Phillips.

Sean Corgan spoke for all the teenagers here: "I don't get it."

"Tommy John surgery," said Lucky. "Pitchers make the same motion a million times and it wears out the ulnar ligament." He pointed at bits of his left arm. "It connects this to that, and if it craps out, they replace it with an extra tendon." The man was suddenly happy Calvin had worn his gym uniform short-shorts. He made a big show of inspecting the boy's ice white thighs. "Which leg they take it from?"

Calvin felt naked. "They didn't. I got one from a cadaver."

"*Ewww,* they put dead-body meat in you?" Reggie gagged.

"Part-mick, part-zombie," said Sean, getting a laugh.

"The tendon came from your ma," Calvin told him. *"She's* inside *me* for a change."

"Knock it off," said Skip. Pointing a gnarled finger at the rough scar on Calvin's inner elbow: "That meatball mess reminds me of battlefield surgery in Korea. What happened?"

Calvin had grown sick and tired of feeling sick and tired about saying he was sick and tired of telling this story. Ryan Phillips jumped in: "We were camping one time when a big storm hit. This tree branch snapped off with a sharp point and went *shooom!"* Ryan karate-chopped a pointed finger into his own elbow. "Cut the ligament in half."

"'Bisected' is how they put it," said Calvin. "They couldn't reattach it and I was too young to donate my own spare piece."

"Ya coulda lost the whole arm," said Lucky. "How's it feel? Pitchers say our arms are stronger after Tommy John. Mine sure was."

"I dunno. There's no pain. But I got nerve damage too. Sometimes my hand tingles, like when you hit your funny bone."

"Tryout's over!" said Mr. Falcone. As the only member of team staff who worked at Axsubeen High (in his Gym Teacher Man role), Fran Falcone got spooked enough to quote policy: "No more 'til he gets his physical. The school board's anal about pre-existing injuries."

Skip nodded. "Dr. Jacoby'll clear him, I'm sure." He stuck his hand out to Calvin. "Welcome to the Axes."

Calvin shook the hand gingerly, expecting it to explode like a pineapple grenade. "Thank you, Mr. Phillips."

"'Skip.' And *just* 'Skip,' never 'the Skipper.' Bring up *Gilligan's Island* and I'll cut off your nuts. Wanna ride home with me and Ryan?"

"Sure, thanks a million."

"When you're ready. Gonna shower first?"

"Not with you."

The old war hero's concrete face busted wide, spraying the air with confettied yuks of laughter.

"Let him keep the orange uniform, Skip!" said Sean.

"White for now. He's way too green for the Varsity. Coach Falcone will love having talent on the J.V. for once." Skip turned to Lucky. "Guess I'll be seein' you more often this season?"

"You bet," Lucky said. "My time'll be well-spent."

"Then get this nasty sumbitch ready, A.S.A.F.P."

⚾ MANAGER'S OFFICE ⚾

After scribbling his home number on the back of a business card for Calvin, Lucky Cheeseboro took his leave. Perry Phillips joined him; the two men exited the gymnasium using doors in the far wall leading directly to the faculty parking lot. Lucky jumped in his showroom-shiny jet black 1988 Callaway twin-turbo Corvette B2K (a convertible but with the top up—it *was* January, deep inside Central Pennsylvania's chilliest butt crack).

As the 'Vette peeled out onto Rte. 666 (Bald Eagle Pike), Skip dashed around to the back of the school with an agility few saw, and none would believe, from a gent of his sixty years. He re-entered via the loading dock and crept down the hallways' alternating pools of light and shadow (the custodian had killed half the lights here too).

Skip slipped into the locker room. The Phys. Ed. Dept. office was a cinder block protrusion jutting out the perimeter wall, installed two years after the school's initial construction when then-Athletic Director Christoph Schultz III realized the Gym teacher needed his own spot. Six feet to a side, one desk, one chair. Phillips had his own key for this office. He didn't teach (he'd worked thirty-odd years as head machinist at Schultz's Lumber) but he'd coached the Varsity football team for a short spell after Korea and took over the baseball team from Axsubeen's legendary village idiot, Toby Stewart, in 1959.

With the office's overhead fluoros off, Skip stood invisible in a back corner. The wide wire-shot glass window provided decent sightlines into the boys locker room: dim, dank, and presently empty.

Soon *The Silence of the Lambs* will come out and Perry Phillips will lose the "Sergeant Slaughter" soubriquet in favor of "Hannibal Lecter." And why not? The old man had killed people and it wasn't a stretch to imagine him eating them, too. Skip could hold his lean frame rigid for long periods with no sign of impatience. He exercised daily, kept his buzz-cut sharp, and wore a thousand-yard stare like other men wear a favorite pair of jeans.

Sumbitch saw into your soul.

The shuffle of unshod feet—Sean Corgan, out of his cleats, moving on stirrup-socks to the locker room's far corner. Skip watched the rich kid hide behind a couple big water pipes, ducking his ginger head under the giant red valve with the equally giant placard dangling on a tarnished brass chain that warned against doing this very shit.

Seanie's knucklehead crew came in from the main hallway. Skip heard *shhh!*-ing and hands slapping the air to signal quiet. "God-*damn*, can't handle that freshmen funk," one said, a phrase only a colored boy would use. Skip agreed with Reggie, though. A moist reek in here.

The targets arrived thirty-four seconds later. The Connor boy was nuclear war on the concrete floor. Skip's son, Ryan, moved with stealth. Connor prattled about a homework date as the boys passed the Phys. Ed. office window. "Just the two of us," he said, "finally."

"If Abby shows up, gimme a call," said Ryan, "I'll rescue you."

Skip knew every kid in town, their names, athletic prospects, chance of growing up wasteful/liberal/queer. Connor and Davey were at war over the Howes' daughter, so "Abby" was Kitty's flabby friend. *Nice of Ryan to act as wingman,* thought Skip, *s'long as that's all it is. Won't have any son of mine chubby-chasin'.*

Connor worked a Master Lock dial and slapped open his locker, the metal-on-metal crash ringing through the damp air. With an instinct that embarrassed him, Phillips reached for a sidearm he never wore. He blinked away the damp Asian battlefield that likewise was never there.

Big Boy pulled a towel out. A homework date meant he'd grab a shower before putting them swanky clothes back on. The Phillips driveway served as the bus stop for kids on his block. Skip saw how Connor dressed lately, saw him eye-fucking the blind girl during Mass.

The fat shit was about to get ambushed and had his head in the clouds. Wasn't no way Davey stormed out of the building after being ejected. Teen boys were so obvious, 'specially the hotheaded ones.

The wildcard was Skip's son. Ryan hovered near but not next to Connor, grabbing a seat on the thin wooden bench that ran down the locker aisle. His head swiveled, casual, but aware. Phillips had drilled that into all four of his boys and was proud to see it in action. The world's a battlefield. Trust no moment of peace.

Some boys were confident naked, others timid. The former tended to be well-hung but it wasn't a reliable predictor. Big Boy did all right, Phillips saw, and had no compunction to disrobe when the audience was only Ryan. Back in the gym, where the bullies were, the fat mick couldn't get that orange uniform shirt over his Jell-O belly fast enough. This suggested timidity in Connor's competitive character. Shit like that cost pitchers dearly.

Blue chip? Yes. Sure thing? No.

Connor had to hold the towel in place over his wide waist. Ryan swept the locker room again to clear it. When his blue eyes hit the office's wire-shot glass window, he stopped.

Skip tensed. *I just got made.*

The bullies blazed in. Davey led the charge from the near end of the aisle. Ryan adroitly sprang off the thin wooden bench, throwing a shoulder into Davey and driving him back into Chicken and Reggie.

With Connor's attention focused that way, shoeless Sean Corgan maneuvered in easily from behind. Some shadow or rustle tipped Big Boy off and he whirled. Seanie threw a fist and halted it at the last instant, a fake sucker-punch.

Connor's flinch sent him twirling about-face, like a cue ball struck with some English. His hairless legs caught on the thin wooden bench and he smacked his forehead on the lockers behind him. The doo-doo brown Axes trucker cap tumbled off his noodle. The tiny towel lost its struggle around his waist, fluttering away.

Seanie was technically innocent but it was a chickenshit move.

Connor rolled on his back, one fist limply cocked to the side. Eyelids dropped half-closed. He was out.

Seanie stood over him and laughed in pride. He never saw Ryan's fist 'til it clocked him above the right eye.

Chicken Ysderrhi untangled himself from the pile of Scoundrels to confront Ryan. Skip couldn't see the foreign kid's face but his body language went from fierce to cowering. Ryan hadn't raised a fist or said anything … Chicken backed off at the mere thought of Ryan's attack. *Must be some history there,* thought Skip, again proud of his boy.

Davey bounced up—and backed off cuz his target was now naked. Pathetic! More concerned about his heterosexuality than getting the kill. Teenaged Perry Phillips would've gone the other way entirely, delivering jabs at Irish's nuts, destroying any chance Connor would have kids.

Ryan stood guard over his felled friend. Seanie got to his feet. He let a second pass. That's a good move. Seanie loves to use it.

When Ryan didn't charge, Seanie knew it'd be safe to call a truce. He said, "Check on him, chief."

FOUL

A bubbly yellow sludge swirled betwixt a hundred aubergine and pine starbursts. A blond head penetrated this Pink Floyd laser light show. "Y'aight, Calvin?" said Ryan.

"Nice pee-pee, Irish," said Sean.

"Is nice, actually," Chicken said, pointing. The beakly freak fielded punches from Reggie and Davey.

"He ain't dead," said Reggie, "see his big ol' belly's breathin'?"

Calvin heard their noise, nearby, miles away. He swept to his feet, swept Ryan aside with a big arm, and swept to his towel so he could cover his nakedness. All that sweeping led to disgorging.

"Ah shit," said Davey, "he yakked!"

The vomit puddle wasn't much. Calvin went to wipe his chin with the towel but the little wanker had put one stirrup-socked foot on the corner. With a mighty roar, Calvin yanked. Sean was just fleet enough of foot to step off and avoid getting hurled through the ceiling.

"Relax, chief," said Sean. "This is your initiation."

"Like in *Revench zovva Nertce?*" sputtered Calvin with spittle.

"Sure. 'Cept it's a team you're joining, not a frat."

Calvin spoke more slowly: "Let's fazt forwerd to the pert where I put on a Derth Vader mesk and fuck your girlfriend."

"Yeah, Kare'll *really* believe your fat ape ass is me in disguise." Sean rolled his green eyes for the Scoundrels' amusement. "Meanwhile I'll be over at Schultz Park fuckin' your sister Rose up the butt."

Calvin boomed his big guffaw right in Sean's face. "Enjoy that V.D., mate!" he whooped, putting up a hand. Ryan waited for it to stop wobbling before fiving it.

Reggie laughed too. He loved a good joke, no matter who told it.

"You got cinnamon toast *burnt,* bro!" he told Sean. He offered a hand for Davey to five, who swatted it away.

Ryan folded his arms at Sean. "How come I never got initiated?"

Sean shrugged. "You're Skip's son, chief. Different rules for you."

"No, it's cuz this is revenge. *Revenge of the Numbnutses.*"

"I deserve revenge for all his beanballs!" said Davey.

"You deserve all my balls, all right," said Calvin.

"The real initiation," Sean said to Ryan, as if they were adults chatting while noisy kids played in the sandbox, "is the team haircut."

Ryan pointed at Sean's flappy red tail. "I ain't gettin' that shit."

"What're you, deaf? Different rules for you, Skipson."

"Sergeant Slaughter didn't say nothing about the haircut," said Calvin.

"Cuz this ain't his rule, it's mine," said the little wanker. *"I'm* the team captain. *I* got you this tryout. *You* ain't an Axsubeen Axe 'til you hit the barber."

Calvin's forehead, red from abuse, crinkled up. "I'll look stupid."

"No stupider than when you had that skater rat thing," said Sean.

"Or when you were all penis-head bowl-cut," said Chicken.

"What about that fugly white mop thing?" said Reggie.

"I'm not doing it," said Calvin, like *that's that.*

"Lemme punch him," Davey said, "give him a black eye."

"Nah," Sean told him. "If you fuck up his face, Kitty'll feel sorry for him and be all, 'Oh lemme kiss it to make it better!' Think how much madder you'll get if you help Connor lose his virginity."

Calvin sighed at how thick the little wanker was. "First off, Kitty can't see a black eye. And second, I'm not a virgin."

"Every dork says they ain't a virgin," dissed Sean.

"He fucked Jenny on your lawn that one time!" said everyone.

Sean let a second pass. "Oh yeah." He reset his poker face. "But we ain't helping you get laid *again.* No way."

"Nice recovery, 'chief,'" said Ryan.

The wire-hairs on Davey's nuts itched. "Stop talkin' about that!"

"Talkin' about what?" said Calvin. "You guys all bein' virgins?"

"No, about you and Kitty! She's mine!"

"The girl who's two years younger than you, that you brag about making out with back in, like, fifth grade? The crippled girl you never leave alone, you pervert?!"

All this yelling made the lad dizzy. He leaned on his locker, then pretended he was doing it to look casual. "Got a date tonight. Gonna get it on, too. When're you lot gonna finally leave Virgin-ia?"

He pointed at Reggie: "Virgin."

At Davey: "Virgin."

At Chicken: "Rapist. Oh I heard rumors now!"

At Sean: "Wanker."

At his locker: "Pants."

He dropped his towel and turned his back on the Scoundrels, flexing his arse as he got back into boxers. "You're all so thick," he went on. "What if I tell Skip about this on the ride home?"

"He'll believe anything I tell him." Sean spoke like this was undisputed fact. "I'm Skip's darling little Seanie."

Ryan picked an odd time to snort down a laugh.

Calvin didn't find it funny. He was still concussed and in mortal peril. He did enjoy seeing the bruise forming over Sean's smug green eye. Ryan got him good. But the real threat was Davey. "You," he said to the goon. "You lost, mate. You need to leave me and Kitty be."

"No, I need to break my foot off—" Davey started.

"—doin' the moonwalk the other direction," Sean finished. "Brion's gonna do that, Connor. *You* need to leave *him* alone, too."

"Done. For the rest of my life, if I can help it."

"Good. Get the team haircut." Sean turned. "Later, chief."

Chapter 7

LA PASSION DU GORILLE.

FOUL

SHRUBBERY BOXED IN THE yellow brick American Foursquare at 40 Liberty Road. Smoke curled out the chimney towards a waning half-moon. The porch lamp had a silly plastic torch-flame diffuser. His eyes had their own apple juice filter. He resisted the innate urge to clear his yellow vision by shaking his head. It never worked.

Calvin knocked. Footsteps and barking. He mopped sweat off his forehead with his noisome scarf of many colors and did one last check for B.O.

The mother always answers. Jill's ma loved him. Jenny's ma hated him. Wren was an exception; her ma wasn't around but her da was and he'd made vague threats about his preferred projectile load.

Ma Howe *chunk!*ed back a deadbolt and opened the door. A plain Sears sweater and slacks. Darkened eyes and big hips. No slutty tattoos like Ma Pedersen (now called by her maiden name, McSween). No snooty tan like "Mrs." MacDonald (she hated Calvin's use of "Ma"). No 12 gauge like Satan Lyons.

Nope. Ma Howe was just a plain ol' American ma.

"Hello, I'm Calvin Connor the Third," the lad said.

Ma Howe's eyes, made beady by spectacles, bounced over his kelly green down jacket, odious scarf of many colors, charcoal gray Irish wool sweater, and Bugle Boy jeans. She peeped his broad belly, long limpen brown hair, and forehead bruise. He toted a text and a Trapper Keeper with a sports car on it. She scanned the street behind him for lurking gangs or trails of corpses.

Satisfied the boy wasn't a bank robber or axe murderer, Ma Howe brightened. "Hello. I'm June Howe. Come in." Confident. In authority.

She *was* a Schultz after all, the younger sister of Konrad III, a.k.a. the owner of Schultz's Lumber Co., a.k.a. Troop 666's "The General." Like many of Axsubeen's legacy Germans, her given name was old-school (Gudrun) and she traded by a common name (June).

Calvin crossed the threshold. Ma Howe didn't let him close the door; she did it herself and bolted it behind him, a little unusual.

"Cold one out!" he said, requisite weather comment.

"We've got the fire going in the living room," she said. Calvin could smell the pleasant wood smoke. "Did you drive here?"

"My sister gave me a lift." Calvin panicked. Did he reek of Rose's Parliaments? Or other things—B.O., jisim, turkey? "She's hitting Logan Valley Mall and coming back to pick me up at 8:30."

A Siberian husky bounded up to him. Its creepy cyan eyes put Art Maguire's icy sapphires to shame. The dog wore a yoke with a stiff hoop-like handle. Calvin had seen this animal from a distance.

"Lewis, meet Calvin," Ma Howe said. The dog snuffled the stranger's jeans, figuring him out, then panted in approval.

"Lewis, heel," the woman ordered, and the beast immediately sat and left Calvin alone. The Connors didn't have pets (Da was allergic) but none of the dogs Calvin had been familiar with, like Sandy's silly pooch Fozzie or the two German shepherds belonging to the Schaefers next door on Maple, were ever this obedient!

Well. It is a guide dog.

"Calvin, this way." Ma Howe said it like that so the dog knew whom she was addressing. That, or she was used to issuing orders.

The Howes had a country kitchen. Shiny brass handles on stained-wood cabinets. Thatched decorations. Nutmeg stench. Gorgeous amber light streaming in the window, even at 7 p.m. in the winter.

No Devil-may-care warped vinyl floors and peeling paint like the McSween-Pedersen shack. No sparkly cathedral-ceiling fixtures like at the MacDonald McMansion. No rifles mounted to the walls like at Mr. Lyons's house (Calvin had never been there but Wren mentioned the guns in approximately 40% of her weekly letters).

The Howe house was a cozy, friendly joint.

That reeked of dog hair.

Ma Howe halted by the fridge. "Kitty tells me you're helping her with French?"

"Mais oui!" yipped Calvin. "She's helping *me,* in fact."

"She's certainly a bright one." The woman's beady eyes inspected him again. He stiffened his shifty hands before they could hide in pockets like a guilty little boy. "You're from Ireland?"

"The accent gave me away, did it?" A standard response to a tiresome topic. Everyone knew but asked anyway. "I was born there and lived there until March of '83. We lived in my mother's village, called Leixlip in County Kildare. My da's from Altoona, but his father was straight from Dublin."

"Your dad is one of my husband's bosses," said Ma Howe.

"And your brother is my da's boss," said Calvin.

"Yep. Funny how we've never formally met. Seen you all down at Saint Brigid though. I thought both your parents were foreign."

"They are now. They're from outer space."

After a chuckle, Ma Howe spread her hands in a late display of welcome. "I'd introduce you to my family, but Eddie's upstairs with his Nintendo and my husband's still at the yard, working overtime."

"My da's always working too."

Ma Howe's face gave away what she thought of the use of the word "work" in relation to management. "Something to drink?"

"I'm fine, thanks a million," he said, turning at a noise.

Through the archway to the living room, a queen in a green woolen sweater made her entrance. Firelight danced up behind her, adding a shiny halo to her long russet hair. A wide smile spread her cheeks, pushing up the pink dark glasses over her eyes.

Barefoot, too.

The Trapper shifted in front of his Bugle Boys. "Glass of water?"

FOUL

"You're a year ahead of me and still have trouble conjugating?"

"Anything '-er,' '-ir,' and '-re' is easy. Like English."

"It's not at all like English. We add endings to the infinitive verb. 'To want: I want, you want, he/she/it wants.' In French, the infinitive has its own ending. You gotta pull that off and put on the one you need.

'Désirer: je désire, tu désires, il/elle désire.' "

Calvin smirked. "You oughta write textbooks."

Kitty snorted. "And you oughta read 'em. If you can do memorization like multiplication tables, you can do French."

"Doing French is like doing Algebra with the book upside down."

A blind person'll get that, he sighed to himself.

"Irregular verbs *are* hard," said Kitty. "That's why Madame Lefebvre covers them so much. They're irregular! Y'know … like you and me." She cocked her head to punctuate that.

Whoa. He assumed her statue-like body language came from her never seeing the head nods and shrugs and shite everyone did. Can't imitate what you don't know exists. But once in a while, like here, Kitty got all Italian and waved her hands. *Are gestures, like, human nature? Or did the Blair County Institute for the Blind train her to do them so she'd fit in?*

He felt guilty for noticing. *Stop making her blindness a focal point!*

"Me and you are irregular," he said, "but we're still conjugatable."

Kitty gave her spritely tinkle of mirth. "Is that even a word?"

"Uh, maybe it's 'conjugal.' "

"Well. We're making up our own language now!"

He gasped in surprise—she'd imitated his "Well." Said at the start of a thought, as a complete sentence with a full stop. He'd never heard any Yank do that. It was a Leixlip quirk he'd never rid himself of (nor wanted to), like the superfluous "now" he put at the end of sentences.

"Let's stick to a real language, love, like French," he said.

"Good idea, love." She lay on one elbow and propped up her head. Orange flickers danced mirthfully over the exposed skin of her soft feet. Long brown shadows fondled the big bumps across her woolen sweater.

Calvin thrust his meaty hands at the fireplace to dry them. The heat felt good on his fingertips, a lite pain. The teenagers had eschewed the living room sofa for the pea-soup green shag carpet by the hearth. Calvin's notes, French 2 text, and a prudent measure of open space lay between them. An agreeable configuration for homework.

Lewis the guide dog sat near the sofa. Calvin aimed his eyes at the husky while keeping his face locked towards Kitty. The dog perked up its snout and looked back. The lad aimed his eyes away, to the kitchen archway (clear of parentage). The dog didn't move. Calvin tested the waters some more, flicking his eyes towards the red brick hearth, the windmill painting, then Lewis's face. The dog only reacted when the Ape's gray eyes touched on its cyan ones.

Succumbing to the Devil, Calvin bugged at Kitty's tits.

Lewis didn't notice.

Kitty didn't, either.

Calvin pulled the Trapper over his crotch and breathed in measured bursts.

Some mouth above the tits said, "Bench bash bah basshun bin bit."

His head dipped as if in prayer. He felt dirty. It was fucking *dirty* looking at those great knockers up close, for so long a blissful stretch, without the fear of getting caught.

Calvin Connor considered Man's inherent nature as one of sin. Sin was who he was. Sin was what he was. He was Catholic after all, taking the Augustinian view that sinners sinned cuz they were sinners. The Protestant approach, that sinners became sinners only when sinning, was just crazy talk. God had a plan but Man controlled his destiny.

There's sin, and **SIN**—like theft, abortion, denigration, apostasy. Those bothered the lad to his soul. Mild crap like fornication and deceit had no lasting effect: confess to Father Sean, say a Hail Mary, and split.

"Boanch boo bagree?"

The lad blinked. "Huh? I'm sorry?"

"I said, French has passion in it. I asked if you agreed."

He looked at the girl. Looked righteously at her face and only her face, cuz Calvin Ciarán was a good little boy. And he saw the Devil's face—nay, *his* face, his stupid face with its prurient grin, wreathed in flames, red spears licking around him like so many pulsating hard-ons—he saw his face reflected back at him from her dark glasses.

"Very passionate stuff now." He turned away, ashamed.

A box of orange flavor Tic Tacs, hers, sat on the carpet between them. Calvin helped himself without asking.

"I have passion." Soft words. Her voice, breathy.

A pop from the fire flung hot sparks at the hearth's chain-mail screen. Calvin jolted, swallowing his Tic Tac with a gasp. Lewis jolted with him. The boy patted his sternum to get the candy down.

Kitty's left hand slid across the shag carpet, reaching for him. He swatted his notes out the way and put his hand in her path.

"I have passion too," he said, his slippery baritone basking in the Tic Tac's melted sugary coating, the voice equivalent of an actress hoisting a suds-covered leg out the bathtub in a Calgon commercial.

Her breath reached his cheek. "It's hot in here." Close words. Her saliva was thick enough to be sticky and make clicking noises.

"Whose bright idea was it to sit so close to the fire?" he said.

"Yours. You were cold. Can you smell our *puff of smoke?*"

"That's us, love. We *appear briefly.*"

"Mmmm," she said, "then *we disappear.*" She slid her fingers through his. Her damp hand was warm. His damp hand was firm.

They officially held hands.

Fucking is sooo inevitable.

Quit it! This is love, not a porno. Phil Collins and shit!

A blush hit his face and joined the bruises and sweat. He crossed himself with his free hand, the left one, the incorrect hand, sinister manus, the Devil's hand. Abby Normal. Strange. Wrong.

Hot. Heavy. His mental movie projector, the Bellend Howl, wobbled as it ran at double speed. His body shed its fat and turned into Myron's honed *Discobolus*. He was become Future-Calvin, the upright hero of his dreams, the star athlete able to woo chicks with a glance. No need for a Lamborghini, muscles under a mesh crop-top, or *Club MTV* moves. All he did was say hi to Kitty and she fell for him.

Did I get her all wrong? She's no timid church girl.

All girls erected a hill of timidity—even Wren, starting with her goddamn name. Kitty had no such hill. This was like if Wren had done her "pretend I said it and get over here and fuck me" routine on Day 1 of summer camp.

"I wanna look at you now," she said, taking back her hand.

He didn't know what she meant. He figured it out, though. She sat upright and dried her fingers on the carpet. "Ready?"

He sat up too. His hands went sweaty like at the baseball tryout. His flute was rock-hard like any hour of the day.

She held out her hands, palms out, fingers curled, a housecat stretching its paws. "Guide me." He moved her paws to his chin. "Now let go." He did, his dexter hand dropping down to keep the open Trapper Keeper tented over his flute, his sinister hand landing quite by accident on her wispy floral skirt, down by her bent knee.

"Hold on if you have to, it might get intense," she said. It was not tacit permission to fondle her thigh, her warm thigh, but a warning that he was about to get rough-handled.

He quickly felt just that as her calloused skin scuffled his cheeks. Using all ten fingers, she danced over his face, working up.

He realized why Kitty's hands were so rough: they were her means to see, always rubbing shite. His own hands clutched tight to his Trapper and her knee. When she reached his eyes, he flinched, abandoning the Trapper to grip her shoulder. "Not so tight," she said.

"Really not used to this now," he wheezed.

Reading the scent in the air, Lewis bounded over and gave a hot happy pant right in the kids' faces.

"Lewis, go away," she hissed. The dog did precisely as told, moving back to the original post by the sofa to sit on haunches.

Calvin felt the light dim as Ma Howe's roly-poly form filled the archway. *Oh bollocks, my hands!* He kept his face aimed front and his hands locked in place. Jerky movement always came off more guilty.

"I'm just looking at him, Mom," said Kitty.

"Okay, dear." After a second, two, three, Ma Howe retreated.

"Lewis will like you now," the girl told the boy, ignoring the topics of his hands and her mother. "He pretty much waits for my approval."

"Thanks a million," he said.

"Oh, like I wasn't gonna approve of you?"

"I was talking to Lewis."

She flicked a forefinger and caught him perfectly on the nose. "Quiet, porcupine!" she said, doing a voice. Not the stuffy Brit lady.

"... was that Moe from the Three Stooges?!"

"Hush, lemme finish."

Her fingertips traced the scar on his forehead that'd come from Jon Oldroyd's flashlight. A fresh smile crowded her wide cheeks when she reached his locks. "Wow, you got great hair. I like that its silky and not full of hairspray."

"Thanks another million. It's pretty long."

And so's my hair!

But seriously folks, I might hafta cut most of this hair off soon, ugh.

Kitty's hands traced down to his neck, around to his Adam's apple, and fell away. She calmly removed his stabilizing mitts from her person and scooched back to an innocent distance. "You're cute," she said.

"I'm an Ape, or haven't you heard? *You're* the one who's cute."

"Do stop embarrassing me in front of the staff, young man," she said, as that haughty British lady.

"Woulda been funnier if you said it like Moe."

"Moe is Abby's favorite. 'Shaddap, lamebrain!' But don't you like Lady Em? It's from a show. Never mind, long story. What made you come talk to me that first time? I'm curious. You're not afraid of this?"

"Whoa, one at a time!" He composed answers. "Lady Em's okay; cuz I wanted to meet you; and I ain't afraid of nothin'."

"I *see*," she said, teasing him.

Her tone changed on a dime: "Oh, leave us alone."

Lewis gave a bark like a fanfare. Ma Howe, out in the kitchen, bellowed, "Don't you dare interrupt them, Edward Mark!"

Calvin scrambled to tug the Trapper Keeper back over his crotch.

"Hey," said Eddie Howe. He tumbled into the living room on puffy bare feet like a Smurf bouncing across the TV screen.

Calvin was of his father's mold: a tall hulk. Eddie was likewise his father's son: a stubby fat fuck. The senior boinged over to the bookcase, expressing lots of vibrations but no convincing purpose whatever.

Kitty flopped on her back petulantly. "Just get out!"

"Shut up, I need the thesaurus!" Fetching the Roget's, Eddie did a terrible double-take, *Oh crap, I didn't know you had company!*

"Hello," the company said, "Calvin Connor the Third."

"'The Third,'" said Lady Em. "How pretentious!"

The wide, red Howe cheeks which gave Kitty's face an endearing warmth also gave Eddie's smile a creepy funhouse mirror look. "I'm Eddie. The first Eddie. The best Eddie. I know your sister, heh."

"And now, I know yours," said Calvin in a naked challenge tone, like *Which one of our sisters is getting felt up tonight?*

Eddie missed that subtext completely. Like all male seniors, he had a hard-on for Rose Connor, reputed super-slut. Eddie couldn't wait for his turn to boff her. Judging by the distant horny gaze on his face, a Rose porno was threading up in the fat guy's Bellend Howl right now.

Calvin muttered to Kitty, *"Put to death, then, the parts that—"*

Kitty issued a spritely tinkle of delighted mirth.

Eddie issued a farty sigh. "You quotin' the Bible? Nice dork you pulled in, Kate." He chucked the thesaurus back on the shelf and bustled out. "See ya, wouldn't wanna be ya."

"Rlluff rrof!" barked Lewis, sounding quite like "Fuck off!"

"That was spooky how you knew he was coming!" said the lad.

"Blindness makes the other senses sharper," said the lass.

"Lewis barked too. Dogs got super-hearing also."

"Are you calling me a dog, Mr. The Third?"

"Christ our Lord, that's not what I meant!"

"Did you notice Eddie's 'goodbye' was 'see ya?' And he didn't even take the book! He's so phony. Check the floor, please. Did he leave anything on it?"

"Uh, not that I can s—behold," said Calvin.

"It's fine to say 'see' in that instance cuz I asked you to use your sight to help me."

"Gotcha. I don't see anything on the floor. Why would he—"

"Cuz I like to be barefoot and Eddie thinks it's hysterical if he can make me step on a hairbrush."

"Jaysus. He would do that to—to you?"

"'—to a cripple,' is that what you were going to say?"

"'—to a little sister,' actually." *Nice save, lad.* "As the little brother myself, I totally get it."

"Oh you have no idea. He hides stuff, takes the bag of Triscuits out of the box and puts in Lewis's dog biscuits." Her arms jerked once, like frustration. "Even now he's wasting our time. Quelle heure est-il?"

He checked his Swatch. "Il est sept heures trente-quatre."

"Mon Dieu! We've blown half an hour?"

He thought of making a pun from *blown,* but not for long. "Flirting's never a waste of time, Mademoiselle Em."

"Lady Em. The title's part of her name. Like I said, long story. Let's get to work. Time to get all conjugal: 'désirer.'"

"I shall conjugate. Désirer: je désire, tu désires, il/elle desire—"

(glance downward) "—nous désirons, vous désirez, ils/elles désirent."

"That was easy, right? Especially since you looked at your notes." She stuck out her left hand. "Fork 'em over."

Calvin almost—almost!—drenched his pants in goo again. "Busted," he huffed, slipping out the second page of his notes.

"Not that one. The real one."

He wouldn't ask. Everyone else would've asked, so therefore he would not. Calvin would be different from everyone else—

"HOW?!"

Lady Em: "Do not refer to me solely by the family name."

"I—*ha!*—I meant 'how,' like 'how did you know?'"

"I heard the papers shuffling. The page you needed to cheat with would've been on top. *Visible.*" This time, her spritely tinkle of mirth had a decidedly *Gotcha!* tone to it.

"And besides, Calvin, ne faites pas confiance aux garçons!"

"Je suis d'accord." Calvin pulled back the wrong page and forked over the right one. "I really am trustworthy, Kitty."

"Well. If you say so." Her one hundredth-and-first amazing smile of the night pushed up her wide cheeks.

Chapter 8

THE NITTY-GRITTY ON GOIN' STEADY.
TUESDAY, JANUARY 31, 1989.

FOUL

AXSUBEEN SCHOOL DISTRICT BUS No. 10 rolled up Third Street to Maple. Jill Pedersen disrespected the code of the streets and cut in front of the row of backpacks marking everyone's proxy position in line. *She's going through some stuff,* Kare had allegedly told Art.

Ryan Phillips, whose school bag was always first since the bus stop was his own driveway, showed up Jill by doing his cool routine of flattening down his black shirt and snapping his fingers across his body, turning them into an inviting hand, like *Be my guest, babe.*

Ryan did the gesture again to let his pal Calvin Connor go next.

The lad nodded thanks and followed Jill. When she mounted the top step, his face was level with her bum. Her thistle-colored jean skirt made them thighs look wide ... but god-DAMN what an arse!

The gangly Art Maguire embarked at the next stop, Cherry Street. Calvin got up so his friend could park his skinny butt in the window seat position. Apes required the extra space of the aisle position.

"What's goin' down in funky town, Charlie Brown?" Art rapped.

Calvin labored. "Uh ... the shite might be tight, all right."

"Damn, you suck! You were s'posta call me last night too. I made a beta of the M.S.S.M. and thought we'd hang out and field-test it."

Art saw the lad had returned to his normal costume: jeans and a sweater (this was the Cosby era, when "normal" sweaters meant polyester excretions of OSHA-violating Crayola upchuck), but Calvin styled his mane *down* to hide a forehead bruise.

"Yesterday was insane," said Calvin. "I had detention, the tryout, and the little wanker offered me a job at Pizza Putt. I said 'get bent!'"

"Oh, Irish here's too good for making pizzas," said Art.

"By Jaysus indeed, the Irish Raging Ape is *far* too good for that now. Anyway, Lucky Cheeseboro was there with a radar gun and I got to hold it, that was awesome. My radar totally made him stiff."

"Wha'ja hit, like 80?"

"91."

"Fuckin' A! Yo, that's awesome! So we're on the Axes together?"

Calvin nodded. Art held a hand up for five. Calvin slapped it.

"Then Ma was up my arse about my grades and 'who's gonna pay for the bloody glove and bat?'"

"You are, my man, cookin' pizzas at Corgan's dad's restaurant. Hangin' out with Jill's momma, the star waitress. Yer gonna get paid to stare at Kimmy McSween's melons!"

"Ma McSween's melons are ancient. She was born in the '50s!"

"So what? It's almost the '90s. Get with the times, bro."

Calvin dropped it. Jill was on the bus and might confront them for talking about her well-endowed ma that way (as if folks talked any *other* way about Kimmy Pedersen [née McSween]).

"Went to Kitty's for a homework date too." Art's enthusiasm for this conversation took an immediate dive but Calvin soldiered on: "She doesn't like when people say 'I see' cuz it's biased but I remembered you being all *'Behold!'* so I used that and she loved it. So I'm gonna 'behold' her again at lunch today. Thanks for the cool new word, mate!"

Calvin held a hand up for five. Art slapped it, cuz he had to.

"She's so good at French, too, way ahead of me."

"Pro'bly cuz of all them silent letters. You can see them so they give ya trouble. She can't so they don't."

The lad thrust out his bottom lip in approval of that theorem. "She can't see Algebra problems either but gets A's in that too. I oughta be, like, inspired by that but it makes me feel 'tarded."

"She gets tutoring. Maybe you should too. I see her and Saint Mark in the library a lot after school."

Calvin sighed. Saint Mark again. And with Kitty again. "In *our* library? But he goes to Bishop Guilfoyle."

"Ain't illegal for him to come in our building. Mark tutors tons of people. He's a pitcher too, you should talk to him." Art's finger pointed at the window. "Behold—the little wanker himself!"

Sean Corgan stood at the Belgian block curb before his Overlook Estates McMansion. "Haven't seen him ride the bus since he turned sixteen," said Calvin. "Did Daddy take the IROC away?"

"Holy shit, lookit! What a shiner! Did you do that?!"

"Ryan did," said Calvin. "How come Kare ain't giving him a lift? She's got a car too. And she lives right on the next cul-de-sac."

"Sack," said Art. The lads shared a giggle. "Kare says things ain't so great between them."

"She didn't say that to *you*."

"Yuh-huh! I talk to chicks, Calvin, you never believe me. We're doin' that Biology project. Good thing Kare's got me as a partner or she'd get an F. She's so dumb." Art's voice dropped to a hiss. "Yo, she asked me about you once, like 'I know he's the Ape but I bet he's not as bad as Jill says.' I was like, 'Actually, he's *much* worse, ha ha!'"

Art shaddap as Sean sashayed onto the bus. The little wanker was all Joe Cool, smooth as silk in his white Members Only jacket and stonewashed jeans. Sean's ginger Davey Dangle tail bounced jauntily. His pale face betrayed no green envy, only sexy green eyes.

And one whopper of a bruise.

He stopped at Calvin's row and glared over at Art. "Beat it, backup," he said, then turned to sit, lowering his awesome glutes in a comically slow fashion, making the lack of space *their* problem.

The Ape hesitated at the idea of shoving the little wanker away by the buttocks—putting his paws too close to Sean's *actual* little wanker—so he crushed in towards Art, forcing his gangly friend against the window glass. To avoid complete pulverization, Art fled up and over into the empty seat in front of them. Calvin helpfully tossed Art's cool satin bookbag over. It sailed by Art's head, barely missing his glasses.

Sean parked his arse without it being touched and gave Calvin a blasé nod. "How's it hangin', chief?"

"Never had a bad day in my life," said Calvin.

"That's bullshit but I like it. We friends or enemies today?"

"You tell me."

"We're the bestest of pals, Cal." Sean inspected the scuffed fingernails on his right hand. So punchably nonchalant. "Just remember, it was your pal Seanie here who got you your tryout."

"Phillips says that's shite, that *he* recruited me."

"He never woulda known about your ability if I didn't call him up."

"Why do you keep making that point?"

"Cuz havin' an Ape with a major league fastball will help us win. You get your physical?"

"I get physical with your ma all the time. And the tryout was last night. Was I supposed to race to Dr. Jacoby that second?"

"Our first practice is Thursday. Come by after detention," said Sean. "Your butt-buddy Davey is suspended so leave the boxing gloves in your locker. And before you ask, dumb-ass, we practice in the gym. Still way too cold for the diamond."

"I get called a dumb-ass for a question I didn't even ask? Wow, the perks of being bestest pals with Seanie Corgan."

"Just toughenin' you up so you'll be awesome against Larsen. We play 'em twice a year. Can't wait to spank them rich boys."

"A rich boy wants to spank rich boys."

Sean shrugged. "You're just jealous."

"See that spot?" Calvin pointed back at Sean's McMansion. "Right there. *That's* where I fucked your girlfriend."

A small smile. "Nice try, Cal. Jenny was *your* girlfriend back then."

"Sorry, mate, guess I accidentally forgot which one of us was dating her on the night I took her virginity. Out on your lawn."

Sean twirled his fingers 'round the Irish Raging Ape's moronic scarf of many colors, implying he'd use it to pull Calvin's face close. "The only reason you ain't bleeding right now is cuz we're talkin' about Jenny. If you do that shit with *Kare*—or if you talk about doin' it, or if you go near her again—then I get one of my dad's guns."

Calvin's beefy hand closed over the little wanker's twirling fingers and squeezed. Sean released the scarf, like *I meant to do that.*

"Relax," said Calvin, sitting back. "You couldn't pay me to go near your conceited Mall Chick."

"You already *do* go near her. Like yesterday, when you told Kare you could see her bra through her banana blouse."

"What?! I never said that!"

Calvin sounded both innocent and guilty. Sean's face shrunk with confusion, like maybe he got the facts wrong. The Ape leapt on it and imitated the little wanker: "'Work on your poker facing, chief.'"

Sean lifted those green eyes to Calvin's limpen mane. "Still ain't got the team haircut."

"Gimme a ride to Steeler's Shears after school today in that hot rod your rich da got you—"

"I'm on the bus with you, you dumb immigrant. My hot rod's at the garage." The little wanker stood and sashayed off. "Later, Studly."

Art climbed back to his seat. "'Studly?' What a homo."

Calvin stewed. "It's what Jenny called me. She musta told him."

"Oh." Art sounded jealous. "What was that about Kare's bra?"

"I've no idea now." Except, he did. Just not like Sean said.

It was an impulse prank. Kare had been running her mouth in the hallway, judging people, her usual. Calvin happened to be behind her and snapped her bra through her shirt to disrupt her flow. When she turned to flay the Irish Raging Ape, he gave a tight grin and quoted Proverbs 13:3: *"To open wide one's lips brings downfall,* love."

That was, like, a fortnight ago, not yesterday. And the Mall Chick had been wearing an electric-magenta number with black starbursts, not a "banana blouse," so Calvin couldn't see the bra underneath. No one could've seen it. He'd merely triangulated the straps' relative positions.

She must've kept mum about it and finally told the little wanker about it last night, and he got the details wrong. Or she obfuscated them.

She's just like Jill now. Hates me and likes me.

FOUL

Mr. Falcone announced a film today. The sophomores in Health squealed in delight. Lights off, no notes, no Gym Teacher Man talking, yay! Falcone was excited too—his fat phalanx of a 'stache flailed up and down like kids with their arms raised riding the log flume.

Twelfth-grader Peter McLlwayne, the A.V. Club President, came in lugging a 16mm reel can and a projector. Not a 27" Emerson tube TV set wobbling top-heavy on a castored stand with a top-loading Sanyo VCR on a shelf below. No sir. Falcone didn't say "tape" or "video," but "film." McLlwayne pushed up the pair of transparent square beer coasters on his face (as a certified '80s nerd, he insisted on calling them "spectacles") and unpacked the projector: a folds-up-into-a-neat-box-complete-with-its-own-handle 1972 Bell & Howell* model 1541. With practiced fingers, the nerd threaded the film through various gates.

Gym Teacher Man's blocky hand killed the lights. Some teenager pinched or fondled some other teenager. "Eeep! Quit it!" a boy said in a girl's yelp. Falcone demanded hands to selves.

McLlwayne fired up the Bell & Howell and left. Gym Teacher Man pumped up the volume 'til it masked the reels' clacking and adjusted the lens to get the title card in focus:

THE NITTY-GRITTY ON GOIN' STEADY.

Twenty groans of "AGAIN?!" or similar.

Billed in the Pennsylvania Dept. of Education's film catalog as "a psychological take on the repercussions of premarital sex," *The Nitty-Gritty on Goin' Steady* was awfully light on the grit. None of that X-rated crap: this movie was PG-13, at best.

At least it had humans. *When Jack and Jill Made Jimmy,* a bio-logical-focused reel, had horny anthropomorphic cartoon mallards.

The class attacked the teen actor's oh-so-ancient feathered hair and bell-bottoms. They went "Hubba-hubba!" at the teen actress with the cats-eye glasses and allergy to bras. They booed when she got cold feet midway through the notorious make-out scene, when the kids got cozy on the parchment-tan vinyl back seat of a 1974 Duster Twister. The girl dragged her wet eyes over the curly James Caan tapestry across the boy's shirtless chest. When she gave in—starting the decline of her future and the moral superiority of Perry King's narration—Health class stood as one to applaud.

This was Calvin Connor III's fourth screening of *Nitty-Gritty.* In seventh and eighth grade, he watched as all did, in muffled immaturity. As a ninth-grader and a veteran of actual relationships and buggery, he watched with open sarcasm. This time 'round, he sweated over not having even a tithe of the *Nitty-Gritty* actor's chest hair (yet he got called "The Ape," go figure). Teenaged Calvin was confused on this

---

* A brand of much repute. Calvin mocked the name as "Bellend Howl," a joke none of his Yank friends got.

point: chest hair was manly, right? Yet every body-builder was hairless with glistening skin. Mr. Falcone, a Phys. Ed. teacher and iron-pumper, had no hair on the toned limbs poking out his polos and short-shorts. Calvin had yet to behold the man topless, and rued the day when circumstances might contrive it, but confessed a curiosity over whose head Falcone's chest would resemble: Picard's or Worf's.

After the bell, Gym Teacher Man pulled Calvin aside to ask about how his arm felt and when he'd get his physical. The lad said he was going after lunch tomorrow. "Get me the signed form pronto," said Falcone, "and apologize to Davey. Do it at lunch. Don't put it off."

Calvin found Ryan slouching in the corridor, waiting. The athletic kid often kept close to the Irish Raging Ape while maintaining a noticeable distance from other classmates. The Suicide Kings were his only real friends. They knew of his book ("The Book") with the pentagram on the spine. They knew of his curious gift of foresight. They knew he prowled in the night like a ninja. They knew if they confessed some embarrassing inner thought to Ryan, he'd keep his mouth shut. Most teens couldn't say the same.

"I got a vision of how Future-Me is gonna be," said Calvin.

"Rotting in a grave?" said Ryan.

"Not that far in the future. If you made a drawing of Future-Me on one of them clear thingies for the overhead, what're they called?"

"Transparencies."

"Right. If you took a transparency of Future-Me and one of Gym Teacher Man and put them on top of each other, they're the same."

"You wanna be a clone of Falcone? A Fal-Clone?"

"That's good. Thought you'd go after 'me on top of him.'"

"Too obvious. Everyone wants a piece of that beefcake."

"Well. Ditch his lame Adidas pants and that bloody mustache, put on Ray-Bans and club clothes, and that's me in five years."

Ryan snorted. "Of all grown-ups, you pick *Falcone* as yer destiny?"

"I don't wanna be a fat pile of shite like Mr. Jourgensen."

"I get that. But you need 'roids to be as big as Gym Teacher Man."

"They're illegal, right? Your brother's a drug dealer. I'll ask him."

"Steve's only got the other kinda 'roids—hemorrhoids. Don't worry, you can't catch 'em, even if you do him in the butt."

"Gross!"

They stood near the queue. The caf crowd didn't tease Calvin today. It hadda be cuz of Ryan, with his all-black shroud and muscles.

That's it—I'm getting in shape! thought the lad. *Wonder if Falcone used to be a teenage fatty too?*

Kitty and Abby showed up out of the blue, startling Calvin. Ryan gave him two-for-flinching on their behalf.

The big girl nudged the blind one. Kitty took her cue: "Hi!"

"Hi!" said Calvin.

"Hi!" said Abby.

"Hi," said Ryan.

The four got in line and cleared throats, twiddled thumbs.

Calvin asked, "Your ma say anything about me after I left?"

Kitty held in a breath. That was her answer.

When the queue moved forward a step, Calvin's free right hand made to fetch her free left hand to help usher her along.

Abby reached from behind him to slap his hand away. He turned to set her straight. Her slanty face mouthed, "She can do it on her own."

"My," breathed Lady Em, "but the young man moves fast." Kitty's left hand reached over to grab his right.

How did she know—whatever, you're holding hands, shaddap.

Kitty hoisted Excalibur snug against her right side and clutched it partway down its white shaft, keeping its metal tip a foot off the tile. Calvin had seen this pose before: she was putting the cane in carry mode so it didn't get in the way as she entrusted another with forging the path. Usually that meant she'd stand directly behind the helper with her left hand on their shoulder. Here, in front of everyone, she stood at Calvin's right, holding his pitching hand.

"She can do it on her own"—ha! He turned and gave Abby a wink.

"J'ai passé un bon moment hier soir," he said, totally unrehearsed.

"J'ai passé un très bon moment hier soir!" she said.

In her pink shades, he saw the goofy face of an Ape falling in love. He turned front to find the black orbs of Cuauhtémoc Ysderrhi.

Troop 666 was a putrescent corpse, slain by the Souviens Affair. Of the four faces on Calvin's Mt. Flushmore of Annoying Troop 666 Arses, three were out of his life. Jon Oldroyd's da's house was in Overlook Estates but the zitty brat lived full time in his dorm at Larsen Academy up in Altoona. The Duffys likewise sent their kids to a private school, Bishop Guilfoyle Catholic High; Matthew "Father" Duffy had graduated and moved on to Saint Vincent College. And the instant Konrad "Inky" Schultz IV had collected his Axsubeen High diploma, he put his Harley under his cock and fucked it on down the road.

The only Annoying Arse left was Chicken. The Davey Dangle didn't look quite as asinine on him as it did Reggie or Sean or even the name-giver Brion because *everything* about Chicken was asinine. The haircut merely blended into the kid's tapestry of asininity.

"What you *see* in him?" Chicken asked Kitty, pointing at Calvin.

"Don't say it like that," said Calvin with vinegar. "And she can't see you pointing at me, anyway."

"No one wants to see anything *he's* waving around," cracked Kitty, and everyone laughed.

Everyone. The whole caf was watching this.

Chicken put away his finger. Was that a blush in his cheek? "Connor no worth your heart. He total dork!"

"I disagree," said Kitty.

Ryan turned to Abby. "I can't understand Chicken's shit."

"Chickenshit, ha," said Abby. Her pig snort laugh was 50% agreement and 50% swooning over the hunky boy actually talking to her.

"Trust me, he dork," Chicken told Kitty. "So much, I say twice!"

"You said it three times, actually," said Kitty.

"Which is the bloody limit," said Calvin. "Belt up!"

Chicken looked past them for a sec. Calvin checked over his shoulder, expecting to see another Scoundrel about to ambush him. He saw only Ryan and Abby behind him.

"Davey love you, Gatáki," Chicken told Kitty. "He put me up to this. You hot for Ape? Davey not Ape or dork. Plus blond. Straw hair so lovely." Again, Chicken looked past Calvin.

Again, only Ryan and Abby were behind them. Both were blond …

Kitty took back her left hand from Calvin and set her right hand in Excalibur's safety loop. *Readying it in case she needs an <u>actual</u> Excalibur?*

"Would you leave us alone, Cuauhmétoc?" she said.

"Not 'kwow·MAY'·tok.' It's 'kwow·TAY'·mok!'"

"It means 'douchebag,'" said Calvin.

"Bring my mamá a douche, and she let you use it on her."

When a goofball like Spazz Watson made ma jokes about his own ma, it was charming. When this awful turd did it …

The line moved up. Chicken moved up. Excalibur went *tick-tick* on the tiled floor and Kitty moved up too. She'd desired Calvin's help until Chicken came on the scene, then suddenly she was Li'l Miss Asserting My Independence. Or was she afraid to show fondness near Davey's pals? Kitty and Calvin hadn't discussed Davey yet.

Chicken stuck out one Adidas high-top. Kitty's cane struck it. The turd went, "Careful!" and swung his arms like Wile E. Coyote trying not to fall off a cliff.

"You did that on purpose," said Kitty. "Rudest person on Earth!"

"Soon to be the deadest person on Earth," said Calvin. Bringing his shoulders up to vulture position (like his father did when roused), Calvin blasted forthright eye contact (again, like Da). "I already wiped out one of you Scoundrels. Wanna be next?"

The beakly freak gave a meek gawk and flailed slappy hands. "¡Adios!" he said, forfeiting his spot and heading for the end of the line.

"Adieu!" said Kitty. She turned her pink shades towards Calvin. She had such a lovely, sweet face. "Est-ce que ça va?"

"Oui, et toi?"

"We're up to 'tu' already? Pas encore, Monsieur Connor, you're still in 'vous'-land."

The queue moved up. "Kitty, tu devrais—"

"Vous!"

"Vous devrais—"

"Vous *devriez!"*

"—bollocks! How j'say 'move up' in vous-landian?"

"Like this: 'move up.'"

Abby's blue New Balances stuttered on the doo-doo brown/pus orange checkerboard tile and she toppled into Calvin's back.

The lad swung around to give her what-for and burped to find Chicken there too, wedging himself between Abby and Ryan. Drool dripped from the turd's tongue. Chicken's fruit bat eyeballs had a greasy glaze, a steamy weaponized horniness. His candlestick dripped hot wax.

And for a second, Calvin enjoyed it all.

Screw Abby. She never liked me, she's fat and ugly with a melty face, and she deserves torturing.

He couldn't let this happen to Kitty's friend, let a Scoundrel ruin this moment. His fist rose to smite—

—Chicken's spine bent this way and that, like a strip of metal being made into a paper clip. Calvin swept Abby and Kitty behind his girth, shielding them in case an alien burst out Chicken's chest, holding the turd's crushed heart in its multiple telescoping jaws.

Chicken fell to both knees, revealing his slayer: Ryan Phillips, rising up like the Kraken out of the sea in *Clash of the Titans,* squeezing the turd's shoulders into powder. Ryan's hot eyes burned the acne off Chicken's cheeks.

"Fuck the fuck off, you fucker!" said Ryan through clenched teeth.

Chicken slithered aside on his knees and pogo'ed away.

The crowd roared. Kitty, jostled between Calvin and Abby, made helpless yelps. "Stop, what's happening?"

Abby moved back to Ryan, her hero. Ryan dusted his knuckles.

Calvin fetched Kitty's hand. Both their hands had gone sweaty. "Tout va bien," he told her.

Kitty squeezed his hand, so glad it was over, so glad he said everything's okay, so glad he *made* everything okay, so glad he'd told her as much in French.

"Are we out of vous-land yet?" he teased.

"Oui!"

He shook loose her hand, cupped her wide cheek, and planted a quick one on her lips. "Bien," he said.

Ryan gave him a game slap on the back. Abby's blubbery arm went around Kitty's shoulders for a congratulatory hug. Other reactions were heard, seen, smelt. Most of the crowd missed it, still zoomed in elsewhere as the lunch monitors Mrs. Barker and Mr. Jourgensen gave Chicken Ysderrhi a dressing down.

"Good Lord, don't do that again," Kitty said, red-faced. "You gave me a heart attack!"

"You mean, I took your breath away?"

"I—certainement pas!"

"Ain't like it's her first kiss," Abby noted from behind them.

Kitty coughed a very definite *shut up!* at her.

Ms. Jonckheere coughed too. The dice-eyes hammered into her skull teemed with disgust at Calvin's lusty behavior. "We got split pea soup and chili con carne," she said, pointing at a steaming green ooze then a steaming brown. The latter looked more like chili con estiércol.

They both got soup. Calvin fetched cardboard half-pints of orange drink for them from the beverage tub. An inspired choice. He hoped she couldn't hear the vinyl cover of his Trapper Keeper squeaking as he crushed it against his flute.

"Who then is she to judge?" said Kitty. "Ms. Jonckheere, I mean."

"We are a *puff of smoke,* love."

Kitty hummed a low trilling note. She loved that. Loved all of this. They skipped dessert.

⚾ **DUGOUT** ⚾

The couple did their "au revoir, *appear and disappear"* routine. It was officially a thing now. He carried his tray into the caf with a goofy smile … then remembered his promise to Falcone.

Everyone watched him. This brought fresh sweat and his sweater's wool threads pricked him like swords. He ignored all the weird noises and comments. *Poker face,* said Lucky in his head, using the wacky Pavarotti voice the guy affected in his car commercials.

I need a fucking lobotomy, thought Calvin.

He reached the Scoundrels Table. Reggie Roberts gave him a welcoming laugh. Sean Corgan ate an orange peel, utterly unperturbed but not nearly as unflappably cool with that huge black eye on his mug. Chicken Ysderrhi was here, banished from the line. He'd convinced Reggie to sell him his popsicle (at twice market price) so he wouldn't starve. Chicken finished it off and licked his fingers clean, drying them through his black Davey Dangle. The skeevy turd seldom employed accouterments. Hands were all the napkins and cutlery an Ysderrhi used.

The fourth seat was empty, giving Calvin an unobstructed view of the next table over. Three of the four Breast Strokers, girls on the swim team, hid sniggers behind their hands. The fourth, a birdlike junior named Shelley Quince, had her big owl eyes aimed at hunky Sean.

Addressing the little wanker, the Ape said, "I gotta apologize."

Chicken stood arms-wide for a hug. "I accept!"

"Not to you, shite-for-brains!"

"Aww. I thought you finally make up for van Halen-ing my face with crunchy gee-tar." Chicken sat and played with his popsicle stick.

Reggie clapped his hands and wiped off tears from his laughter.

The little wanker said, "Davey ain't sittin' with us today," issuing a tiny bob of his ginger-haired head. The lad followed the bob … to the Rejects Table. Brion Davey sat stone-faced, finishing his chili, as original tenets Mia Pintcure, and Mike "Leggers" Clegg looked put-out and flatulent respectively.

"You drive him to hari-kari," said Chicken. "I get vengeance!" He dabbed the naked popsicle stick in Reggie's chili to gather sauce on the tip and bent the stick as if to catapult said sauce at Calvin.

The target made a nasty face like, *Don't you dare.*

Only then did Chicken let fly.

Calvin wiped his face clean and moved towards the Rejects Table.

Sean flung a Puma to block the path. Emerald orbs broke poker face protocol, flaring a warning. "Don't poke the sleepin' bear, chief. You're battin' .500 against us and we ain't gonna take it much more."

"'Batting five hundred' means 'fifty percent,' right?"

"And they say you're flunking math. Add two and two and apologize to him tomorrow."

⚾ CLUBHOUSE ⚾

Calvin sat with his Suicide King mates, enjoying his split-pea soup quietly. He levitated in style, his arse literally floating above the chair. And disproved Kitty's theory that he could stand to lose a few pounds.

"That's some serious zero-g yer pullin' there, Zero Caliber," said Spazz Watson. "What'cha all stoned about?"

"Think I'll ride Kitty's bus home today." Calvin checked his Swatch. "We'll be makin' out in like three hours."

"You got detention," said Art Maguire.

"He's stoned all right," said Spazz. "Only thing tiny on this fat sumbitch is his pupils!"

Ryan Phillips's blue eyes locked with Calvin's grays, like *They missed what you did.*

Calvin's eyes were like, *They missed what _you_ did.*

Ryan shrugged and tried a joke: "Blind leading the blind?"

Calvin guffawed.

Art was befuddled. Ryan told him, "You hadda be there."

"He *was* there, that's the funny bit," said Calvin.

Art was tart. "C'mon guys, what're ya talkin' about?"

"Calendar Method's puttin' the moves on his new squeeze," said Spazz. A hand went to his temple. "I can see the future, and it's them two puttin' those bedsprings to the test! Literally a *ton* of squishy fun!"

"No fat jokes 'bout me and Kitty," said Calvin.

"Or Abby," said Ryan.

"'Or Abby?'" mocked Art.

Calvin said, "Cue the Art Maguire speech about standards."

"I *got* standards, at least."

"That no girl ever meets. Maybe girls aren't for you, mate."

That hurt. Art focused down on his lunch, and Calvin (in true Catholic style) felt guilty.

"Everyone's got their muse," Spazz noted. "Like how Señor Buck-Buck-Ba-Guck keeps chippin' away at Flabby Abby's armor."

"Oh," Ryan said to Calvin. "They *did* see it."

"One of them did," said Calvin.

"See what?" said Art.

"Big Tail Abagail is sweet on Ryan!" said Spazz. He held folded hands down low, stretched his neck up and backwards, made kissy lips, and flittered his eyelids at the sky; the only thing missing was a halo of hearts. The pose was known to all kids: Pepé Le Pew, swooning.

Calvin felt an instinctual urge to check himself for body odor.

Spazz smiled at Ryan. "Settle a bet, Landfill-ips—ya think Cal-Vlad the Impaler's put his saucer of man milk in Kitty's kitty?"

"Sure," said Ryan. "I got video of it."

"Homemade pornos?" said Art. "Uh … can I borrow it?"

"Bollocks," said Calvin. "You work in a video store. You'd totally make copies."

"I'll invite all my buds over like our *Faces of Death* parties," said Spazz. "First homo who looks away has to eat a tin can of Alpo!"

Art's blue eyes popped out his gray glasses. "A tin can! *That's it!* I been using sheet metal for the shotgun-shell mine casing. A tin can would work better. It'd be stiffer."

"A tin can'll make you stiffer?" said Calvin. "What a loony!"

Spazz suddenly shot to his feet and pointed. "Egads! The Rejects want Davey Dope-face out of their sewer!"

All eyes went to the Rejects Table. Purulent Mia Pintcure was nominally the Head Reject, a gawky girl who hated everyone and everything (soap for example). Mia just wanted to eat lunch and read her Barbara Hambly novels in peace. Davey must've said or did something cuz Mia was *pissed*. Her seat faced the room; her pus-pasted cheeks shone red in rage.

The caf grew quiet to try and hear the argument. Any teens still blabbing got shushed by others.

Spazz cupped his hands. "Yo Mia! Eat him like an Eloi!"

A murmur swept from one end of the caf to the other as a new player emerged ...

... Jill Pedersen, the plum-colored princess herself, leaving the Mall Chick Table with her lunch tray and making her way towards the Rejects Table.

Art gasped like he'd taken his dying breath.

Jill took the open seat by Brion Davey. Then put a hand on his arm.

"Jaysus," said Calvin, barely able to cross himself.

Spazz jittered like a kindergartener shown an ice cream sandwich. "The Morlocks are gonna dine well tonight!"

FOUL

"The back wall had two hundred sixty-six 'concrete bricks,' as we say in Ireland. Yanks like you call them 'cinder blocks.'"

"Two hundred sixty-six, is that so?" said the late show host.

"Indeed, Dave. Had lots of detention. Counted them many times.

There's fourteen rows with either nineteen or eighteen bricks each."

"Nineteen or eighteen? Which is it?" The audience laughed, so the late show host fed off it: "Do we gotta send you back to school for remedial math, Calvin?"

THUNK!

Calvin jerked his head to an awake-looking position. Official Detention's overlord, Mr. Walsh, glared at him over the top of the latest issue of *Time,* checked out from the school library. The newly inaugurated forty-first President was on the cover.

The Irish Sleepy Ape resumed his study of the Economics Room's rear wall. Seven rows of nineteen perfectly spaced cinder blocks, interlaced with seven rows of eighteen cinder blocks spaced so one needed to be halved at the left-hand corner. Should those half-blocks count? Fractions reminded him of Algebra, reminding him of the test he got back Monday with the fat red F, reminding him of explosions and death. His eyelids closed, shutting out the nasty world.

"Mr. Connor?"

That didn't sound like Dave's voice. Or Paul's. Or Bud Melman's.

It came from the doorway. He had to look past the stare of Brion Davey, who he'd not yet apologized too, to find the source of the voice.

A man in grave gray. "This way, Mr. Connor."

Fartin' Martin strode down the hall, dress shoes clicking on the checkerboard linoleum. Calvin shuffled out after him, sweating. As was standard following the final bell, every alternate bank of lights had been switched off to save power. Mr. Martin pointedly stopped under active fluorescents so any passing pupils, staying late for study, club, or athletics, would behold the naked execution of his authority.

"I reviewed your file," said the man, "and your signature is on the *Student Handbook's* List of Policies form."

"Uh ... guilty as charged," the lad shrugged.

"Indeed you are," said Martin, "of violating the public behavior statute. Open displays of affection are explicitly forbidden."

"Cuz I held Kitty's hand? She's crippled, in case you missed it."

"The accepted term is 'handicapped.' And holding Miss Howe's hand for the purpose of locational guidance is unnecessary."

"In the caf? With all those chair legs and seniors sticking out their foot and stuff? Do us a favor."

"Miss Malone manages to provide assistance in that setting without holding hands. That act is tangential: the charge was 'display of affection.' Do you claim to provide locational guidance with a kiss?"

"Well." The Principal had him there.

"The fact that your rival was in the cafeteria to witness it was pure coincidence, I'm sure."

The lad now got why Brion Davey had left the Scoundrels Table—one of them made a joke about Calvin smooching Kitty, so the goon got away from them before his rage landed him in a hotter tub of water.

This corridor's walls were covered in vibrant paint, student art of Axsubeen Pride. Rising behind the Principal's solemn silver hair was a cartoony axe, double-bitted, half-moon-bladed, in glorious pus orange set within a circle of doo-doo brown. The borough's motto curled atop in white: NO LANDS UNTAMABLE. The phrase, with its missing apostrophe and questionable spelling choice, was loved by the millmen and farmers, and loathed by the pedants and English teachers.

Fartin' Martin's stentorian blare lost no menace when taken in before this collage of immature color. "Your baseball tryout last night irked Mr. Davey into suspendable acts. Now the kiss in the cafeteria. Quite the cunning plan to obliterate him completely."

Calvin fixed his eyes down at the little man's nerd spectacles; a housecat menacing a mouse. "I could care less about Davey. *He* started all this! *He's* the one who can't accept that Kitty don't want him anymore. Why am I getting all the blame?!"

The mouse planted his feet resolutely. "Ever the victim, the small child caught purchasing banned breath spray. I await the weeping."

Calvin gave up. There was no way to beat this cunt!

"Discipline for a first offense is a reprimand." The Principal didn't bother adding, *which I am now giving you.* "You will no doubt report this conversation to Miss Howe, the spirit if not the letter, and that will serve as her reprimand.

"And, Mr. Connor? Things will only change when you do. Depart." The mouse turned on his heel and strode off.

Calvin felt like Tom after he'd gotten his whiskers plucked by Jerry.

Chapter 9

Now, promenade!
Wednesday, February 1, 1989.

⚾ TRAINER'S TABLE ⚾

JACOBY FAMILY PRACTICE WAS located at 16 Main Street, a converted Queen Anne, long ago the home of the borough's third mayor, Wilhelm Schultz II. With its mason staircase, creamy wood siding, and wraparound porch complete with swing seat, this lovely 1885 piece was an island of organic warmth in a sea of soot-smeared red brick rowhomes and shophouses that stood shoulder to shoulder along Railroad Street, Main Street, and the western terminus of Bald Eagle Pike. Simply having a few feet of grass out front set the doctor's office apart.

Axsubeen's main drag had other non-brick structures but they were all cold boulders. Like the grand train station at 1 Railroad with its Renaissance Revival quarry stone, lofty entrance arches, and red mansard roof. It looked like the world's biggest Pizza Hut. There's the 1950s yellow brick Borough Fire Station at 5 Main and the rickety old horse stable behind it (the former home of the former Troop 666). Let's not forget the houses of worship: the sedate charcoal gray stone of Good Shepherd Lutheran Church at 24 Railroad and the serene gray charcoal rock of Saint Brigid Cathedral at 40 Main. Let's *do* forget about the local branch of Blair County S&L, a Richardson Romanesque monstrosity rising like a Gothic ingot cock at 101 Bald Eagle.

When Calvin Connor III got the stitches removed from his forehead after Camp Souviens, it was inside the Queen Anne. When the lad found a strange raw spot on his inner thigh, it was here that the good doctor assured him he suffered neither AIDS nor the Winter Wiener Plague but an ingrown hair. The Irish Ape switched from tighty-whities to boxers, raging that his first body hair was an ingrown cunt.

When Calvin, age 12, had his first ejaculation while inspecting his boner in the shower, it was inside Jacoby Family Practice that he learned semen's role in making babies. He'd never gotten "the talk" from his father. His mother gave plenty talks, light on the process details and heavy on its consequences: "Don't make me a feckin' grandmother, boyo. Not for many decades!" All of Calvin's sexual knowledge up to that point had come from playground taunts and some porno mags found under the bed of Ryan's eldest brother, Trevor.*

Thank the Lord for Claudius Jacoby, D.O.

Doc was the right kind of adult: he listened to concerns, was indulgent with his time, kept embarrassing secrets, and didn't dismiss Calvin's opinion cuz of his youth. Other men (Fartin' Martin, Father Sean, Art's da, Ryan's da, even his own da) didn't check off that whole list. Some, like a certain Troopmaster, missed 'em all!

The lad sat on the lumpy exam table, paper crinkling under his butt. The whole building was noisy: floorboards creaked, doors squeaked, words could be discerned through the nearest wall and sometimes the next nearest. The normal-house feel of the layout went a long way towards making Calvin comfortable.

His study of a gloriously graphic "Effects of Stroke" poster ended with door hinges screeching. Dr. Jacoby was a squat man with a shiny pate and a face splotched with red puffs. He looked like a latticed cherry pie. Unlike his son, the roly-poly Gus, Claude wore a tightly wound girth; nothing wobbled or shimmied. Doc was blessedly unhindered by stench.

"Calvin me lad," he said, in the most offensive Oi-rish accent possible, "top of the evening to ye!"

Calvin shook hands. "Keep telling you, us Irish never say that!"

"Ain't that the straight craic, so it is."

"Stop! 'Craic' is legit Irish but from my grandmother's time."

"Just breaking the ice." Doc made saucer dish eyes at the paper on

---

* A life-changing stash: three *Playboys,* the distressed back half of the October 1982 *Oui* (Ryan woulda adored the cover with Linda Blair), and a glossy text-free masterpiece called *Cum* featuring full hardcore. Ryan and Calvin borrowed from Trevor Phillips's library often 'til acquiring their own.

his desk. "A sports physical?! Wow. It *does* say 'Calvin Ciarán Connor' here. Sure this is for Calvin the Third?"

The lad guffawed. "Calvin the First is no longer with us. And Calvin the Second is way too old for high school."

"Calvin the Second might as well be a ghost to me."

"Da has this thing with doctors." The lad pointed at the form with pride. "Believe it or not, I made the baseball team."

"How a-*bout* that?" said Dr. Jacoby, doing a Mel Allen impression.

It was totally lost on Calvin. "Lucky Cheeseboro was there," he said, "and his radar gun said I threw ninety-one miles an hour."

"Ho-ly *cow!*" said Doc, doing Phil Rizzuto this time.

Once more, the baseball reference went over Calvin's head.

The floorboards creaked as Nurse Maier led another patient past their door. Calvin's attention left the Doc and fell into his own mind, some ribald scenario. Nurse Maier was a grown-up but kinda hot.

Doc pointed at the kid's right elbow. "Show Lucky your scars next time. He had the same procedure back in the Bigs."

"Too late, Doc. We compared scars at the tryout. That's when Falcone stopped it, freaking out about the school board."

"Falcone freaked for nothing. Your surgery was years ago."

"Lucky says pitchers love it, that their arms are twice as strong. Why don't they just get the operation first?"

"*Before* an injury? That's unethical. We don't install bionic arms!"

"Only a thought." Calvin's arse shifted, crinkling the paper. The flop of hair over his forehead moved aside.

"Just happened to change hairstyles in time to hide that bruise, eh?" said Doc. "You steal Sean Corgan's girl again?"

"Nothing like that. But it *was* Corgan, sticking up for a friend of his. Who, uh, I stole a girl from."

Doc pulled back Calvin's hair to study the wound. "A cerebral contusion can have effects long after it happens. You promised me you'd take care of that noodle." They were so close he smelt Doc's Listerine. "Any trouble remembering words or events?"

"Nothing like that, sir."

"Don't make me beg, Irish. Out with it."

Calvin sucked in a shameful breath. "My memory is good.

Sometimes I hear echoes, like flashbacks. Not much. Don't last long."

"Outbursts? Changes in mood or behavior?"

"Well. I don't have patience anymore. I get annoyed with my friends and I feel guilty about it."

"Typical teenage petulance, don't worry about it. Vision issues? Blurring, seeing yellow, seeing stars?"

"Recently?"

Jacoby's eyebrow dipped and Calvin knew he fucked up. "You're having aftershocks," said Doc. "How many blows to the head have you had? Big ones that give you the yellow blurring and purple stars?"

"Three."

"Number four might be your ass. What were the circumstances?"

"The first one was back in Troop 666, when I got this scar." He traced it under the fresh forehead bruise. "The second one was the next morning, when I got mad at Oldroyd's bollocks and nearly passed out. Then on Monday, at my tryout." Calvin laughed sheepishly. "Tell a lie, four times: one time Jenny was over and I hit my head pretty hard on that wood thing on the bed. Behind the pillow."

"The headboard."

"Oh. Duh."

"Musta been soft wood. The headboard, I mean, not you."

The kid got the ribald joke and his guffaw followed.

Doc plucked his scopes (stetho-, ophthalmo-, and oto-) and did the exam routine. "Who's the new squeeze?"

Calvin's eyes did a dance over the splotchy red parts of Doc's face, wondering if he should trust him. "Kitty Howe," he said at length. "If I was in school right now, we'd be in the lunch queue talking."

"She's a sweet girl, God bless her. Don't take her to Schultz Park. Place has bad memories for her."

"It does? Why?"

Jacoby dropped it, feeling he'd said too much. "You still sexually active?" he asked. Casual. One guy talking to another.

"Not since Halloween," said Calvin. Just two guys talking.

"Same here. Old lady cut me off."

"Valentine's Day is coming up."

"Thanks. If I forgot again, I'd be bunking on that exam table." Doc pulled up Calvin's sweater, a teal/gray one with geometric fiddlybits, to clear space for his stethoscope's pickup. "When girls get the frying pan out they aim at your head, laddy, so run away. Breathe normal."

The kid strangled back his laughter and dutifully drew air.

"Ever see stars or get headaches when you ejaculate?"

"Just that one time with the headboard."

"Sounds like it was a great night. Taking precautions?"

"I am."

"Good to hear. There are no accidents, Calvin the Third, there is only a lack of precaution. I have condoms if you need them."

"Thanks a million. We play cards every Saturday and I'm out."

"Ah yes, the safe-sex poker chips. Each one is worth a buck?"

"Two, cuz they do double-duty."

"Very clever." Jacoby parked his fireplug on the exam room's stool and glossed the sports physical document.

"Am I gonna be all right, Doc? We're, like, way past talking about the physical."

"You want me to say 'yes you'll be fine' but I can't rightly say for certain, Calvin. Provided you keep your noggin safe, you shouldn't have future problems." Jacoby moved his pen quickly across the paper. "Speaking of futures, what's your plan? College? Still wanna be the first astronaut from Éire, or Blarney, or whatever?"

"'Ireland' is the term in common use. And I dunno, Doc. Kinda worried about today for now."

"I get it." Doc forked over the form. "If this was for football or wrestling, I'd reject it."

Calvin got off the table, crinkling the butt-paper one final time. "Why? You're saying I'm not okay?"

"You'll be fine. Stay hydrated, drink plenty of fluids. Gus tried out yesterday too. He made the J.V. as a catcher. You treat my son fair, unlike the other kids. This is my way of sayin' thanks."

The lad was embarrassed. Blobby-blob Gus the freshman made no secret of looking up to Calvin. Hearing it from Gus's dad was awkward.

Doc poked about a cabinet for prophylaxes. "Given your history," he said, letting his bedside manner get the best of him, "I bet you quit the team before the season starts. Or get kicked off it."

Outrage flooded the Ape's face. "Appreciate your faith in me."

Jacoby forked over five Trojans. In his Oi-rish accent: "Skip won't let ye destroy the Axes like ye did Troop 666, Calvin me lad!"

The Ape made every floorboard squeal as he stomped out.

⚾ FAMILY SECTION ⚾

A suitor supplicated his sweetheart's assertion that they shared a savor suitably similar to sequentially fissured stripes. Ma hummed along in that pleasant, unobtrusive hum only mothers pull off.

Calvin sighed in that annoyed way teenagers do, especially teens stuck riding with Ma. The woman listened to the worst shite on the radio: easy listening (WFBG) or news (1240 AM). She drove precisely the posted speed limit: if the sign said 25, her Volvo wagon went 25. Not 35 like everyone else, not 26 ... twenty-fucking-five. She tolerated neither tomfoolery nor superciliousness: passengers were prisoners, not compatriots.

Hence Calvin's silent, dead-inside gaze out the passenger window at "downtown" Axsubeen while his mother hummed with the song.

If Ma likes Phil Collins, you know he's rubbish!

Then something in Phil's timbre struck a chord. Calvin set his chin in his beefy palm and gave the tune a good listen.

Ma got the Volvo into the left-turn lane at the junction with Bald Eagle Pike, the direction everyone else was going—Rte. 666 went that way. She looked over, saw her younger son's hazy eyes, and instantly knew everything. "Swooning over this new lass, are we now?"

"Kathryn Amelia Howe is her name," he told her. Saint Brigid Cathedral was at this intersection. Calvin felt like popping in to ask Father Sean a few questions about Kitty. *Doc brought up Schultz Park—you know what the deal is with that?*

He felt that parental gaze on him. "Quit staring, Ma."

"She's *really* got hold of you." Ma declined to join the parade of cars zipping left slightly after the light went red. "Look at those mushy eyes! Just like your da's when he met me."

"Da never had 'mushy eyes.' Go on!"

"He did when we first met!" said Ma. "Been on dates with this

Kitty, then? Don't take her somewhere pointless like the cinema!"

"Whoa, you know she's blind?!"

"The Howes go to our Mass. *Of course* I know Kitty's blind." She finally turned left onto Bald Eagle Pike and shifted the Volvo to low gear for climbing the Big Hill.

"Kitty's more than just 'the blind girl,'" the lad sniffed. "She's a person. And she's awesome."

"Awesome, so she is. Tubular. Gnarly."

Calvin ignored this desecration of the sacred slang. "She's not like the others, Ma. She's got lots of brains."

"I agree, lots of 'brains' under her cardigans."

"It's not like that! We got some kinda unique magic going."

"'Magic,' is it? 'Magic' is what *girls* say."

"Maybe Da said it too back when he had mushy eyes for you."

Ma did something singular: she took her eyes off the road to glare into his soul. "Your da has done something with his life. What has my youngest done? He's my most famous child, and for what? Saving a baby from a housefire? Oh that's right, for the unmentionable episode on the Corgans' lawn."

"The unmentionable episode you mentioned AGAIN? Ma, do us a favor and stay outta my life." He stared out the window furiously.

Phil Collins buggered off *and Butch Cassidy and a babe bustled in bestride a bicycle.* Rte. 666 (the Bald Eagle Pike section) was a windy affair, sharp curves around ponds, lots of dips and hills, old-ass trees leaning over the power lines, bracken cumming in the gutter ditches. The farms and homes along this stretch were old and looked it, but at least there weren't any eyesores like the abandoned steel forge at the south end of Railroad Street, the de facto trash dump with decades of old fridges at the bottom of that one hill on Roaring Spring Pike, or Old Man Mueller's dilapidated, fire-scorched barn.

Nope. This was the nice part of town. A few of the steads along Bald Eagle Pike had rose trellises over their rustic gates or cutesy bogus street signs at their driveways: Petunia's Pass, Gilly Gulch, My Way Hwy.

The one with the Daddy-O Drive sign belonged to Toby Stewart, the infamous town fuck-up. Part of Toby's legend was the perpetual green light shining out his Dutch Colonial's second story window.

Indoor weed farm, said Robbie.

Yog-Sothoth summoning spot, said Ryan.

Romulan orgy room, said Art.

Who gives a shit? said Rose.

"I'd like to visit this mythical place where parents take no interest in their kids' lives," Ma droned on. "Particularly when it's a boy and the first word he uses to describe a romance is feckin' *magical.*"

"You're just too old to remember the magic, Ma," said Calvin.

"If you end up with this Kitty, it won't be for the magic but for the right reasons. You *won't* end up like all these sinners and cravens and malingerers, Calvin Ciarán. I'll see to that!"

"Lovely, I'll end up like you two."

"Oh right, me boyo doesn't want to be 'boring' like Ma and Da. Boring gave us our house, this car, the heat, the food. Wise up! You're too old to drift along. You'll be licensed soon. You'll need a job for dates and gas money and insurance. Pick a career yet? A college? How about Point Park? I hear Saint Francis is nice and Catholic."

She took a break to hum with the radio in that unobtrusive motherly hum. *"Rain-hmm hm hmm-mm hm mm hmmm,* and this Kitty better not be another MacDonald wench."

"Don't hold back, come right out and say it."

"None of that cheek. You wrote that Jezebel a poem and she crumpled the paper up in front of you. Evil!"

"The word is 'fickle.' With Jenny, nothing matters 'til it does. Only felt like I was in the same room with her when we were bickering."

"She dumped you for that rich boy Corgan. Evil!"

"The first time we were dating, that's true. The second time, *I* dumped *her* ... for being fickle!"

"This Kitty will be your fourth girlfriend by age sixteen. Define 'fickle,' please?"

"Quit throwing Jenny in my face! It's over. I got the last laugh."

"Do not look for revenge but— "

"*—leave room for the wrath?* Done. Jenny is God's problem now."

Traffic came to a crawl. An Oldroyd Heating Oil truck, making a delivery, blocked their lane. Ma refused to pass until it was safe enough to breakdance around the tanker.

"One-sixteenth impulse power, Mr. Crusher," muttered Calvin.

"The MacDonald wench came back begging once already," said Ma. "Close that door but *firm*. You've a wandering eye, boyo. I see you down at the bus stop teasing your *first* ex, the purple daughter of that pizza slut McSween next door. And you got another love letter in the post today from the diabolical redser. Should've thrown it in the bin but I put it on your desk."

"Thanks a million, Cliff Claven."

"Bloody cheek. You don't act like the other boys and I love you for being your own man and not chasing their favor, but *Lorrrrd* do you act the eejit when some lass is involved."

"I keep telling you, it's different this time. Even when I was all *me-me-me* around Kitty, she teased me and I felt dumb. But it wasn't judgment like with Jenny, or with you. Kitty was, like, helping me out."

"Well," said Ma, reluctant to give Calvin a point. "It sounds like she tolerates your shite because you're good to her and show promise that you'll learn from mistakes."

"… thanks?"

A reedy man on WFBG recited artist and title and gave way to a manly man making big promises over gunfire, fanfare, klaxons, and ass. "No job? No money? No buns? Bad credit? No credit? In jail? Get'cher buns down to Lucky Cheeseboro GM Chevrolet in bun·YOO′·tee·full al·TOO′·nah!!"

The Connors pretended not to hear this obscenity.

"The Howes seem a trustworthy lot, if a little overweight," said Ma. "Though the lass has the least mass."

"What're you, Run-DMC now?" laughed Calvin. *"The lass with the least mass / got an ass that pass the gas?"*

"Why is that now?" Ma went on to herself. "You'd think Kitty would be the least active. Can a blind person exercise, play sports?"

"She 'watches' her weight!" The lad employed the teenager's trademarked you-wouldn't-understand,-old-person laugh.

"Yet I should think Kitty was raised to face the truth. If she can't run around like the others, she needs to eat less. They'll have told her. Can't gobshite a crippled child. She's probably quite sharp." Ma gave her boy a nod. "Not a bad catch."

"Thanks a million. Don't worry, I act like a perfect gentleman."

"'Acting' is 'lying.' Women are not objects. You will *receive her in the Lord in a manner worthy of the holy ones!*"

"Aye aye, Father Sean."

"Jesus weeps at your insolence, Calvin Ciarán! You need to be responsible for once—Kitty Howe is crippled!"

"*You're* crippled. Deaf."

She slapped him once.

WFBG returned to the easy listening with *the Alan Parsons Project, deploring the diaspora's dismal daily diversions.*

Ma's thin hand flicked the indicator lever about three-quarters of a mile before the school. Calvin checked his hair in the sun visor's vanity mirror and sighed. There had to be a way outta this. "Thinking of a new look. There's a team haircut, see."

"Army buzz would suit. Can't believe you joined the 'base ball!'" Ma gnashed the word in twain like a kid snapping into a Slim Jim. "You were my last hope of raising a true Irishman."

"Ma, there weren't any spots open on the school's hurling squad."

"Bloody cheek."

"And you raised a perfect Irishman in Robert Críostóir."

"Robbie's as Irish as that cold cereal with the leprechaun. All his 'ye'-ing and his bard ballad bollocks. He's a prancin' fool, embarrassing his name and his roots, and for what? A pint or some hoor."

Eileen Connor's offspring were never cordial/smart/Irish/Catholic/studious enough for her. "On behalf of my siblings," he said, "I hereby apologize for us lot being such utter disappointments."

Ma finally made the right off Bald Eagle Pike into the Axsubeen School campus, where both the Elementary (K–6) and High (7–12) Schools were. "Straight home afterwards, Calvin. *Children, obey your parents.* No girls and no explosives with that Maguire."

"I have detention again so 'straight home' is like 4:20."

"Not a second later. It's Saint Brigid's Day so we need to keep the traditions and make crosses. If I'm to foot the bill for bloody base ball kit, you *will* be home and doing your homework so you're eligible."

Calvin deliberately opened the passenger door a second before she completed the stop, just to drive the woman insane.

FOUL

Three minutes was the school's limit for switching classes between bells. Said interval applied to late passes; sign in at the office and get where you belong, stat. Calvin needed more time than that so he ignored the Office for now.

He strolled into the gymnasium to find it was Square Dancing Week for the seniors. Peter McLlwayne's favorite time of the year: the A.V. Club President got to hook up the gym's permanently requisitioned phonograph player to the P.A., spin the school's vinyl copy of Kimbo's 1968 release *Modern Square Dancing (with calls),* and, best of all, the bespectacled bastard got to pick which babe to dance with. All the lads did. Boys' prerogative.

It was the best, or the worst, class ever.

Calvin delivered his physical to Mr. Falcone and made taunting eyes at his sister Rose. She hated life so bad right now: her little brother was here, she wore the white short-shorts and doo-doo brown Gym shirt, and she was forcibly *do-si-do*-ing with fat-ass Eddie Howe.

Calvin got his Office pass. He now had three minutes to rejoin Algebra class, which the Office clock said ended in five. He cooled his Reeboks so it'd take precisely three minutes to reach Room 227.

Walking the lonely halls during class was 80% cool (not in a lesson), 10% thrilling (peering into the doors' wire-shot windows at mates stuck in class like chumps), and 10% anxiety (any grown-ups encountered became Berlin Wall sentries, asking for papers).

Three of the Mall Chicks rounded the corner before him: his ex and neighbor Jill Pedersen, future prom queen Kare McGillicutty, and hanger-on Rayche Schultz.

Why the girls were permitted to roam the halls during class was anyone's guess, but they moved full speed and in full clucking blather and so ran right into the foot-dragging Irish Raging Ape.

Like, *ran* into him, colliding as one.

Squeaks—Jill's lavender Chucks on the tile as she scooted back, disgusted at being so close to him. She booked around him, out of sight.

Shrieks—Rayche's *"OhmyGOD!"* as she was thrown to the tile, then *"Ewww* yuck I touched him!" as she ran back whence they came.

Peeks—Kare's eyes, facing front and squeezed mostly shut.

The rich girl had been in the middle. Kare was the Queen of the Mall Chicks and always stood in the middle. She'd taken the brunt of the collision, smooshing right up into the Ape.

Kare stood frozen, stunned, mouth open. Her wad of Big Red had flung onto his teal/gray sweaterfront. Her arms had carried forward; her right hand wound up around him to grasp his back, while the left hand got jammed awkwardly between his Trapper Keeper and her thigh.

Sorry, not her thigh—*his* thigh.

Sorry, not his thigh—his *crotch*.

His rapidly fossilizing flute slid upward, pushing a tight bulge of Bugle Boy denim into the palm of her hand.

Sorry, not her hand—her grasp. She let go, then re-engaged. *Yep, that's the Ape's bone, all right,* is how he interpreted that second squeeze.

Calvin's left hand had wrapped behind Kare's back just as hers had gotten behind his. Miss McGillicutty wore a willowy affair today, black, with Keith Haring-like pipe-cleaner squiggles resembling red doggies and blue television sets.

The shirt looked great on her. Totally Mall Chick-ish.

His sweaty fingers flicked through her shirt's polyester. *That's the Mall Chick's bra, all right.* He gave it a pinch, meaning only to snap it.

His fat fingers unfastened it instead.

Focus came back to Kare's hazel eyes and with it, a fire. Her mouth clicked shut, taking away the lingering scent of cinnamon freshness. When he moved his Trapper to set her free, she slid that hand up, wiping her palm along his sweater, and fetched her Big Red wad off his chest. She popped it back in her mouth.

Sorry, not her mouth—*his.*

The Ape didn't realize he was so agape. He gave the gum a chew. "I hear you need help with your Biology," his baritone purred.

She peeled herself off him like she was extricating a Fruit Roll-Up from its cellophane. "So what," she said. "I don't want to get an F."

"Oh, you want an F now."

Kare's mouth twisted to its usual Mall Chick sneer: "You're

disgusting, Ape." She slapped her binder and Science textbook into his hands, reached behind to refasten her bra through her shirt, grabbed her school shit back from him, and hustled off.

His boner died seconds after getting to Algebra and beholding polynomials on the homework handout.

FOUL

"Yer such a hairy little ballsack, dude."

The sweetness of Mike Love *proclaiming to his paramour (prior to proof to prevent aspersions) that his piston-penis pumped more pell-mell than other players' in the pueblo* went sour under the devastatorious duress of Rosaleen's American accent. Unlike Robbie and Calvin, *this* Connor kid left Irishness behind the second some Yank boy snorted at "arse."

Calvin looked up from the Algebra that he was totally doing. "Been called worse. How do you make percentages from fractions?"

"Like this—I'll only beat one half of yer ass if ya eat 100% of my shit." Rose was all chewing gum smacks and crackling pasty neon yellow lipstick. She could make no more noisome an introduction lest she be naked and juggling her used diaphragms.

"Good thing Eddie didn't fall on you in Square Dancing. He woulda turned you into bread-and-butthole pudding."

Her cud-chewing smacked to the beat of Bon Jovi's *trial of a toxicant so treacherous that it tee-hee'd at the tincture while tallying a trio of turbulent traits.* This was the death knell for Calvin's tunes. Brian Wilson's lifeless head crashed against the piano keys, a dagger made of watermelon Hubba Bubba wrappers jutting between the shoulder blade folds of his white and gray vert-stripe shirt.

Calvin shut his radio off to spare the Beach Boys further ignominy.

"You *hadda* come into my Gym class at that exact moment," Rose pissed. "My friends were all, '*Ewww,* your baby-brother the Ape!'"

In a David Attenborough voice: "Notice how the carrion-feeding Rosaleen weaves a fiction: the telltale phrase 'my friends' gives it away."

Rose cocked her hips, making the belly-cut of her four-sizes-too-big Bruce Springsteen shirt swing side-to-side like a church bell. "Eddie Howe ain't left me alone since ya beaned Davey with that orange. Took me forever to figure out why! Matty told me Pete Hennessey said during hockey that ya hit on his fat fuck of a sister."

"Justine Hennessey's a stick figure, not a fat fuck."

"I meant *Eddie's* sister, not Pete's. Moo-moo Mrs. Magoo."

"Oh how original now. And who the hell's Matty?"

"Matt Winowski ... my ex-boyfriend, asshole!"

"Your boyfriend, Asshole? Wait, *ex*-boyfriend? C'mon Sis, how long did that last, a whole week? And you dare judge my love life!"

Rose's gum, lipstick, and mouth did a Devastator: the three separate entities transformed into a single unified bitch-face. "The Howes are so fuckin' gross. Eddie's like gnarly rotten olive loaf, all sweaty hands and stinky, except for his matchstick dick, *that* was like a goddamn twig pokin' my side—hey! I'm talkin' to you!"

Calvin had turned back to his fraction equations.

"And someone keeps calling here and, like, breathing hard."

"Horny seniors," said the lad. "Round up the usual suspects."

"Maybe it was Kitty. Pro'bly ran outta breath just walkin' across the room to use the phone." Rose folded her arms, knocking about the most suckled teenage breasts in Axsubeen. "She'll dump you a month from now, dude. Then you'll be all like—" She adopted a scary accurate Calvin-voice, the crackly one from his puberty: "'Don't leave me like Jenny did!' And Kitty'll go, 'We can still be friends.'"

Calvin flew from his seat and grabbed her. He was much bigger and had been for years. If he thrust Rose's shoulders together, he could collapse her into a crunchy pulp. "Don't be jealous of true love!"

"*Pfft!* Talk about less than a week! I can't wait to tell all my senior friends how sad ya look after that Bible-bumper ditches yer fat butt!"

"You'll hafta take a break from giving them head to talk to them."

"Admit it, ya picked the blind one cuz she won't mind ycr face."

"I mind *your* face, you bloody menstruating cunt, so remove it." He shoved her out to the Usonian home's Pac-Man-maze corridor and shut his door. Since it had no lock, he wedged his desk chair under the knob.

Rose stomped back to her room and slammed her own door, cackling like the Joker the whole way.

Chapter 10

AN IRRATIONAL FETISH FOR RATIONAL NUMBERS.
GROUNDHOG DAY.

FOUL

CALVIN LEFT OFFICIAL DETENTION for the final time and hustled down the corridor. He was sick to death of those two hundred sixty-seven cinder blocks. Or was it two sixty-six? *Five days in that room and I forget already! What a colossal fucking waste of time.*

He popped into the gym around 3:57 p.m. to find eighteen boys and nineteen girls standing on one of the hardwood's lines. He expected them to be in baseball kit like at the tryout but everyone wore standard Gym unis: white short-shorts and doo-doo brown T-shirt.

A troop of grown-ups stood in front of them: baseball coaches Skip, Mr. Falcone, and Sheriff Steve; softball coaches Mrs. Geoffries and Miss Siess; and the groundskeeper guy with the tan skin and the weird name (Spuy). Skip and Geoffries were outlining the team rules.

When Skip caught sight of Calvin, he did a two-finger whistle—the sound was unreal, piercing to the point of pain—and waved Calvin to one end of the line. The lad stood next to ninth-grader Gus Jacoby and felt silly being the only kid here in his unsweaty street clothes.

"Rule five," said Skip. "The F-word's off-limits."

"The C-word too," said Geoffries. "Take note, Irish."

A peal of teasing laughter echoed. Calvin had never once interacted with Mrs. Geoffries and *that* was the cherry-breaker? What a cunt!

"Rule six," said Geoffries, "no foreign substances on pitches."

"No sign-stealing," said Skip. "Or bean balls!"

"No tagging runners in the face," said Geoffries.

"We will not stick up for you if you cheat," said Skip.

"The Axes and the Lady Axes play fair ball," said Geoffries. "That said ... "

"... all of that's part of the game," Skip finished.

These two were like a well-rehearsed vaudeville act, sans the humor. Calvin wondered if this would end in a pie-fight.

"Last rule," said Skip. "This ain't from Axsubeen High but from the West Penn Conference—the equipment standards. They got an obsession over numbers and colors."

Geoffries picked up a stack of Xeroxed guidelines and walked down the line, handing them out. "The '88-89 uniforms will be the same as last year. Varsity softball wears a brown shirt with a pink number. Varsity baseball, orange shirt with a black number. J.V. softball, white shirt, pink number. J.V. baseball, white shirt, black number."

"Girls wear white pants, boys wear brown pants," said Skip. "We all wear the brown caps. Your shoes can be white, black, or the school colors. Good luck findin' cleats in brown and orange."

"These guidelines are super-important," said Geoffries sternly. "The other team can challenge it if our players don't have the right shirt or shoes on. That could mean ejection or forfeit."

"J.V. players can play in Varsity games," said Skip, "but they gotta keep their J.V. shirt on."

"During a J.V. game, everyone on both teams'll have a white shirt cuz only J.V. players will play," said Geoffries.

"During a Varsity game," said Skip, "some of us'll have orange shirts and some white, while the other team'll have boys in white shirts or in blue ones or whatever their school color is."

"That's so confusing!" said ninth-grader Rhonda Adams.

"Both teams could be in plaid with purple polka dots," said Geoffries, "but it'll be *obvious* who's on your side. If we're fielding, all of us will have hats and mitts on. If we're batting, we'll have helmets and empty hands."

"Wait wait," Gus Jacoby said, putting up a whale of an arm. "How comes we can't all wear orange during a Varsity game?"

"Cuz of that whole cheatin' and breasts thing back in '81," spat Skip. "It forced all these new rules!"

"The what now?" burped Calvin.

"Yeah," chirped Holly Watson, "the 'breasts thing?'"

Mr. Falcone jumped in here: "Up at Altoona Area High School, a girl softball player taped down her chest, put on her twin brother's number 19 shirt, and played on the baseball team. She looked just like him and was a way better hitter."

The line of kids erupted in comments.

Skip did his sharp whistle again.

The comments slowed but didn't stop:

"Wasn't it Portage High?" said Jennifer Adkisson.

"I heard it was her boyfriend, not her brother," said Nick Oelwein.

"No, they *were* twins," said Steph Millar. "Both had the same uniform number but one was in baseball and the other in softball."

"Didn't they find out cuz she got hit in the, uh, y'know, but she wasn't wearin' a cup?" said Sammy "Zedz" Dzedzy.

"I heard it was the other way around—a dude put on a bra and falsies to go play with the girls," said Spazz Watson.

"That's your fantasy, not reality," said Geoffries, getting a laugh.

"Cross-dressing is disgusting," said Roni Vogel.

"Girls pretending to be boys, yuck," said Josh Adams.

"Sneakin' peaks in the boys locker room afterwards," said Spazz.

"Shut it, Watson!" said Skip.

"It's so stupid," said Anna Schultz.

"What's stupid is, they woulda got away with it," said Ryan.

"If not for those meddling kids?" joked Paddy Millar.

"If not for judgmental people. She was hitting homers and the baseball team was winning games. Some Bible-thumper turned her in."

"Cuz some boy's degenerate dad was getting cheated," said Skip. "You can't put in a ringer and expect gamblers not to figure it out!"

"Hang on," said Calvin, "people bet on these games?"

"The 'why' doesn't matter," Geoffries said patiently. "The rules are the rules. We still have a big one to cover: numbers. All four teams— softball, baseball, Varsity, J.V.—pick from the same list so there's no duplicates."

"0 through 99," said Skip. "No fractions, no decimals, no NASCAR crap like '06.' And we won't have names on the backs of our shirts like the Pirates, for budget reasons."

Coach Falcone brandished a clipboard. "Line up in order by birthday. Gender don't matter. If two of you have the same birthday, then it's rock-paper-scissors."

Calvin laughed. No one else did. The lad was about to learn how irrational everyone was about their number. In football (the real football), the keeper wore 1, defenders 2 through 5, and so on. In baseball you got to keep the number forever, no matter what position you played. It was personal, an identifier, a possession.

Numbers had backstories.

Some kids took their favorite or lucky numbers. Lucky Cheeseboro took 1 3 back in the day to prove just how lucky he was. Gus Jacoby's favorite number was 2 5, for Christmas.

Some kids wore the number of a pro player hero: Sammy "Zedz" Dzedzy took 2 0 for Mike Schmidt, who in turn had worn 2 0 to honor *his* hero, Frank Robinson. Art Maguire had a similar story for 4 2 but an older white kid named Adams kept getting it, forcing Art to transpose the digits to 2 4. "Adams graduates this year," he said. "Next year, Jackie Robinson's 4 2 is mine!"

Some numbers had deep personal ties: Valerie Crenshaw took 0 cuz, as a trailer park kid, she always heard she was nothing and worthless. Calvin thought that was oddly maudlin until he found out why Brion Davey wore 8 9—he'd flunked ninth grade and was now Class of '90. Calvin had to give the gap-toothed arse credit for wearing such a brutal truth literally on his sleeve.

Some kids made a joke of it. Spazz Watson with his 6 9, for example. Detta Roberts explained her 7 7 like so: "I'm tall, I'm black, and I'm so fabulous I need *two* lucky sevens on my back!"

Some kids didn't care at all. Philomena "Pony" Ysderrhi, Chicken's sister, went full random; she played AD&D and brought 2d10, rolling 'til she got something Falcone said was open (5 0).

And Calvin? Well.

"I'm Calvin the Third. Let's go with 3."

Falcone: "3's taken. Chicken has it."

Chicken: "You can have the 3 for crisp three-dollar bill."

Calvin: "There's no such thing as a three-dollar bill."

Chicken: (a shrug) "Oh well, no tienes suerte, wah-wah-*waaah.*"

Falcone: "You can transpose it, Calvin."

Calvin: "I'm not dressing up like a girl for it."

Falcone: "No no, trans*pose:* swap the digits. With a single-digit number, put a zero in front of it, then swap them around."

Calvin: " 3 0 's fine."

Falcone: "… er, it's taken. Sorry."

Calvin: "Whatever, double it up: 3 3."

Falcone: "That's gone too."

Chicken: "Thirty-three for 3. Transpose to bucks. Final offer."

Calvin: "Get bent. How about 1 2? One and two make three."

Falcone: "That's good. Too bad it's gone too. So's 2 1. How about you pick something with a three in it, like 3 7."

Calvin: " 3 7 's gay. I like 1 3."

Falcone: "It's retired."

Calvin: "It's … what?!"

Falcone: "That was Lucky's number. The great players get their numbers retired and no one can wear them again."

Calvin: "Whatever. Let's transform that shite: 1 3 to 3 1!"

Firmly: "No. That's the cursed number. No one wears it."

Chicken: " 3 not cursed. It's lucky for you, Connor? Make it lucky for me, sell me sister for it. Rose give it away anyway."

Calvin & Falcone: "Beat it, Chicken!"

Calvin: (sweaty hands through hair) " 8? Spazz says an eight looks like dog balls, but I say it looks like two threes sucking face."

Falcone laughed. "I like that! Fits the three theme! But it's taken."

Calvin: "Jaysus Christ with Gravy Fries, what's open?!"

" 4, 7, 1 0 —"

" 4!" Calvin cupped his hands to announce, "I AM 4! AND IT DON'T MEAN CRAP! IT'S RANDOM BOLLOCKS!"

Skip didn't like that one bit. "Don't piss down the backs of the Baseball Gods and tell them it's a rain delay."

"Baseball has its own gods? Blasphemy!"

"It's just a joke," said Michelle Cullen, one of the Proverbs Patrol kids, a good li'l Catholic girl.

"A commandment-breaking joke—the *first* commandment, that's all now. And graven numerals on our backs!"

Felon Adkisson said, "I can see ya wantin' 3 cuz you're the third dickhead loser named Calvin Connor. So why pick **4**?"

"Why not?! The girls are rolling bloody dice for their numbers but suddenly mine has to mean something? Go and shite!"

Sean Corgan got right into Calvin's space. "Are you insulting a Varsity player, rookie? Someone who's got the team haircut? Now tell him why you picked **4**! And you better make it good!"

This could get violent. Yet Falcone, Skip, Geoffries, and Siess, the adult coaches, wore flat faces, had arms folded. Typical grown-ups: "Fuck you, kid, you're on your own!" Even part-time assistant coach Sheriff Steve, a paid keeper of the peace—standing there in his fucking peacekeeping outfit—didn't seem likely to peacekeep.

"You're **2**," Calvin told Sean. "I picked **4** cuz I'm twice as big. Ask your ma."

The Axes went wild: some laughed at Calvin's balls, others went *Oooo!* at his impending doom, and most of the girls clicked their tongues at his vulgarity. Roni Vogel tried to start a *"Fight fight fight!"* cheer before getting shushed by Coach Geoffries.

Sean's poker face was a rock. "We'll see how big you are come game-time, chief."

FOUL

Skip did his two-finger whistle at 5:19 and Mrs. Geoffries had the teens line up facing the far wall. Calvin had never noticed the 6′ x 4′ Old Glory hanging next to the gym's wall-mounted scoreboard. The lad had also never recited the Pledge of Allegiance outside homeroom. If that wasn't creepily American enough, Skip made them go to one knee and pray to God. Thankfully it was silent and not some movie speech prayer, coming out the mouth of a man crowned town hero for murdering Koreans. Skip *did* end practice with this: "We come in hungry to win, and leave patriotic and penitent." Calvin nearly vomited.

Lucky Cheeseboro had arrived around 5, straight from the dealership, and showed Calvin some new finger grips, stretches, exercises, and baseball lingo. Sean Corgan popped on his catcher's gear to field Calvin's throws. When the little wanker brought up the Davey Dangle haircut—again—Lucky offered to take his protégé to the barber in his

Callaway twin-turbo.

"Can I drive?" asked Calvin, gray eyes bright and thirsty.

Lucky smiled. "You like the Detroit muscle, champ?"

Eyes on the prize, the lad said, "Italian's my dream. Lamborghini. I mean, I'd drive a Ferrari if no one's looking."

That leathery face cracked in two with a big laugh. "Once in a long while, I get something like that in a trade-in. Would ya settle for a Camaro? You can get bright red to match your boyfriend Sean's."

"Wouldn't wipe my arse with an IROC-Z, sir."

By 5:29 Calvin's unwiped arse was in the passenger seat of the 1988 Callaway twin-turbo Corvette B2K, marveling at the all-black interior, the crisp (and fuckin' freezin') leather bucket seat, all the buttons and dials, the three digital-ish readout screens showing numerals and graphs in white, electric blue, and what Jill Pedersen would call "heliotrope."

Lucky fired it up and revved the engine. "Eh? Eh?" he said. "She's one smooth bitch!"

"Sounds lovely," the lad drooled.

"It's a 5.7-liter V8, that's 382 horses—more than any Eye-talian jalopy can offer ya, buttercup!"

"The Countach has 425," said Calvin defensively.

With an economy of movement that suggested he'd done this a thousand times, Lucky's non-pitching hand flicked on the cabin light and pointed at a small plaque on the center console, below the stick:

1988 TWIN-TURBO CORVETTE
CONSTRUCTED BY
CALLAWAY ENGINEERING
OLD LYME, CONNECTICUT 06371

NO. 13 / 400

Calvin nodded with a thrust-out bottom lip. "Thirteen, of course."

"Of course! Hadda pull strings to get it. You'd think for the extra twenty-seven grand they'd give ya the number ya want—"

"This is only twenty-seven grand?"

"Shit no! The base model's sticker is thirty-five. For a Callaway, you gotta put down almost double." Lucky backed the black beast out of his spot and shifted into first. The Corvette burped across the faculty lot to the exit on Colonial Drive. The car moved so fierce, so fast, that Calvin swore they'd left the macadam.

Sixty thousand! he thought. *Guess the car sales business is good!*

His Trapper slid away as the 'Vette burned up Colonial. Calvin reached down with one hand to park it under a Reebok. His fingers came off grimy; the floormats were as pasty with crumbs and old fluids as the floor of Rose's two-decade-old Bug. *You'd think a bloke would keep his baby shiny and clean, or at least get his people to do it ...*

"Yer pro'bly thinkin' to yerself, 'I can't afford fifty-seven grand, that's as much as a rancher,'" said Lucky, "but trust me, you can. Well not yet, yer just a kid. But keep fryin' my radar gun and you'll have fuck-you money faster'n you can say, 'Yee-ha!'" Lucky put it into third and cooked those cylinders.

"Eff-you money?" asked Calvin.

"Yeah. Like, 'Fuck you, loser, I got cash and you don't, eat my dust.'" When speaking through a character, the weary man lapsed into that redneck opera singer twang he employed in his TV ads.

"You mean, I'll get eff-you money betting on the team?"

"Nah, only the degenerates at the Biergarten do that. They'll bet on *anything*. Guys that gamble ain't ridin' in a sweet machine like this! But *you* will, Calvin. You'll blow past yer neighbors while they sit in traffic in their used Toyotas and used Volkswagens, jealous as hell."

"My brother's got a used Toyota pickup and Sis has a used VW Beetle. You spying on me, or was that a 'lucky' guess?"

Lucky laughed. He got on Rocky Road, which climbed over one of the Valley's two tit-hills. This was the long way back to town. Lucky was showing off. The 'Vette's high beams fired long white streaks to penetrate the darkness deep and hard.

"So what do yer parents drive, Calvin?"

"Da has a brand new Caddy ..."

Lucky did a shrug. "Fine for old guys."

"Ma's got a Volvo station wagon."

"Not just a Vulva but a wagon? *Boring!*"

That hit home with the lad.

They crested the hill's nipple and careened down Rocky Road's western end, a section called "Suicide Slide" by the locals. Calvin peeked at the dash and saw 63. "That's high-falutin' how it's got both the numbers and the graph thing."

"Digital *and* dial readouts for speedometer and tachometer, yep."

"What if I don't fry the radar gun?"

"Huh?"

"I mean, what if I suck in real games?"

"In that case we can do financing, don't you worry."

"I'm not talking about the Corvette, Mr. Cheeseboro."

"What're ya, a judge? It's 'Lucky,' or ain't ya heard?"

In no time they were off Rocky Road, down Barley Street, and peeling right with a rolling stop at Roaring Spring Pike. "We're goin' to the barbershop in town, right? Old Man Mueller?"

"Well. *Frank* Mueller cuts hair. *Hans* Mueller is the one we call 'Old Man Mueller.' He owns the farm on my street."

"Too many fuckin' krauts in this town! One of the reasons I split."

"You don't live in Axsubeen?"

"Couldn't wait to leave, sweet pea. Bet ya feel the same way. I got a place up in Bellwood."

"Where's—"

"Nice suburb north of the 'Toona. Keep forgettin' I'm talkin' to a teenager here. How old are ya?"

"I'll be sixteen in a fortnight or so."

"Christ, my daughter's age. She's just like you: knows all about Bon Jovi and *The Wonder Years* but no basis in how the world works."

"Bollocks, Lucky, I'm from overseas and I've seen some shite."

At the junction with Rte. 666 (where the Big Hill was, at the end of Bald Eagle Pike), Roaring Spring Pike became Main Street. Lucky got lucky with a green here and strolled the 'Vette through town. He got in the left turn lane at the T-junction with Railroad Street but neglected to put his turn signal on. Calvin noticed the man hadn't put on his seatbelt either.

"Okay, then picture this," the guy said. "You, in a ride like this, from my dealership. Where are we?"

"Uh, Axsubeen?"

"Not L.A.? New Orleans? Miami? Somewhere hot *and* cool?"

"My dream is to move to Miami."

"Great. Now: who's in the passenger seat?"

"Me."

"Yer killin' me, hoss—*fantasize!*"

"Kitty Howe. She's kinda my girlfriend."

"Is she hot? Stacked? A great face that you don't see too often cuz she's so busy suckin' yer dick?"

Why do "cool" grown-ups embarrass themselves and talk like that? moaned the teenager. He didn't have the words to rebuke Lucky's porno flurry.

"There's a certain kind of babe who gets in the passenger seat of a Callaway twin-turbo—Christie Brinkley, Teri Weigel, Ginger Lynn."

"I fancy Lisa De Leeuw myself."

"Ah, *biiig* tits, a man of culture." Lucky turned onto Railroad Street, went a block, crossed over the double-yellow and parked the wrong way right outside Steeler's Shears.

Calvin pointed out how illegal that was, like a diligent know-it-all.

Lucky rolled his eyes at him. "If Sheriff Steve came past right now, y'know what he'd do?"

"What?"

"Offer to park it proper for me." He spread his leathery face into a showroom smile. *"This* is how the world works. My world, anyway. Could be yers too ... after I teach you a four-seamer."

Chapter 11

THE ORIGIN STORY.
FRIDAY, FEBRUARY 3, 1989.

FOUL

THE IRISH RAGING APE'S Davey Dangle debut was a smashing success. Calvin did a little catwalk stroll up and down the bus stop at the Phillips driveway. Pete Hennessey made sarcastic hoots. Eighth-grader Justine Hennessey told Calvin he was handsome. Ryan's gape and wide blue eyes were totally Ralphie peering in the shop window at that Red Rider B.B. gun. Jill Pedersen gave him her fashion critique, thinking she'd sound knowledgeable and sarcastic but everyone there heard the undertones of psychotic jealousy. She'd only praise his hair-style when she viewed it looking down at him in his open-casket.

A fat hand across his forehead pushed away the sweat and bangs, but found no bangs. Young Calvin went through this once a year, chang-ing hairstyles and needing a few days to adjust. Remembering he needed but a smidge of shampoo in his palm, not a full-on blob. Davey and the others had a close buzz on top, but Sean Corgan wore it a bit longer and spiked it up with gel. Don Johnson had a similar thing going a couple years ago on *Miami Vice*. Calvin went with that variant but after twenty minutes' fucking about with his own product, then Rose's unguarded Studio Line by L'Oréal, then Robbie's leftover Aqua Net, the Ape ended up with a sticky clump, like he'd cum on his own head and ne-glected to wipe it off. Forced by time, he rinsed that shit off in the sink and ran paper towels over it.

Mr. Mueller had left the lower back of his mane alone; eight inches of silky brown hair caressed his neck like a velvet scrotum.

"Part of the team now," said Skip. Calvin hadn't noticed the old man appear out of thin air, ninja-style, in the front doorway of his house, despite wearing a very non-ninja costume of boxers, wife-beater, and tin coffee mug from his Army days. "You look gorgeous, Irish."

"Go and shite, sir," said Calvin. "It looks stupid."

"That's why I won't let my boy get it. And you *paid* for it, too."

"All the money I had in my wallet." Which had been eight dollars. The lad turned desperately to Ryan. "You got any cash, mate? I've nothing for lunch until I can tap MAC!"

Ryan shook his head no, but only cuz his father was there. Perry Phillips hated loans and usury. He owed no one and no one owed him. One of his sons wanted tuition? Better get a job, kid.

On the bus, Ryan hooked up Calvin with a five-spot with no vig.

FOUL

No practice on Fridays; too many kids bailed for dates and dances and cruising and Logan Valley Mall and ColecoVision and whatever else teenagers did. Riding home after school on Bus No. 10, Calvin pictured himself driving.

... to summer school. Another Friday Algebra test, another likely F. No job, no future, borrowing lunch money ... *what kinda ride am I gonna get financed at Lucky Cheeseboro GM Chevrolet?* He scrubbed his hair and was annoyed anew at the Davey Dangle.

And you paid for it, too.

"—field-tested three versions of the M.S.S.M. and none of 'em work," Art droned. He dusted his fingernails on his chest and did his Calrissian purr: "Hey, even *I* fail sometimes. Then the light bulb went on over my head. I have bells at Saint Brigid on Wednesdays and I was walkin' out and saw Shawn Crowe's dad's pickup goin' down Main Street and he hit that one pothole and I was all, *whoa, lookit the wheel goin' up and down!* I raced home and grabbed the Chilton for my dad's Bronco and looked up shock absorbers to see how I could apply—"

Art tugged down his gray glasses to peep at Calvin over the frames. "You *do* know what a shock absorber is, right?"

"I do!" said the lad. "It's like a cylinder with a short rod inside it and a spring. Like a pen, a click-on pen, what're they called?"

"Retractable. Damn, that's a much better way to explain my new design! See, I wanna fix a spring to the shell's firing plate so when ya step on it, it'll add velocity and *ka-blooey!*"

"Won't a spring *absorb* the pressure from a trespasser's foot? You'll have a shock absorber for real!"

Art sucked in fresh oxygen to push down a look of failure. "The mad scientist will make it work. You'll see."

Calvin changed the subject before Art started blubbing. "Does Lucky have a baseball card?"

"Sure, all players get one. I got a couple Topps Cheeseboros. He's a common, they ain't worth shit."

"Lemme check them out sometime."

"No prob, bro. They're kinda lame. He's got a stupid mustache and it don't even list his jacket on the back."

"His jacket? He's been busted?"

"Grew his own Kentucky green grass. Failure to pay child support. The usual crap."

"Well. Makes sense. Everyone says car dealers are crooks."

"Ballplayers too. Lots of cocaine busts. That shit don't happen where I'm headed in computer-land."

"Hot chicks aren't into nerds, mate."

"When I'm Black Bill Gates, I'll have *cash*. Steve Jobs, Peter Norton, they're all billionaires. I'll have Madonna in my penthouse."

"No Whitney Houston?"

"Ugh, no way. If I'm gonna do a sister, it'll be Janet Jackson."

"If I'm gonna do a sister, it's that Cosby girl. Not the skinny one."

"Tempestt Bledsoe? That's cool." Art searched for a really far out one. "I'd bang all them girls on *You Can't Do That on Television.*"

Calvin gaped. "Even the porky motormouth?"

"Lisa. *Especially* her. I'd totally bang Moose too, the one with the big hair and big tits, what was her real name? Christina? Christine?"

"Like I know? I'm not fucking ten anymore!"

The bus halted at Cherry Street and Calvin chose to debark here to continue this conversation. "So," the Ape said, all casual, "how exactly does your report card scam work?"

Art posed by the curbside mailbox at the end of his driveway, flipping open its door. "Your report card comes in the mail—"

"Not mine. Don't sales-pitch me. Let's say Moose from *You Can't Do That on Television's* report card."

"Fine, Christine McMoose's report card comes in the mail about a week after every marking period." Art shut the mailbox and led the way to his garage lair. "They're done on dot matrix printers, which use tiny pins in a six by nine grid. Certain pins poke the ink onto the paper and it makes all the different letters and numbers."

Calvin had noticed COMPUTER-PRINTING before. "You use your mechanical pencil to fill in dots and change the grades."

Art flopped in his drawing board's chair. "My work is flawless."

The lad waved at the black bookshelf with the hundreds of duped cassette tapes. "Probably cuz you got lots of practice writing all them fiddly perfect labels."

Art put proud hands behind his head. "I bet you said that to offend me but I'm gonna take it as a compliment."

Calvin sat in his usual milk crate chair. "If Moose's parents—"

"Barth and Valerie Prevort."

"—who?!"

"The parents on the show. Rem'ber?"

"Fuck off! If Moose's parents know she's failing, why bother surgicalizing her report card into straight A's? They'd never believe it."

"I can't do A's at all. I can only add dots to turn D's into B's." He sifted through a shoebox with many innocuous article clippings on top.

"You do it on your own report cards too?" said Calvin. "I bet you laze-out and get D's in every class!"

"You know how hard it'd be to get straight D's? Might as well do the goddamn homework!" Art found a report card in the shoebox and set it out on the drawing board for them to analyze. "Which one's fake?" He pointed at two B's in the second semester column.

Calvin peered close. "Both of them. Trick question."

"You're right but it's *not* a trick question. This is my report card from eighth grade." Art tapped the top B. "I shocked the world and got a D in English. I added these three dots in the middle, making the D into a B." Art tapped the bottom B. "Then I added a dot to this, a *real* B, to close that gap on the right side." He flipped the card over and sketched a quick version of a matricified B, circling the gap in the middle right of the character, where a B's bowls met.

Calvin took the report card back and examined the front closely. He fingered the top, where the homeroom teacher was listed. "You filled in that dot here too, for Mrs. Baker."

"Right on, Perceptor. Gotta hit 'em all or the jig is up."

"You can totally change *that* into a B." Calvin indicated the F in DRAFTING, a Shop course Art had taken to sharpen his design skills.

"Nope. That top part goes too far out and makes a right angle down." Art went ahead and filled in the dots on that F to turn it into a B.

A clearly phony B. "The bottom bar's gotta match the top one or it's top-heavy. But the finished result don't look like a B anymore, it looks like a fuckin' refrigerator."

African gave Irish a shrewd eye. "I can't help anyone who's *really* failing, like gettin' F's on Algebra tests. You gotta get to a D."

Calvin sat back with a sigh. "Moose is the one who's failing."

"Right, I forgot. Here's another point—if Moose is failing, doctoring the card that comes in the mail only fools her parents. It won't stop the administrators declaring her academically ineligible." Art gave his suave smile. "But I don't tell customers that."

"You keep that detail secret?"

Art waved at his black bookshelf. "Blank tapes cost, bro. I wouldn't turn down Brion Davey if he asked. He stole Jill from me, but I'll take his cash." He played with his report card, then held it up and indicated the third and fourth semester columns, which were blank. "Another thing I leave out—the old D's show up every marking period."

Calvin's steel gray eyes went wide. "That's right! Each new report card shows all the old grades too!"

"That's the *real* money-maker, bro. If Moose gets a D in the first marking period, she pays four times, *cha-ching!* Ten bucks is a big chunk of cash but desperate kids'll go for it. If I tell 'em it'll eventually cost forty, they get cold feet." He pushed down his glasses again to peer over them. "If they were *smart* they'd see that recurring charge coming— but they ain't smart, else they'd have good grades. And the girls get the most desperate. You should see them! Kare says that Rayche Schultz is bombing in Social Studies *and* English and wants my help. I'll practically own her!"

"You always wanted your own slave," said Calvin.

"Massa Art'll be crackin' a whip!"

Calvin *almost* said, "This ruthless thing you got going is why you win at poker." At the last second, he realized that'd be tipping his hand.

Let Art keep thinking you're dumb.

FOUL

Calvin was dumb.

A smart kid wouldn't need to ask about report card surgery. A smart kid would've gotten off the bus near his house and not had to walk home via the Millar/Mueller farm fields. The wind picked up, tear-assing through the valley. Smelt like snow was coming.

The lad came in his back door at the kitchen and spent a minute soaking in the heat of home before peeling off his kelly green down jacket and revolting scarf of many colors. He put the kettle on.

His mother was seated at the dining table, going over the local weekly. "You made the *Distorter* twice, laddy."

"Did I now?"

Her slender hand snapped to page 3. Legal notices. Imminent foreclosures. The police blotter had a fine issued to crazy Mr. Adkisson for burning leaves in his driveway (again) (in February, no less) (no mention of who phoned in the anonymous tip [Eileen Connor]).

Near the bottom was the "Dunce Cap Blotter." After the big Binaca scandal of 1986, angry, frightened parents demanded all administration-level punishments, no matter how minor, be printed as a matter of public record:

```
Calvin Connor 3d, 15, soph: 5 days Official
Detention, disorderly conduct, 1/27/89
```

"They didn't mention the orange." Calvin put the kettle on. "Typical *Reporter,* leaving out the facts."

Ma flipped to the sports page. Under BASEBALL sat a triptych: Sean Corgan in catcher's gear; Lucky Cheeseboro outside his dealership, smiling wide; and Calvin's yearbook photo from ninth grade (taken four months after Souviens; his stupid punk 'do had three inches of brown hair with nine inches of cadaver white). The story:

> girl to wear the number 99 . . . Calvin Connor
> (yes, that Calvin Connor) tried out for the
> Axes' pitching staff Monday. Despite never
> playing baseball, Connor, 15, wowed pitching
> coach Lucky Cheeseboro with fastballs reach-
> ing 90 miles-per-hour. That's not a misprint.
> "He's got great stuff," said sophomore
> catcher Saen Corgan. "I wish he could play on
> the varsity team right away." Cheeseboro was
> likewise impressed: "He'll be a star, mark my
> words!" . . . Axsubeen may officially retire 31

"Ha ha! They spelt the little wanker's name wrong."

"Never mind that—'yes, *that* Calvin Connor?!' Like my son was Hitler!" Ma fingered the byline. "Radcliffe wrote it, the poof!"

Calvin felt a bit giddy. "It's praise. My photograph, even."

"The shittiest one available. I knew I should've forced you to dye that hair." The woman threw her short arms in the air. "Now it lasts forever. This edition will be on microfilm at the library!"

"Hitler's ma would simply burn the library down." Calvin poured steaming water into his mug. "And have William C. Radcliffe shot."

"Oh I've considered it, so I have." She fetched the scissors. "I'll save it anyway for your scrapbook."

"My jacket, as they say in *Miami Vice*. Ooh, gotta set the VCR for tonight." Calvin dunked a bag of Earl Grey and pointed at the clipping. "If I play in the majors, that'll be worth something."

"Fat chance. You know how many kids say that?"

"Lucky says kids get drafted for throwing in the nineties."

"Drafted, like for the Army?"

"That's how kids enter sports leagues. They have a draft and the clubs take turns picking 'em. Like in Gym class when we pick teams."

She squinted at him. "Did you really throw that fast?"

"Plenty of witnesses. A few tried to kill me right afterwards."

"Well. I had to ask—it is the *Distorter* now." She closed the paper, and the topic. "Your father needs to talk to you. He's downstairs."

Calvin felt cold again. He would've seen Da's Caddy in the drive if he'd gotten off at his own bus stop. "What's, uh, he doing home?"

"Schultz's let out. It's supposed to snow at dinnertime. Warm up that shovel, laddy."

"Snow? Kitty's coming for dinner!"

"Oh is she now? Thank you for letting us know, young man!"

"Bollocks, I swear I told you."

Ma opened the larder and stared at its shelves. "'Coating to an inch' they said on 1240. It'll be a bloody foot. What shall I make?"

Calvin sipped his tea. "I dunno."

"Come now. What's her favorite food? What does she hate?"

"She's a vegetarian. She loves cheesecake but no cherries." He held his mug in front of his crotch for no discernible reason.

"I'm not making a fucking cheesecake!" Ma went to the fridge. "'Vegetarian' is useful, though, glad you paid attention. Suppose I'd gone and made blood sausage?"

"On Friday? You already tempt the Lord with toad in the hole!"

"Hot dogs are *not* meat." Ma got out two Pyrex pans and sprayed them with Pam. "Toad in the hole it is. One without hot dogs for the precious vegetarian."

"Why not something Irish? Like colcannon."

"You want colcannon? Fetch me a cabbage." Ma's steely face took on a pleading slant. "And don't talk about yourself all night, 'oh my picture was in the paper.' Ask Kitty *about* Kitty. Find out who she is. You'd be surprised how much a lass likes that. Now go see your father."

FOUL

Da spoke about once a year. 1989's lecture was coming early.

Son found Father in his usual post-workday position: down in the telly room, parked in the Barcalounger, large baleful eyes aimed at the 25″ Quasar, bottle of Heineken, bag of Benzel's Sourdough Hards, pack of Merit Lights. Calvin Ciaran Connor II was not exactly fat, just large. When standing erect his shoulders rose up and out like a vulture's folded wings. Da literally filled doorways. He had the same limpen, sandy brown hair as Calvin Ciarán Connor III; not that you'd ever know, since Da kept it seriously slicked black. His sober speaking manner—just this side of stentorian—made people shit themselves. He was a feared boss down at Schultz's Lumber.

Calvin the Third had spent a lifetime dealing with him and still shat himself. "Ma said you wanted to talk to me."

Da worked a remote, lowering the volume on the hi-fi. He always ran the TV sound through the component receiver and tower speakers, even for *The Flintstones.*

"Sit," he said. His voice sliced clean death. Clean like a surgeon's blade. Death like death. Da could kill at a word.

Calvin sat in the middle position of the sofa, not too far away from the Barcalounger, and sipped his Earl Grey.

"Your mother tells me you got the male-Connor horny look in your eyes," said Da. Not quite how Ma had put it! "We should discuss why *you* are 'Calvin the Third' and Robbie isn't."

Calvin arched his brows. "Never thought about it, really."

"Traditionally, names get passed to the firstborn son. I woulda been 'Oliver Connor Jr.' in that case. But Aul' Olly never saw eye-to-eye with tradition—things like marriage, gainful employment, sobriety, legal residency, raising his child."

Must be why we don't talk about him, Calvin thought, then realized Da was actually talking about him. The lad decided to pay attention.

"Aul' Olly vanished when his wife Molly got pregnant. Olly's cousin Calvin took Molly in. It was the Christian thing to do. Molly was so grateful she named the child—me—Calvin Ciaran Connor II. Naming a kid 'the Second' is how you honor someone who isn't the father."

"Buuut," the pedantic teenager butted in, "you're my father and I'm not 'Calvin Junior.'"

"Imagine 'Calvin the Second' with a son named 'Calvin Junior.' How tired would you get of explaining that?"

The lad looked down at his tea, shamed into silence.

"Calvin the First and Molly got married and he adopted me," Da went on. "You can get technical like Calvin the First was my second cousin once removed and also my stepfather, but that's legal bullshit. He was my dad, period. The only one I ever knew. I never met Aul' Olly, the goddamn bum. Hopefully he's dead. Causing no more trouble."

Whoa. Da finally talked about Olly ... and wished him dead.

Da's baleful eyes flicked to the TV. Fred and Barney were at the Water Buffalo Club. "When I was your age, I got determined to be the good Christian. The same sort of man as Calvin the First. I told him I'd pass his name to my son as a tribute, and he actually cried."

A sweet mist filled Da's eyes, the kind of mist that produces rainbows. He turned to his son. "I see him when I look at you. You're not his blood, but the resemblance is striking."

Calvin the Third gulped at the compliment. It felt like the precursor to a judge banging his gavel. *Does Da have cancer?!*

The mist evaporated. "As you know, I met your ma in Ireland over July 4th weekend, summer of '69. The '60s in a nutshell. Draftees like Art's dad spent America's birthday in 'Nam killing people. This draft dodger spent it in Ireland making people."

Calvin sputtered in his tea cup. *Is Ma pregnant again?!*

"I was twenty-two, my last year at Penn State, questioning my good Christian lifestyle. July 4th was a Friday. I went to O'Donoghue's Pub to see some troubadours sing about peace and shit. Your ma was up from County Kildare with some friends. I bought her a Guinness. Then she ordered us 'two of the Dew.' And we spent the night together."

Da's butt shifted in the Barcalounger. "You know what I mean?"

Carefully: "I do. We've had Sex. Ed. the last three years."

"You've also had sex the last three years."

Everyone knows. "Ma gave me the big talk last summer—"

Da's snort was like a .357 magnum's report. "When she took you and Robbie to Ireland? I'll bet she did. She hates reruns. Anyway, Eileen and I exchanged addresses before I left. Three months later I got an aerogram from Leixlip. They did the rabbit test and it died."

"What's the rab—"

"Don't interrupt. It's how they checked for pregnancy in the Stone Age. Now the girl buys a stick at Schoenberger's Pharmacy and pees on it. Back then, they tainted a rabbit. If it died, the girl's pregnant. And Eileen was. The aerogram ended with, 'It could be yours.'"

Da fumbled for his Merit Lights.

Calvin wanted a smoke too. Like any teenager he rued the image of his parents porking, but to hear talk of other partners, painting Ma as promiscuous …

There's more of Rose in Ma, and vice versa, than Ma wants to admit!

Da took a drag, the cigarette tiny between his big fingers. "The Christian thing was to marry her. I sure as hell wasn't gonna do to Eileen Ní Dubhthaigh what Aul' Oliver Connor did to Molly Georgeson—but she lived in a foreign country. Tell me, Calvin, how's that work?"

The lad was so off balance: history, bombshells, don't interrupt, please answer the question … "Uh, call the embassy?"

"Ours? Ireland's? The State Department? Do I fly over and turn myself in to the Garda?" Da gave his snort laugh. "I had to find all that shit out. Then there's the paternity matter. Eileen figured only two men could be the father: me and this Brit named Charles."

Only the two, thought Calvin. *Fucking hell, Ma is Rose.*

"She was gonna have the kid, no doubts there. No abortion in Ireland. Until she popped, she considered me and Charles both responsible. When the time came, I flew back over and we waited. I sat around your grandparents' sitting room in Leixlip. Very uncomfortable. Lots of quiet meals. It got worse when Charles came."

Calvin gasped. "Maimeó Clodagh let a Brit in her house?"

"A Tory—Charles told your grandmother that the Republic was stolen property of the Crown."

"I mean … what was he doing in Ireland in the first place?"

"Exactly." Da issued a curt nod, as close as he got to slapping his boy on the back and saying *Good job*. "Worked out for me though. You know the old saying: 'Always replace a bum.' Clodagh was never going to see me as a choice cut for her only daughter, but the other guy was a pro-Ulster monarchist bringing the Troubles right to her sitting room."

Da stamped out his smoke and blasted Dristan up each nostril. The man spent ten bucks a week on nicotine and oxymetazoline. "Eileen went into labor," he said, licking the roof of his mouth. "Back then fathers weren't allowed in the delivery room so me and Charles gave a little blood for type-testing and got blind drunk at a pub. Couple hours later, the barman took a call. Robert Christopher was B-positive, my blood type. Charles bought cigars for everyone."

"I'm sure," spat Calvin. "Happy not to have a filthy mick son."

"Probably. But Charles had a look in his eye, a sad look, like he wanted to be the father after all. Like I always say, you never *really* know what people are thinking, what goes on in their lives …

"Long story short, I married Eileen at Our Lady's Nativity and we listed my name on Robert's birth certificate. Eileen had been set on the name Robert or Rosaleen, neither of which satisfied your maimeó. She wanted proper Irish names. Your ma did not. Ma's real name is Eadaoin, you know that, but what you might not know is how much she hates it.

"When it came time for a second child, I told Eileen I wanted to name him after Calvin the First. Clodagh made us promise if there *was* a Calvin the Third, we'd at least spell and say 'Ciarán' right. That's why you have that stupid dash over the A."

"You don't?"

"Nope. Neither did Calvin the First, not on his U.S. documents anyway. And he and I both said it like KEER′·in. Yours is pronounced keer·AWN′."

"I didn't even know it could be KEER′·in. That's a girl's name!"

"The day over in Leixlip when me, your ma, and her ma talked about naming our next kid 'Calvin the Third'—that very day—Calvin the First died here in Altoona."

Da's eyes went misty again, a soft pall on his brow. "I meant to stay in Ireland a couple weeks to help your ma but now I had to fly home for your grandad's funeral. As long as I was back, I finished the semester and graduated from Penn State. Didn't get to Ireland again 'til June, and Robert was already so big. I wanted to make Calvin the Third as soon as possible. Funny how death and birth can move a man."

He took a breath. "Of course, the second child ended up a girl. Robbie and Rose are only eleven months apart—'Irish twins.' I got my work visa and my first job with the E.S.B. and we tried once more. It took a while but here you are. Calvin the Third."

The man sat back, evidently done talking for 1989. Maybe for 1990 too. He chomped a Benzel sourdough pretzel and watched Gazoo play tricks on Mr. Slate.

FOUL

"Do they give you your shirt number in baseball, or do you pick?"

Calvin had no memory of climbing the stairs or nuking his tepid tea. "I picked," he said, blinking. "I'm number 4."

Ma made a disappointed face. "Why not wear 3? You're a third child, and you're the third Calvin Connor."

"So I heard." Nuking his tea had made it sour. "Hell of a story."

"Indeed, it is. Don't you start a 'story' of your own, Calvin."

"Y'know, Da didn't say I'm obligated … but I'm going to name my first son Calvin Ciarán Connor IV." It just fell out his mouth.

Ma's reply rocketed out of hers: *"You fucking will not!* Not for years anyway! When you have sex again—a decade on when you're newly-wed—you'll wear protection, so you will!"

A teenage eyeroll. "Every wife's dream."

"Bloody cheek." Ma returned to the stove. "Do learn from your father and I. We didn't have the perfect start. Two countries, married, one child, suddenly two, and we barely knew each other beyond one night at the pub. Frankly it's a miracle we've lasted these twenty years."

Calvin's skull was so thick: Da needed a whole family history, with a profane recap by Ma, simply to remind their son *Don't go knocking up your new girlfriend.*

"How many times I gotta say it?" the lad sassed. "This one isn't about sex. Kitty's what I've been searching for all this time."

"She's feckin' magical." Ma set down her juice glass, which Calvin freaked to behold had a measure of Tullamore Dew in it. That stuff *reeeally* loosened his ma's tongue. "You don't even know this girl! I'd say you're too young for sex but that cat's been out of the bag for years now. You'll be driving soon and 'parking!'"

"Such an old person's word," said the lad.

"Five minutes of parking can change your life forever! The 'magic,' the 'spark,' the 'heat,' call it what you will, that's the Devil's work. That's the starting point. It puts a spell on many children and they end up stuck in bad relationships."

Calvin dumped out his tea. "Ma—"

"Look all around us. The Sandmillers, that Pedersen hoor next door—back to using her maiden name, McSween—the Daveys, the Adkissons, Perry Phillips down the street—all divorced."

"Sergeant Slaughter didn't divorce Ryan's ma. She's dead!"

"He damn well divorced the two wives before her! And you know *why* all those divorces happened, laddy?"

"The Devil. You just said."

"*Selfishness.* The ultimate sin. Not a one of them tried to stick with the marriage and make it work for the kids' sakes. They took the Devil's candy and turned their backs on the Lord." She shook her head sadly. "And all of their kids are fucked-up."

Calvin didn't like his ma when she drank. "No religion or politics talk at the supper table, isn't that the rule?"

Ma had another belt of whiskey. It came back as mist on her breath. "I make the rules so I can break the rules. It's important to me to be good Catholics! I know you take Jesus seriously. Keep doing, son."

"Me and Kitty are both good Catholics, Ma. She's smart, classy, has Jesus in her heart ... we quote the Bible to each other. You'll approve of her. Of us. I just know it."

The phone rang. Ma was busy cooking so Calvin answered. "Connor residence, this is Calvin keer·AWN' the Third speaking, the one with the stupid Irish dash over the A." He laughed when Ma did a foot-stomp. "Behold you soon, love!" He hung up. "She's on her way."

Chapter 12
TWO SETS OF FOOTPRINTS.

◗ **FAMILY SECTION** ◖

ROBBIE CONNOR KICKED OPEN the front door, jostling his slender body and guitar case through. The two had a hard time fitting simultaneously so he applied force. There was much scraping.

Once inside, he shuffled past the freestanding glass block wall and found his mother perched on the sitting room's Chesterfield. "I wondered where those scratches came from," she pissed. "Pay no mind to my house, laddy; come as you please, use the washing machine, eat our food. Who uses the dorm room we're paying for?"

Robbie had heard all this before and killed the latest performance by poking a Camel Light into his mouth.

"Don't you dare smoke in this room, Robert Críostóir!"

He shrugged like *whatever* and dusted the snow off his locks.

"Captain Picard, report to the bridge!" came Calvin's voice from the kitchen.

After some whispering, a new voice came. A girl's. "Ahoy, Captain Robert Christopher, welcome aboard!"

Robbie lowered his brows and poked his head in the kitchen. Calvin and the blind girl sat on the far side of the table at a (sudden) respectable distance. His little brother's notes were scattered about and a French textbook was tented innocently over his lap.

"Homework on a Friday night?" Robbie teased. "Sounds fishy."

"Watch it, Excalibur's there," said Calvin. Rob turned. Kitty's white cane was propped against the fridge, the handle securely snuggled in the gasketed space between the freezer door and the unit proper.

"Ye pulled the sword from the stone, young king," said Robbie.

"Knock it over and you'll get the guillotine," said Calvin. "Ooh that's a French word, isn't it? La guillotine!"

"Mais oui," smiled Kitty.

Robbie said, like a smart-ass: " 'May we' what?"

"Stop," Calvin told him. "Meet Kathryn Howe. Kitty, meet—"

"Robert Christopher," said Kitty, "I heard. Nice to meet you."

"A pleasure," said Robbie. Like everyone in town, he'd seen the blind girl from afar. Now the young man of nearly nineteen drank in a close-up of the girl of barely sixteen. She *did* look gorgeous, long russet hair, charming wide-cheeked face, canary-and-eggshell cardi bulging at all the right areas. Robbie wished for a French textbook of his own.

What killed it—what reminded Robbie that Kitty was a girl and not a woman—was how her airy full-length black skirt sat high above her waist, pulled up to just below her bra. That's how children dressed themselves. *Or, let's face it, how blind lasses with no fashion sense do.*

"Robbie's home from college for the weekend," said Calvin.

"Oh?" said Kitty. "What's your major?"

"Applied Narcotics," said Robbie.

She didn't laugh. Or notice that it was a joke.

"It's a line he stole from Monty Python," said Calvin. "Robbie pretends to go to college so his band can get gigs there."

"You're in a band?" said Kitty brightly.

"I *was*," sighed Robbie. "We just broke up."

"Again?" laughed Calvin.

"Piss off." Robbie checked the fridge, found a fresh Tupperware. "This'll be the usual Friday. What did ye think of toad in the hole, Lieutenant Howe?"

"*Lef*-tenant," giggled Kitty. "It was okay. Your mom made a vegetarian version for me. Can't believe you guys eat hot dogs on Friday!"

"Hot dogs are not meat," said Calvin and Robbie.

"Oi!" yelled Ma from the sitting room. "That's enough cheek!"

"Surprised you didn't make something Irish, Ma," Robbie called back. "Like blood sausage."

"*Ewww!*" eeked Kitty. "*Blood* sausage? With real blood?!"

"And real sausage. Irish meals are all meat and cabbage, meat and potato. Meat and two veg, ye might say."

Calvin kept his breath and posture normal while his body temperature and middle finger rose. "Kindly eff off now, we're busy."

"But not too far, Robert," called Ma, "you can give your parents a break and take on chauffeur duty when it's time for Kitty to go."

"Ooh that's French too," said Robbie. "'Chauffeur!'"

"Oui!" said Kitty.

"Ye come too," Robbie told Calvin, "ye can get some learner's permit time in. Three will fit in my pickup." He winked. "There's a French word for *that,* too: ménage à tr—"

Calvin got up and slid over on his woolen socked feet to hip-check his brother out to the sitting room.

"Holler when ye're done," said Robbie, sticking the Tupperware under one arm and miming putting on a condom.

He fetched up his guitar and rucksack and stomped to his room. Piles of stinky flannel. Overflowing ashtrays. Tattered rock star posters drooping on the walls. John Lennon seemed put off to be part of it.

Drag. Exhale. Sigh. The Places might've broken up for good this time. The drummer (Ace) brought up that his favorite food was toast. The keyboardist (Doogs) told him toast is only good for breakfast. The bassist (Gooey) said breakfast can be toast, but toast isn't necessarily breakfast. The frontman (Robbie) called them all Yank shite-stains since it's not "toast," but "toasted bread." The rhythm guitarist (Ripper) called Robbie a pompous Oi-rish asshole. Doogs called Ripper a fucking fuck-face. Robbie called Doogs a shite-stained fuck-faced arse-taster. Five pairs of fists flew. Gooey kicked them out of his garage.

Time to move. Dublin. New York. L.A. Go where the action is!

He stubbed out his butt and picked up the Tupp. *Oh bollocks, forgot a utensil.* Passing through the sitting room: "What ye readin', Ma?"

"Jackie Collins," said Ma without looking up from the page. "Are you eating in my sitting room?"

"Not yet. Are ye sitting in my eating room?"

Now she looked up. "Kindly feck back off to your room, Robert."

He gave his shite-eating grin. "I'll leave ye to spy on them."

"Don't eat in this room, boyo."

Robbie defiantly showed her the still-sealed Tupp and buggered off back down the hall. He saw light under Sis's door and peeked in.

The girl had on her audaciously oversized (yet belly-cropped) BORN IN THE U.S.A. T-shirt with Bruce Springsteen's sweet ass on the front. Rose surely wore it at dinner to annoy Calvin. She surely asked Kitty what her opinion on the shirt was. She surely felt like an eejit when the blind girl had no real opinion on something purely visual.

Rose stood at the far wall. Two tubes fed from under her coarse frizz of black hair and combined at a pickup. Her room adjoined Calvin's on one side and the kitchen on the other. She slithered the pickup this way and that, searching for the sweet spot. Eyes inundated by yellow-silver makeup went squinty. The balloony sleeves on her shirt kept bunching up; the wide collar kept rolling off her shoulder. She tore the thing off and chucked it on the bed to complete the operation in just her bra. That's when she finally noticed Robbie.

"How's the reception?" he barked.

She got the Springsteen shirt back over herself. *"Shhh!"*

He popped the lid and forked cold food into his gob by hand. "Can ye hear 'em?" he hissed. "Is it English or French?"

"Not anymore, he put the radio on."

Robbie stilled himself and picked up noise from the little TV/radio set atop the fridge. The noise had a beat, and not the Beach Boys kind. "Why fuck about with a stethoscope then?"

"Cuz I wanna hear. Duh!"

"Let us have a go."

"No way, get your own stethoscope!"

Despite being wispy featherweights like their Ma (not big bears like the two Calvins), Robbie and Rose could do considerable damage to each other. She reared back to whip him with the stethoscope.

A challenging grin tickled his unshaven face. He held out his hand.

"Fine, fuck you," she sighed, handing the instrument over.

Robbie examined it: a cheap model, entirely made of plastic and rubber. "Where'd ye get this, then?"

"Matty's dad is a vet," Rose said.

"So he is. And, who's Matty?"

"Matt Winowski. My ex-boyfriend, asshole."

"Your ex-boyfriend, Asshole?"

"Shut up, that's Calvin's stupid joke."

Robbie set his dinner on her bed and stuck the binaural bits in his ears. Plunking the pickup against the wall, he got a bassy fuzz with regular, sharp beats. Like that Van Halen song *where the gent juts out a grasper to jostle his groovy jalopy's gun-turret to a jauntier gradient.*

"This Kitty must be special indeed," said Robbie. "Not even 'the MacDonald wench' got Wacky 103 privileges!"

"Not there, the fridge radio is right on the other side." She aimed a nail covered in florescent yellow polish. "Put it down here."

"Ye say that to all the lads." Robbie took the stethoscope off and yanked it roughly with both hands, successfully breaking it apart.

"Hey, what the fuck did you do that for?!" wailed Rose. She socked him one on the chin.

He whacked her in the face with the diaphragm bit, knocking her frizzy black hair askew. "Shh, Sis! Calvin might hear ye!"

She punched him in the chest. "I can't believe you protect him!"

"'—from eavesdropping perverts.' Finish the sentence."

"Bloody hell!" roared Ma from the doorway.

"He's trespassing!" said Rose, pointing.

"She's eavesdropping!" said Robbie, pointing.

"Tais-toi!" Calvin yelled through the wall to the kitchen.

Now that Calvin knew, Rose didn't care anymore. "Fuck you, Robbie!" she said. "And fuck Calvin and fuck Miss Piggy!" She loosed her shriek, a fanfare announcing *I'm gonna ruin everything for everyone!*

FOUL

When Ma and Rose went at it, Calvin likened it to two dump trucks loaded down with TNT playing chicken on a road paved with landmines. He was used to the profanity and explosions, but Kitty wasn't. The calliope and caterwauling and steam and shrieks out in the sitting room quite overwhelmed the lass. Kitty's trembling shook the kitchen table. *This needs to end, quick—Da's gotta charge upstairs and lay down the law like he does at work.*

'Cept Calvin the Second had already spoken this year.

Calvin the Third prayed for a meteor to drop and shatter the sitting room's glass block wall, shedding shredding cuboids of justice.

"Out!" shouted Ma. "Leave my house at once, Rosaleen Sorcha!"

"It's fuckin' snowing out, Mom!" shouted Rose back.

"I'll not have you disturbing my peace any longer!"

"My Beetle can't do snow! Anyways, yer wagon's parkin' me in!"

"Robert, you go and take her somewhere!"

"I'd need a ten-spot for fuel," said Rob, his voice full of leftovers. "I'm on fumes."

"Feckin' worthless!"

"Indeed—I'm worth nothing. I can blow my own sousaphone, Ma, ye don't hafta toot it for me now."

"You—get your coat. You—make yourself useful for once and watch them, and get the lass home by 8:30."

Kitty and Calvin listened to a closet door slam, feet stomp, a hand slap a cheek, and Rose sizzle hotly about how Ma protected Calvin *waaay* more than she ever did for her, Ma's only daughter.

The front door shut, an engine fired up, and it was over. A trickle of the snowy air made it to the kitchen to cool their damp faces.

Robbie came in with his empty Tupperware and greasy fingers. "Right, you lot," he said, puffed up and faux-deep-voiced, like Terry Jones playing a stuffy police constable in a sketch about a boil on his semprini, "no funny business!" Robbie chucked the Tupp in the sink, belched, and headed down the stairs to join Da in the telly room.

The kitchen radio added a series of farts and wheezes that, through clever editing, combined into "We're whacked out of our minds! W-A-C-K 103.1 FM, Altoona, Pennsylvania ... we're Wacky 103!" Then a Def Leppard ditty: *ditzes dishing dextrose down disposed dudes.*

"Wanna see my room?" said Calvin.

"Yes," said Kitty, standing, "I desperately want to 'see' it."

He dumped his textbook atop the table, left the radio on and her cane by the fridge, and led her back through the house. He wanted to pull her by the hand but the Pac-Man-maze corridor was too tight and required them to go single-file formation, she behind him, her left hand on his shoulder. For once, Calvin didn't blaze across the Usonian's hardwood like Paul Coffey leading a power-play charge. He crept in his woolen socks, she in her white hold-ups. He always wore socks—he found feet disgusting, especially his own, with their fatty ankles and lack of hair. He loved that she always had hose on.

"I only got the one chair plus my bed," he said, guiding her in and shutting the door behind them.

She probed to find the edges of the bed, then shrugged him away and cast herself on her back. The springy mattress bounced her way up and her head *thonk!*ed the wall.

"Jaysus!" he said with a laugh, "you okay?"

"I'll survive," she giggled, patting her noodle. Finding her hair splayed all over, she tugged it together to lay over one shoulder.

Down over one boob.

Calvin's eyes snagged on his desktop, on a Polaroid of a black-haired lass thrusting her yummy fanny at the lens. He bolted to hide it under his magazines and junk … then stopped.

He needn't bother.

"What's a matter?" said Kitty.

"Thought something was gonna fall off my desk. I'm kinda messy." He poked about the papers for a Right Guard and surreptitiously did one pit, then (remembering) blatantly did the other.

"That smells nice," she said, with a spritely tinkle of mirth.

"Busted! Things got hot out there. Y'know, I'm just realizing how tricky my house is for you. We shoulda brought Excalibur with us!"

"I didn't wanna bring it at all but Mom insisted cuz this is a new environment. I kept sayin' you would guide me. She hates the new name, by the way. 'Excalibur is a weapon, your cane is a tool.'"

"Excalibur was more than a weapon. It was magical. And a symbol for the whole Camelot kingdom."

She didn't give a fuck about all that. "You got no idea how nice it is when I can leave Excalibur back at the castle. I feel free then. Ooh, don't let me forget it when I go."

He looked at her lounging so comfortable on his bed. She was smiling so much tonight. Surely her cheeks hurt.

"Your first time at a boy's house?" he said, collecting homework off the floor and nonchalantly parking it overtop Wren's ass photo.

"Yep. Daddy's all, 'Homework on a Friday night? Sounds fishy!'"

Calvin sat on the bed with his back propped against the wall, next to her. But not too next. A gust from the snowstorm outside shoved a tree branch against his bedroom's only window, a thin slice of glass at the top of the wall, making him smile. "We did some homework," he said. "It's official."

"Mais bien sûr, we did some conjugaling!" Following his voice, Kitty sat up alongside him. But not too alongside. "My dad's big-time suspicious of you, Calvin."

"Is he a da-with-the-shotgun?"

"We don't own guns. Is 'Ma' a mom-with-a-shotgun?"

"Is she ever now. You saw it." He slapped himself. "You *heard* it."

"I smelled it too. The alcohol."

"She had a belt o' whiskey before you came. Believe it or not, she was toning it down at supper! But she likes you."

"I guessed that. She kept trying to get you to ask me questions about my condition and things. Why didn't she just ask herself? Me and you already talked about blindness over at my house."

Calvin blinked. *We did?*

"How's your memory?" Dr. Jacoby asked, his breath tingling of Lister- ine. "Any trouble remembering words or events?"

"Your room's okay," said Kitty. "Feels cooler than mine. I like the sound of that tree hitting the window."

"Me too, I love it. I don't have a TV. No Nintendo or VCR. I like to put on music and 'get away,' you know?" He remembered Ma's advice to shaddap about himself. "What's your room like?"

"It's bigger."

Carefully—he asked all such questions with care—"How can you tell?"

"The sound. You have a lot of junk around, soaking in the echoes, but I can figure out the size. My room's upstairs so it's very warm. I got a TV. And a carpet. Your house is all wood floors, I love that they're cool on my feet but they're *sooo* noisy."

"You have a VCR, too? Or a boom box?"

"I have a little tape player. Abby says it is *not* a boom box. No VCR, no phone. Last Christmas, Daddy gave us the choice: a TV or phone. Eddie and me both went TV. I like hearin' people talk, y'know?"

Kitty's body did a rigid sit-up-straight move with rhythmic hand-opening. "Seems stupid I didn't pick the phone," she said through the spasms. "Instead of listening to people talk, I coulda actually *talked* to people. Be part of it. And honestly? TV sucks!"

Calvin's big guffaw ricocheted. "I still like *Miami Vice* cuz it's all seaside and beaches." Those are visuals, mate. "And the music."

"I got my Johnny Depp on *21 Jump Street* on Sundays." Kitty shifted to "face" him. The angle was off, so he moved to put himself in front of her dark glasses. "If I wanna give you a call, I gotta sneak in Mom and Dad's room or downstairs. I've been avoiding them, they're totally annoying lately, always asking me about my business."

He felt like he should hold her hand to show he cared. "Dealing with family is such a pain in the arse, Kitty."

"Totally. When I have kids, I won't be annoying like them."

"I'm not going to be like my parents either. So *boring.*"

"Exactly. There's a whole world out there." Her hand searched for his. "I just wish I picked the phone."

He gave her hand a squeeze. "Here's one thing I've learned in life: regretting the past is worthless." She perked up at this, so he expanded on his policy: "When I think about the past, it makes me depressed. I did some stuff, y'know, things happened. Then I get all, like, afraid to mess up again. That's no way to live. Life's all about moving on.

"You shoulda picked the phone over the TV, but … you didn't. So what! Learn your lesson and move on. It sounds like grown-up bollocks but it works, I swear it does. I hate the past. I've fucked up more than once—maybe you heard!—but I never let it get to me."

He finished there, waiting for her reaction.

When she didn't smile or nod or say "I agree," he started sweating.

She took back her hand and dug in her canary cardigan's pockets, producing a little green spray can. "I was gonna surprise you," she said. "But if it reminds you of the past, I can throw it out."

He took the Spearmint Binaca from her hand. "My favorite flavor! How'd you know?" He pumped a squirt in his gob. "Robbie says if anyone offers you a breath-freshener, they're telling you to use it!"

"Tell *me* something: are you a virgin?"

He pulled away, choking on the crisp boozy mint mist. "No!"

He felt stupid for denying it like it was murder charges.

He felt shocked that someone—anyone!—didn't know about him

and Jenny over at Corgan's party that one time.

"Oh I knew the answer," she said, reading his mind. "Just testing! I wanted to hear if you'd lie to cover up the past. Y'know, that thing you hate so much."

Calvin felt tricked. "What about you? Still a virgin?"

Fast and firm: "Yes."

"No one ever says 'yes.' At least not that fast."

As Lady Em: *"Who then are you to judge,* young man?"

As Kitty Howe: "I say 'yes' that fast cuz I'm proud of it."

"Well," said Calvin. "It's the good Catholic thing to be."

"So, you're a bad Catholic?"

"Sorta. I try not to be."

"Well. We hadda talk about that one time at Corgan's at *some* point. You know I hate rumors. So I was like, go right to the horse's mouth."

He laughed. "I'm more of a horse's arse."

"Lots of people say it was revenge against Corgan and you staged the whole thing."

"We woulda did it in Corgan's kitchen then," he said, in the verbal equivalent of rolled eyes. "Y'know, that was the only party he didn't invite me to."

"He's never invited me to any of them," Kitty admitted.

"Exactly, that's my point, he don't invite *everyone*. Then he started dating Kare and suddenly I was off the list."

"You were dating Jenny. Sean's ex. So, why did you guys show up unannounced? Like a prank?"

"Revenge. It's childish, so sue me. I figured we'd show up and see the stupid look on their faces, Corgan and Kare's faces, and they'd kick us out. The end. But Kare held the door open, 'C'mon in,' cuz she wanted to rub it in Jenny's face that Sean was *her* man now."

Kitty said nothing.

Calvin surged on: "We had a bunch of drinks and I say to Jenny, 'let's slip out for some privacy,' and Roni saw us out the window and was all, 'Hey look everyone.' They could all see us out there. We didn't stage that! Jenny lives like a block away on Canyon Curve. We coulda gone to her place. Or anywhere. And who wants a whole crowd to see you naked? Can't people see how dumb that is?!"

"Pretty dumb. Even I can 'see' that."

"Holy crap—sorry. I *am* trying to stop being so biased!"

Kitty said, "What I meant by 'staged' was, people think you staged it to get back at *Jenny,* not at Sean."

"That's … people are wrong. I swear. From the horse's mouth."

"They say you and her broke up right there on the lawn."

"'They' are wrong again. It was the morning after. I had had enough of Jenny."

"Sounds like you had just the right amount of her."

"Can't you se—er, haven't you heard how Jenny manipulates people? 'I'm an acquired taste,' she likes to say."

"Did you use Binaca to get that 'acquired taste' out your mouth?"

Wow, I do look like the bad guy, he thought. *Kitty's seeing herself in Jenny's shoes. Her future, it appears, will be just like Jenny's past.*

look seeing appears

briefly and then disappears.

"Me and Jenny are over," he stressed. "I can't change the past. And like I said, I don't dwell on it."

She pulled away.

He went to fetch her hand and found he was still holding the Binaca can. He tossed the thing on the desk. "Don't be that way, Kitty. I like the way we, uh, communicate. It scares me when you're so quiet."

These words, so honest and direct, touched the girl. And gave her the courage to speak her mind: "I don't want to hear any more about Jenny MacDonald. I don't like her. Never mention her again, got it?"

"Way ahead of you, love."

"That goes for Jill too."

"Done with her also, but she's still my friend. And besides, she's not that kinda girl—"

"No more girls from your past," said Kitty. "I hear all about your past from my folks and Abby and Roni and Sean and everyone."

"Sean? As in Corgan, or Father Sea—"

"Listen to me. I don't wanna hear about you and other girls from anyone. Including from you. Especially from you." Her wide cheeks got hard. "Same with Karen McGillicutty. I heard Corgan's mad at you cuz you, like, talked to her or something? You stay away from her, Calvin."

Three or four emotions sat on each other's laps atop Calvin's brain's lap. "Whoa, heave to! One thing I hate is when people hold stuff over my head. My ma and Art do that shite all the time. I mean, I did the right thing here—I told you the truth. I am done with Jenny forever. But Jill's my neighbor! Our desks are close in homeroom, we ride the same bus ... none of that's my fault, and I *have* to talk to her cuz of class and stuff. If Abby runs to you and says 'Calvin was talkin' to Jill in Health,' you can't automatically assume something's going on. Besides, she hates me. And she's all lovey-dovey with Davey now."

Kitty's arms did a frustrated jerk, up and down. "Good Lord, never bring Brion up around me! That topic is off-limits!"

"Oh, we don't get to talk about *your* past? Davey tried to kill me the day I met you—we should probably discuss him, don't you think?"

"No. I don't want to talk about him."

"So what? I *do*. I hear things. Everyone says you and him made out back in sixth grade, what's the story with t—"

"I never did anything with him, *it's just a rumor*. Shut up, Calvin!"

That stung. A girl telling a boy to shut up always stung.

"It was *fourth* grade," she went on, "and y'know, I don't need to defend myself over a rumor. It's the past. I get to hate the past, too."

"That's fine, but I'm talking about the present. Davey still looks at—*beholds* you from a distance. And *I* behold you with Saint Mark, all the time."

Her reaction to that was electric, like he'd buzzed her with a cattle-prod. "He's my tutor," she said. "That's different!"

"How? What if I need help about something from a girl? I can never talk to girls or about girls, but you can do whatever with boys?"

"You're jealous of Mark," she said. Panted.

"Should I be?" he said. Accused. "Kitty, listen to yourself now. How can you not see how crazy all this is?"

"Shut up!" she said, accidentally casting spittle in his face. "The problem is, you can't 'see' how dumb you are! Get out!"

"'Get out?' It's *my* room!"

"GET ... "

She didn't finish. Couldn't. A sighted girl would've turned away, would've hidden her crying face in her hands. Kitty just sat there, tears rolling down from under her dark glasses to moisten her wide cheeks.

FOUL

He wobbled down the dark hallway, blinking, parched. After downing a cool glass of water, he saw Excalibur propped at the fridge. His first instinct was to break the stupid thing. That'd solve nothing and he felt awful for having the impulse.

King Arthur broke Excalibur fighting Sir Lancelot. The Lady of the Lake restored it ... once Arthur admitted his mistake.

Even a King fucks up once in a while.

puff of smoke

Pinwheel Pippi asked Michael Hutchence to give her a spin sometime and *the intriguing individual invited your infrastructure to invade him for an instant.* Calvin recognized this band's sound, if not the song proper, saw a white T-shirt with **INXS** stretched across a pair of—

appears briefly

He slapped off the radio. He could now hear the TV in the basement, Robbie's laugh, Da's snort. He left the empty water glass on the counter, not caring that Ma would yell at him for not putting it in the dishwasher. Woolen socks slithered over the sitting room's hardwood. He peered out the wall-size window. Their driveway had two "lanes." Robbie's Toyota pickup had parked in Da's Cadillac. In the other lane, Rose's Bug; behind it, a dark patch of blacktop, growing white with new snow. Two sets of footprints, walking as one until they'd reached the Volvo, divided to either side.

and then disappears.

Art would call this a "movie moment." That bastard saw John Hughes scenes in real life all the time.

Calvin tried it. A pop song swelled in his head.

```
MUSIC (v.o.): Heart, "Who Will You Run To."

                                            CUT TO:

CLOSE-UP of CALVIN looking out the window at
the snow. He is weepy, sad, lost.
```

"Balls on that shite." He turned away. He'd seen his reflection in the slab glass, with his moronic new baseball team haircut and damp cheeks, and hated everything about himself.

Kitty's list of demands was stupid. They needed to address it like young adults, not start the perpetual fire like the one that had burnt he and Jenny. Kitty needed to see his side—to *behold* his side of things. She feared that he was chasing other girls. *I am not!*

Oogling Jill's thistle-colored jean skirt—god-DAMN what an arse!

Kare let go, then re-engaged. "Yep, that's the Ape's bone, all right."

He slid up the Pac-Man-maze corridor. He'd overreacted. He should ask forgiveness. Tell her he loved her. Ask for head.

Something.

He slipped through his door kinda facing sideways and shut it tight. He turned and Kitty crashed into him, her arms finding his edges and wrapping around him so tightly that he couldn't move his own hands.

The dark glasses lay on the bed; her head thrust against his chest. Tears wetted down his sweater. He pried a beefy hand loose to lift her cheek. Her eyes—blank, staring, dead-to-the-world, useless, worthless, bright, big, glowing, green like Virginia pine in the sun—blinked like mad to wash away her tears. He wiped some away for her, trying to be tender. She lurched forward, clumsily pushing him back into his door. He nearly thumbed her left eye out.

"Do they scare you?" she croaked. Her damp hands fumbled up to his head and squeezed it down towards her face. "People say my eyes give 'em the creeps."

He wet his lips. "Who cares what people say, mon cerise?"

They tried to kiss but her long hair got in the way, strands of it catching like Velcro on Calvin's newly buzzed sides. Four hands swiped that shit aside. Their hips checked in ways hockey players never dared. Smooches quickly became tongues dancing to a beat, to a music of their own devising.

Calvin's big hands went down and grabbed Kitty's thighs to hoist her up. Her wispy skirt got the hell out of the way and she hooked her legs together behind him. "Oh my," said Lady Em, the only discernable words for some time. Her arms squeezed to keep from falling, frightened, ecstatic. He dropped them both on the bed, testing the springs.

They were up for the job.

The kids' wide bodies pretzeled like braided loaves, neither one officially on top.

Heartbeats gave pace to this action, adrenaline rushing. She refused to stop kissing him. When she ran out of air, he drew some through his nose and passed it across the tight seal of their liplock. She squealed in childish glee. She'd never experienced that before. It didn't really help her breathe but it was terribly exciting.

His flute betrayed him, but how could it not?

He got up, flicked on his boom box, and tuned in Wacky 103. Phil Collins *supplicated his sweetheart's assertion that they shared a savor suitably similar to sequentially fissured stripes.*

The tree branch smacked his window, saw the glass was foggy, said "'Scuse me," and swayed the other way for the balance of the evening.

Chapter 13

PSYCHOTIC AND BORING.
SATURDAY, FEBRUARY 4, 1989.

⚾ **CLUBHOUSE** ⚾

CALVIN'S SWEATY RIGHT HAND wiped itself dry on the linen sheet drawn tightly atop the drawing board. His other hand held five blue-backed Bicycles. Benzel's pretzels sat in a little bowl on one side, his tin cup of coffee on the other. The kerosene heater—it was white and red and roughly astromech droid-shaped, so the boys called it R5-D4—made ominous ticks behind him. Tunes from the *Eclectic III* mixtape purred out Art's boom box: *Phil Collins boasted about the banknotes in his britches bursting ablaze.*

"I could go the rest of my life without fucking Phil Collins," said the lad. He held A♠ 9♦ 8♦ 6♦ 2♥. He shoved his last quarter and condom into the pot, cuz bluffing is what poker players do.

"You'd love to spend your whole life *fucking* Phil Collins," Art cracked, making the call.

Though it was not his turn, Ryan swept his stack of cash, coin, and condoms off the drawing board.

"Pattin' Phil on the bald head while poundin' his bass drum!" said Spazz, thrusting his skinny hips as if buggering, and thereby buggering the whole poker game.

When angled parallel to the floor, Art's drawing board was perfect for poker. Its massive supports were not so perfect for active teenage legs. Spazz's fake-fucking shook the setup off the Richter scale, knocking over Calvin's tin cup.

"Way to ruin the cards, asshole!" said Art, smacking Spazz's nose.

"I like when you hit me, Pop-Tart!" Spazz made his hands flappy to playfully slap back.

Art skirted away, yelping, desperate to protect his glasses. They gave him a more precise view of the world while simultaneously making him feel more fragile in it.

"Sorry, Dolly Art-on," said Spazz, "Forgot ya don't like it rough!"

"Art's ma does," said Calvin.

"No mom jokes—house rules!" said Art, scrambling for napkins.

"Wish there was a 'no Phil Collins' rule too," said Calvin. *Did I make that joke already?* The likely answer, *I can't remember,* was too much to deal with right now.

He wanted that coffee back in the tin cup. He *needed* that coffee in his belly. "Belly-coffee," he said, using his abominable scarf of many colors to wipe his single coin and condom clean. "Bell-offee," he said. "Boffee," he said, and laughed and laughed.

"We lost him, over," Spazz said into an imaginary field radio.

Art gave up drying the playing cards. They were positively dripping. He noticed Ryan's stack was missing from the table. "Funny how you picked that up *juuust* in time … "

Ryan's left hand patted a pocket on his puffy black down coat, where The Book rested close to him. "Game over," he said, drawing back his 25¢ ante bet from the pot. Spazz joined in, flicking the coffee off his rubbers before wiping them on his denim jacket (the one with the huge Iron Maiden patch on the back).

Fearing an exodus—and an end of his chance to win back the $5.25 he was down (that is, two Ramses Extras and five quarters)—Art got desperate. "I'll get another deck! I'll put a different tape on! C'mon guys, let's keep playing poker!"

"I'm out," said Calvin.

Once he lost Irish, African knew the Suicide Kings would follow. He threw the blue-backed Bicycles into a trash bin with a pissy huff and swept the wet linen sheet off his drawing board.

The chilly, oily Maguire house garage steamed with hot disappointment. Calvin looked at the quarter in his hand. One fuckin' game of *Rampage* down at Pizza Putt. He loved to play George the Ape—incorrectly, Art would point out, since all Calvin did was pluck the blonde lass in the red dress out of the high-rise apartment window and hold her. "The object of the game is to use the giant monsters to destroy cities," Art would say.

Calvin didn't care. He liked to be a benevolent Ape for a change.

Still. One must *have* change to waste it on video games. Sighing, he popped the coin and Trojan in his Bugle Boys' pocket.

"You used to come to poker with a big ol' bag of prophylactics," said Spazz. "Whatever happened to them?"

"I used them fucking your ma," said the lad.

After the laughter, a sticky voice said, "Stop being silly, guys." It was Valerie Crenshaw, busying herself at the workbench with *Super Mario Bros. 2* on Art's Nintendo. "What would *you* do with a big ol' bag of rubbers, Bill? You never use 'em!"

Spazz said, "Damn right, rubbers are for liberals and faggots! I let my mighty man mist, the Spazz-razz-matazz, spray where it may."

"Like, in your lap?" Art said, eyebrow cocked at Calvin.

Calvin needed a second. "Fuck you, Maguire."

Val had no comment. The matchstick slip of a girl was engrossed with the game. She floated Princess Peach around the same couple of platforms over and over. Like Calvin, Val was an early pioneer in emergent gameplay, the wish-fulfillment version. Val was a skater but could never get the sort of air seen in *Bones Brigade* tapes.

Princess Peach *could,* and Val loved being part of it.

"Got a fag?" Calvin asked Spazz.

"Talkin' to one right now!" said Spazz.

"You know the rules!" said Art. "No smoking in the mad scientist's lab! This whole room is full of shit that'll blow up."

Spazz waved at R5-D4. "That droid fireball's fine though?"

"It's a controlled blaze. You wanna freeze your ass off in here?"

"You test your shotgun-shell bombs near that thing?" said Calvin.

"I don't test *primed* cartridges inside, you moron! Just dummies!"

Calvin, Spazz, Ryan, and Val all made jokes about "dummies" that cancelled each other out.

Spazz got his 'Bros. "Goin' rate's a quarter a fag, Calvin Congo."

"Bollocks! A dollar buys a whole pack!"

"Then walk yo ass to the sto'. Oh wait, you don't have no dollars no mo'. Lost it all with two pair to my flush."

"I can tap MAC. Drive me over? It's on your way home."

"I don't want no one to see me toolin' around with *you,* Calvinubo, now that ya gots a Davey Dangle!"

"I'll lend ya a buck, Calvin," said Val from the Nintendo.

"He already owes me one," said Art.

"And me five," said Ryan.

"On second thought …," said Val.

Sighing, Calvin forked over a quarter. He and Spazz headed for the door. Val set the Nintendo controller down. Ryan made to come too but Calvin put up a hand. "Gotta talk to Val and 'Bill' alone. Privately."

"Val ain't for sale," said Spazz, half-joking.

"Bill is," said Val, not joking at all.

Everyone laughed.

"We'll be right back," said Spazz. "Just goin' out for a smoke. And a belt o' rotgut. Maybe a couple lines on the way back." He snorted an imaginary rail of coke out into the cold Axsubeen morning.

FOUL

Spazz's skinny hand showed the Ape a Marlboro Red and a joint. Calvin accepted the street legal one and a flame from the wild-child's Zippo. "Why is Bill short for William?" he said. "Where's that B come from? How come James isn't shortened to Bim, or Daniel to Ban?"

"Or Calvin to Bal," said Val.

"Or Valerie to Bal," said Calvin. "In Ireland, most blokes called William use Liam, the back half of the name."

Eyes twinkled from under Val's skater-bangs. "I kinda like Liam!"

"Me too!" smiled Spazz. "Makes me sound like an aristocrat!"

The kids trudged down Art's back yard to the phalanx of trees along the border with the Millar farm tract. "Keep an eye on the door to make sure Ryan doesn't slip out," said Calvin.

"Good call. Hairdryin' Ryan is a super-ninja and we gots to keeps tabs on him." Spazz lit the joint.

"Ladies first!" said Val, swiping it and taking a hit. "I see Ryan at the trailer park. He's all creepin' between cars or up in that one tree."

"'Doin' the Devil's dirty laundry' is how African puts it." Calvin toked on his cigarette. The taste of the paper, of spice's names, of sliding face first on dry grass. *Mmmm.* "Dirty laundry is what I wanna talk about. I'm trusting you guys with this."

"Cross my nuts and hope to die," said Spazz.

"My lips are sealed," said Val, "unless you ask me to part them."

"Just go ahead and blow 'im already!" said Spazz.

Val stood tippy-toe to give her man a smooch. Their long blond hair drifted together in the cool winter breeze.

"So I hung out with Kitty last night," said Calvin. "And it went pretty well. She's really into me, and I like her a lot."

"They did it," Val stage-hissed.

"Two Jabbas bumpin' uglies," Spazz hissed back. "Bet it looked like one elephant shitting out another."

"She brought up Jenny and that night at Corgan's," said Calvin.

"We totally saw your dong," said Val.

"The whole world did," said Spazz. "Ran into Old Lady Mueller one time and she's like, 'Is it as small as everyone sez?'"

"Fucking hell, would you two shut up?" Calvin took a drag of clean air for a change. "I told her the truth about what happened. All of a sudden, she's screaming, 'Never talk to Jenny again! Or Jill or Kare!'"

"Kare wants to screw you," said Val. "I see her lookin' at you."

"Who *don't* want to ride a slice o' Crispy Bacon-nor?" said Spazz. He put a hand to his temple. "I can see the future—"

"No sighted words, that's biased. You can 'behold' the future."

"That's cooler-soundin' anyway—I can *behold* the future, and it's got an 'athlete meetin' and cheatin' with fleets of sweet chick meat in the back seat' written all over it."

Giggles and red eyes squinting. The weed indeed kicked in with speed. "She thinks I'm doing stuff with every girl but I'm behaving," said Calvin. "That's not good enough for Kitty. I gotta live like a monk, she says. These chicks are tempting *me.* Can I help that?"

Tittering, Val said, "The Butt-Sex Girl wants to screw you, too."

Calvin made retching sounds.

Spazz said, "Does she want the Spazzster too?"

Val's tiny hand, with fingers like the half-pencils you get at miniature golf courses, slapped him. "Don't even joke about that, Liam. You get near Lorey Adkisson's butt and *my* butt is outta here."

Spazz's headbanger hair rocked in disbelief. "You get near all kinds of skeevy dudes—Sicko Ricko and Perv Griffin and Pedophile Kyle!" He turned to Calvin. "You see the double standard, Triple C?"

"That's my whole point," said Calvin. "We haven't talked about her history yet. I see Saint Mark hovering around her, plus Art says he made her a mixtape—"

"Wow," said Val, "I asked Art for one a while back and he got all snotty, like 'No way, girls don't appreciate good music.'"

"I tried to ask Kitty, 'what's the deal with you and Davey?' And she fucking freaked out on me."

"Talk about skeeves," said Spazz. "He's had her flag on his pole since elementary school."

"They made out in like fourth grade or something?" said Calvin.

"Fourth grade for *her*. He was in sixth."

"Kitty hates him," said Val. "She likes *you*. You're doing *juuust* fine, man."

"Why'd she make out with him in the first place? She says she didn't but I dunno. Now Davey's being sweet on Jill but is it so he can get close to me? I live next door to Jill. I don't wanna go outside and behold his toothless arse right there."

He flicked his smoke into the snow. "The whole night was crazy, we were close, then apart, we were loving, then fighting, then loving again. She's independent and tough, she's blind after all, and I admire that. Don't give me gay looks, her strength is admirable. But she's treating me like *I'm* the wife here. 'Do this, don't do that, and that's final. I am Kitty, I have spoken!'"

Val and Spazz gave knowing laughs.

"Nah, she's just bein' a *fee*-male," said Spazz. "She got it out of her system and now she'll move on."

"That's how we are, man," said Val. "Sometimes we talk a lot and other times we don't wanna say shit."

"Pay attention to *eeeverything* the pussy says," said Spazz, "but don't be bringing up every little detail later. Pussy don't like that!"

"The secret is to be there when she needs you, and get lost when she doesn't," said Val. Her slow drawling speaking manner reminded Calvin of Mr. Rogers, and he felt like a little boy looking at her all wide-eyed. "We don't like being crowded, know what I mean?"

"What you mean is, 'girls are all fucking insane,'" said Calvin.

"Girls aren't *all* insane, man."

"Bollocks. There's only two kinds of girls: psychotic and boring."

"Guess which type my Val is!" said Spazz. He galavanted in the snow, did cartwheels, and dribbled a finger over his lips.

Ignoring all that, Val asked, "What kind am I, Calvin?"

"Well. There's *levels* of psychosis. But boring is just boring."

Val's little mouth smirked at him, teasing him, judging him, dismissing him, desiring him, like she didn't know (or care) what he meant, like she knew (and found delicious) some secret in the back of his closet. "Ooh I like that!" she said, syrupy and thick.

"*That's* what I mean!" said Calvin, waving a beefy hand. "Your man's right here but you're coming onto me! You're all nutters."

"The nutters is where the butter comes from," said Spazz, giving his crotch a languid massage.

Val hid her eyes, aiming them down at her duct-taped Chucks. "Anyway," she said. "Next time you see Kitty, tell her you'll do better."

"Tell her you'll do her in the butt," said Spazz.

"Something in the middle seems prudent," the lad said.

Chapter 14

THE SCOUT.
SUNDAY, FEBRUARY 5, 1989.

FOUL

THE CONNORS ARRIVED EARLY enough for Mass to park in Saint Brigid's lot for a change. Calvin the Third had time to dash across Bald Eagle Pike to the fugly-ass Blair County Bank.

He felt like a grown man, fetching his leather wallet from his suit's arse-pocket and slipping out the royal blue Money Access Center card. Calvin's pin number was 0219, his birthday. He hit **Check balance**; a wimpy **$8.06** blared bright on the monitor's green phosphor.

He felt like a little boy, making the minimum five-buck withdrawal. So much for paying back Ryan and Art, renting a movie at Video On-slaught, or grabbing the Swimsuit Issue (on newsstands Monday); he'd need every cent for his ice cream date with Kitty. He hung his head and saw the fat end of his tie was too short. He looked like Oliver Hardy.

He took his spot between Ma and Rose in the pew. "How old you gotta be to own a car?" he asked.

"Eighteen, I guess," said Ma. "That's the Yank age for everything except Beelzebub's Urine."*

The Bachner family strolled down the aisle. They preferred to sit close to the pulpit, on the left. Ma pointedly clammed up 'til the lawyer, his Gossip Gertie wife, and their two girls were well out of earshot.

Only then did Ma tell Calvin, "We are *not* buying you a car for your sixteenth, boyo."

"I'm not asking for a car," said Calvin. "I brought it up cuz Lucky Cheeseboro tried to sell me one the other day."

---

* *BEE'·zil·bubs yer·IYN'.*

"Can't make a sale without making a *pitch,*" said Rose.

"Lucky never said I had to *buy* the car."

Ma's agate eyes sent shockwaves out. "What in God's name did he ask in return for it, then?"

"Nothing, I dunno! I'm not even sure what he meant." Calvin felt stupid for bringing it up with his mother around.

FOUL 🏏

He sat at a picnic table enjoying a black cherry cone in the company of the girl of his dreams. She fancied pistachio.

"That shite oughta come with a Mr. Yuk sticker!" he cracked.

"We use them too!" said Kitty, spooning down icky green stuff flecked with icky tan nuggets. "Eddie can see them. He's the one dumb enough to drink bleach. Daddy cuts out little circles of sandpaper and glues them around the Mr. Yuk stickers. That way *I'll* know."

"Wow, that's awesome."

"Did you get cherry cuz of your new nickname for me? Ta cerise?"

"Naturellement. Plus I love it."

Calvin's eyes lifted to the glass panes behind them. His da hadn't come but Ma and Rose did, sitting with Da and Ma Howe at a table in the interior seating section at Schultz's Farm Market. Ma Howe had made noise about it being too cold out for her daughter (it was) and the picnic table seats had crusty snow and ice since they'd not been properly swept after Friday's squall (true). "I notice that no one *else* is fool enough to eat outside," agreed Ma Connor.

But Kitty had insisted. "We just want to talk, alone."

Ma Howe forced her daughter to take Excalibur and to sit where they (the Ape) could be seen (monitored). That worked both ways—Calvin saw the two mothers pointing at them (him) and talking (bringing charges).

The lad raised his black cherry cone in front of his mouth, like a pitcher did with his mitt when talking strategy with the catcher. "Your ma won't take her eyes off me," he muttered.

"Now you know how I feel," sighed Kitty. "She's afraid of you. Totally thinks you'll take my virginity."

Calvin sputtered mid-lick, sending flecks of cherry onto her. The kids laughed. The lad balled up napkins and cleaned her off.

"You missed a spot," she said, turning her mittened left hand over.

It was unsplattered. He got it, though, playfully dabbing the soiled napkin in her palm. She closed her hand around it like a Venus flytrap over a beetle. The soiled napkin went *splat!*

"Now there's a spot," he said. "You got cherry all over you."

"Isn't it weird how we say, 'take your virginity?'" she said, using a Father Sean voice at the end.

He mulled that. "Is it not yours to give?"

"It's not a possession at all. No one 'takes' your childhood when you turn eighteen."

"The barber 'took' my hair."

"I'm still annoyed that you cut it!"

"*You're* annoyed? I'm the one who gets the stares and comments."

This got Kitty all excited. "Ooh I got a new quote about rumors! After Mass, Abby was talking about someone and Saint Mark said, 'You do them a disservice by talking about them behind their back.'"

"That's an okay quote, I guess," said Calvin, like a jealous boy.

"Oh absolutely, Mark's full of good advice like that." She set down her half-eaten bowl and took off both mittens so she could hold his hand skin-to-skin. Their fingers were damp from sweat and bright pink from the winter air. "Everyone talks about me. I'm sick of it," she said, and quoted from today's Bible Study: *"Why should my freedom be determined by someone else's conscience?"*

Sometimes we talk a lot and other times we don't wanna say shit.

She leaned her face close to his.

Her parents were right on the other side of the glass behind them. He had never kissed Jill in front of her parents, or Wren in front of Mr. Lyons (and his shotgun), but he had tongued Jenny a hundred times on the Belgian block sidewalk in front of her McMansion (Jenny's idea; after pissy ol' "Mrs." MacDonald forbade the Ape in her house, Jenny took him just past the borders of the property).

He leaned close, eyes closing, lips puckering.

"There's some old railroad tracks back here," she whispered.

He froze mid-pucker. "Around the side," he whispered, "I know them." *Maybe we'll make out over there!*

"Let them know we're going for a walk." She stood, corralling Excalibur where she'd parked it—between her legs.

Calvin was all about making out but didn't wanna lose out on that sweet black cherry goodness. He shoved the remaining two-thirds of cone in his mouth. Part of it hung out, like the hind leg of a hyena dangling out the jaws of a victorious lion. Only far less majestic-looking, and lots more drool.

The lad faced the window, waved at their families' disgusted faces, used two fingers to mime walking like in the Yellow Pages commercials. He pointed in the snow-pasted scrub beyond the picnic table section and threw in a couple of steam locomotive *"choo choo!"*s.

"I'm sure they get it," said Kitty with a snicker.

He plucked out the cone before it could suffocate him. "We got a minute, tops. It's gotta be the quickest makeout session ever."

"We aren't making out, Calvin. I want to show you something."

His flute filled like a firehose once the hydrant's nut was loosened.

"Not *that,* either," she teased.

"I wasn't thinking it was *that.*"

"Liar. Your breathing told me what you were thinking!"

A dozen former Pennsylvania Railroad sidings dotted the borough, train tracks that had served coal mines, farms, and workshop concerns in Axsubeen's halcyon days. Some lines had been cleared and some still had rotting ties, rusty rails, and ballast strewn with bracken.

The tracks behind Schultz's Farm Market were of the latter variety. She followed his lead with her left hand on his shoulder. "Mind the pickers," said Calvin, steering them aside before her nice church skirt got snagged.

"You have a jingle bell at home? Like from a Christmas decoration. Sew it on this." She tugged at the yucky scarf of many colors around his neck. "Then I'll always know where you are."

"It'll go *jingle-jangle* like a dog collar!"

"Exactly. You'll be another Lewis. Stop here."

He did, and took a position on her left. "W—"

"Shaddap, lamebrain."

He shaddap. They'd gone fifty feet from the Farm Market, facing a bracken-choked meadow and light woods.

"Listen to them," she said.

All he heard was Rte. 666 (Hollidaysburg Pike) nearby, tires crunching the parking lot gravel behind them, and people blathering.

"Filter out the noise," she said. "Your mom says you never hear anything she tells you. Do it here. You totally can. It's in Filipinos 4:13."

"Eh? You mean 'Philippians?'"

"Whatever. *'I have the strength to do anything through him who empowers me.'*"

"Ooh that's a good one. I'll have to rememb—"

"Look it up later, now hush! Filter out the traffic and listen."

He shaddap. He filtered the racket and listened.

Wind. Some branches moving.

"Do you hear them?" she hissed. "They're chatting."

You gotta pay attention to <u>eeeeverything</u> the pussy says.

Feeling silly, he shut his eyes to experience this as she did … and immediately heard them. They were chatting!

"Ah!" He opened his eyes and located them: crows, standing out in the field, making little warbly calls. They'd been right in front of his eyes, yet he only now beheld them.

"Aren't they beautiful, Calvin?"

"I wouldn't pick that word, but sure."

"What word would you pick?"

"Mystical? Harbingers of doom? Crows are always evil in stories. They're not pretty like parrots. And they eat dead things!"

"That's vultures. You need to let go of your bias, love."

"Bias?! Cuz they're black?"

"Maybe. If crows were white like doves, how would you feel?"

"Trapped," he said, and shaddap.

She hugged his arm. "You know what a family of crows is called? A 'murder.' This is a murder of crows."

"Oh what bollocks!"

"It's true. Lots of animals have funny names for groups of them. Know what a group of apes is called?"

"I'm afraid to ask."

"A shrewdness."

"That's so made up, Kitty."

"If you say so, love."

They listened to the crows make little *rwrk!* sounds to each other as they pecked about the bracken meadow for grub.

"Sounds like they're gossiping about us," he said. "Shall I quote them some Book of James?"

"Crows are like nature's police department. The murder keeps tabs on each other with that *rwrk!* noise. The other call they do, the *caw!*, that's like a siren, letting everyone know there's danger around."

"Us two are right near them—humans, mankind, rulers of the animal kingdom. And they don't even care."

"A lot of birds would fly off, yes, but crows know better. We are no threat. The real threats to them are hawks." She fetched his hand and squeezed it. "Daddy's a birdwatcher. He says one crow always sits way up high to be the scout. He protects the others while they eat."

"Oh, like a lookout."

"Calvin."

He shaddap. *Lookout* was, obviously, a sighted word.

"Find him for me," she said.

Calvin scanned the trees. "Ah!" he said again, spotting a crow perched up a leafless maple.

This one was quite aware of the teenagers; his dark face turned to and fro, watching the murder, then the kids, then the murder, the kids, something behind the kids, the murder …

The lad peered over his shoulder. He was both surprised and not so to see Eric Howe. Kitty's da was a roly-poly fellow with a balding pate and a silly walrus mustache. He stood by the farm market's picnic tables, keeping his distance, keeping an eye on his daughter.

"Daddy's being *our* crow scout," she said.

Calvin checked his gasp. "How—"

"I'm not helpless. I have my own radar but don't need it when it comes to my parents. They *always* stick close to me. I hate it."

"Well. They're concerned."

"It's more than that. I … I'll explain later."

"Something *else* we'll talk about later?"

"Yes. I'm trying to understand how to deal with you and the other girls in your life. Please try to understand how to deal with me and the things we'll talk about later. Okay?"

"What choice do I h—" He cut himself off.

Tell her you'll do better.

"Okay," he said, "I'll do better."

"Great." She did an about face. "Let's go back."

"Aye aye, Captain Howe."

They met up with her da at the picnic tables and Kitty told him about the crows. "I'm glad you got to hear them, Smiley!" the man said. The three of them trekked around the building to the parking lot.

A yelp from the market's front door: "No, Brion!"

Davey, out of his church costume and back in his usual jeans and snarls, turned away from Schultz's entrance and stomped their way. Jill Pedersen pulled on his arm, digging her lavender Chucks in the parking lot gravel, her concord Minnesota Vikings jacket billowing behind her.

The lad moved to place himself in front of Kitty; so had her father, and the two bumped into each other.

Seeing Kitty's da, Davey gnashed his tooth. He spun 'round and barged into Schultz's. Poor Jill nearly got slammed in the face with the Farm Market's glass door.

Calvin told Kitty, "I don't know how to describe what happened," he said. "I can't mention a certain name."

"Please don't. Kiss me goodbye," she said, her tone adding, *so this will have a happy ending.*

He got it, and pecked her cheek.

Chapter 15

PUS ORANGE, ORANGE PUSS.
MONDAY, FEBRUARY 6, 1989.

FOUL

THE SOPHOMORES IN MR. Browne's homeroom whooped about the Pens big win against the Broons (Rob Brown had a hat-trick) and the funny cartoon bits on last night's *Tracey Ullman Show*. Calvin's concentration helmet did its job on that but failed versus Art's verbal orgasm over his newest homemade landmine design.

"Forget springs, *elastic* is the key! Rubber bands holding the thumbtack against the firing plate, puttin' on the pressure—"

Then the mood of the room took a sharp dip. "Holy shit on a stick," whispered Art. Calvin heard that and re-entered the world.

Brion Davey entered a homeroom that was not his, escorting his girl, Jill Pedersen, to her desk. The one directly in front of Calvin's.

The Mall Chick stood facing the Ape, her petunia-and-gray blouse buttoned tight at her neck, her fuchsia jeanskirt angled to starboard as she cocked her hips to port. An excited flush shone right through her ultra-marine blush. Her shit-eating smile was framed in cerise lip gloss.

Mr. Browne left his desk to usher Davey back out, but the goon was already highstepping it outta there.

Browne therefore had his back to Jill as she revealed the one non-purple/non-neutral color about her: the orange in her hand. Like the one that'd been on Davey's lunch tray (and then his face), this orange was cleared of all the peel except the stem points holding it in one piece.

Jill set the orange on atop Calvin's Algebra text and spun 'round to plant her big ol' buttocks in her seat.

On his way back to his desk at the head of the class, Browne said, "That food needs to leave at once, Mr. Connor."

"She put it here! Tell me you saw that!"

Browne leveled a puffy finger. "Now, Calvin."

The Irish Raging Ape palmed the orange and debated between three targets: Browne's pumpkin-headed face, Jill's puss, or Jill's arse.

OFFICE OF THE COMMISSIONER

Calvin and Jill sat in the Principal's Office, in the interrogation chairs, alone. Mr. Martin was busy reading the morning announcements over the P.A. and trusted the teenagers to behave.

"Everyone's gonna laugh so hard at how the great pitcher missed."

Jill did not act like she was in a John Hughes movie: that is, she didn't say her line while facing front, then turn towards camera (Calvin) to give a biting second line with an undertone of cheap sexual tension.

The girl just said it and that's that.

Calvin, however, *did* reply in John Hughes-style:

"I tried shoving the orange up your arse ..." he said through a front-facing stare. Then he turned towards Jill, did a horny power-sneer, and purred: "... but your fat head was already up there."

He grinned at destroying her. Proud of it. Just so proud.

"Puh-*leeease!*" said the Mall Chick. "Admit it—you missed!"

"It's a miracle seeing how big a target your bum is."

"Shut up about my 'bum.' It's all cuz your fingers were too fat to get inside my waistband! Ha ha! Like Mrs. Kelly says in English class, there's symbolism in that."

"That skirt's locked on you tighter than a chastity belt."

"Brion would knock you out if he knew you were talking to me about this. I'm spoken-for, Connor. Get over it."

He choked on the irony. "Me?! *You're* the one who never stops growling at me for dumping you, staring at me across the bus or in the window of my house when you walk by ... still coveting me!"

"Finally got my revenge on you for ruining my magic lilacs. Ha!" Her laugh flitted between them like a dust mote.

"What are you on about?" he said, mystified.

"My magic lilacs! You remember."

He did not.

"My lilac-color panties—'knickers' you call 'em—that you tore off of me when we went to Old Man Mueller's field that time."

"That time fifty-eight years ago? They were *magic* knickers?!"

"*You* called them that! Your face *lit up* at Logan Valley Mall that one time we went into Gadzooks and I saw them. I told you how hard it is to find girls' underwear in grown-up sizes in my colors. And you were like, 'You brought *me* this time and there they are—knickers in your color. It's like magic!'"

"You're psychotic. All you girls are! The reason we're in the Office is cuz of some old *purple knickers?!*"

"Lilac, not purple. You always do that. There's *shades,* dummy."

"You and your shades, always making it sound so grand, 'mauve' and 'eggplant' and 'imperial.' It's all purple, Pedersen!" He pointed at her face. "Except that lipstick you got on. That shite's red!"

"No it's not, it's cerise!"

He was caught short by that.

"Cerise is a purple shade," she went on, "like dark cherries!"

His steel gray eyes zoomed close to her mug, inspecting her lip gloss. She put up a hand, bopping her palm on his beak. He sat back with a snarl. "You desecrate the word 'cerise,' Jill."

"Like *you* desecrated my magic lilac panties. The only pair I ever owned. You ruined them! And you don't even remember."

Well. Calvin did remember. Kinda.

In a midnight dalliance,* Calvin snuck Jill out of her house to a shady copse in Old Man Mueller's fields. Jill gulped down Calvin's Tullamore—she rarely drank—and let him get farther than when they'd dated—she wasn't that kind of girl.

In his Raging Ape haste to get her panties down, he'd ripped them.

Editor-Calvin spliced this particular muff-dive into his Bellend Howl's highlight reel and reviewed it. Under a tree in the dead of night with a new moon … panties in such lighting would need to be magical indeed, shining iridescent like an energon cube, to make any impression on a seventh-grader whose tongue stampeded towards her clitoris.

---

* Taking place in late June '87, after Calvin and Jill broke up but while Calvin was dating Jenny MacDonald (the first time). It's worth noting that Jenny still attended Axsubeen High back then and was reigning Queen of Jill's Mall Chicks clique.

"And for the worst muff that I ever dived," he said aloud. "Or is it 'that I ever dove?' Gotta ask Mrs. Kelly."

"Brion is *sooo* much better than you in every way. He ain't flunkin' math. He's skinnier, he's American, he's blond, he's got a pickup."

"You hate trucks."

"I hate that *Momma* drives one. It's so 'trailer park' for a woman to drive a pickup! Now, Brion … he is all man in that truck!"

"I bet his truck's missing a wheel, like he's missing a tooth."

"I told him I'm sick of riding the bus. It's full of losers like you."

"You *think* you're talking about him but you keep mentioning me! Just bang Davey's brains out already and forget about me."

"I'm not that kind of girl," she sniffed. "That's not what I want."

"It's what *he* wants."

"Nut-uh! How would you know?"

"We're both boys. Davey wants to do it, and if you don't, then he'll dump you like I did." He pointed at the inside of his left thigh, way high up. "You got a mole right here, Jill. I bet Davey never beholds it."

"*Beholds* it?!"

"Sees it. You know what I mean. Out of respect for Kitty, I stopped being biased and using sighted words."

"Never had respect like that for me." She stuck her nose in the air. "Brion will 'behold' my mole. Someday."

"Davey's face will never get close enough. Think he's the muff-diving type? He's all about *him*."

"Ugh, you're so gross."

Fartin' Martin strode in. The kids straightened out, sat up, pushed hair off shoulders (in Calvin's case, that scrotum flap in the back).

"Miss Pedersen," the Principal said, taking his seat. "We will dispense with your rehearsed excuse. The obvious truth is you meant to tease Mr. Connor about your newfound romance with Mr. Davey, using a symbol made legendary by the victim himself."

"I'm the victim?" burped Calvin.

"Await your turn, Mr. Connor." Martin turned to Miss Pedersen.

"I have no excuse, I'm sorry," Jill said briskly, like she was talking to a waiter. "That's exactly what we did. We brought it all full circle."

"There is no 'we.' Mr. Davey has not been summoned here. You brought the foodstuff into Mr. Browne's room. You set it on Mr. Connor's desk, hoping to tempt him. Or make him weep for mercy."

Calvin scoffed at the Principal's *constant* references to him crying.

"*Fiiiine,* Mr. Martin, it was just me, whatever." Jill wanted to pop a gum bubble at the stuffy man but had no Bubblicious. "I plead guilty."

Mr. Martin turned to Calvin. "Your side, Mr. Connor?"

"Did I hear you right? You said I'm the victim here."

"You were, indeed, 'sitting there minding your own business.' Until you fell victim to yourself. To your desire to dominate."

"My desire to *educate.*"

One silver eyebrow lifted precisely one millimeter skyward. This was as close to a gasp or scoff as Principal Martin ever got. "Mr. Connor, did I hear *you* correctly? You want me to believe that lodging a citrus fruit in a defenseless girl's backside would teach her a lesson?"

"Jill isn't innocent—"

"I said 'defenseless,' not 'innocent.' "

"And I didn't lodge the orange—"

"Oh come now, it's beneath even you to deny the facts."

Calvin turned to Jill. "Did I lodge a citrus fruit in your backside?"

"Yes," said the Mall Chick, automatically.

"No," she said, a moment later. "You got the story wrong, Mr. Martin. He *tried* to lodge it in my—God, I'm not saying the word. He tried to grab my skirt's waistband and tried to jam the orange down but his hands are fat and he couldn't get a grip—"

Martin was not amused. "I stand corrected, Miss Pedersen."

"—so he spiked it on the floor like a football player does when he gets a touchdown."

Calvin opened his hands. "All I ended up doing was making a mess on my Reeboks. There's a lesson in that."

"No doubt there is, Mr. Connor," said the Principal.

"I'm confused." The Ape turned to Jill. "Why would you do the crime back in homeroom, then stick up for me in here?"

Jill sputtered. "I'm not sticking up for—"

"Sure you are. You were going to lie, then you stopped." He turned to Mr. Martin. "It may not be obvious but Jill is—dare I say it?—she's my friend. I worry about her. She's never been in this office, she doesn't get detention. Now Davey's a part of her life and she's going bad!"

"Would you quit it!" hissed Jill through her teeth.

Calvin put a hand to his heart and the other out, like an opera singer belting a solo. "I keep telling her Art likes her, he's a good lad but shy. She goes for bad boys. Did you not say in this very room, Mr. Martin, there's no worse thing than to be tied to the likes of Davey or me?"

Jill hopped to her lavender Conversed feet. "Shut up!"

"Be seated, Miss Pedersen," Martin ordered. His perfect monochrome delivery sucked all the cabernet and wisteria from Jill's face, not to mention the cool whites out of the fluorescent lights.

"Mr. Connor," the man said, his body language signaling withered tolerance, "what is your point?"

"Child abuse. Neglect. I don't know the terms," said Calvin. "Jill's da is gone, her mother isn't the best at parenting—I mean, you should see their house—"

"Jesus!" seethed Jill. "I hate you!"

"—*who then am I to judge?* Well. She's my friend. And she's never gonna mature properly. Me either at this rate. I tried to put an orange in her butt in homeroom. Goes to show how much more I have to grow."

"*Please* grow up," said Jill. She turned to Martin. "Everyone says to me, 'You're so immature,' Momma and Kare and Rayche, but I *am* mature! That's why I turned my back on this Ape even though he's *always* there, at my bus stop, in my homeroom, living next door ... "

Fartin' Martin's other eyebrow rose 1½ millimeters.

"That's why you're falling so hard for Davey," said Calvin. "You think being with him will get you away from me! But here's the truth— whenever you're with him, you'll be thinking of me. And he won't be thinking about *you,* he'll be thinking of Kitty."

That stole Jill's air. "Nut-uh. *No.* That's not true."

He looked at his lap. "I'm not saying that to 'dominate' you. I'm sorry, for all of it. Never should've brought up that secret mole—"

"Oh my GAAAWD!" Jill hid her face in her hands.

He turned to the Principal. "I was gonna shove that orange so far up her arse, Mr. Martin. Like a depository. Suppository? I pictured it before I did it—orange squishes open, Jill falls down, broken pelvis or whatever, everyone laughs, juice all over her fancy Logan Valley Mall fashion. This is all Lucky Cheeseboro, by the way, he's been teaching me to picture my pitches before executing them. It works."

"What needs executing," said Jill, "is the Irish Raging Ape."

"Probably. I get why you're ... well, why you're *you,* Jill. I'm sorry for what I did back in Old Man Mueller's field, and for every time I called you names and treated you like one of the guys instead of a girl, I know you hate that. Like Jesus says, *I love my neighbor and my enemies.*" He opened his hands. "And I do. Can you do it back?"

Jill's brown eyes got moist. Her cerise lips opened.

🎥 FILM ROOM

Here's how this scene will end in the *Foul Territory* movie:

```
             MARTIN
     Ahem. I don't believe any
     further punishment is
     warranted here.


                          PULL BACK:


CALVIN and JILL stand and exit one at a time.

MUSIC (v.o.): Simple Minds, "Don't You (Forget
About Me)."

             ADULT CALVIN
               (v.o.)
     We both learned something that
     day, something about
     condemning the nihilism of
     Salinger's Caufield, about
     turning our backs on the
     Satanic consumer culture of
     MTV. Lessons not taught in
     Social Studies or Sex Ed.


                          DISSOLVE TO:
```

105 EXT. AXSUBEEN HIGH SCHOOL - DAY

    CALVIN exits the school and blinks up at the
    sun.

                    ADULT CALVIN
                 (v.o., CONT'D)
          We learned to love thy
          neighbor. Just as Jaysus
          would've.

FOUL 🏏

... but this is the book:

Jill's brown eyes got moist. Her cerise lips opened, and she said, "Fuck you up the ass, Connor."

Mr. Martin put his hands flat on his desk blotter. "Enough. Miss Pedersen: three days Official Detention, classroom disturbance; an additional day will cover that explicit outburst.

"Mr. Connor: Miss Pedersen asked neither for your friendship nor an evaluation of her life, but Mr. Browne did ask you to remove the vittles from his room. Whether you strike the target or not, brandishing fruit is assault. Your repeated malfeasance advances you to In-School Suspension. Three days, beginning at once. We'll send notes to your teachers. Depart, both of you."

FOUL 🏏

The Hole was a basement room, a literal dungeon, a pedagogic graveyard. Cubicles, not desks. Some college-lined paper and a pencil. No books, no napping. All homework and tests failed automatically. No talking, no farting. The cinder blocks were factory showroom gray, not a single coat of Institutional Hwite on them.

And there were so, so many cinder blocks down here.

The other I.S.S. prisoners were the dregs. Anytime his ma said, "Keep this up and you'll amount to nothing, so you will!", Calvin wanted to show her some of this lot. Kids like Jessie Hackett, a ninth-grader perpetually doing the Kubrick glare from under his eyebrows. Destined to hold up a liquor store. Maybe next week.

And Lorey Adkisson, a senior of considerable notoriety. Lorey was the Butt-Sex Girl. No one knew where the tale originated. No one cared if it was true. Kids said it behind her back, to her face. The lad felt kinda sorry for her, especially after hearing that Wren had gotten a similar rep up in Connecticut.

From the next cubicle over, Lorey dropped a note to the doo-doo brown/pus orange tile, nudging it his way. He left the folded-up paper alone. It was probably contaminated with herpes. It *reeked* of Kools.

Coach Falcone came down to The Hole between classes and pulled Calvin into the hall. The man's chest-high wall of a mustache was so forlorn it seemed to seriously consider divorcing Falcone's face to spend a quiet life in a log cabin somewhere. "You're more trouble than you're worth," he told the lad. "Lucky gave you his number, right? Call him tonight so he knows not to come to practice tomorrow."

"But Tuesdays and Thursdays are when he works with me."

"This ain't your first rodeo—no extracurriculars during I.S.S."

"Kitty'll be standing in the caf at lunch, waiting for me."

"Don't screw up and you won't have this problem."

The lad bit his tongue to stop blubbering.

"I'll tell Ryan to let her know. Now, can you stop this crap?"

"I'm doing my best, Coach."

"Your best ain't good enough. Gotta do better."

Tell her you'll do better.

He went back in the Hole. The note was still under his cubicle but had mysteriously unfolded itself. WANNA? was all it said.

He pinched one end with the toe of his left Reebok and shredded the note in two with his right Reebok.

FOUL

Bus No. 10's route served the outlier ramshackles first, pulled off Rte. 666 (Bald Eagle Pike) for the ostentatious Overlook Estates, and finished with the ranchers along the northern ends of the tree roads. Calvin had the window seat since Art wasn't there. Neither were Ryan,

Jill, Pete Hennessey—the baseball/softball players were at practice.

Riding the normal 2:30 p.m. bus home felt weird now. The traffic and skies were lighter this early. A bunch of popular ninth grade girls— too young to drive, too young to have boyfriends with cars—loudly gossiped about the girls who *did* have boyfriends with cars. Justine Hennessey, the eighth-grader who lived across the street, turned around and smiled at Calvin.

He wanted Abby to be here. She lived on Pine Street on the east side of town. Abby was still nasty ol' Slanty Face but she'd have the pulse on what Kitty felt about today's shocking events.

Is she with Kitty right now? In the library or something.

With Saint Mark. Getting "tutored."

He ran hands through his hair to clear his mind and felt annoyed anew at how little there was on top.

A girl sat down on the vinyl seat next to him. She was a sophomore bombshell with a bright face smattered with freckles, bouncing blue eyes, and natural blonde hair under a spell by Studio Line. Though her padded bra told lies, the girl maintained a truth-telling toned figure, bronzed even in the dead of winter (Mother owned tanning salons in Newry and Duncansville).

This lass never wore a demure smile, low-cut tops, slutty skirts, fuck-me pumps—but boys sure as shit acted like she did. Photos might show the lass seated at a pew during Mass in plain blacks, or standing straight in a floppy Adidas tracksuit holding a volleyball trophy ... but boys saw a hot babe licking her top lip, curling a finger at them, hips cocked like *come and get it.* Boys went all fizzy-pop with boneritis in her wake, their heads embroiled in clouds of tiny mouth-atoms opening, tiny heart-atoms popping, and tiny erection-atoms splooging.

Jenny MacDonald.

Her folks pulled her from Axsubeen High and put her in Catholic school in November ... just after the Corgan Lawn Incident. The MacDonalds stopped going to Saint Brigid, too; now they went to Saint Patrick in Newry, five miles north up Rte. 666 (Hollidaysburg Pike).

Axsubeen Bus No. 5 made daily afternoon trips up to Altoona to pick up kids like Jenny who lived in town but went to private schools in the city.

This bus, as has been noted, was No. 10. It only went to Altoona in the mornings.

"What're *you* doing here?" Calvin spat at her.

"Intramurals." She made a big show of fixing her navy plaid skirt so it rested over her knees. Her navy wool cardigan with the embroidered crest of Bishop Guilfoyle High School was visible under her neon yellow Nike windbreaker. Her athletic legs were wrapped in orange Coloralls to keep them warm.

"I thought the weather didn't affect cold-blooded creatures," said the Ape.

"Heard you got a crush on Kitty Howe," said Jenny, all blasé. "Good for you, *Studly.*"

"I don't need your approval, *Bunny-Buns.*" He thrust an arm out to shove her off the seat.

"Stop it." When he didn't, she yelled, "Don't touch me, Connor!"

Everyone was staring. He stood. "Up there. In your usual seat."

When this was her regular bus, Jenny liked to sit right behind the driver, Smoky Joe. Mother got annoyed at the smell of Joe's Pall Malls on her clothes. Anything that annoyed Mother delighted Jenny.

Calvin went down the aisle first to show that she wasn't dragging him along. Jenny was all about appearances. He put a *shhh!* finger over his lip at Justine Hennessey, telling her not to gossip. Justine was the only one here impressionable enough to listen to such a plea.

Jenny strolled up the bus aisle like she was doing it a fucking favor. Lesser girls got mocked for having a duck walk. Jenny, unable to shed them fanned-out feets, made the duck walk her trademark. She swished her Catholic schoolgirl skirt side-to-side with pride.

They sat down. There were five or six stops before the bus would pull up in front of her McMansion on Canyon Curve.

He said nothing. Poker face.

She let a sunbeam kiss her freckles and make her neon windbreaker pop. "Why fall for the blind girl when you could still have this?"

Poker face? Bollocks! This required a reaction: he flapped his lips.

"I mean, *ewww!* You kissed a cripple!" she went on. "One that made out with fugly Brion Toof-Face, too. That's gross. I'm serious."

"Seriously mental," the lad said.

Her eyes had the absolute-zero cold of outer space.

The bus stopped on Rte. 666 at one of the homesteads to let off Stefan "Steve" Schultz VI.

"Her name is 'Kitty,'" said Calvin tartly. "The way you say 'the cripple' and 'the blind girl' … she's not a sped!"

Jenny's eyes ran for cover, down to her lap. "You're a sped. I left you for Sean Corgan. All the girls want Sean. He's hot. You left me for a handicapped porker. She's a hog. That's, like, demeaning to me."

The bus made a stop. As Brenda Schoenberger went past their seat to exit, Jenny bunched up against Calvin and slid her hand over his Bugle Boy trouserfront.

He judo-chopped her hand away.

"It's soft, Studly. You musta been thinkin' about Kitty. All three hundred pounds of her." Jenny's breathy voice used to get him hard. Now it pickled his anus. "A couple of fat fucks is all you are."

"Gave *you* a fat fuck, love, after you dumped me for Pizza Boy."

"What a letdown, too," she teased, holding up one small pinky.

This *really* burned him. Jenny had offered a different opinion about his flute at the time. Same with Wren. Those comments had filled the lad with confidence. Yet the more porno tapes Calvin saw, the more anxiety he felt. Those dudes were *muuuch* bigger. Were the girls he'd gotten with lying to stroke his ego? He suddenly swore not to use the Irish slang "flute" anymore. *I have a shillelagh, goddamnit!*

The bus pulled onto Overlook Lane to begin door-to-door drop-offs for the rich kids. Jenny lived on the third of five culs-de-sac.

"I wish we never went to that party," she said. "It ruined everything. I only wanted to make Kare jealous. She's such a bitch."

"Why do I get the feeling," said Calvin, "that if I talk to Sean, he'll say you've done this exact same thing to him recently?"

"Yuck. Screw him."

"I'll pass."

"So did I."

"Can't you, like, find someone new? Aren't there any hot boys up at Bishop Guilfoyle?"

"The boys there suck. They're all posers, or 'rebels,' or Bible-beaters like Saint Mark. Ugh."

Poker face. *Do not tell her that Mark tutors Kitty!*

"Think I'll come to your Valentine's dance," said Jenny.

"You can't come," said Calvin. "You don't go to Axsubeen."

"I could if someone asked me!"

"I'll give Art your number."

Her big blue eyes shrank. "I don't want a *nerd* to take me."

He put the poker face on but it didn't fit the contours of his snarl.

"You don't understand how much it hurts to get replaced, Calvin."

"Oh what bollocks! You literally replaced me, dumped me days before summer camp and went racing out with the little wanker."

Her big eyes drowning in tears made Calvin feel evil where he had no cause to. "Sean was a mistake," she said, wiping her face. "Kitty's a mistake too, you watch. Sean didn't complete me. You did."

"Complete this." He pumped his nuts at her.

"Sean wasn't for real. He barely listened to me. All he wanted was to get me in the sack. He didn't even give my parents discount pizza."

The rich MacDonalds—they of inground pool, basement billiard table, multiple Jaguars—"Father" and "Mother," who found Calvin an unsuitable match for their only child, calling him a syphilitic illegal immigrant—*those cunts* asked for a discount at Pizza Putt?!

"You accused me of that, Jenny. Remember?"

"Of wanting discount pizza?"

"Of only wanting to get you in the sack!"

"You wanted more than that." She snorted up some snot.

"Did I, Bunny Buns? I dumped you the second I got it."

Her wet face reddened. "Stop making me feel so ... inferior!"

It was never a case of *Will Jenny guilt trip me?*, more like *How many guilt trips will this whore's hole work in?* If Spazz were here, he'd be taking bets from the other kids on the bus: "The line's four! Over/under four guilt trips from the built bitch Gently McDone-hole!"

"This act you're doing, it's just pathetic," said Calvin. He pointed out the windshield at Cloven Cape: "Behold, Corgan's yard."

"Behold?! Whatever, dork. Let's fuck again."

That last, said so abruptly, knocked the lad for a loop. He turned away, then bugged at her hand on his thigh, then looked at her wet orbs. He saw the tears boiling off to steam from a fire in her blue eyes.

The fire of desire.

Désirer: je désire, tu désires, il/elle desire—

"Go and shite!"

Smoky Joe levered open the door at the MacDonalds' driveway. The girl slammed Calvin out the way with two hands and stormed off.

There was a burst of applause from the other kids on the bus. Girls laughed as Jenny ran for her front door, boys pointed out she had her face covered in both hands.

Calvin sat back down behind the driver. "Hey Joe, can I bum a smoke?"

Smoky Joe's dry voice raked Calvin's nerves like a steel bristle brush. "Ain't worth my job! Go steal yer old man's!"

FOUL

Calvin's old man was working so it was no surprise the Caddy wasn't in his driveway, but no cars were there. Whole place to himself. He used the kitchen phone to call Kitty.

After four rings, Ma Howe's voice came: "You've reached the Howes. We are not home right now. Please leave your name and number and we'll call you back."

Beeeep.

"Hi. This is Calvin Connor the Third, calling for Kitty. I, uh. Well. Please call me back. You know the num—"

The line crackled and Kitty came on. "Hello, Calvin!"

"Hi! You're home!"

"We just got in," she said.

"We?"

"Me and Abby. We have homework to do."

"So you're downstairs?" They were still being recorded by the answering machine up in her parents' room; it would be broadcasting both their voices loud enough for Abby to hear.

"Yes. Abby told me what happened," said Kitty, meaning Jill and the orange. "It's all anybody talked about today."

"I don't suppose we can talk about *this* past in the future?"

"No," she said. Her voice had a little scorn and a little mirth.

"Let's add this to it: I got confronted on the bus home by Jenny."

Her breath hit the handset's pickup in a snippy snoot. No more mirth. "Why was *she* on your bus?"

"She said intramurals, whatever that is. She's psychotic! She threatened to come to the Valentine's Day Dance to annoy everyone."

"That won't apply to us," said Kitty, "since we won't be there."

"Sure we will!"

"You have to ask me to go first."

"Well. Will you go with me, mon cerise?"

"That depends. Will you try to get revenge on Jenny if she shows up? Or bring an orange to throw at Jill?"

"I—"

"You remember the Doseman?"

What does this have to do with me? "Of course. He picked on all the little kids. I'm glad he's in juvvy."

"He used to pick on me, too. He'd come up beside me in the hall at the grammar school and kick out my cane. Kids have tried to take the dark glasses off my face and steal Excalibur from me since day 1, my whole life—but I turn the other cheek. Y'know, like Jesus.

"But this one time, I didn't. Doseman kicked the bottom part of the cane away and the tip caught on a locker or something. I heard the fiberglass break. I felt the end of the cane hanging down, still attached by a thread. I knew it was Doseman cuz he *smells*. Like, garlic and poop. He was *sooo* gross. I got so mad, Calvin. I hate Excalibur but I *need* it! It's how I get around!

"So I turned toward where his smell was and I swung the cane. I wanted to *kill* him. I wanted that *so bad* ... but I missed, or he ducked, whatever, it doesn't matter, and I hit Gail Bachner in the neck. The broken bit that was, like, hanging by a thread? That snapped off and went flying down the hall and almost hit Mr. Adler."

"Holy shit."

"The school nurse said Gail was fine and I was lucky the broken bit didn't stick right in her throat. My parents were so pissed off. The Principal too. I had a long talk with Father Sean about it in confession. He was the only one who forgave me. But he read Matthew 26 to me, you know, *all who take the sword die by the sword*. Or *perish*. The exact words don't matter. The point is to not let yourself reach that point."

He forced down a dry gulp. "Right."

"It's hard, Calvin, so hard, I get it, but you can't give up and lash out. And you *certainly* can't try to pull down some girl's skirt to shove an orange up her butt."

Tell her you'll do her in the butt.

Tell her you'll do better.

He felt ashamed that Spazz's quote came first.

came first

"The temptation is strong," he said.

Kitty said nothing. Poker face.

"I need my own crow scout, Kitty. To keep an eye on me."

He slapped himself. *Asking a blind person to keep an "eye" on you?*

"Crows pair-bond," she said. "That means they stay together forever. That's why one of them is willing to sacrifice dinnertime to be the scout up in the tree. If *you* need someone to watch over you, there's always Jesus."

"Right."

"When are you out of I.S.S.?"

"Wednesday's the last day. Behold you at lunch Thursday?"

"Peut être."

"'Maybe?'"

"Oui. Adieu." She hung up.

Adieu. Not au revoir.

Chapter 16

FOUL

"... PETER NORTH'S ONE OF the X-Men. He's not just *splish-splish,* he's all WHOOOSH!, *splat splat splat,* the jisim never stops ..."

Calvin never wanted a Walkman more desperately than right now. Kitty wasn't talking to him, his final I.S.S. day lay ahead, Bus No. 10's suspension was extra bouncy, and Art Maguire kept on blathering!

"... down to Steeler's Shears. Me and Mr. Mueller talked firearms while he fixed my fade. He says the gatling gun changed warfare but I say it's the M1 Garand."

Calvin focused on Jill, seated near the front. She'd gone from constantly giving him quick glances to never doing it at all.

"... the clips only held eight rounds but it was reliable and cheap. Notice I said 'clip,' not 'magazine?' It's actually a 'clip' on the M1—"

"Let me pontificate," whispered Calvin.

Here we go again. The lad only said these words before making a firm case that Art was wrong about something.

African went rigid with unease. Irish nodded up at Jill. "She'll end up hating Davey. She's totally rescuable," he hissed. "Call her tonight, ask her out."

Art, at normal volume: "I got bells at church tonight."

"Not 'take her out tonight'—*call* her tonight."

"Hope ya did the Algebra homework," said Art, loud and smooth, since he and Calvin were discussing school and not anything untowards like girls. "If you wanna play baseball, ya gotta get passing grades and shit."

Meanwhile, one of Art's gangly hands rummaged in his cool black satin bookbag and withdrew a calculator. The device was so complex-looking for 1989 that other kids thought he acquired it from the future. The Casio *fx*-7000G was an amazing gadget with fifty buttons and a huge screen (2½" by 1⅓", *huuuge* I tells ya). Its $130 price tag— $82,053 in 2024 money—did not compute with many parents.

Art proved time and again he'd gotten his dad's money's worth.

The *fx*-7000G was programmable and had memory slots to hold algebraic formulas. Art exploited these slots to store plain text, such as answers for a test, phone numbers, or notes to a friend, proto-text-messages, passed along by "lending" the device over.

Art opened the first memory slot (kept free for messaging) and quickly dashed off text with both thumbs. He forked the calculator over:

```
WHO WANTS A USED
CAR WITH THAT
MANY MILES?■
```

Calvin thought, *Now you don't want Jill? Make up your mind, Art!*

That reply was too long. You gotta downshift your mind to express yourself on the *fx*-7000G. The Ape hit ALPHA-LOCK then hunted and pecked. The alphabet was a tertiary label on some six rows of buttons. He and Art never deleted the original message, instead adding a standard one-space separation followed by the reply. It took the fat-fingered lad forever, using one hand to type and the other to hide the screen from Art's ice blue eye.

Calvin's messages always lacked the polish of Art's punctuation and manual word wrap:

```
WHO WANTS A USED
CAR WITH THAT
MANY MILES? BOLL
OCKS HER MA HAS
A MILLION MILES
JILLS ODOMETER I
S ALL ZEROS■
```

Art quickly typed his response. Bus No. 10 reached the Axsubeen School campus and turned up the High School's entrance. The kid triumphantly held the *fx*-7000G up instead of passing it over.

```
WHO WANTS A USED
CAR WITH THAT
MANY MILES? BOLL
OCKS HER MA HAS
A MILLION MILES.
JILL'S ODOMETER
IS 1/10TH OF A
MILE COURTESY OF
MR. MUFF-DIVER■
```

Art repurposed Calvin's message to make fun of his cunnilingus record *and* corrected the Ape's syntax, adding an apostrophe to JILLS.

Calvin grabbed the calculator. He couldn't think of a clever and vicious reply so he typed FU.

Nothing happened. He checked he was on ALPHA-LOCK. He hit random letters. Nothing.

Then he realized—all 144 bytes of this memory slot were taken. That ball-bag Art used 'em all up on purpose!

Surreptitiously, Calvin cycled through the other memory slots. A couple had genuine equations or formulas. At last he struck gold: a list of initials and phone numbers. Kitty's was on there, he was irked to note. The last one was:

```
K.M. 107-3139■
```

He committed it to memory, cycled back to the message slot they'd been using, and gave back the *fx*-7000G with a sigh.

Art was laughing his arse off. "Never go in against an African when death is on the line!"

"Well. At least *I* know what muff tastes like."

Chapter 17

SIZES AND COLORS TO SUIT EVERYONE.
MONDAY, FEBRUARY 13, 1989.

⚾ FAMILY SECTION ⚾

"I NEED TO BORROW money for this, Ma."

"Of course you do."

"Not just the baseball stuff, but a gift for Kitty too."

"Come to a full stop, laddy, none of your rampaging through."

"I'm already on thin ice cuz of the I.S.S. thing. Me and her are talking again, you saw us at Mass, but her parents must've seen the *Reporter*—"

"'3 days In-School Suspension, sexual harrassment!'" quoted Ma.

"—which is bollocks, even Jill said so."

"I have to front cash for a make-up gift too? My money, my Volvo, my gas, my time, future trips to base ball practice and matches."

"'Games.' Baseball doesn't have 'matches.' Duh."

"I do hope they have your 12½ at the shops, Lord knows it's hard getting you plain tennis shoes. You never indicate, boyo! That's the whole point of the signal lever!"

Eileen's station wagon barreled into the Millar farmhouse's dirt lot. "A fiver, please? I'll pay you back, Ma."

He hopped out (engine still running, which was okay with the cold so nipping, but he failed to set the parking brake) and met Paddy Millar. Eileen knew him: second son and third child of Michael Millar, himself first son and heir apparent to the Millar farming concern. Paddy was that rare Yank-Irish kid: one with a proper Irish name (Padraig).

Paddy was loitering by the greenhouses. Her son traded the fiver for one rose. "What a bargain," sighed Eileen.

Calvin got back in and passed the rose to her. The cabin light turned itself off once he'd closed the driver's door but she reached up to snap it back on. Her agate eyes grew large. "Would you look at that," she said, dazzled. The petals were kelly green—obviously (but cleverly) dyed from an original white.

She turned to her second son and third child, her heart all but melting. "How thoughtful!"

"It's not for you, Ma! It's for Kitty! We were just saying. But I can't hold it *and* drive."

Eileen choked back her disappointment. "Seatbelts!" she said, the standard order when anyone got in a vehicle with her. She didn't want to hold the rose the whole way up Rte. 666, but also didn't want to set it down on the dash or back seat and watch it get damaged. She tried the cupholder but the stem was too long.

"A lovely treat for your girl," she said.

"You told me to listen to her, Ma, and that's how I know green is her favorite color. Thanks a million for the tip."

"How can she have a favorite color if she's been blind since birth?"

Calvin cleared his throat. "Her eyes are green so maybe that's it."

"*Of course* you don't know. Still, credit for the bare minimum."

"I *try* to listen. Half the time I don't know what she means, or she doesn't explain. But I *try.*"

"I see."

"Don't say that. It's biased."

"It's what now?"

"I've been training myself to stop using sighted words like that."

Eileen abhorred society's recent pussyfooting around common language but beamed at her son's attentiveness towards Kitty's needs. Futzing with the rose, she plucked the thorns off. "Poor lass's hands won't stand a chance."

"Good thinking, Ma!"

Eileen sniffed the rose (its natural aroma had an artificial kick of sugar), gazed out the passenger window, and wished for some bygone era when Calvin the Second used to get her flowers.

Calvin the Third parked near the Mall Cinema, like his father would, and not right outside Hess's, which is much more sensible in terms of walking distance and didn't involve making a left onto 666

South on the way out. He pocketed her key but left the fob hanging out, dangling against his hip. That lovely little leather fob he'd made for her ages ago in Leatherworking merit badge. She adored that thing.

"Lucky says that kids get drafted from everywhere," her son was saying. "You don't need to be from a big city or a big college. If you're *that* good, he says, you'll get attention from scouts fast."

"How nice of the fellow to indulge your fantasy," she said.

"Ma, he knows what he's talking about. He went to Axsubeen then Penn State and got drafted. I saw it on his Topps card. He played on three teams. He got traded for himself once—now that's big-time!"

They passed through the revolving door into Logan Valley Mall's warm concourse. Eileen had no idea what Calvin was on about but at least she'd no longer have to listen in the blustery chill.

"Lucky says it helps a pitcher's stats when his team doesn't suck. I told Art that and after poker Saturday we went to the library to check out old copies of the *Distorter.* Guess what? The Axsubeen Axes suck, Ma. We *suuuuck!* Skip, Mr. Phillips I mean, he's been the coach for like a hundred years but the Varsity team record is pretty shite."

"Language, laddy."

"The best records in our conference are Altoona and Larsen."

They passed the Hallmark shop and Eileen made a note to ditch Calvin and slip in here to fetch a birthday card for him.

"Art says Larsen's student body isn't much bigger than ours."

"It doesn't matter since we can't afford it."

"Altoona Area High School is free."

"That's not how it works in the States, Calvin. Children can only attend a free public school in the district they live in. Otherwise you pay, just like private and Catholic schools."

"We could move."

"Go and shite! You want us to pick up and move to Altoona so your base ball team will be better?"

"Better hitters score runs and help the pitcher win," said Calvin, a little miffed at her automatic dismissal.

"Better students score better grades and get accepted to colleges."

At Herman's World of Sporting Goods, her son picked out a glove (a "mitt"), an athletic protector (a "cup"), and a gym tote (a "bag").

Doing the cost arithmetic in her head, Eileen needed a whiskey (a "belt"). Lucky told him to skip the bat, he wasn't going to focus on hitting anyway and he could just borrow someone's. *Thank the Lord!* she thought. *How can an aluminum stick cost so much?*

At the shoe department, Calvin told the very fit young man at the counter that he needed baseball cleats. They had to be black, white, or (in his words) "doo-doo brown or pus orange."

"Don't sell too many pus orange men's in 12½ but lemme check in the back," the Very Fit Young Man said. He came back a minute later with two boxes, a black Nike and a white Converse. The Nike fit better, Calvin said. *Of course they do; they're ten dollars more.* She went into her pocketbook for the Discover card.

"My first sneakers that aren't white," her son lamented.

"These ain't sneakers, hoss," said the Very Fit Young Man. "Only wear 'em on out on the diamond, or those cleats are toast."

Toasted bread, thought Eileen. She signed the receipt and told Calvin she needed to go into Fashion Bug and would meet him by the Hush Puppies. That successfully kept him away as she backtracked to Hallmark. When they reunited, Calvin had somehow come up with enough coin to buy an Orange Julius. A large one.

"Hans and Franz recognized us," he said. "That muscle guy at Herman's. He's like, 'Yo, say hi to yer sister. Tell her she's got her mom's hair.'"

"How would *he* know her? That young man was too old to be Rose's classmate!"

In the parking lot, she fetched the leather fob dangling at his hip. She didn't want to hold the green rose on the way home or watch Calvin sip his drink while driving.

Chapter 18
THORNS. AND RICK SPRINGFIELD.
VALENTINE'S DAY.

◯ BLEACHERS ◯

MULBERRY SHADOW HALOED JILL Pedersen's eyes but couldn't hold back her anxious squint. One of her trademark upper thighs, robed in denim the color of creeping phlox, jiggled from foot-throbbing.

Everyone else at the bus stop was laughing. Calvin showed up with his stuffed-full gym bag, new cleats dangling from one hand, Trapper and texts in the other, and a long stem rose between his teeth. A trickle of blood ran down to his chin; his mother hadn't plucked *all* the thorns.

Jill wanted to laugh too. But that rose ... that rose, dyed green ...

What're the chances Brion got me a rose dyed purple?

What're the chances Brion got me a rose, period?

Or anything, period?

Her eyes met the Ape's and saw empathy in him. And a little shrug, like he was saying, "You made your choice, Pedersen."

When Bus No. 10 rolled up, she nearly ran away.

FOUL ⚾

Back in eighth grade, Jenny MacDonald wanted something odd for Valentine's Day: "Get me that Rick Springfield album—"

"Rick Springfield?!" sneezed Calvin. "Jaysus!"

"—pay attention, *not* the new one with Spuds McKenzie on the cover, the other one with Rick's cute face. The one with that song he did at Live Aid. But you gotta give it to me in school. Valentine's Day is Saturday so bring it Friday. And, like, wrap it up and all, so I can open it up in homeroom and make everyone jealous. And get the record, not the tape, cuz it's bigger and everyone'll see it!"

Jenny had delivered this dictum early on Wednesday, February 11th, 1987, giving the lad two evenings to acquire the gift. The kids had been on exactly one date: Sock Hop Saturday, the night of February 7th. They'd only bloody *met* the Monday preceding, February 2nd.

Calvin had gotten in Ma's Volvo (the back seat this time cuz he was 13 and Rose called shotgun) and blown his allowance at The Listening Booth buying the *Tao* LP. He stood at this very bus stop that Friday the 13th, trying to hide the gift-wrapped album from the upperclassmen: Ryan's older brother Charlton, his own older brother Robbie and Pete Hennessey. Calvin went to Jenny's homeroom and made a big presentation. She unwrapped the record, got the reaction she wanted from her Mall Chick friends, kissed Calvin on the cheek, and said, "Hold onto this 'til the final bell. Don't break it!"

The fucking thing didn't fit in his locker. Anytime he set it down, some senior prick was right there trying to draw Groucho glasses on Rick's portrait. Young Calvin carried around that Rick Springfield record all day. And, as Jenny'd said, *Everyone'll see it.*

"She let people know," Ryan told him later. "Pointing you out."

"Sounds like *that's* what she really wanted for Valentine's Day," said Robbie Connor. "To show she rules ye."

This Valentine's would be different.

Kitty sat in the front row of her homeroom, Excalibur braced against the desk's edge with one hand. The jingle bell Calvin had safety-pinned to his ghastly scarf of many colors alerted her long before his arrival.

Everyone shut up to watch. He put on a show for them, kneeling at her desk. His gym bag bopped against his knee. "Gimme your hand," he said. He was getting better at telling when it was fine to take her hand and when he should ask first. This was an "ask" moment. She was on the spot. She heard the quiet anticipation around her.

She held out her left hand, the free one. He put the rose in it. "Oh my God, what's this?!" Her right hand shot up to grip the stem too. Excalibur, hanging by the wrist loop, swooped over the next desk, nearly slapping Abby Malone in the face.

Kitty tickled the petals and took a deep sniff. "Smells like cereal!"

"Dipped in Lime Kool Aid," said Calvin. "It's the only way I could get you a rose in your favorite color."

The girl nearly melted out of her desk. "You got me a green rose for Valentine's Day?"

"I pulled off the thorns so you don't prick yourself," he said. Someone in homeroom sputtered at his employment of "prick" *(v.)*.

"Aww, you think of everything!"

"Give it time, I'm due to screw up!" He tilted his left wrist to check his White Window Swatch, sending his gym bag into his own face. "Gotta run, love. Don't wanna be tardy."

"Most tards don't," said Abby, and they all laughed.

Calvin gave her a nod like *Good one!* and saw the girl's slanted face was slathered in makeup. Far more than usual, covering up her eyes.

"Happy Valentine's Day!" said Kitty, one hand making a grabby motion, to pull him close, keep him here.

"Behold you at lunch." Calvin's Reeboks squeaked on the doo-doo brown and pus orange checkerboard tile, heading out to the hallway.

"I love you!" she called out.

WHOA! It was the first time one of them said that! "I love you, too!" he said over his shoulder—

—and collided with Brion Davey. The blond butt-face's butt-face got indignant. "Get offa me, faggot!"

The Ape tear-assed away, making no apologies.

He rounded to his hallway and dashed in his homeroom. "Here comes the 'Ape' Train, all aboard," Jill cracked to a general laugh.

Calvin did an ungracious pirouette into his desk. "I'm here!"

"I'll alert the media," said Mr. Browne, getting no laughs. He wasn't one of the "cool" teachers.

Calvin turned to Art and did an exaggerated brow-wipe, like *Whew!*

Art studiously worked his mechanical pencil over graph paper. *I don't got a girlfriend on Valentine's Day, but that's cool cuz I'm totally too busy for pussy. Working on the M.S.S.M. here. Version 4.1. See?*

Jill turned around to face Calvin. "Did she like it?"

"She did now. Ran into your boyfriend right afterwards."

She faced front, fiddling with her iris-colored bracelets.

Chapter 19

T RIAL BY FIRE IN THE COURT OF THE DIAMOND.

FOUL

T HE ATHLETIC ARENAS SAT across Rte. 666 (Bald Eagle Pike) behind the dirt and stone, pot-holey student parking lot. Axe Field hosted soccer, lacrosse, field hockey, track, and Friday night gridiron under four Musco light standards. Axe Park was lit by the sun alone and used by the baseball team alone. The girls' softball team had to bus to the little league field near Saint Brigid.

A shoddy and shaky six-row bleacher rose behind each dugout. No admission was charged since no one attended apart from girlfriends and parents. A thirty-foot-high backstop was installed in '87, ending de-cades of broken windshields. No press box, radio booth, clubhouse, electronic signage, or P.A.; all that bollocks required power.

In the '70s, some students painted Axsubeen High on the concrete roof of the home dugout and No Lands Untamable! on the visitors'. The dugouts were ground level, not sunken, with warped bat racks, splintery wooden benches without padding; without electric fans, foul ball screens, or toilets. For that last, a concrete bathroom shed was situated by the concession stand way over at the football field.

The playing surface was grass* but as it was still winter, the outfield was brown. Spuy, Axsubeen High's strangely named groundskeeper, had his work cut out for him. The home opener was in six weeks.

Schultz's Lumber, Pizza Putt, Millar's Farm Stand, Oldroyd Heating Oil, Schoenberger's Pharmacy, Mueller's Farmstore, Schultz's Hardware, Lucky Cheeseboro GM Chevrolet, the Law Firm of Bachner Esq., Schultz's Farm Market, O'Sullivan's Wallpaper &

---

* Stating whether a ballfield is grass or turf is required under 15 U.S.C. § 12.

Paint, Jacoby Family Practice, Merk's Super-Merket, Video Onslaught, and Steeler's Shears Barbershop all had placards on the outfield's rusty chain-link fence. The proceeds helped pay for the team uniforms.

A scoreboard rose above the fence in right, wooden number boards changed by student volunteers. A billboard behind left displayed all the Axes'/Lady Axes' retired numbers:

ꓯ — Bart Twain	1 3 — Richard
5 — Wilhelm	"Lucky" Cheeseboro
"Big Billy" Schultz V	2 9 — Charlotte Meier
5 — Honora Tracey	3 6 — Jack Stiles

The single bullpen mound sat in a slice of foul territory along left. Calvin Connor parked his arse on it. The odorous whalespawn Gus Jacoby, the J.V. catcher, sat downwind.

"What's the ꓯ about?" Calvin asked.

"Dunno," said Gus. "Maybe he had a letter and not a number."

"If that's the case, ol' Bart shoulda worn a 'T' for Twain."

"I'll ask Lucky, he knows everything." Gus spoke with reverence. Pro ballplayers were heroes. The ballpark was a battlefield to Americans, the diamond sacred ground. They even honored the fallen dead with shirt number headstones.*

A couple years ago, Calvin Connor III saw a felt banner immortalizing his name for incompetence and knew it'd outlive him. He didn't care; he said, "I'll never see it again." (He never would.)

Same here: if his 4 joined the numeral graveyard, Future-Calvin would never gaze wistfully at it over his Ray-Bans. What for? He'll be floorin' his Countach across Miami as some bikini babe blew him.

"Whaddaya wanna be when you grow up?"

"Good enough for a retired number, and too cool to give a fuck."

---

* Gus'll never remember to ask Lucky so here's the scoop: Bart Twain played before the school started wearing numerals (1940), so his retired "number" was the cap insignia. Honny Tracey wore 5 after it was retired for baseball but before the West Penn forced the teams to use the same pool of numbers, so it was later retired for her too. All the players listed had either made the Show (Bart, Big Billy, and Lucky) or passed away before graduating (Honny, Charlotte, and Jack; coincidentally, Honny and Jack died on the same day).

FOUL

Exhausted from prep for the coming Presidents' Day Sale, Lucky Cheeseboro took his sweet damn time climbing out his black Callaway Corvette. He came down Tuesdays and Thursdays to mentor the blue chip. The warm air (49°) and sharp sun made it feel like baseball. Lucky wore his usual costume: skinny khakis, salmon showroom polo with burger/car/tits logo, glistening gold Rolex, and navy blue ballcap from a former employer (today, the Minnesota Twins' interlocked "TC").

Passing through the rusty gate near the third base dugout, Lucky waved at the kids taking B.P. and shagging fly balls. He made a finger pistol and shot Gus Jacoby. The roly-poly kid hustled for his catcher's gear. The Ape pulled on his mitt. He'd oiled the thing and beaten the crap out of it with Ryan and Art. It felt foreign on his hand.

Lucky waved him on like *Get started*. Calvin threw warm-ups with Lucky right at his side, watching. The collar of the man's dealership polo was frayed. His long rear locks almost covered it up.

Distracted, Calvin's next warm-up went wide. "Axsubeen's the 412 area code," said Lucky. "Keep them balls out of 717, cherry pie."

The Ape held up his mitt and made it pucker like *blah blah*. "I've beheld your Topps card," he said.

"You've *beheld* it?!"

"It said you went a whole season with only eight strikeouts."

"Sure, the year I got this." Lucky showed off the Tommy John scar splitting his elbow's baked-potato tan. "*You* still ain't got a single K."

"You'll know when I finally do. It'll be in all the papers."

"Like that story with our pictures in it? Nice of Radcliffe to pull a stock photo of me at work. Free advertising!"

"You didn't ask Radcliffe to use it?"

"Nope, just like you didn't ask him to use that pic of you. Can't believe ya *liked* that hairstyle. Okay, let's get started. A four-seamer, then a circle-change, then repeat. Don't bother hiding the ball in yer glove, show me the grip each time. Remember to follow through."

"No radar?"

"Sorry, stretch, left the gun in the 'Vette. Got yer license yet?"

"My birthday's on Sunday. The test place is open late Tuesdays and Kitty gets tutoring then—that's my chance."

"Come by the dealership after yer test. It's on the way home. I'll set ya up in something nice."

"You keep saying. I can't afford it. *My* da don't own Pizza Putt like Sean Corgan's da."

"Plenty ways deals can be done." Lucky grabbed a ball and stepped in front of him, pretending to show him a new grip. "Don't move off the saddle, dusty. There's a scout here."

Calvin immediately moved off the mound, scanning the bleachers.

"Yer killin' me," said Lucky, waggling a finger like he was telling him off. "You must be the worst poker player ever. Be smooth, would ya? Guy's in the first base bleachers, second row, on the left."

The man stepped aside. Calvin scoped the bleachers before continuing his throws. The fellow so indicated wore a tan woolen pea-coat and a gray flat cap—standard costume for a lorry driver at a pub back in Leixlip, but a far cry from, say, Art's da in his black satin Pirates windbreaker and Vietnam Vet trucker cap.

"You talked about scouts but what are they, exactly?" the lad asked. "And don't say 'go camping and tie knots.'"

"Paid peeping toms," said Lucky. "They check out players, their skills, form, the shape they're in, how well they deal with crap."

"For who? For what? This is just practice. Not a game—practice."

Lucky fetched a pinch of dip. "Push down that stiffy, lemon slice, this dude ain't from the Yankees. Probably just Larsen Academy."

Gus, crouched sixty feet off, had been listening in. "Them rich kids are already afraid they'll lose to us farmboys!"

Lucky slit his throat at him, like *Shaddap, dumb-ass!*

Gus made the biggest show ever of shadding ap. Even Skip, all the way over at second base, noticed Gus shadding ap.

"Could be some local weirdo," said Lucky. "Yer an attraction, tiger. Folks ask me every day if yer the real deal."

"I'm getting that too."

"I'd love for you to be seen driving a nice ride from Lucky Cheeseboro GM Chevrolet." The guy popped his dealership polo.

"'To be seen?'"

"That's what I said. I won't use a nerd-word like 'beheld.'"

"You want me to be your own personal billboard? Lemme guess, that's how the world works: you scratch my back, I scratch yours."

"Teenagers and liberals look at it like that."

"Cuz that's the truth," the know-it-all fifteen-year-old said.

Lucky's shrug was well-rehearsed and powerful. He used it when a potential customer picked function over fun or Jew-ed out on a plush trim package. Sometimes Lucky added a glance at his watch and said some or all of this: "Did I mention this is a Rolex? Have ya seen me in my 'Vette, the envy of other dads, surrounded by the heaving cleavages of babes? Think you got any chance of that in a Corsica hatchback?"

The shrug was all Lucky gave Calvin ... and all it took. The lad automatically felt inferior. He gave it away by resetting the white J.V. mesh pinny over his shirt so it didn't bunch up and make him look fat.

"I don't make deals," said Lucky, "I have relationships. Like me and Skip. I love helping Perry out. The kids love my help. The school pays Skip a fee to do this. I don't get a dime."

"I'm sure you get *something* back. Like a free ad," said Calvin, waving at his dealership's placard on the outfield fence.

"Nah, I pay for that shit. Same with the corner spot on the Pizza Putt place-mats. Y'know what's more valuable? That big photo at the cash register of me and Tony Corgan deep-sea fishing. Pizza Putt customers ask him all the time about it. It puts 'Lucky Cheeseboro GM Chevrolet' in their minds. I'm not using Tony, or Perry. They're my pals. Like I said, it's a relationship."

Lucky nodded his head at the stands. "Them people never notice the outfield ads, but they *do* notice when I stop by during a game, when I meet parents in the stands, when I shake hands with the coaches on other teams. Some kid's dad'll ask me what it was like in the Bigs. I knew Hank Aaron and Carlton Fisk personally, man! Then I'll ask what they drive, and tell them it sucks compared to the Sierra's 4.3-liter V-6. It's got 160 horsepower, 235 foot-pounds of torque, and a stepside body so the cargo bed's nice and square."

Calvin said nothing, afraid to look silly again.

Blunt as a billy club: "You ain't gettin' on TV with me, Calvin, and you ain't gettin' a free car. But you in one of my cars *is* worth somethin', which means a big discount for you. And your parents."

"My parents?"

"Gotta be eighteen to sign. And to own a car."

This felt like a trap. He wanted to bluff or raise or something. "Lambo or bust, buddy," he said, imitating Lucky's TV ad voice, that operatic cowboy. "No shit-ass Chevy stepside for me, pardner!"

With a charming salesman grin: "We'll find the right fit for ya, shortcake! Now, if yer done breakin' balls, show me yer breaking balls."

FOUL

Perry Phillips ended the B.P. B.S. and put the Axes through one of his patented intrasquad simulated games. Batting orders, base occupations, and squads were subject to the manager's whimsy. Skip might throw a kid into a fielding position he'd never played, or ask the slowest turd to steal home; an exercise in, "Show me what you got!"

For Calvin, it meant sitting on the bullpen mound, watching.

Fans, on a midweek afternoon, in the biting cold, attended practice. Players who had a parent or gal-pal in the stands tried harder. Calvin felt left out. His father never came to extracurriculars: the seventh-grade production of *Romeo and Juliet*, any of Troop 666's pancake fund-raisers, that silly Junior Olympics thing his school back in Ireland did in 1980. Da had missed every event of Robbie's and Rose's, too. Calvin's eyes glazed over whenever Da talked about how much work he had at Schultz's Lumber or the Poolbeg E.S.B. Station before that. Even when the man took time off, it was for a strictly planned family vacation or house project. And where was Ma? She didn't work. She might enjoy coming and spying on other parents here. Calvin's only "fan" was some mysterious, dispassionate scout.

His gray eye caught two girls waving in the front row—Kitty and Abby! They huddled close in their big coats, russet and blonde hair swirling in the breeze. Kitty's salmon-pink pom-pom hat stood out. Calvin heard them calling his name. He popped the foamy doo-doo brown trucker cap off his head and waved back.

"Oooo!" Gus said, the universal kid noise for *Yer gonna be in trouble!* "We're spose'sta ignore the stands!"

Too late. "Only fans wave, 4!" said Skip from his lifeguard spot at second base.

"Sorry." Calvin put that cap back on. It fit better with less hair.

"Get'cher ass warmed up!" said Skip. "You're goin' in!"

Lucky called back, "He's warm! I'll go get the gun." The lanky dude danced back to the student lot.

Calvin looked down at Gus. "Well. This is it. Pitching for real."

Gus looked up at Calvin. A bloop of snot ran to the boy's upper lip, the kind of thing only a six-year-old would leave to dangle on his face. "You'll strike 'em all out, Calvin."

The Ape headed out onto the field of play, shaking himself to keep the blood moving. He mulled throwing a prayer at God, but let it go. He wished for a towel to hang off his belt to wipe the sweat off his palm, but Lucky said that was a serious no-no. The rosin bag was all you got.

Skip set up Calvin's first live action against the heart of the Varsity lineup: Paddy Millar, Ryan Phillips, and Brion Davey. The one, two, and four hitters.

The three hitter, Sean Corgan, stayed in as catcher. "Yeah, this'll be fun," the little wanker said when he reached the mound. "Me and him ain't gone over signals yet, Skip."

"No time like the present, Seanie."

Sean showed Calvin: "One finger means fastball, two for a changeup, three for a curve. If I pat my thigh, it means throw it to that side. Then you nod so's I know you understand. We do this cuz I'm pickin' the pitches for you, and so's I got an idea where you plan to throw the ball so it don't fly right past me."

"Focus on the catcher," said Skip, "not the batter or the chatter."

"I'm ready," said Calvin, steeling himself for this test.

"Bullshit, 4. Nothing like a little trial by fire!" Phillips went back to his lifeguard position at second and stood ramrod straight. His short sleeve ARMY T-Shirt and old man skin told the cold to go fuck itself.

Sean's doo-doo brown catcher regalia clattered as he ran back to the plate. Coach Falcone pulled down his umpire's mask.

"Play ball!"

His teammates and the two dozen fans cheered. As a right-hander, Calvin had the third base side in view. Jill Pedersen was among the fans in those bleachers. *What's she doing here? The girls got practice too!*

He tucked his glove under one arm to rub the ball with both hands, like Lucky showed him. He got on the rubber and looked at the plate. Paddy Millar, a switch-hitter batting left against the righty, got in the box and stared back with his salt-of-the-earth farmboy face.

Sean Corgan got in his crouch and signaled for a fastball.

Calvin Connor envisioned the pitch he wanted to make, then made it. The ball left his hand easy and a little high.

"Ball," said Falcone.

Lucky was at the backstop with his radar gun. "89!" he yelled.

"Only call 'em out if he breaks 90," said Skip.

Sean signaled for another fastball. Calvin threw it low this time. Paddy planted his foot but didn't swing.

"Two and nothing," Falcone said.

"90!" said Lucky.

"I said," gnashed Skip, "only if he *breaks* 90!"

Sean called for a third heater. Calvin threw it right down the middle. Paddy swung, late and low, popping it *waaay* up. Jason "Doggy-Door" Pearse, the third baseman, easily nabbed it in foul territory.

Claps from the bleachers. The first at-bat from the Next Big Thing was a success. "92!" Lucky said.

"66!" Skip called. "If you strike out, you're walkin' home."

66 was Ryan Phillips. He couldn't wear 666 so he picked the next best thing. He got in the batter's box, wearing the face of a cold killer. Friend or no, Ryan wanted the first hit off the blue chip.

Sean Corgan signaled with no fingers.

Calvin put his hands up like, *I missed that.*

"Ah shit, forgot that one." Sean signaled for time-out from Falcone and stood up. "That's the trick signal. It's a bluff. You shake your head like, 'No.' Then I make another signal and you nod. Got it?"

"Wait—I can tell you 'No?'"

"No you can't, chief. You're a brain-dead sped out there. You throw what I call for. Got it?"

Giggles from teammates. Calvin turned away.

The catcher signaled with no fingers. The pitcher said, "No!"

"No talkin' on the mound!" said Skip. "Shake or nod!"

Calvin was used to comments and questions during practice.

Game-time was evidently quiet-time. He shook his head at Sean.

Catcher signaled no fingers again. Pitcher shook his head again.

Catcher signaled one finger. Calvin got it now—Sean was using dirty game-day tricks against his own squad.

The fastball screamed out of Calvin's right hand, scorching the cool mountain air. Ryan wasn't sure what was coming and threw his weight into a swing that had no chance of catching up.

"3-2!" said Lucky.

Sean called for a fastball outside. Calvin painted the corner and Ryan reached for it. "Strike two!"

One of Lucky's speeches came back to him: "With yer stuff, you'll be in 0–2 counts a lot. If ya try to ring up the guy with a heater, you'll risk an extra-base hit. Waste a couple pitches first. Maybe he'll chase."

Sean disagreed. He signaled for the exact same outside fastball.

Ryan was so stressed over becoming Calvin's first strikeout victim—and the prospect of walking home, for Skip didn't make idle threats—that he swung wildly, so wildly his ass ended up on the dirt.

"Strike three!"

"3-4!"

A big cheer from the players. Ryan got up and dusted off his pants, ignoring his father's cries: "You swung at that? Are you blind?!"

Sean trotted out to the mound and covered his facemask with his mitt. "You broke your cherry. Ready for butt sex?"

"Butt sex?!"

The little wanker shoved up Calvin's glove-hand. "Goddamnit, it's mitts-up when we talk here! Do that in a game and it'll cost us big-time. And wipe that fuckin' smile off your face. Hitters see a pitcher smiling and their dicks get hard. We want them dicks *limp!*"

The lad dropped his glove down from his face. He wore a flat-eyed glare. A distant look, one that purred, *You talkin' to me, wanker?*

"Yes, that's gettin' *my* dick hard," moaned Sean. "I forgot to pack one of my dad's pieces today so no throwin' at Davey's head."

"You bring a gun to practice?"

"Pay attention, chief. Paint the corners. Cut the plate in half and Davey'll hit that shit to Pittsburgh."

Next up, the cleanup hitter, number 8-9 ... Brion Davey.

His swagger meant business. His glaring eyes meant ugly business. His gap-tooth snarl meant fugly business. Davey started at right guard and defensive tackle. He wrestled heavyweight, hurling fat Altoona Area High School fools out the circle like he was hurlin' some pesky prick's Science textbook in the trash. It was no secret Brion Davey took steroids. He had a deep voice, hairy forehead, pimply cheeks, shrinking penis, and passed for age twenty-six.

And for all that, the junior-shoulda-been-senior never seemed as old, as tall, as sculpted, or as confident as the little wanker Sean Corgan. Insecurity turned even the gooniest goon into a small boy.

"Gonna hit this faggot's fastball to the moon!" said Davey.

Calvin didn't take the bait. Poker face. He fetched the rosin bag. The gritty powder was ice cold on his skin.

Sean signaled for a fastball, a little inside please. Calvin stood and made the pitch. The ball slipped, bouncing to the plate. Davey hopped to avoid it. "Ball," called Coach Falcone.

"Not used to fastballs that *slow*," said Davey.

Snorts and giggles from the crowd, including one from Jill in the third base bleachers. The wind defeated Jill's Aqua Net, creating a wide curly explosion of auburn hair around her head. Her brown eyes were fixed on her man Brion at the plate. Her mouth opened a tad. Calvin fancied he could behold her tongue.

on his shillelagh

Calvin snuck a glance at Kitty and Abby in the first base bleachers. His girl's pink cheeks shivered. Abby was upset; her crush Ryan had been crushed quite badly.

He zoomed his vision back to home plate. He picked at the protective cup. Suddenly the straps felt too tight.

Sean signaled fastball outside. Calvin made it outside, all right. Sean leaned to snag it, then made a *calm down!* motion with his hands. "Frustrated pitchers strangle the ball," Lucky once said. "A calm pitcher handles the ball delicately, like a classy girl's right tit."

Kitty's tits were amazing. Round and fittingly heavy, the right size areola, the right color nipple. Everything he'd ever wanted. *Thank you, Lord,* he thought. It was a sin but c'mon.

Sean called for fastball away.

Calvin fired his best fastball to date.

Davey swung through it, and in what was becoming a motif, fell over. The goon had faced five fastballs from Calvin (two at his head, three at the plate) and 60% of them put him on his butt.

"85!" said Lucky from the backstop.

Cheers and woofing. "Same pitch, faggot," said Davey. "Do it!"

Hell no, Sean's two-finger signal said, *time for a changeup.*

Calvin shook him off.

The little wanker called for the change-up again.

Calvin shook it off again, making his eyes tight. *I wanna blow him away,* his un-poker face said.

"Throw the goddamn pitch I'm calling for, Connor!"

Sighing, Calvin hid his hand in the glove to change his grip the ball: an O.K. symbol with thumb and forefinger along one side and the remaining three fingers overtop.

The lad peeped at Jill. She was antsy, wiggling of her arse. *Hmmm, that arse!* Calvin's shillelagh whistled Dixie against the athletic cup.

Kitty's quote from "Filipinos" 4:13 came to him: *I have the strength for everything through him who empowers me.* He fired. The circle-change was as good as any he'd done in practice. The ball wobbled, knuckleball-ish. Most guys woulda held up, or swung early.

Calvin cut the plate in half, so Davey hit that shit to Pittsburgh.

Reggie Roberts, J.V. center fielder, raced back. Axe Park was 385 feet in dead center, the deepest outfield in the West Penn Conference. When his feet found the warning track, Reggie braced for impact. He jumped, glove high in the air, and smashed into the fence.

The ball landed about ten feet past him in the meadow beyond.

Defying Skip's longstanding order against homerun trots during simulated games, Brion Davey trotted the bases. No whoops or taunts or fist bumps. A big smile was all.

Calvin kicked the crusty infield grass in frustration and winced as the movement triggered pain under his stressed-out cup.

He retired the five hitter, Felon Adkisson, on three strikes, ending his inning. Thirteen total pitches. Only four balls. One run, no men left. Two strikeouts. One ejaculation.

Chapter 20

SCARING OFF A MURDER.
WEDNESDAY, FEBRUARY 15, 1989.

⚾ __CLUBHOUSE__ ⚾

THE SUN SHONE BLEAK orange on a curl of woods. A low breeze swayed the tired trees, sending shadows slow dancing across the snowy earth. A crow scout, standing high atop a bald maple, went *"Rrwk."*

Art Maguire's calculator watch beeped. "Top of the hour here on News Radio 1240 AM," he cracked.

Calvin Connor checked his White Window Swatch, the black face and hands barely readable in the gloom. "Mine's old-timey, no beeps."

"Mine's digital like his," said Ryan Phillips, "but I turn the beep off so it won't give away my position."

"Very tactical, Phillips Eclipse," said William Watson. "The Spazzster don't wear no timepiece—it's how the Man keeps ya down!"

"Shhh!" said Valerie Crenshaw. "You'll scare 'em off, Liam. They're *sooo* cute!"

"They already know we're here," said Abby Malone, her slanted face craned up to admire the crow.

"Crows are okay with humans being around," said Kitty Howe. Parked on the snowy ground with Calvin, she tilted her head to aim an ear towards the edge of the copse, where the rest of the murder noshed.

"A lot of humans ain't so okay when crows are around," said Art.

"Like farmers," said Calvin.

"And white folk."

A ripple of embarrassed laughter raced through the kids.

"Don't make this about that," said Calvin.

"In my life, it's *always* about that," said Art. "One time I was walkin' across these fields and this freight train was comin'—"

"Ooh did it have the kitty on the side?" said Abby. She reached over to lovingly grab Kitty's arm.

"Yeah, it was a Chessie System one," snapped Art. *"Anyway.* The engineer leans out the window, shakin' a fist at me, and he was all, 'Get the fuck away from the tracks, you dumb nigger!'"

"That never happened, mate," said Calvin.

"Blow me, Irish! You weren't there!"

"Neither were you, African, cuz it never happened. Freight trains are so bloody loud ... but you heard the driver yelling over that?"

Abby nodded at this logic. Spazz blew a snot rocket in concurrence.

The Ape went on: "Up close and standing still, no one can tell you're black, but some prick in a speeding train could?"

Art's long face dripped down, an ice cream cone melting. "You never believe me."

Val went *"Aww,"* at Art like he was a sick puppy.

"I believe it," said Ryan. "If it happened in your mind, Art, then it happened. Somewhere in the infinite reaches, it happened."

Abby perked up. "In some parallel dimension? What an awesome idea! Somewhere, there's me with a million bucks!"

"And me with a Lambo," said Calvin.

"And me with sight," said Kitty.

"And me with all of Maiden's albums on CD," said Spazz. At their gawks: "What? Mirror Universe Spazz has realistic goals!"

Art always had to come out on top when it came to weird examples: "And me married to Mary Jo Powell."

Abby sputtered. "The *Action News* lady?"

"Hell yeah. She's got that Janine from *Ghostbusters* thing goin' on. Nerdy girls want some of what I got!"

The others laughed.

Calvin said, "There's a dimension where you're actually black."

Art said, "I *am* actually black."

"Where you *look* actually black."

"But I still *am* black. You keep denyin' it but I'm black. I'm stuck between two worlds here. You wouldn't understand."

"The half-American bloke born in a foreign country has no hope of understanding," said Calvin, rolling his eyes.

"Just shut up."

"Y'know what I don't understand?" said Kitty. "Racism."

"Duh, cuz you can't see it," Art said, snippier than called for.

"Exactly. Close your eyes and everyone's the same. But people see colors and judge. That's why it's so stupid."

Art mulled that over and changed his mind. He lowered his glasses to peer over them and issue an appreciative nod to her.

"He nodded at you, like *thanks,*" Abby supplied.

Kitty smiled between her wide cheeks. "You're welcome, Art."

"Wait up," said Calvin. "We say a dark stormcloud is bad but a fluffy white cloud is beautiful. Is that *only* cuz of their color?"

"See how racism is embedded in the way you think?" said Art.

"'See' how sight is embedded in your talk?" said Calvin.

"'See' how colors lead to generalizations?" said Kitty.

"Okay, I gotta stop you there," said Art, getting snippy again. "The color of a cloud isn't just pigment. It says something about the nature of it."

"The dark ones bring storms," said Calvin.

"Is that bad? Rain is good for crops."

"I get what you mean," Val said to Art, "but it's, like, instinct too. Bright colors make little kids happy. Dark rooms make them scared."

"My mom is bright white and my dad is dark," said Art. "As a little kid, I was never scared of him. I was happy to see them both."

"*Hmmm,*" the kids said, mulling it over.

"Quit it, all of you," Kitty said, whipping her hands up and down at the elbow, her Arms of Frustration gesture. "Clouds and people are beautiful. Quit putting *bad* things on them. We're all God's creations."

"Even my herpes," said Spazz, scratching his nuts. "My beautiful Godly herpes."

The crow scout cast an eye down at him and went, *"Rewwww."*

Art said to Kitty, "How do you envision color?"

"She don't 'envision' anything, you arse," said Calvin.

Kitty grabbed his arm to calm him. "No, I get this a lot and Art wants to understand, so let me explain."

Calvin sighed like *Okay, whatever.*

"I've never had sight so there's certain concepts I can't grasp," the lass told them. "Like how pictures don't just show a person but also how the photographer took it, the lighting and angle and stuff.

"If there's two sheets of paper that are exactly the same except one's red and one's green, I'll never know, but most of the time there's other differences. People see mold on fruit and know it's bad. I can smell it a mile off. People think that when hair turns white, that's the only difference, but I can feel it. Hair that's lost its color *feels* different."

"That's cool and all," interrupted Art, "but I wanna know why green is your favorite color. How you can even *have* a favorite."

"I'm allowed to have a favorite, Art."

"No you can't, if you've never seen it!"

"*Yes I can,* cuz long ago I was taught how to make associations. That's how blind people 'envision' color—we are taught to tie each color's name with concepts that will define it for us."

Art gave her a snotty look.

Abby told Kitty, "His face says you're full of shit."

"Green," said Kitty, "is the color of grass and leaves, of things that grow, vegetables that are fresh, springtime after winter. Green makes me feel happy and ready to take on challenges. Green says *Go!* at the traffic light. It's the color of Christmas trees, when kids get excited and tear off the wrapping paper. I love that sound. Very few people have green eyes and they're considered special and beautiful."

"Okay," said Spazz, warming up to the idea, "but green's also the color of rotten flesh and snot and toxic waste and alien goo."

"And money," said Val.

"Too right," said Calvin, "greed and envy."

"Yes," said Kitty patiently. "Every color is tied to good things and bad things, or what people call good or bad. Green's still my favorite."

"How 'bout red?" asked Spazz. "Blood an' fire an' heat an' sex?"

"What about purple?" asked Val. "Grapes and kings?"

"Blue?" said Calvin. "Water and fish and floating?"

"Brown?" said Spazz. "Mud and squishy and havin' the squirts?"

The kids flooded Kitty with every color they could think of and everything they could associate those colors with. Abby, who'd been Kitty's friend their whole lives, helped answer the questions.

When it died down, Kitty took a breath. "You didn't ask about black or white," she said …

     … to Art. "Yo, I'm afraid of the answer!"

"What you *think* I'm gonna say is, adults taught me to stereotype them—white equals good and hope, black equals evil and despair," said Kitty. "But I don't do that. Black to me is cold, like at night. Mystery, like the night sky. Poetry and knowledge, like the ink on the page that forms the words. Silence, like in death. White is emptiness, like that blank piece of paper. It's cold and frozen, like ice and snow."

"I associate black with looking bad-ass," Ryan put in, sweeping a hand down his attire. Every stitch was black.

"For me, black is heavy metal!" said Spazz, making devil horns with his hands and banging his head.

"Sci-fi space battles and spiders and witches!" said Val.

"Guinness," said Calvin. "You all hate it but stout is God's gift!"

"For me, black is beauty," said Art. "Power. Strength. The hammer head and the anvil that break the chain. Black rules!"

"Unless it's in yer stool," said Spazz. "That means ya gots blood ups yer butt."

"*Ewww!*" they all went, then all leapt in the air as the Axsubewa Valley got rocked by a deep, groaning HONNNNNK!

A second groaning HONNNNNK! came, and a third, one every other second, echoing off the tall ridges surrounding the borough.

"It really is the dumbest fucking sound now," Calvin guffawed.

"It's the scariest noise I've ever heard," said Art, dashing to the edge of the copse and scanning the horizon for smoke.

"It's annoying is what it is!" said Abby, gnashing her teeth.

"I hear it in my nightmares," said Val.

"Me too," Art called. "That noise means people are in trouble. And other people, like my dad, are running *toward* that trouble." He came back to join the others. "Firefighters die all the time."

"Axsubeen Fire Brigade needs to get a normal alarm," said Calvin.

Spazz nodded. "One that don't sound like no rhino cumming."

The girls all went *"Ewww!"*

This gang's crow scout, Ryan, sat up abruptly. "Mummy alert!"

A loud *BOOM* rushed into the copse and the murder of crows dashed off, *caw!*ing crossly. The kids got to their feet. Art's gangly hand tugged at the strap holding his .410 across his back, debating whether he should brandish it or not.

The "mummy" left the sun-lit fallow farm fields for the copse's shade. It was Old Man Mueller, in the flesh (er, wrappings). His baggy duck canvas clothing creaked in contempt. His back was bent from years of servitude to the earth. Thick and shiny skin, like PVC piping. The mummy had no eyes to speak of. He carried his trusty Winchester Model 12 before him, keeping the dangerous end up and to his left. A wisp of smoke dribbled out of the barrel.

"Hey, Mr. Mueller," called Art, as friend and not foe. He dusted his hands to cancel out the invisibility afforded by his white arctic camo.

The other teenagers stood to form a clean row with Art. Some were nervous. Kitty smelled the anxiety and clutched Calvin.

"That you, Maguire?" Old Man Mueller's voice was crisp and crazy. He halted four paces away, close enough to be point-blank range but far enough to not get showered in ricochets and spatter. "Yer on the wrong side of the tracks again."

"So's you know," said Art, "I got my .410 across my back."

"That a fact?" Hans Mueller racked his shotgun. The spent cartridge flew out the ejection port, bounced on the snowy mud, and landed near Calvin's Reeboks. The fleeing crows laughed over their shoulders.

Art raised open hands. "You got coyotes in your woods!"

Spazz held up hands like a haunting specter. "And ghosts!"

"Ghosts?" the old man said. His teeth were on vacation.

"All the tunnels under your land," said Val, "from the old mines!"

"Christ almighty," said Mueller. "There ain't no tunnels under my land, I ain't buried no granddaughters in my pond, and there *ain't no ghosts* in my woods! You kids need to quit that shit about the Maggot Man. He's been dead goin' on seven, eight years now!"

The mummy's dry, crumpled face suddenly noticed Abby and Kitty in the line of kids and went pale, like he'd seen a ghost himself. The girls held each other but dared not breathe.

The barrel of Mueller's scattergun motioned at Spazz. "Off my property, you girly-haired gay!"

The headbanger and his skater chick turned and bolted. Val said,

"Good luck you guys!"

Mueller snorted. "That other one was a girl?"

He'd directed that at Calvin. "She does make that claim, sir."

Mueller snorted again. "You boys're always doin' stupid shit on my land. Snooping around. Testing contraptions. Going down on the neighbor girl. Sampling my corn."

Ryan, Art, Calvin, and Abby were each taken aback in turns.

The old man had nothing to say about (or to) Kitty.

"But 'least ya ain't brung no Millars over the border. Nothin' but lazy half-breeds, them Millars, spawn of a mick loser and a traitor whore ancestor of mine!" Old Man Mueller hitched the barrel of his Winchester on his shoulder. "Speaking o' the worthless Irish, I hear *yer* a big stink on the mound, Connor."

"Just rumors," said Calvin, "but thanks a million."

"Rumors? It was *news*—I saw it in the paper. A *rumor* would be how ya balled that rich girl out on the grass over on Faggot Lane."

"Begging your pardon," said Art, "but if he 'balled a girl on Faggot Lane,' wouldn't that be the most heterosexual thing ever?"

Wacky cackles left Old Man Mueller's dry throat: "Heh heh heh!" His breath slapped their faces, reeking of putrescent bacon.

"Don't bring that up again," Calvin told him, not checking his anger. "My girlfriend's right here."

"I'm glad *one* of you queers gets hay for his donkey."

"Please stop, Mr. Mueller," said Kitty.

The old man lowered a ridge that once was an eyebrow. "Oh … all right. Maguire—why'd ya bring this posse to my property, anyway?"

"I was gonna do a field-test," said Art.

"Another one? Go across the tracks and blow up Seamus's limp-dick trees, why don't ya."

"I like your trees better, Mr. Mueller. They're stiffer."

"Heh!" Mueller waved a hand like, *hurry up, ain't got all day.*

Art rallied his friends: "Yo, let's do it." Abby backed Kitty off to one side. Ryan fetched an RCA camcorder and got it rolling. Calvin pulled his wretched scarf of many colors over his mouth and readied a tin bucket; the water inside had been salted to halt freezing. Art fetched a nylon cord up and drew out the slack; the taut line fed to a wooden apple box ten feet up a nearby oak. Below the box, in the target zone, a Maguire Shotgun-Shell Mine version 5.0 lay buried. It had rubber bands holding the cartridge in a skirt made from a bent tin can with the tip of a penny nail fixed under the firing plate (the latest alteration; Art finally noticed the thumbtacks on all his prior betas had bent tips).

Art fixed a pair of old pilot's goggles over his ice blue eyes. "Stand by!" he cried. Without further preamble, he yanked the ripcord.

A trapdoor under the apple box swung open and six large rocks plummeted down. One of them set the M.S.S.M. off!

"Finally!" yelled Art. He dashed to the test site, Calvin at his heels, ready to douse. Abby and Kitty gave some applause.

Ryan's camcorder zoomed in—the fallen rocks were scarred by the pellets of buckshot. A whisper of white smoke oozed from the frayed cartridge shell poking out of the earth. Art put out an arm to prevent Calvin from dousing it. Dropping to his knees, the kid unearthed the spent M.S.S.M. with his bare hands. "Yo, not even hot!"

Calvin dumped the salted water and lined the bucket with an old towel. Art set the M.S.S.M. inside and held the bucket like an infant.

"Whoop-de-doo," said Old Man Mueller. "Don't go blowin' your balls off. Not like you'll need 'em."

Chapter 21
THUNDEROUS STAMPEDE OF PUSSY.
FRIDAY, FEBRUARY 17, 1989.

⚾ **CLUBHOUSE** ⚾

BUS NO. 10 LEFT at 2:37 full of teens hyped for the big dance tonight or feeling like losers cuz they had no dates. The Suicide Kings sat as a group: Art with Calvin, and in the seat behind, Ryan with Spazz.

"That was cool what Kitty said about racism being bullshit," said Art. "Wish I knew she was so open-minded. Woulda asked her out."

Calvin was nonplussed. "Odd thing to say to her boyfriend."

"I know. Just how I feel right now."

"Feel that way about some other girl. Who you taking tonight?"

"Ain't goin'. White girls won't go to the dance with no negro."

The lad sighed at him. "First off, notice how you don't hear *me* repeating that one word they all call Irish people?"

"You *should* say 'mick,'" said Art. "You take away its power then."

"Take away *your* word's power by not calling yourself that!"

"Calling myself what?"

Calvin made flat lips. "Nice try, mate, I'm not saying it."

Art pushed up his glasses. "It's fine when my friends say it."

"I thought you'd be, like, appreciative that I *won't* say it."

"Yeah, thanks. Whatever."

"You're as bad as Kitty! I can't say things like 'I see' cuz it upsets her, but when she asks me to be her eyes, then it's fine for me to say 'I see.' It's aggravating to constantly double-check my words!"

"We all got words that piss us off," said Spazz. "Like 'Journey.'"

The Suicide Kings turned as one to bug-eye him.

"One time I brung my CD boom box to poker to blast heavy metal music, and Sweet Tart here sez, 'You mean like Journey?'"

"It was a joke," Art yelped.

"Oh no," said Spazz, swinging his blond locks like a pendulum. "Oh no no *NO*, Artificial Hearty Farts, you were NOT joking. You actually think them heiny-hobbits in Journey are metal!"

"I hate that word," said Ryan.

"Which word, Phil-Leaps-the-Dips?"

Ryan's stark stare chilled them. "Heiny-hobbit. It's stupid. Who cares if people are gay? Let people be themselves."

"You're a poof all of a sudden?" said Calvin.

"Champ-een of the limp-wristed queens," said Spazz.

"Only fags stick up for fags," said Art.

Ryan reached over the seat and popped him on the shoulder.

Art was indignant. "Ain't my fault you're all so thin-skinned."

Calvin felt like punching Art's shoulder too. *"We're* thin-skinned?! You're the one who's all, can't say this, can't say that, can't complain at your jokes, can't bring up our chicks cuz you're single ... "

"I don't mind being single. Got time to do shit."

"Lemme rephrase that: can't bring up *sex* cuz you never get it."

"Fuck you, Connor. That's so uncalled-for."

"Your *standards* are uncalled-for. Shut your eyes and stop *seeing* the girls that you say aren't good enough. I bet one of them is."

"Here comes the sales pitch for Abby."

Ryan barked a single laugh. "She's not available, dumb-ass."

"Bro." Art looked over his shoulder with a scoff. "Yer actually serious about her? I thought you were just humorin' her to get her away from Kitty. And to keep Chicken from pervin'."

Ryan squinted, like *You thought wrong.*

"No offense, Ry," said Art, "but Abby ain't good enough for me."

"What's that?" Calvin yelled, hand cupped to his ear. "Can't hear you over the thunderous stampede of pussy headed your way!"

"Abby's a thunderous stampede all on her own, asshole!"

"My next punch'll 'stampede' your two front teeth," said Ryan.

"Sorry," said Art.

After a sec, Calvin said, "Me too. I never realized what a raging ape I was until Kitty came along." He offered to shake hands. "I'm sorry."

Art shook the hand and let his shoulders slump.

The bus stopped at Saint Brigid for kids who lived on this part of Main Street or nearby Cemetery Lane. Spazz debarked, yelling, *"I* ain't sorry, you Journey-lovin' heiny-hobbittin' mick-dickin' son of a coon!"

Art gave Calvin a friendly pop on the arm. "You can talk about Kitty. It's cool. I'm proud of ya. You guys get along. Not as in, makin' out and bumpin' uglies, I mean like a real couple. But it's hard to like a guy who's gettin' it on when my prospects suck."

"The lake's full of fish," said Calvin. "Just put a hook in."

"All the fish suck here. Back in Aberdeen I had choices. Here in Axsubeen I ain't got shit. Even Altoona's a washout. I hate this place."

"Me, too! I'd move to Dublin tomorrow. But I can't, so … I make the best of it. I'm doing good, wouldn't you say?"

"Gee, *wouldn't* I? Guess that means I'm fuckin' up royally."

"By doing nothing." Calvin pulled him down so they were hidden in their seat. "You want Jill, to ride and get inside?"

"Yes. But she's taken."

"Take her away. Give her that Lando Calrissian smile, that 'wink which makes the panties wet.' Davey can't stop you trying. If he does, great, I bet she'll love having boys fight over her."

"Too much work. 'Sides, she's stained now that Davey's got her."

"You got her first—behind the shed at Corgan's party."

"Not puttin' *my* long-schlong-a-ding-dong anywhere *he's* been."

"Well. Uh, what about Detta Roberts?"

Art issued a hollow laugh. "You mean the only sister in town? Who's a senior, to boot?!"

"Then pick a sophomore. Or a freshman."

"If I take a white girl to the dance, Paddy and Felon and them farmboy crackers'll dangle me from a tree." Art turned away. "'Cept Mia Pintcure. No peckerwood's gonna lynch me over Mia Pintcure."

"Do us a favor, Art. You can do better than Mia Pintcure."

"How about you put in a good word for me with Jenny? I think she'd say yes, cuz datin' me would get her closer to you."

Calvin threw up his hands. "You fucking cunt! This is your problem, not mine!"

Art slapped him. *"Shhh!* Everyone can hear!"

"Ask a girl out, any girl! It gets easier after the first one."

The bus slowed down for Cherry Street, Art's stop.

"Jill's right up there, Art. Ask her to the dance on your way—"

Art was all, "Nah," as he vaulted over to the empty seat in front of them. Over his shoulder: "See ya at poker tomorrow."

The Irish Ape tried not to rage.

FOUL

At the Maple Street stop, Pete and Justine Hennessey and Ryan Phillips headed straight home. Jill Pedersen hesitated, watching Calvin.

"What I do this time?" he said. "Wrong color shoes for a Friday?"

"No, white shoes are versatile. It's those pants!" She waved at his Levi's; he'd dribbled bleach on them in a lame attempt to recreate the expensive brands' professionally bleach-dribbled jeans.

"I'll take them off right here if you like." He grinned. "Maybe *my* knickers are lilac too."

Jill whipped around so huffily she lost her grip on her books. Her Social Studies text sailed into the snow on the Phillipses' front yard.

He fired off his guffaw. Dipping a shoulder, she said, "Can you *pleeeease* get it for me? I don't wanna get my lavender Chucks wet."

"But it's fine if my Reeboks *do* get wet?"

"… like I said, white shoes are versatile."

"Girls're so greedy."

"But you're my friend, Calvin. Dare I say it."

Grumbling at that, he hopped over the snow to fetch her book. He stumbled during his hurtle back onto the driveway. An old crow loafing in a bare Japanese maple went, *"Whrr-tsssh!"*

Jill nearly wet herself. "That bird did a whip-crack sound!"

"Piss off, cunt!" he said. At her glare: "I was talking to the crow."

Her lips, lathered in boysenberry liniment today, went, *"Suuure."*

The kids headed home side-by-side. With no sidewalk and knowing Jill's fear of traffic, the Ape positioned himself on the outside.

"What do you wanna be when you grow up?" said Calvin.

"Far away from here," said Jill. "College, then married, with a family, in a real nice neighborhood."

"Davey's too dumb for college. He'll be intimidated by a woman with a college degree."

"He ain't afraid of nothing, Connor. Shut up. What do *you* wanna be? The fattest ape at the zoo?"

"Fuck off. Once upon a time, you *dated* this Irish Raging Ape."

"Don't remind me."

"You Mall Chicks suck at picking men in general. Kare acts like she won the lottery, the way she's so proud of Sean, but I hear she's totally bored with the little wanker's crap."

"Where you get your information from, huh?"

"I got my spies. And I behold her droolin' at me."

"You and your 'behold,'" laughed Jill. "Wake up and smell the coffee, dude, Kare'll never drool over a talking ape."

"She looks at me like how *you* used to look at me. Maybe she's the one who's been calling our house and hanging up."

"That's happened to me too. Whoever's doin' it should stop." She dropped a hand to pull the hem of her white denim skirt back down. Mall chick fashions never forgave Jill's puffy thighs.

"You should wear that tonight," he said. "Looks good on you."

"I got an awesome dress for the dance. Wait up, did you just compliment my fashion?"

"You're having a wet dream, Pedersen."

"Goddamnit, *stop* talking to me like I'm one of your guy friends. Give me some respect as a person!" She popped him with a fist.

They passed the driveway at 32 Maple, home of old Ray and Laurie Schaefer and their two ancient German shepherds, Piper and Aldo.

"I'll make sure me and Brion stay far away at the dance," she said.

"Thanks a million, we'll keep our distance too," he said.

"Going to Corgan's party afterward?"

"We can't. This is Kitty's first dance and her da is chaperoning. He'll never let her out of his sight."

Jill smirked. "That'll force you to take things slow. Like I do."

"With Davey, you can't go slow enough!"

"*Awww,* are you jealous?"

"Gimme a break. I just don't want that prick procreating."

"Ugh."

"I'm stunned he agreed to go to a dance. 'Only faggots dance!' Ha,

I can totally behold him saying that."

"Don't talk about him like that. He's better than you think."

"He couldn't be any worse." They reached his driveway, at 34 Maple. "Well. Hope you two have a good time now."

"Thanks." She nodded at him. "I kinda like New-Calvin, who's my friend, dare I say it. No one else tells me they hope I have a good time with Brion. They judge. They make jokes."

"I'm dating a blind girl. All I hear is judgment and jokes."

"Y'know what Momma says to me? 'Brion's okay, but he's nothing like my kiddie kindred soul next door!'"

Calvin bucked. "Your ma still calls me that?"

"I think *she* wanted to date you."

"What a gross concept."

"Momma's happy I have a boyfriend but wants me to be more like her, and go from guy-to-guy. No way! I'm not that kinda girl!"

"You already *do* go guy-to-guy. This is your third in three years!"

"My *third?* You, Brion, and who?"

"Art, that one time."

"Maguire?! Yeah *right!* I'm no nigger-lover."

"Again, you already *are.*"

Jill crossed her arms. "What're you talkin' about?"

"Art told us all about that time you two got hot and heavy behind the shed in Corgan's back yard."

Her dangling jaw, her flat eyes …

Calvin instantly knew Jill had never lived through this scenario.

"What else did Maguire say?" she prompted. "Did we do it?"

"You didn't get the chance. He said you guys were making out, 'titty under the shirt,' then Zedz puked on the shed. You ran inside and passed out on top of Kare and they took Polaroids."

"And you believed him? I mean, you ever *seen* these Polaroids?" Jill headed for her house up at 36 Maple. "I know ya only do girls on Corgan's *front* yard, but if you go tonight, check out his *back* yard."

FOUL

Ma stood sentinel at the glass block wall and slapped him across the face with an envelope. "Write this fake redser back and tell her no more. You should *not* be getting post from other girls. Or talking to your ex-girl-friend in the drive—*oi!* Where are you going?"

He shut his unlockable bedroom door and hoped Ma didn't barge in. The envelope had no photo this time, only a single page written in shlurpy pink ink, for Valentine's Day. Too drained to read it all—Wren's letters had lots of rhetorical questions—he skipped to the end:

> Maybe your desparate for a date.
> Checking dishrooms all thru ~~Axsu~~
> Axsubeen haha. But look here, my
> single ray of sunshine, <u>I'm</u> getting
> desparate yelling at a dude 1000
> miles away cause he ain't writing
> me back!!

He usually heard Wren's voice in his head, reciting with her little laughs between sentences. He didn't this time.

He set the letter aside.

FOUL

His built-in operating system (BIOS) had boy presets (wear whatever) that'd been overwritten by Jill and Jenny (call girlfriend before dressing). God forbid he wore something too similar/contrasty!

He called Kitty. She wasn't home, naturellement. She'd gone shopping for last-minute stuff with her older brother Eddie.

The Ape stood before his closet and put his bruised brain to work. It's a formal, right? Wear black. But Valentine's has its own colors: red and pink. He owned no red or pink. Neutrals, then. Jill's rule: white and gray go with pretty much everything. Jenny had bought him a silver silk club shirt cuz it matched his gray eyes and lacked a fag-tag.* He had

---

* Or "locker-loop." Many '80s button-downs had a hoop sewn on the middle-back to allow the shirt to be hung on a hook. Jenny MacDonald *hated* them. And after witnessing a Homecoming prank when some senior speared an unfurled condom on a bent paper clip and hooked it to a freshman's fag-tag, Calvin hated them, too.

white Wranglers from last year and tried them on. They fit his waist but rode his ankles way high, like *Revenge of the Nerds* high, even before pegging them. The correct resting point for pegged cuffs was an inch above the shoe; pegging these Wranglers took the cuff above his sock.

"She's blind, she won't notice, she doesn't know about fashion." All three statements were true. He hated how much he thought about her blindness. He just wanted to be with her.

"Other kids will notice, tell her, and make fun of you." All three of these, likewise true. He hated how much he cared about what other kids said about him. He rolled down the cuffs and sat on the bed. The jeans looked like capris now. *You don't care.* Except he did. *You don't!*

Sucking in a breath, he kept the Wranglers on.

The Davey Dangle came off stupid no matter what he did to style it, so tonight, he decided not to bother. No gel or mousse. No Aqua Net splash-damage sticking to his forehead. In fact, he vowed never to use that dumb shite again. Next time, he'd ask for a man's short buzz, like Fartin' Martin's butch thing. Save millions on Prell alone.

He went to Rose's room. "Well. How do I look, Sis?"

Rose laughed so hard she nearly swallowed her Hubba Bubba. "Queer," she said.

"So do you," he said, lamely.

She looked stylish, in fact. Her teased and shellacked hair bounced in jolly black clumps. Her pink dress had a single white stripe across the bumps. Its lacy skirt poofed out, showing lots of white-hosed leg.

"Easy access for hands and/or penises," he said. "Who's your date then? Your ex-boyfriend, Asshole?"

"Pfft, I ain't goin' to no dance. I'm not a child like you."

"Then you're going to Plastique Chic."

"Under-21 clubs are for losers like 'the MacDonald wench.' I'm goin' where a girl can get a stiff drink."

"Eons, then. I hear a girl can get a lot of stiff things there."

"Eons blows! We're goin' to Wanker's."

Calvin still couldn't believe there was a club in Duncansville called that. "That'd be funny, you jerking off guys in a place called Wa—"

She two-handed his chest to get him the fuck out of her room.

Chapter 22

WHITE DENIM, BLACK LABEL.

FOUL

DAYS LATER (IT SEEMED), Da Howe pulled up in a sapphire blue '87 Chevy Celebrity wagon. The novelty front plate had "Eric & June" with a rose forming the ampersand. Calvin was so embarrassed that this was their ride to the dance.

Some girls went crazy dolling up for dances and formals. Kitty had the same plain straight hair, wore a typical outfit of white top, pink cardi over it, wispy floral-print skirt pulled up a bit too high on her belly, white thigh-highs, pink flats. This was her first dance.

Ma Connor posed the young couple by the glass block wall for a flash photo with her Kodak Instamatic 60 while Eric Howe and Calvin the Second bullshitted about the Pirates. The team had a bright future: Bobby Bonilla, Andy Van Slyke, Bobby Bonds's kid, Doug Drabek. Kitty's head turned when Calvin's da mentioned John Smiley.

The lass sat up front in the wagon, Calvin in the back. Da Howe didn't let them share the back seat. Just to be a lad about it, Calvin held his shillelagh the entire trip.

"I brought change to call for a ride back," he said.

"Abby offered us a ride home, too, Daddy," Kitty added.

"It's okay, I'm gonna drop you off and go park," said Da Howe.

"You don't hafta stay!" Kitty said. Whined. Upset.

The man's mustache wobbled. "Smiley, it's your first dance. You don't even have your cane tonight."

"Cuz it's a *dance,*" she said, as if talking to an idiot. "You can trust Calvin to take care of me. He's got a jingle bell on and everything."

The lad had safety-pinned a jingle bell to his scarf as a locator beacon but she'd brought a new one tonight, fastened to an earring hook. He refused to pin it to his collar ("I'm not a dog,") and she refused to let him put it on his belt ("I'm not one either!"). They settled for his left breast, where the silver club shirt's pocket would've been, had it not been a club shirt.

"How will you hear it with all that jungle music, Smiley?"

"Daddy, we talked about this."

Da Howe made eye contact with the lad through the rearview. "I'll stay outta the way," he said. The words, for her. His glare, for Calvin.

The high school lobby's fluoro banks shone out into the dark night. The Office and the hallway to the gymnasium likewise shone bright. Every intersecting corridor was a dark cave mouth. Chaperones stood everywhere, even at the locker room entryways (they were the closest bathrooms), teachers and parents, men like Da Howe with daughters to keep an eye on, women well aware of the tricks boys pulled to sneak off for a hip flask hit, a spliff sniff, a geek depantsing, a titty fondle.

Arm in arm, Kitty and Calvin strolled towards the echoes of laughter and pop music. She wore her dark glasses. No Excalibur; a treat for her but extra responsibility for him. That was fine. He wanted this. He wanted to be with her.

"This is exciting," she said, her voice swimming in joy.

"We'll hear plenty of comments," he said.

"Who then are they to judge?"

"We are a puff of smoke, love."

Perry Phillips stood by the gym doors, his son Ryan nearby. Both filled Sunday suits with puffed chests. Calvin said hello and Kitty followed his lead. Skip was on duty tonight, grim thousand-yard stare homing in on Kitty's tight hold of Calvin's arm.

"Ryan, is Abby here?" Kitty asked.

Sergeant Slaughter shot his son a glance. Calvin led Kitty into the gymnasium at once. "I don't think Skip approves of Ryan and Abby."

"Dads suck," was Kitty's assessment.

The gym was dark. Two strings of red and white paper lanterns ran crisscross, drooping weak pools of light on the hardwood. The Student Council blew it on that one! The far bleachers were racked shut and festooned with pink streamers and hand-painted banners. The near bleachers had been pulled out. A dozen of the cafeteria's small tables sat nearby, each covered in pink tissue with a centerpiece flower made of curled and stapled construction paper.

The D.J. was Base Master Brent. He originally traded under the name Bassmaster Brent but grew tired of phone calls about fish. Brent had a pair of dialed-in PARcans on T-stands with crusty red gels. The rig was *waaay* chintzy, but full overhead scaffolded lighting arrays were verboten at Axsubeen High after *Carrie* came out. The Base Master himself, a slender youth of twenty, cued up vinyl for the next song and bopped his head bodaciously. Some might say, bogusly.

"He's got a Jackson Jacket on!" Calvin filled the gymnasium with his big guffaw. "An honest-to-God Michael Jackson Jacket!"

"So many zippers," Ryan supplied.

Even Kitty hadn't heard him sidle up. The jingle bell on Calvin's shirt jangled to the beat of his heart attack.

The speakers screeched: *"Alll riiighty!* Yer hangin' with me, the main man, Base Master Brent! Welcome to the 1989 Valentine's Day Dance at Azzubean High School! How is everyone tonight?"

Sixty kids gave a collective fartish noise.

"Is that the D.J. or a chihuahua?" burped Kitty.

"'Master of bass,' my arse!" said Calvin.

Ryan barked a laugh. "More like, 'trainee of treble.'"

"You early birds all know," Base Master Brent went on, "the early bird gets the worm ... in the bottom of ... every bottle of ... "

Brent let his turntable go, playing *that saxophone song with one word of lyrics that is also the title.**

Abby Malone arrived in a billowy red dress, red lipstick, and too much metallic pink eye shadow. Her blonde hair was balled-up, reminding Calvin of a crumpled snot rag. *Why do girls always wear their hair so dumb for formals?* thought the teenaged boy with a buzzcut featuring a nutsack backflap down his collar.

The big girl took her spot next to Ryan. Around that slice of beefcake, the only slant to Abby's face was upward in delight!

Spazz Watson and Valerie Crenshaw sloped up in matching tuxedo

---

* Making an alliterative synonymic puzzle not possible. The only clue you get is Base Master Brent hopping on the mic to say, "I'm a loner, Dottie. A rebel!"

T-shirts, black jeans, and red Chucks. The bone-thin, breast-free duo smelt of Marlboros and rye whiskey.

Sean Corgan and Karen McGillicutty deigned to stop by on their long circuit of being nice to every attendee's face. Kitty and Abby's friend Roni Vogel came up in a Mario Lemieux Penguins jersey (home white). Her doofus junior boyfriend Bob Mueller also had a Lemieux jersey (away black). Ryan kinda loved it—each jersey had six 6's.

This crowd became its own little party. Things got spicy when Roni Vogel said to Calvin, "Couldn't help notice you and Jill havin' a chat after you guys got off the bus today!"

Kitty gripped Calvin's hand. The kids all went *"Oooo!"*

"You two-timin' son of a shamrock," said Sean Corgan.

Spazz jumped in for the defense: "Chill with that jazz, Corgandalf! You slander my pal Conn-feti here and I'll nuke yer ass!"

Val flung her pipe-cleaner fingers out, like *Bwsssh!*

Roni sidled up to Kitty. "Me and Bob drove right past Irish here and he didn't notice. Guess the talk was too hot and heavy!"

Calvin sighed at her. "You wanna know what me and Jill talked about? You won't believe it."

"What?" asked everyone.

"We talked about how people jump to conclusions and spread gossip and try to ruin each other's Valentine's Day."

"Seems convenient," laughed Roni.

"I believe it," Kare hooted. She was a hooter.

"We're not *gossiping* here," said Abby. "We're asking you flat out."

"May God strike me dead," said Calvin. "We also talked about whoever's been calling our phones and hanging up."

A universal reaction—every kid was like, "Yeah, that happened to me too!" All except Val, a denizen of the trailer park with her Granny. The old woman rarely had enough cash for the phone bill.

"If only we could trace the call like cops in the movies!" said Bob.

"Who here's buddy-buddy with Sheriff Steve?" asked Sean.

"Oh, we *know* who's making the calls," said Kare. She pulled in the other girls: Roni, Val, Kitty, and Abby. As unlikely a fivesome as Axsubeen High ever saw but the Mall Chick Queen was rounding up a posse. "You're all invited to the party at Sean's tonight," Kare told them, "and if Jenny MacDonald crashes it, if she shows her goddamn face, we kill that bitch. Right girls? We kill her."

"Yeah!" said the girls, plus Calvin and Sean (exes of Jenny, whose currents were right there).

"Jenny ain't invited," said Sean. "She's been banned from my property ever since that one time—"

"When you caught her stealing the silver?" Calvin zipped in, before the wanker could mention his front yard.

Kitty was excited to be invited to the party and told Kare thanks. The Mall Chick Queen shooed the Irish Raging Ape away so she could give Kitty a hug. Abby said, "Aww."

"I hope you come," said Kare to Kitty ... while looking up from Kitty's shoulder at Calvin. Giving him *that* look.

The lad's blood froze, except for a boiling half-pint or so down low.

Base Master Brent spun that Jazzy Jeff/Fresh Prince *funny fable about funky frights freighted in the flesh from fantasy to their freeway*. When the boys started debating which *Elm Street* movie sucked hardest, Kare pulled Sean away to resume their greeting tour of the plebes.

Abby scored an open table for her and Ryan and Kitty and Calvin. "Oooh we gotta figure how to get away from my dad," said Kitty. She took Calvin's hand again, gripping it to powder. "I've never been to a real high school party!"

"There'll be a lot of smoke and puking," warned Calvin.

"And booze and leftovers from Pizza Putt," said Ryan.

"And Spin-the-Bottle," said Abby. "But they'll only play it until the bottle points at Ugly here. Then it'll break."

Ryan laughed. Calvin knew where Abby could shove that bottle.

"I don't think we should go," the lad said. "Lots of temptation."

"Oh bullcrap," said Kitty, "what're you, Father Sean?"

"I have to behave, love. Part of the new me. And I'm responsible for you and all."

"That's the point. You'll be my crow scout there. It's not fair that you got to go to parties and I didn't. This is my chance!"

Calvin looked at Ryan and got a shrug.

He looked at Abby and said, "Back me up on this?"

"Back you up?!" said the big girl. "I oughta back you out the goddamn door!"

"Stop," Kitty told her. "I think it's sweet. He's trying."

"If you wanna go, love, then I guess we'll go," said Calvin. He stood up. "Who's thirsty? 'Scuse me a sec."

The snack table was on the far side of the dance floor, where a few kids wiggled their hips and did white-boy overbites. Calvin looped the perimeter, aware of every gawk and comment, every swoon and smile, every finger pointed at the high unpegged cuffs of his white Wranglers.

He paused at the D.J. table and made a request.

Treble Trainee Brent gave an insouciant nod, like *Maybe, pal.*

Ryan joined Calvin at the snack table and they gathered up four cups of punch and a paper bowl of chips. "No way Kitty's da will let us go to the party," said the lad.

"Wrong. Follow my lead." Ryan headed for the gym entrance, where Perry Philips and Eric Howe stood as crow scouts in their own way.

"Hey, Dad?" said Ryan. "Karen McGillicutty invited us all to a party afterwards."

"Yeah?" said Skip. "Who's drivin'?"

"Abby has a car."

Da Howe's walrus mustache went prostrate in distress. "I dunno."

Calvin said, "Kitty's real excited to go."

"I heard about these parties, Calvin."

Who hasn't? gulped the Ape.

"This one's not at the Corgans' house? It's at Karen's?"

"Kitty says she's never been to a party before," noted Ryan.

Da Howe looked over at Skip, who said, "What time you gonna be back?"

Ryan and Calvin exchanged a shrug. "Midnight?"

"Before then. Junior license expires at midnight."

"Great, thanks," said Ryan, turning and leaving.

Calvin stood there alone, awkward, and told Kitty's da, "I'll tell her you said yes."

"No, wait … I'll drive you two there."

"We have a ride, Da Howe."

"I want to come. And look around and make sure it's safe."

"You want to *go* to the kiddie party, Eric?" said Skip with a smirk.

"Don't worry," said Calvin, backing away from the men. "Abby'll be there too, and tonight I'm Kitty's crow scout."

He hustled to catch up to Ryan. "Fuckin' A, it worked! We just bluffed Sergeant Slaughter!"

"Not a bluff," said Ryan. "We made a big bet and watched them fold. I knew my dad would say 'fine' and that put *her* dad on the spot."

The girls cheered the good news. Ryan drew a silver flask from his black suitcoat. "Who's in?"

Abby made wide eyes. "Me me! Kitty? Spiked punch?"

"You don't have to," Calvin told Kitty. "No pressure."

Kitty needed a moment. "Yes. But gimme only a little bit."

Ryan blooped Johnny Walker Black in three of the drinks. Calvin said no. Abby distributed the cups, giving Kitty the weakest one.

"Sláinte!" said Calvin.

Kitty asked, "What is that, Gaelic?"

"Irish. It means 'your good health.'"

"Pray for mine!" Kitty took a sip and coughed. *"Ewww!"* she wailed, and her free hand did that herky-jerky thing.

Calvin purposely spilled his cup on the table's tissue cover, giving him an excuse to stand up and block Kitty's actions from her da's eyes.

"Smooth," said Ryan. "I'd high-five you but I'm not an idiot."

"It was literally a splash of booze, chowderhead," Abby told Kitty in a Moe Howard voice.

Calvin placed his palms on the table. "I'll get water for you."

As Kitty: "No, it's fine." As Lady Em: "I shall manage. I am just not used to it." She sipped with caution.

Abby stuck out her tongue at Ryan, who stared at it like he'd never seen a girl's tongue and wondered what it might taste like.

"Never slow danced before," Kitty suddenly said.

"I have," said Abby. "At summer camp. 'Member Li'l Joey?"

Kitty smiled at this memory. "Yes, I loved Li'l Joey! I hope he's still little. I hope my first dance is …"

"… magical?" Abby finished, cocking her head.

The D.J. came on the P.A.: "Let's slow things down for all the love birds out there." Warbly piano notes filled the gym.

"Cool, he played it," said Calvin, fetching Kitty's hand without prior verbal permission. "Voulez-vous danser avec moi?"

She corrected him: "'*Veux-tu* danser avec moi!' We're not in vous-land anymo—oh *oui!* Oui, allons danser!"

As Phil Collins *supplicated his sweetheart's assentation that they shared a savor suitably similar to sequentially fissured stripes,* Calvin Connor took Kitty Howe to the floor for her first slow dance. Kitty held him tight, head on his chest. She was alone with him at last.

The Irish Slow Dancing Ape did not want the song to end.

⚾ CLUBHOUSE ⚾

Kitty's cheeks glowed with excitement. "Can't believe we're actually going to a party! I totally thought Daddy would say no!"

Calvin checked over his shoulder. The rear window of Abby's 1982 Honda Civic was crusty with pollen from being constantly parked under a tree. The cars behind them on Rte. 666 (Bald Eagle Pike) could've been a Chevy wagon, or anyone—Calvin didn't know one headlight package from the next.

"He took convincing," he said. "He was all, 'I want to come.'"

"Daddy wanted to *come* to the party?" said Kitty.

"Not just come, but come inside."

"That's totally off-limits."

Calvin tugged at his collar.

"He doesn't trust you yet," said Kitty, "but he had to face the facts. I need to be on my own tonight. And you'll be my crow scout."

"*Caw.* I'm more afraid of *Ryan's* da showing up. Dropping out of a tree in his camo outfit with a dagger between his teeth."

Abby's slabby hands worked the wheel, turning the Civic into Overlook Estates. "Which way? Never been here before."

Ryan, riding shotgun, waved ahead. "Straight. At the end of the development there's a Y. Cloven Cape is the one on the right."

"What kinda stupid name is that for a road?"

"They're all C-words: Crest Cay, Canyon Curve, Cove Court."

"Except this street—Overlook Lane," said Calvin.

"The only non-C-word," said Kitty, "is a sighted word."

"Well," joked Abby, *"this* C-word says they're dumb names."

They all laughed.

"Goddamn you got a loud laugh, Irish," said Abby.

"Irish." Not "Ugly." Calvin told her, "Thanks a million."

Abby turned the little sedan down Cloven Cape. It was a dozen homes on a short lane ending in a cul-de-sac. "Park here," said Calvin. "The driveway's always jammed."

The big girl cozied up to the verge and put her little sedan in park. Ryan and Calvin tried to open their doors but the tall curbside Belgian block went *Scrrrch!* "It's fine," said Ryan, "do the clown car!"

The girls got out the driver-side doors and the boys slithered out behind them. The night was alive with the thump of pop music, teen girls laughing, teen boys going *"Whoa!"* The kids left their coats in the car. Abby clutched Ryan for heat—it was too bitter a night for only a dress. Calvin wanted Kitty to go by his side, but on this unfamiliar turf she insisted on following behind him with a hand on his shoulder.

Overlook's McMansions had horseshoe driveways with a siding to the three-car garage. Pizza and water ice with family fun (arcade games and mini-golf) was such a cash cow that the Corgans splurged for the inlaid brick driveway. A dozen cars were jammed along the horseshoe. Kids passed a dozen drinkable and smokable things around.

"Is that cigarettes?" asked Kitty. "Smells funny."

"Got me," lied Calvin. He gave the Burn-Out Buds a silent nod.

The front door was wide open; the little wanker was evidently born in a barn. Clusters of teens in the entrance foyer had a gander at the freaky foursome. Ryan, fit and famously Satanic, cute in his suit, drew looks of intrigue. Calvin and Abby got sneers, like *Who invited the heifers?* Kitty got pointed at like she was some strange primate, *oh look, the proboscis monkey is real, isn't it funny how it moves, ha ha.*

Japes and wails carried up the curvy staircase to the second floor landing and cathedral ceiling beyond. Careless young hands tested fate, flailing beer cans just past a giant goldfish bowl resting atop a marble pillar in the center of the foyer's slate tile floor.

There were upperclassmen, recent graduates, and/or friends of Sean's sister Amy. Axsubeen was a small town—the high school held about 500 total pupils in grades 7–12—yet to Calvin, older teens were mere faces. He was good at identifying which legacy families the Mueller and Millar and Schultz kids were from (if bad at recalling their given names and suffix numerals).

Later in life when his social map will become more densely packed, Calvin will form a theory on why he never learned these older kids' names: "If they weren't already my friends, didn't go to my Mass, and I didn't want to fuck them … then who cares."

He *did* know a few. Like Heather Buschfeuer—the puffy senior lass stuck out in any crowd with her flaming red hair and permanent OshKosh B'Gosh overalls. Seeing Bonnie Vaupel made him do a double-take and say, "How've you been?" Bonnie had been Anthony "Sandy" Sandmiller's first girlfriend; last year, she transferred to Portage High. And he knew Shelley Quince, one of the swim team girls (the Breast Strokers). Shelley had chicken legs and ostrich feet but it was her chest, puffed out like a sage grouse, that ruffled all the boys' feathers.

Kitty didn't notice Calvin's turned head but Abby did. The big girl gave the Ape a slap on the back of his inane Davey Dangle haircut.

Calvin & Co. went single-file into the living room and past the Corgans' famous gold-leaf sun painting. Art Maguire said it was the same design as on King Arthur's chest in *Monty Python and the Holy Grail*, "only stupider." Music blared from a fancy hi-fi, *Bobby Brown contending that no clearance from the crowd is compulsory for his choices.*

The Irish Raging Ape huddled his shrewdness and told them, "Let's get a drink! Follow me!"

The kitchens in these McMansions were larger than Calvin's whole Usonian house. A marble-topped island thingy with six stools sat in the middle of the room under a pendant lamp (with the classic Tiffany cherry blossom shade). A separate table in a nook sat five comfortably for quick meals and had its own Tiffany (pendant inverted). The fridge had a mirror finish; the stovetop was some kinda *Star Trek* shit with an all-glass surface. A marble countertop wrapped around two walls, featuring a double sink and a built-in water dispenser. A wall-cutout gave easy access to the stately dining room. On the marble floor tile beneath said cutout, three Igloo coolers sat filled to the brim with drinks on ice. Every flat surface had Pizza Putt boxes; the hungry teens had destroyed most of the pizzas. Lots of bottlecaps and cigarette butts.

Many ball players were here: Felon Adkisson, Zedz Dzedzy, Paddy Millar and his sister Steph, Anna Schultz, Detta Roberts, Snatch Mueller, plus boy/girlfriends; Sean Corgan was holding court. When Calvin & Co. entered, the little wanker called them over.

"Great to shee you, thanksh for coming! Grab a drink and mingle! Kare'sh around shomewhere." Sean scanned for his girlfriend. "Oh, Jon Oldroyd'sh here! He livesh nearby. You guys know him, right?"

"What about Davey?" asked Calvin. Kitty clutched his arm.

"What about Chicken?" asked Ryan. Abby clutched his arm.

"What about your parents?" asked Kitty. Calvin rolled his eyes.

"What about everybody chill out?" said Sean. His words stank of booze. "My folks alwaysh go outta town on Valentine'sh Day to the no-tell motel. And I promish the Scoundrelsh'll be on our besht-esht behavior." The little wanker blinked his emerald eyes. "Asshuming them fuckersh ever *get* here. I mean, was Reggie even *at* the dance?"

"Chicken better stay away from me," said Abby.

"'Chill out,' I shed!'" slurred Sean.

"Shed," said Calvin to himself. His head spun 'round to the sliding glass door that led to the back yard.

"It'sh a party, chief. We're all gonna get along *juuuusht* fine."

"Unless Jenny shows up," said Kitty.

As has been noted, real life wasn't a John Hughes movie. The music didn't stop, there was no record-scratch, people didn't stop talking/dancing and spin 'round to glare at Kitty.

But they all heard her.

Karen McGillicutty, gleeful and wasted, flung her little arms around Abby and Kitty. "If she does, we'll just have to kill her! Now let's party!"

FOUL

Based on her scrunched cheeks, Kitty didn't exactly find her Bartles & Jaymes peach cooler delightful. Based on her squirmy hips, she needed a pee. "Suis-moi, mon cerise," said Calvin, setting her free hand on his shoulder and leading her to a short corridor with four outlets: Sean's da's home office, the cellar stairs, the garage, and a half-bath that was double the size of the Connors' sole full-loo. There was a queue.

"Takes me back to the day we met," joked Kitty.

Calvin's guffaw startled the girl in front of them. It was Philomena "Pony" Ysderrhi. She was a senior but barely half Calvin's size.

"Where's your brother at?" Calvin asked her.

Pony pushed her glasses up at him. "Dead, I hope. I love your shirt. So shiny!"

"Thanks a million." He stepped aside to reveal his girlfriend. "Pony, this is Kitty Howe. Kitty, this is—"

Pony got out of line and whisked herself through a random exit (the garage). Calvin burped, "What the hell?"

Kitty's pink cheeks dipped. "Well. Remember I said people try to take Excalibur? Pony would do it back when we were little. She's afraid of me now." She sipped on the wine cooler again, then gasped for air.

"Wine is arrogant, strong drink is riotous," said Calvin. *"None who goes astray for it is wise."*

"Whatever! I'm at a party and I'm having a drink. *You* got caught buying Binaca at recess! *Who then are you to judge?"*

"Touché!"

The loo finally freed up. Calvin tried to go in and show her where the facilities were. Kitty reminded him that she was sixteen and quite capable of locating the toilet and seating herself on it. The Ape fretted over the window: who designs a loo with a window at waist height, facing the back porch? Some prick had puked in the sink and tried to use the window's curtain as a towel, tearing it down and warping the rod. The frosted diffusion over the glass would've made some measure of privacy, but it didn't matter since the bloody window was up and refused to go down!

"It's fine," said Kitty, "it lets out the stink anyway!"

The lad stood guard outside the locked door, wiping away the sweat from his labors. Kitty took forever. He looked for Abby and Ryan to make conversation but they'd vanished into the crowd. He sipped from his Diet Pepsi can, played with the jingle bell on his silver shirt, and felt like he'd never find the right level of protectiveness for his crippled girlfriend. He couldn't even shed all his sight-biased language.

Shed.

A minute later they were in the dining room and Kitty insisted on playing Sips-for-Pips. "That's a bad idea," said the lad. The lass told him to zip it. She wanted to be in the game like the other kids, damn it.

All six chairs at the dining room table were occupied, with Sean and Kare sharing one. The little wanker accommodated Kitty by forcing Zedz to forfeit his spot. The flabby guy tugged at his bleach blond hair and shat a string of expletives as he stomped out. Calvin saw why Zedz was so annoyed—his chair had been across from Shelly Quince's. The Breast Stroker's breasts were fighting a Pyrrhic battle with her dress.

Calvin and Kitty were too wide to share the chair and Lady Em would *never* deign to sit on the young man's lap.

Sean explained the rules to Kitty, getting them wrong, then getting them wrong on purpose, then getting interrupted when Brion Davey and Jill Pedersen showed up.

Davey's asshole dad had made the goon wear a shirt and tie to the dance; the noose had found a trash can hours ago. Jill wore purple even for Valentines' Day; her aubergine dress was a sassy number with its single shoulder strap and rows of frills from waist to hem, just above the knee. Her pumps were bright byzantine. Their faces were moist, cheeks red from the cold night, noses red from having a drink or two. Calvin was shocked to see Jill toting a can of I.C. Light—she never drank.

The lad was standing behind Kitty's chair (with his hand on her shoulder for a change) and felt the lass go tense. Then, warm. Then, loose. Kitty was determined as hell to have fun, no matter what.

She patted his hand to tell *him* to calm down.

Well. He *was* energized at seeing Davey. And Jill looked kinda hot in that dress. He pushed close to Kitty's chair to hide his shillelagh.

The goon demanded a seat of his own but the little wanker told him to wait his goddamned turn.

"Speaking of 'goddamn turn,'" said Kare, picking up the die and shoving it in her boyfriend's face. "Yer holdin' up the works, Corgan!"

Sean rolled and got a 3. He took three sips from his Bud Light can and passed the die along. Kare got a 6 and everyone cheered. Sips-for-Pips' rules were akin to strikes in bowling: she'd have to do six sips plus whatever number the next player rolled.

Kitty rolled next and got a 1. Everyone booed the lame outcome.

Davey's boo halted when he saw Jill not booing. "I don't want Kitty to get drunk," she whispered to him. "She can't even see!"

His hand tipped up her can of beer, like *Drink up.*

Kitty took her one sip. "Ugh!" gagged the lass. "I love it!"

Everyone cheered.

For her seven sips, Kare polished off her Seagram's. The Mall Chick wiggled the empty bottle at Calvin, *Be a dear and get me another.*

No way Calvin was leaving. It'd be just like these pricks to tell Kitty she rolled a 6 when she really rolled a 2. The Ape took Kare's bottle and handed it to Davey. "Make yourself useful, 8 9."

Davey would've smashed the bottle over Calvin's noodle if Jill hadn't taken it away and gone to fetch her Mall Chick friend a fresh one.

The die was rolled and players sipped and spectators hooted and made fun of each other. Calvin caught his girlfriend sipping between turns and told her to stop, but she was thirsty and having fun and defiant of him to the point of shrugging away his hand from her shoulder.

Davey saw that and laughed. That killed the Ape's boner. Kitty and Jill and Kare and Shelley could all be topless now and it wouldn't matter.

Paddy Millar rolled the die off the table, forcing kids to scrounge for it. They all went "Ha ha." Then Shelley's roll caromed off Kitty's wine cooler and fell by Calvin's feet. Sean made a new rule—lose the damn dice and you lose your damn pants.

Sitting there in her fetching pink Valentine's Dance dress, Kare hooted, "What if we don't *got* pants?" She gave that famous Mall Chick look: flat hand held out, sneering mouth, all like *What're you, retarded?!*

"Then you lose your pant*ies,*" said Sean, giving that famous Jock Dude look: fist pumped, salacious smirk, all but screaming *Take 'em off!*

Calvin cheered like the rest of the boys, then came to his senses and tried to pull Kitty out of the game. "No way," the lass said. "New rule—if it's me who loses the dice, then *Calvin* loses his pants."

The whole party laughed at the Ape.

"Well," he said. "I will *not* be held responsible if your girlfriends feint at the sight of my—"

The heckling drowned him out. Jill's comment, "I left my microscope in the Biology room," was loudest of all.

Red-faced, Davey pulled his girlfriend by the arm out into the living room. "Relax, chief," said Sean over his shoulder, then stopped caring.

On her very next turn, Kitty's roll sent the die off the table. Sean tried to catch it—he was the catcher, after all—but only ricocheted it up and through the wall-cutout into the kitchen.

"Smooth move!" said Kare. "You *both* lose your pants on that!"

"*Take it off! Take it off!*" chanted the kids.

Putting on his poker face, Sean stood and pulled down his Bugle Boys. The little wanker wore sparkling white briefs.

Calvin's big foot caught on the tight white cuff of his Wranglers and he planted his poker face right on the corner of the dining table. He wore heather gray boxers but kids had to crane their necks to see them on his crumpled corpse.

Kitty quit the game to take care of him. Jill raced back in the room to snare the vacant seat, kicking the Ape's white jeans under the table.

FOUL

Being pantless and defenseless and under a lass's protective care wasn't so bad. Kitty was tender and checked his face for blood/bumps and wanted him to feel better.

Then someone in the kitchen said it was snowing out.

She forced him to lead her out the sliding glass door to the patio. He lurched them too far right and they both scraped the doorframe.

"I should've brought Excalibur and let *you* use it!" she said.

"I'm sorry. I'm feeling a little concussed. It'll go away."

"That *thunk!* when you hit the table was like a car crash. Are you sure you're okay?"

"Never better. My head's full of rocks, or haven't you heard?" He brought them to a stop. "Well. Technically, it *is* snowing."

"Oh. Just flurries?"

"I wouldn't go that far."

A few kids were out here on the sprawling flagstone patio, smoking or making out. They bugged at the blind girl's pink shades and the Ape's hairless legs going just as pink in the chill.

"We need an open section of the back yard," said Kitty. "No trees or lawn chairs or swimming pools or anything."

"Tons of space." The Ape scanned the wobbly horizon for a shed.

"Hey Connor, find a better hiding spot than last time!" some senior kid joked. One of the Muellers. Calvin made a fist at him.

"Mind your own business," Kitty told the guy. Planting her hand on Calvin's shoulder, she said, "Lead on, mon gâteau au fromage!"

Calvin laughed at that and got them onto the grass. He felt woozy. His vision clouded, like someone had thrown lemon pudding in his eyes. He'd neglected to put his shoes back on and his socked feet didn't dig the crusty frozen lawn. These back yards were humongous. "Okay, mon cerise, how about here? There's nothing around us for miles."

"I don't need *miles*. Just, like, ten paces in every direction." Her voice was disappointed. "'Cept ... it is *not* snowing."

"I mean, it *is,* but there's a meter between each flake."

She made the vocal equivalent of a pout. "Never mind."

He pulled her close. Her head fit under his. "We can go skiing another time," he joked.

"Not *skiing*. I'll explain sometime when it actually *is* snowing." She noticed his head kept panning side-to-side. "What's up?"

"It's not here."

"What's not here?" Her voice dropped. "Can anyone see us?"

He shuffled them further away from the house, towards some trees. "I wanna check over here." Overlook Estates was built in a former woodsy hollow nestled against the cliff-like edge of the Axsubewa Valley bowl. Every McMansion's back yard ended with a tasteful selection of spared firs and maples and then the ridgeline.

"It's not here," he said again. He turned them 360° for one last sweep. At degree 340, he got dizzy and fell. Kitty went splat nearby.

He moaned. She laughed. Not her usual spritely tinkle of mirth but a throaty roar of booze-boosted belly-laughs. Scrambling on all fours, she found him and kissed him. "There's no shed," he told her, "it don't exist, 'cept in some parallel dimension in Art's head—"

Kitty didn't give a fuck about all that. She felt his warmth and wanted to make out. Just as they started Frenching, a tiny snowflake died on the pink skin of her cheek. She moaned at that. Her thigh crossed over him, draping his naked legs with her wispy skirt.

The blender under his boxers went from chop to grind, then to aerate. He no longer felt cold with her heat on him. He wasn't the type of boy to keep his eyes open while making out but he couldn't resist a few peeks. All he got was lemon pudding over his vision.

He felt dizzy again, but in a different way, like when you've pushed your lungs to the limit. He forced his head away from hers and sucked in a chilly breath. Then another. And another.

The frozen grass under them had melted.

"What's going on here?"

A man's voice. Coming from a boy.

"Mark?" said Kitty, sounding guilty. And annoyed. She both pushed away from Calvin and clutched him close. Thankfully, her skirt stayed draped over his boxers.

From Calvin's vantage point on the ground, Mark Duffy seemed twenty feet tall. In reality Saint Mark was shorter than Calvin and weighed half as much. The guy's ego outstripped the lad's by a factor of ten; it was that bloody Yank Christian righteousness.

Mark's sober Polo khakis and sky blue button-down Oxford made him a '50s throwback in this '80s world of color insanity. Calvin had no doubt there was a fag-tag on the back of that Oxford. And while every kid here had a wine cooler bottle, beer can, or soda, Mark carried a pink pint carton—whole milk, like he was Mike D or some shit.

"Popped by to behold how the other half lives?" said Calvin.

Saint Mark said, *"Someone's* gotta save the sinners," in his holy tone mixing bright friendliness and stiff judgment.

"Plenty of them inside, mate. That's why we came out here."

"Into the cold, minus jackets? That math don't add up. Speaking of, I hear you have trouble with Algebra. I'd be happy to offer tutoring."

Calvin muttered to Kitty, "This is the kind of thing you've been missing by not coming to Corgan's soirées."

Kitty said, "Mark, this is a party. Don't bring up tutoring!"

"Corgan always invites me," said Mark. "Maybe he thinks it's funny, but Jesus entered the house of the Pharisee to forgive the sinning woman." He moved around to stand next to the prone lass.

"Very clever," said Calvin. "That's the one where the woman fell to the floor and cried on Christ's feet and kissed them. Mark even put his feet near you, Kitty! His *British Knights,* ugh." He nuzzled up to her ear. "You can be friends with this prick, but if you kiss his feet—"

Mark butted in. "Kitty, the Ape 'christened' the front yard with Jenny MacDonald. Now he's doing it to the back yard with you—"

"Both of you shut up," said Kitty. Her hands de-clutched from Calvin's torso to do the herky-jerky Arms of Frustration, accidentally bopping the lad's nose. "We didn't do anything, and he's not *forcing* me to be here, Mark! I wanna be here! This is my first party!"

"The party's back there, Kitty."

"We heard it was snowing and I wanted to go swooping! It doesn't matter—I can go where I want. Besides, Daddy gave me permission."

"To lie on the grass with a half-naked Irish Raging Ape?" said Mark, brows arched like he was humoring a little girl. "Is this how you *Honor your father and mother?*"

"I'll have you know," said Calvin, "the reason I'm half-naked is cuz my jeans died defending her."

Saint Mark couldn't help laughing his reedy little laugh. The snaps of his snobby sniggers sounded to the heavens.

"Mark," said Kitty, desperation in her voice, "don't tell my parents about this. *Who are you to judge?*"

The guy was taken aback. "Who am *I* to judge? Why, I'm your tutor, I'm your mentor, and right now I'm your crow scout."

"Bollocks on that, *I'm* the crow scout here!" said Calvin. "How does he know about that, Kitty?"

"Doing a real great job, Connor. Can't even watch over your own pants." Mark leaned close to her. "I'm going to help you up."

"No!" she yelped. "I'm fine, I'm safe, and I *was* having fun!"

"He's right, mon cerise," said Calvin. "It was a bad idea to come. We should leave."

"S'il te plaît, mon gâteau au fromage! We are *staying!*"

"Then we'll need some privacy." The Ape got to his feet in stages. The lemon pudding in his eyes squirted cold down to his belly. He bent at the waist, hands on knees, about to puke.

"Lookit, Irish is drunk," said Mark. "What's new?"

"No he *isn't,*" said Kitty. "He hasn't drunk at all."

"Then whose booze breath do I smell?" No longer waiting for

permission, Mark's hands slipped under Kitty's arms to hoist her to her feet. "It's cold out here and you don't got a jacket—you're freezing."

"Okay," the lass said, frozen in a new way—panic. "Just get us inside to warm up and we can talk there. Him too, Mark."

Calvin swung up erect. "Get your hands off my oof—"

He didn't feel the blow but he *did* smell the Palmolive soap on Mark's hands. He saw crushed blueberries appearing inside the lemon pudding over his eyes.

⚾ __SHITHOUSE__ ⚾

The next five minutes of Jill Pedersen's life would form a perpetual background, ghostly, ghastly, lasting years. Decades.

It began when Brion Davey dragged her a second time away from the Sips-for-Pips game, this time into the kitchen. "Brion, what the fuck?" said Jill, planting her heel down on the marble tile.

The report turned heads. Her boyfriend was unperturbed by the witnesses and uncaring of her feelings. "Yer drunk, Jill! Gettin' all sweaty in there cuz guys're takin' off their pants!"

She laughed at him. *"You're* the one sweatin' over that! Like you're afraid it'll make you gay."

"I saw ya kick the mick's jeans away. I saw ya lookin' at his boxers."

"Cuz it was fuckin' funny, Brion! You laughed too!"

"If Sean caught that dice, his pants stay on. But no, he flicked that shit a mile away ... " The boy's eyes went cold. "You *planned* this!"

Jill was first attracted to Brion when he tried to kill the Irish Raging Ape. She liked how he fed off his passions, that he was big and strong, that he took charge.

Right now, all that felt dangerous to her.

"Corgan's in it with you," said Brion. "It's so obvious."

Jill couldn't believe what she was hearing. "You're sayin' we planned it so the Ape's pants would come off?!"

"Corgan wants him on the team so he can get to States. He'll do *anything* to help him, including shit on me. *You're* workin' with him." Brion moved closer to her and she edged back towards the marbletop kitchen island. "It's so obvious now. You don't care about me. You don't even like me. But if I'm 'occupied' with you, then I ain't smearin' queer-ass Connor's face into the garbage disposal."

Jill's back nestled roughly against the kitchen island, making it wobble. An aluminum bowl of fruit quavered. Beer cans fell over. A pizza box, open and empty, drifted to the floor.

As calmly as she could, as calmingly as she could, Jill laid a hand on her man's cheek. "Brion, would you listen to yourself? I *do* like you! That's why we went to the dance together, why we're here now!"

His voice was as cold as his eyes. "I don't believe you. You been laughin' at me this whole time, you and Kitty and Connor and Corgan."

"It's not a *conspiracy!*"

"Heeey, did I hear my name?" said Sean, sliding between them. He held his Bud Light can up like the Statue of Liberty's torch. "Shettle down, kiddiesh, it's a party!"

"I'm sorry, Sean," said Jill, "I can't play Sips-for-Pips anymore."

"That'sh cool. Shay, if you kidsh wanna get cozhy, my room is upstairsh, shecond on the left—"

"She's done playing your games," said Brion. "Me too."

Sean thrust out his chin. "Do me a favor and looshen your jock shtrap, chief!" He looked at Jill. "He's *sooo* wound up!"

"Speakin' of jock straps," said Brion. "That first scrimmage, when I hit the homer off the mick? *You* was watchin' from the bleachers, Jill … and Connor had a fucking boner out on the mound."

Jill's squeaks were like a little girl rubbing dry fingers on a balloon.

"I shpend every practish lookin' at that fat Irish fuck," said Sean. "That'sh what the catcher doesh, he looksh at the pitcher—there wash no boner! If there was a boner to shee, I woulda sheen it!"

"He was pushing it back down!" Brion demonstrated by shoving the crotch of his khaki pants down.

Sean told Jill, "I give up. Now thish guy'sh sheeing bonersh!"

"Holy fucking shit," drawled a sticky voice behind them.

Spazz and Val, with their black tuxedo T-shirts and red Chucks and bloodshot eyes. Val's little hand pointed at Sean's ginger Davey Dangle. "Pop Rocks're growin' out his fuckin' scalp!" she said, orgasmic awe.

"Get outta here, you goddamn stoners," bade Brion.

"Wavy Davey From the Navy needs to come take a hit with us!"

said Spazz, brandishing a joint.

When Brion's hand swept out to swat the joint away, he did an inadvertent Three Stooges slap across Sean's face, then Spazz's face, then Val's. The skater girl fell to her knees, shrieking in terror.

Saint Mark came in the sliding glass door with Kitty holding onto his shoulder. At the shrieking, Mark held out his pink milk carton like Father Merrin wielding a crucifix.

Spazz squared off with Brion. "Don't hit my squeeze, ya buck-toothed butt-face! She's dosin' and now she's gonna have a bad trip!"

"What's going on?" said Kitty.

"Drugs and chaos in here," said Saint Mark, "the Devil's work."

"My dick's itchin'," Spazz told Brion, making fists. "And when *that* happ—"

"Go away, faggot!" said Brion, jostling him back.

"Calvin?" Kitty called behind her.

"He'sh not there," said Sean. "You two-timin' him, Kitty?"

"You told me he was following us, Mark! You jerk!"

Saint Mark said, *"Be quick to hear, slow to speak, slow to wrath—"*

Kitty didn't care. She followed the feel of cold air behind her.

Mark spun 'round to slide the door shut and grab her arm.

"Let go of her!" said Jill.

Brion said it too and turned towards Saint Mark.

Spazz got back up and shoved the little wanker into Brion.

"Chill out, kiddiesh!" said Sean. "Don't make me get my dad'sh gun!"

"Let go of me!" Kitty told Saint Mark, who did the opposite; he used his firm grip on the lass to position her between himself and Brion. Like a shield. Or an offering.

Behind them, the sliding glass door flew off its guide tracks and clanged onto the patio's flagstone, shattering into confetti.

"Holy shit," Abby told Ryan, and desire was in her voice.

"Don't wreck the joint, Shkipshon!" said Sean. "Shome of ush gotta live here, chief!"

Ryan and Abby came inside, Calvin dangling between them. "Mon cerise!" said the Ape.

Kitty swooned. Brion bristled. Val shrieked again.

The McMansion kitchen burst asunder. The precise details of the battle are lost in the mists of time and wine cooler bubbles, but it ended three seconds later with Sean Corgan splayed on his ass and two of the three Igloo coolers upturned. Val tried to hide from the flying ice and Pop Rocks zombies by climbing inside Kitty's cardigan. Calvin and Spazz's limbs flew at Brion and ended up tangling inside the same kitchen island barstool. Brion lost his balance; he tumbled down, flailing his claws for purchase. They caught on Jill's frilly aubergine dress and tore it cleanly off her body.

Everyone pointed and laughed at Jill's white panties and red face. A single-strap dress necessitated going braless. She hadn't sprung for a tanning salon like Kare and Rayche did so her pale chest shone.

She covered herself with her arms and screamed for Brion, still holding the torn dress in his fist, to give it back.

Brion was no longer there. In his place was Davey, the goon. He balled up the dress, chucked it through the wall cut-out to the dining room, and laughed at her.

She'd never felt so humiliated in her life.

It was only Minute 2 of 5, too.

FOUL

Someone winded a war horn from the other side of the house.

"KILL HER!" roared Karen McGillicutty.

All and sundry felt themselves drawn out of the kitchen and towards the foyer, like the flow of retreating floodwaters after a tsunami. The pop music, loud enough to drown conversation, was itself drowned by rude, explosive, violent racket. Doors slammed and glass broke and drywall was penetrated.

Abby charged to help kill Jenny. Ryan was torn between loyalties— watch Abby's back or help Calvin? The kid suddenly cocked his head, looking for all the world as if he was getting a transmission via an earpiece. He handed Calvin off to Sean and took off after his date.

The little wanker was in no shape to support the weight of an Irish Raging Ape, even one unencumbered by trousers. Sean propped the lad on the kitchen island. Calvin saw an orange in the aluminum fruit bowl and fetched it; this cost him his grip on the marble top and he slid down over Jill. The naked lass had curled into a ball, using the island as cover.

The pudding filter over the lad's steel gray eyes robbed him of her nudity but his arm, draped over her back and shoulders, felt hot bare skin. "What the fuck is happening?" he said to the orange in his hand.

⚾ __SHITHOUSE__ ⚾

Jill pulled the Ape close and wept. He was warm. The floor was cold with ice and melted ice.

She got up and realized how drunk she was when the world did a ratchet-wrench thing, ticking three slots to the left before jerking back to its original position. She noticed how unclothed she was when the wind carried flurries into the doorless patio exit. Calvin the Pantless was both her support and her burden, his limbs limply draped over her shoulders. Everyone had rushed off to kill Jenny so this was her chance to go … where? Not outside. They wore too little attire and witnesses would have a field day. The bathroom? Someone was in there, the door locked. The cellar? No escape.

The garage? That office?

She chose the latter.

Minute 3 would've been the final one had she chosen the former.

Mr. Corgan's home office was tight and tidy. The Ape flung himself into the fancy leather desk chair, went *"Whee!"* as it rolled away on its casters, and passed out when it thumped the bay window's shelf.

Jill shut the door and threw her back against it. She couldn't get the lock mechanism on the doorknob to work since it had none.

She saw Davey, grabbing her dress, tearing it off—

No clothing or towels or anything to drape over herself here. She peeked out into the hall. The coast was clear. The door to the little bathroom down the hall was open now. *There'll be a towel in there.*

Davey, laughing at her, throwing her dress through the cut-out—

She tumbled drunkenly out and into the dining room. Her dress was on the floor near the passed-out body of senior Josh Adams. She saw Calvin's white jeans and snagged them too.

She got lost heading back to the office but made it. Calvin was still in the leather chair, his naked legs sticking out, his eyes shut, one hand gripping an orange, the other limply dangling.

"Don't look," she told him, in case he was faking. She put the dress on but the lone shoulder strap had torn in two and the waist-seams were so loose that the thing refused to rest on her hips.

Feeling tears coming again, she went through the office drawers for something to fix the dress with. Anything.

She checked one drawer and found paper clips.

She checked another drawer and found paper clamps, but they were too small and wouldn't grip the dress's fabric.

She checked another drawer and found Scotch tape but so much of her was damp from sweat and tears and all the icy water on the kitchen floor so she couldn't get the shit to stick anywhere.

She checked another drawer and found a stapler. That worked to reconnect the shoulder strap. For now. It wouldn't last. She unhinged the stapler's base and held the device in her right hand like a gun.

She checked the last drawer and found a revolver.

She shut the drawer, then yanked it open again. A snub-nose .38, silver metal with a black grip, rested neatly on bundles of banknotes whose paper bands covered Lincoln's, Hamilton's, and Jackson's faces. Her free left hand reached for, and picked up, the gun.

"Why you bring straw hair chick?" said Chicken from the hallway. "Now we have World War III!"

"*She* called *me*, man," laughed Reggie as they passed into the garage. "How was I s'posed to know that Kare put a hit out on her?!"

Jill barked in panic and turned around.

The office door was still shut.

The Swingline was still in her right hand but the Smith & Wesson flew from her left, sailing over to strike Calvin right on the prepuce. With no denim layer to soften the blow, the lad felt the full force of steel on 'nads and flew out from the desk chair. "Jaysus!" he said, eyes bulging. The revolver's trigger guard hooped into the boxers' relief hole, the snub-nose's dangerous end pressed against his junk. The Ape's fat mitts (one still gripping the orange) squeezed over his crotch.

Jill heard a squeak and turned back to the door. It was open. Davey filled the doorway.

She aimed the Swingline at him. The staples in her shoulder strap came loose and her dress fell. She groped to pull it back up and stumbled over herself, falling forward.

This was Minute 4 of 5. The last sixty seconds were the hardest.

FOUL

Bare-legged, wet-socked, Calvin stood with both hands over his sore nuts, barely aware an orange was in there, totally clueless that a revolver was too. Crushed blueberries and lemon pudding rubbed over his eyes like crunchy quartz. He barely breathed.

Others had come and gone. He heard pain and felt squealing. No, that's not right. He heard the squealing and felt the pain. The squealing was far off but the pain was in his bollocks.

He saw an open doorway, and beyond it a hall, and in that hall another door, which he knew led to that half-loo, the one with the window at waist-height that wouldn't close—

His hand still held the orange and therefore wouldn't get all the way 'round the loo's knob. "Fuck it," he said, and kicked the door in.

The squealing stopped.

Brion Davey was at the toilet. His back was originally to the door but at its destruction he'd whirled around. His pants were down.

"Picture yerself makin' a good throw," Lucky always said at practice. "Don't think. Yer mechanics should be robotic, the same each time, bang-bang-bang, strike, strike, strike."

Calvin started a robotic recitation of his pitching motion. His poor boxers slid off his hips, dragged down by the weight of the .38.

"Put away your dick, faggot!" Davey shouted.

The orange hurled towards the goon's face.

The revolver struck the floor and discharged.

Chapter 23

WIPING WITH WETTED WADS OF T.P.
SATURDAY, FEBRUARY 18, 1989.

FOUL

HIS TONGUE FELT LIKE a limp bit of leather. A rug scraped his face. Low carpet, not the furry kind. Every breath smelt of feet, dirt, his own used breath. His lips opened to curse and tore each other apart, *sooo* dry. His brain kicked his skull like it wanted to break out. He knew the smell of gunpowder from being around Art and he smelt it now.

"Fucking hell," he said, letting himself into the world at large. It was dark and close. A few moans. Some weeping. He shuffled towards the light. *Goddamn I'm hard.* A beefy hand grabbed his hot and bothered shillelagh to comfort it but found a blanket in the way.

The only light source was one of those desk lamps with the green-glass shade featured in every porno scene set in a library. Full dark with some wind-swept flurries out the bay window. His White Window Swatch showed both hands straight up. It was waterlogged. Dripping.

The opposite of himself. *Sooo* dry.

A bath towel was balled up at his balls. His right hand had worked itself under there, pumping. He stopped that shit cuz Jill was here, sitting Indian-style on the bay window's shelf, looking out at the snow.

Calvin tried to use the castored desk chair as leverage to stand and it turned into a Charlie Chaplain pratfall routine. He gave up and grabbed the lip of the bay window shelf, yanking his hands back when one of them landed on Jill's bare thigh.

His cheeks went red under the carpet indentations.

"Your eye looks so bad," she whispered.

Calvin rubbed his left eye and it made his head hurt all over again. He glossed the surfaces of the desk and shelves for water. The only liquid was White-Out; he wasn't quite so parched.

Jill had wrapped a bath towel around her torso from the armpits down. She was otherwise bare; Calvin peeped no bra straps.

"Where are your pants, Pedersen?" he whispered.

The Mall Chick whispered back, "Where are yours?"

Calvin checked himself. Pale beef with a minimum of man hair. His white boxers bunched at his itchy nuts. "Good question."

"You don't remember," she sighed. She pointed at his jeans, lying on the floor. "Right there. And I told ya a million times—neutrals are the *canvas,* not the painting. You ever watch that afro painter guy on PBS? You start with white and work your way out. Get some color in there! I mean, white jeans with a silver shirt?! What a dweeb!"

He took the jeans and put one leg through. His big foot with the stinky wet sock could not make it through the cuff. He jerked the jeans off and inspected them. "These are girls jeans! Jordaches."

"Oops. You took yours off during Sips-for-Pips."

"Oh that's right," he said. Every word poked a new fissure in his cracked skull. "Kitty dropped the dice, I lost my pants. What'd you do to lose your whole dress? Throw the dice into the pool?"

"I don't wanna talk about it." Her scratchy words reeked of booze. Her brown eyes were crossed. Her makeup was all messed-up, like two bunches of ripe concord grapes had collided with her face.

"You sound knackered," he said. "Drunk."

"Beer and tequila and California Coolers," she said.

"Barf."

"Davey made me drink the orange one. *You* know why." She suddenly reached out and grabbed him by the neck.

To hug him.

He slowly hugged her back. "Nice corpse-rot breath. You could really use a hit of Binaca."

"Ha. Thanks for saving me tonight, you Ape."

"…from?"

"Y'know," she said, letting go of him, "part of me's *reeeeal* glad you don't remember. *Aaack!*"

He knew that noise and covered up in case she puked on his face.

Nothing happened. He peeked. The noise had not been a prelude to vomiting, but crying. Tears ran down the violet sludge on her face.

He snared the white Jordaches and wiped the tears from Jill's cheeks, pulling away a measure of that purple schmutz.

She gave the faintest, briefest smile of thanks.

Then puked on him.

"Fuckin' gnarly!" Calvin cried, and in so doing, allowed a blob of throw-up into his gob. He retched himself and ralphed into the Jordaches, getting her purple makeup on his lips.

"Oh my God," she laughed. She put a hand up to cover her mouth but laughed right through it. A latecomer vomit bloop slithered between her fingers.

He shut his eyes to let his brain re-coagulate. "If you go bragging about upchucking on me, I'll kill you."

She hoisted up a revolver.

He froze. "Uh ... just kidding! I'd never kill you. Or anyone. Ha ha. You're kidding too, right? Is that thing real?"

"Yes. I wanna kill Davey."

The Ape went jittery, too shocked to tell her off, too concussed to simply take the gun from her.

She got up, found the desk drawer with the cash, and put the revolver back.

"You got that ten thousand bucks you owe me?" joked Calvin.

She shut the drawer. "Ha! Must be nice to have fucking stacks of cash lying around."

"And an IROC," said Calvin.

"And a pool." The girl saw her obliterated dress on the floor and kicked it. She flopped into the chair with a sigh.

The lad got to his feet. "Where's Kitty?"

"Upstairs with Valerie Crenshaw. They locked themselves in Sean's parents' room's bathroom."

"What the fuck for?"

"It's a long story. You missed a lot of shit, Connor. Spazz broke a stool over Davey's head. Corgan fell on the ice and broke his ass. He was all, 'My butt is broken!'" She laughed. "Then Jenny showed up. They killed that bitch, Calvin. They *killed* her."

He felt like he'd missed a whole season of some show. He switched the TV off. "Here's what I'm doing: finding water, pants, and aspirins. Then Kitty, then coats, then out the door."

"Did you drive? Take me too! I ain't walkin' all the way home. It's like four in the morning and I'm naked here!"

"Four in the morning?" He checked his Swatch. It was still waterlogged. "You said Val's here. I'll take her Yugo. I don't care." He turned his head. "Fix your towel. Lemme know when it's safe to look."

Jill's towel had come loose when she sat in the chair. It still covered her but would've flown open if she'd gotten right up. "Don't look," she said. "And don't look at my reflection in the window!"

"Eh, seen it."

"Fuck you. Ready." The towel went from her bosom down to a few inches below her ass. Plenty of wide American thigh on display.

He tried to lead her like Kitty, her behind him with a hand on his shoulder, but she still had the ratchet-wrench view and kept tumbling aside. They went arm-in-arm instead. Her heels clicked and clocked.

"I better not have boned you, Pedersen."

"I'm not that kind of girl."

"If I *did,* I better not've blacked out and forgotten it."

"Ewww, you fuckin' Ape! Shut up!"

Beholding the kitchen, his leather tongue scraped eagerly over dry lips. He bugged the countertops and island table for a drink but every vessel held a murky liquid ashtray. The kitchen was freezing; the sliding glass door was open. Wrong, he squinted, it was missing entirely.

Jill's head poked in various cabinets. "You would do that? Cheat on Kitty, like you cheated on Jenny with me?"

"This is the new me," he hissed. "I behave now."

"Sure. Kitty's so sweet. I never really talked to her before. You two are a nice couple."

"You and Davey are not a nice couple. He's about as sweet as salt."

"Fuck him." She found a clean brandy snifter and held it up like the Stanley Cup. Both sinks had mounds of dirty dishes and she couldn't fit the glass under the tap. Then she remembered the counter's built-in water dispenser and laughed as air bubbles went through the big glass bottle going *gloop-gloop.*

She drank first, deep, spilling most of the water down her towel and bare legs. "Smooth move, Ex-Lax," he said.

"Eat me."

"I did, remember? That one time."

"Ugh, don't remind me." Refilling the snifter, she fed Calvin like a baby, making goo-goo noises and laughing all drunkenly. The cool spring water softened his tongue to wet gravel. His gray eyes looked up to say thanks and dry-humped her naked shoulders.

"Fuckin' freezin' in here," she said.

"Too right, let's book," he said.

They shuffled to the foyer. Some dude slumped against the far wall like he'd been shot and rag-dolled there. A ski jacket was draped over him as a blanket. Calvin brought them to a stop at the marble pedestal. It'd somehow survived the Battle of Hastings out here when Jenny showed up. The goldfish bowl on the pedestal was full of keychains; Sean's method of managing parking. Despite horseshoe driveways with spurs to three-car garages, plus copious curbside, there were *always* annoying games of 1) "Whose green Tempo is blocking my Saab?", 2) a manhunt for the perpetrator, 3) said perp getting pissed at being interrupted while necking in the closet, 4) dredging the whole 3,900 sq.-ft. house to find the perp's coat with the Tempo's keys in the pocket.

Screw all that: everyone left their keys by the door. If the need arose, someone else moved the offending car.*

"The answer to our prayers," said Calvin, jamming his fat hand in the bowl. Right on top was a keyring with a leather fob cut like a teardrop. The **E** stamped on the shiny side used to be colored green but Leatherworks badge at Lucid Pond Campgrounds had been a long time ago. "My ma's keys. I know *she's* not here so Rose used her car?"

They started up the grand staircase. "I guess," said Jill. "She came with Pete Hennessey."

"I'm sure she did." Poker face.

"Gross me out!"

"We need to jet before Sis finds out."

"She's gone, Connor. Left with someone else. I'm glad it's *your*

---

* Future-Jill will see this set-up years later while watching a movie on cable, but the context was far different. Future-Calvin, he of the Lambo and Ray-Bans, will host such a "key party" in the chronicle's next volume.

mom's car and not my mom's."

"Me too," he said. "Pickups are shite in the snow."

"I hate that Momma drives a truck. It's trashy. You'll never see *me* driving a pickup!"

"Not even a purple one? Hard to port here!"

A left put them in the upstairs bathroom: two sinks, a medicine cabinet with analgesics for their headaches, and a large mirror. Jill went to it and wetted wads of T.P. to wipe off her face.

Calvin *finally* got to the point where he didn't look in a mirror first thing in the morning and go "AAUGH!" at his silly-as-shite Davey Dangle. Today, he went "AAUGH!" at the dark halo over his eye.

The noise disturbed some cadavers hiding in the tub. They stood and opened the shower door. Just Ryan and Abby. Not zombies.

"That fuckin' dining room table did this to my face?!" said Calvin. He put a hand on Jill's bare shoulder and felt her body go flush. "You sure I didn't get in a fight too?"

"Please let go of me. I don't wanna be touched." Jill was trembling. Like her tears in the office, this was real shite.

He let go at once.

"You tried to fight but ended up humping a bar stool," said Abby. She put her cold slabby hands on his cheeks to inspect his face. "Damn, you hit that cement-head of yours *hard!*"

Calvin looked at her and could hardly believe his eyes. Or form the words to confirm what he was seeing. "Is that … blood on your lips?"

"Barbeque sauce," said Ryan, hastily wiping his own gob.

"Quit squirmin', baloney-face," Abby said in her Moe Howard voice, "or I'll squeeze the cider from yer Adam's apple!"

"Let go, Malone," said Calvin. "I don't wanna be touched either."

Abby from last month would've taunted him to death about that, and called him *Ugly* a couple times too. This Abby let go of him at once.

"My jeans died defending Kitty," he said.

Said again? I can't remember.

"I thought you were going to be bad for her," said Abby. "But you're a really great guy, Calvin."

"Yeah," said Jill, "the Irish Ragin' Ape's a fucking Boy Scout."

"Shut up, Pedersen!" said Abby.

"Kids, let's not fight," said Calvin. "You're both right."

"Thank you," said Jill.

"Thank you," said Abby.

Calvin said, "Very good. I'm glad we're all friends now."

Jill put up a threatening finger. "If you call me your friend one more time, I'll punch you. Dare I say it!"

"Listen up," said the Ape to this shrewdness, "I need to drain the main vein. You lot can bugger off, or stay and behold it if you want."

FOUL

Tony and Helena Corgan's bedroom door was shut but not locked. They found Saint Mark lying on the California king in a cross pose, on his back, arms thrust out, snoring.

"I say we crucify him on the front lawn," said Ryan.

At the sound of the jingle bell pinned to Calvin's shirt, Kitty yelped from the en suite bathroom. Valerie Crenshaw was in there too and conducted a three-minute interview through the locked door in a voice seared by shrieking. Satisfied the people outside were *not* zombie rapists with ill intention, the skater rat unlocked the door. Her freaked eyes yelped at passing dust motes that sang Prince songs to her.

Kitty boinked Val aside and cut a direct path to the jingle bell. After her hugs and sighs of relief and apologies about being responsible for Calvin's pantlessness, Kitty wanted to conduct an interview of her own.

"Later," said Calvin. "We're all in this together. Let's go!"

Val said they needed to find Liam first. It took them a sec to remember "Liam" was (part of) Spazz's actual name.

They formed up like an AD&D party and searched room-by-room. Ryan helpfully pointed out to Val the utter lack of zombies. Just harmless, passed out teens.

They found harmless, passed out Spazz in Sean's older sister's bedroom closet. The wild-child giggled to find himself atop a pile of girly sneaks, flats, and heels. "Fell into a foot-fetishist's fantasy here!"

Jill took advantage of that closet to get clothed again. Amy Corgan was taller but a quick search scored some rags that fit. She took them to the hallway bathroom and came back in a candy apple red long sleeve shirt, royal blue sweatpants, and her orchid heels. "Yuck," she said.

No pants would fit Calvin, not one pair in the whole house. All the Corgans were slim and short. Spazz exhibited a willowy white skirt of Amy's that had an elastic waistband and preened, "This'll make ya *faaabulous,* Californicator."

"It's something, anyway," said the lad.

"Oh shit, I wasn't bein' serious!"

"I am seriously cold, mate." Calvin jumped into the skirt but the waist wouldn't stretch enough to get over his Ape arse.

"Trade with Kitty," Abby suggested. "Hers might work for you."

"I can't believe what's happening," said Jill. "We're all drunk, on drugs, drinking blood, naked, turning into transvestites—"

"We gotta do what we gotta do!" said Calvin. "Mon cerise?"

"Everyone out," said Kitty.

A minute later, Calvin came out with Kitty's floral skirt begging for mercy over his hips. Kitty followed in the longer white number that would've matched her hold-ups if it hadn't hid them completely.

"Anyone laughs and you're dead," the Ape said. The floral skirt's hem made it past his knees.

Abby dug through her party clutch purse for her keys. Calvin jingled his ma's keys, Spazz produced Val's Yugo's key. "Fuck that fishbowl!" he said.

"We need our coats," said Kitty. "They're in your car, Abby."

"Mine's in the foyer closet," said Jill.

"Me and Val already got our jackets on," said Spazz, plucking at the tuxedo pattern on their black T-shirts.

They found the landing by the staircase blocked by Saint Mark. He looked scared to confront them en masse and bugged at Calvin's skirt, but determined to keep the faith. "I'll get Kitty home safe," he said.

"She'll be safe once you're gone!" said Val.

Calvin turned to Val and saw violence in her eyes. Behind him, Kitty also roiled in fury. "What happened—" he started to ask.

We can talk about the past in the future.

"Move," he told Mark. "Before I push you down the stairs."

"No," said Kitty. "Not like that, Calvin."

I try to turn the other cheek. Y'know, like Jesus.

"You're drunk," burped Saint Mark. One hand was out like *Stop!,* the other trembled on his bed-head hair. "It's safer for her if I drive."

"You don't have a car, Mark," said Kitty.

"I'm taking her home," said Calvin. "I'm as sober as Father Sean. Gimme a bible to swear on."

"Then ... let me come with you."

"So you can tell my dad?" said Kitty. "Stop ruining my night!"

"You ruined mine!" Mark said to Calvin. "I rode with Michelle Cullen and the Proverbs Patrol, and when I went out to look for you and Kitty, they left and now I'm stuck here ... "

Saint Mark sputtered for more to compel them.

Ryan's body expanded, disenfranchising the stitching of his black church suit. "The power of Christ compels you," he said.

Mark flattened himself against the wall. They zoomed past him.

Jill got her Minnesota Vikings jacket from the foyer closet and happily enveloped herself in purple. Spazz swept up the ski jacket draped over the corpse (it was Felon Adkisson) and found that he and Val both fit inside it. Calvin was jealous that he hadn't thought of it.

The stars were out. A near-full moon too. The barest slice of yellow scratched the horizon line. Bitter chilly. Winter in Axsubeen was bad news, especially for an Ape in a wispy skirt and wet socks. The party double-timed it down the driveway into Cloven Cape's cul-de-sac. Calvin the Concussed led the way, with Kitty behind him gripping his left shoulder. Then came Spazz and Val, tripping (and tripping). Then Ryan, his hand trailed back to grasp Abby's. Jill the Drunken Mall Chick gripped Abby's waist and tried to keep up. Last, and least, Saint Mark traipsed on his Docksiders along in their wake.

Val's Yugo was on the other side of the cul-de-sac so she and Spazz left the train. Ma's Volvo was street-parked behind Abby's Honda. Abby unlocked the driver side door and froze when she opened it.

"Oh no," she said. The dome light didn't come on, and she saw why: the front passenger door was still stuck on the Overlook Estates Belgian block curb. "Fuckin' A, Ryan! Now what?!"

"You'll ride with me," said Calvin, holding up Ma's keychain.

"You can't drive, you don't have your license!" Abby told Calvin.

"And your birthday isn't until Sunday," said Jill.

"Correct," Kitty said, clipping it. She didn't need to hear her fella's *ex* pointing that out.

"It's an emergency and we need to get to safety." Calvin got the coats out of the little Honda's back seat. "Abby can drive."

"Yes, good idea," called Saint Mark from his respectable distance.

"Never driven something that big before," said Abby.

"It's a station wagon, not a Mack truck!" said the lad. "I did most of my learner's permit practice on this car. But if you lot don't trust me, I'll get you home another way."

"... I trust you," Kitty said at length.

"Me too," said Ryan. Abby nodded along.

Jill made eye contact with the Ape, or tried to, and nodded.

"Us too, Calvin Con-vertible!" said Spazz. He and Val gave him puppy dog eyes.

"Bollocks, you got your own ride now!"

"Yeah, so, about that," said Val. "It's a Yugo."

"Sumbitch don't turn over in the cold," said Spazz. "Just like her owner here! Woof!"

FOUL

Calvin turned the radio down before starting the engine (Rose always drove with tunes blaring). He fired it up, got the heater on full, and went back out to scrape the icy anuses off the windshield. He threw up a little from all the back-and-forth motion.

The others divvied up seats. The front ones were buckets: Calvin and Kitty. The back seat was a bench: Abby, Ryan, and Jill, who refused to ride lying down in the hatchback cargo spot ("I'll puke again.")

Saint Mark, with a sigh he hoped reached the ears of God, got in the hatchback with the druggy kids Spazz and Val.

Calvin's bare shins were bright pink and his socked feet shuddered on the cold floor pedals. The digital clock on the dash said 5:01.

"Seatbelts!" he called for the very first time. And you were there to behold it—for as long as he lives, Calvin Connor III will say this every time he drove a car and had someone to say it to.

Every. Time.

Kitty already wore hers. She wiped her red cheeks. In the back seat, Abby and Jill, too, looked miserable and misty but belted in. Ryan fished out the goofy middle-position lap harness. "We'll hold onto something stiff," called Spazz, pointing at Saint Mark.

The car was nice and toasty. Volvo heaters rocked. Calvin adjusted his seat and fixed the rearview. "One-quarter impulse power," he said, shifting to drive. The flurries were done and hadn't accumulated so the roads were fine. The kids sat quietly.

Calvin stopped at Rte. 666 (Bald Eagle Pike) and got them across it to pick up Colonial Drive. "How do we do this, love? I can't take you to the front door with a skirt on."

"I'll take her to the door," called Saint Mark.

"Open your gob again and I'll jam the spare tire in it."

"Yes, Matthew told me how violent you are, how you almost choked Inky to death. Why do you think I'm afraid for Kitty's safety?"

"He's still talking," said Calvin, pulling over.

"A woman shall not wear an article proper of a man, nor shall a man put on a woman's dress," said Mark. "Deuteronomy 22."

"You have a quote about cross-dressing memorized?" said Kitty.

"It's sad that I need to, but that's the world we live in now."

"Got any Bible quotes about fellatio?" said Spazz.

"Ryan, the spare is actually under the mat where Mark's sitting," said Calvin, "so do us a favor and hold him while I get it out—"

"Okay, fine!" said Mark. "I'll be quiet. I promise."

"You better." Calvin got the Volvo back to cruising speed.

"Everyone shut up," said Kitty. "I swear, boys always have to be macho. Silly boys! We have a real problem here! And it isn't your skirt, love, but this car. If we had Abby's Honda, she could walk me up no problem. But Daddy will watch her to make sure she leaves safely and he'll see her get back in this car. I gotta make it inside my house before Daddy knows I'm back, and the only way to do *that* is to make sure Lewis doesn't hear us."

"That can be done?" said Ryan, the hobbyist sneakabout, always prowling in his ninja costume. He considered dogs his biggest tripwire.

"Yes. It can. Calvin, park on my road but way before my house."

The Howes' modest American Foursquare was worlds away from

the Corgans' McMansion in terms of price, but only a half mile on the map. A few quick turns had brought them to Liberty Road. "Answering all-stop on other side of the street, Captain. Number 40 mark 3."

"Nerd!" said Spazz.

"You mean 43 Liberty Road?" said Kitty. "That's perfect. Turn the engine off. Someone'll notice it running."

Calvin killed the lights and ignition and hoped the heat would last.

Kitty said, "Jill? You need to guide me."

"Me?" said Jill, aghast. "I've never been here. I've never guided a blind person. And I'm, like, fucked-up drunk!"

"Let me be your guide—"

Everyone turned around and made urgent hisses to Saint Mark to clamp it before he got clamped Old Testament-style.

"Abby should do it," said Calvin.

"She makes too much noise walking," said Kitty. "No offense, Abby. And Lewis is attuned to you."

"I'll go," said Ryan. "I'm good at sneaking."

"No. I need Jill to do it."

"What about Val?" asked Spazz.

"Skinny helps but stoned does not," said Kitty. "Duh."

"The Spazzster's thinner than an Ethiopian on a diet! I'll do it." Spazz slapped himself. "Oh wait, I'm stoned too."

"What about your cane?" asked Jill.

"I didn't bring it. It works by sound anyway," said Kitty. "Lewis'll bark the second he hears it ticking outside. Lewis is a guide dog and hears ten times better than any human. You people have no idea how much noise you all make—stop moving and just listen!"

Everyone listened at their own heavy breathing. Jill gasped at how goddamn noisy her Minnesota Vikings jacket was.

"All it takes is one foot crunching in the snow," said Kitty. "But we can do this, Jill. We go on the sidewalk, then my driveway, then you get me to the landing by the front door. Just to the landing. The brick part. Then I'll wait for you to leave. I won't get out my key until I can't hear you anymore. Then I'll let myself in, the dog will bark, Daddy'll come running, but you guys will be long gone."

"That house there, Pedersen." Calvin pointed into the gloom, as if it'd help. "I should do it, mon cerise. I know the layout."

"This is *sooo* not a job for an Irish Raging Ape," grinned Kitty, "especially one wearing his first skirt."

The party laughed until she shushed them.

"But why me?" said Jill. Nervous.

"I need someone who's had plain gâteau au fromage," said Kitty.

"Sans cerises!" smiled Calvin. "I *have* been watching my weight, y'know!" He turned around. "She's saying you're skinny, Jill."

Jill loved the sound of that. "Thanks!"

Kitty reached back towards Jill. "I need you."

Jill took her hand. "Let's do this!"

"Wait up! No jacket. Go barefoot, your heels are like gunshots. It's cold but we'll only be a minute. No talking, no whispering, no—" (Kitty made a series of vocal expressions: sucking air through teeth, clicking her cheek, going *bup-bup-bup* as when nudging someone.) "—nothing like that! We walk single file. I'll hold onto your waist. If the lights come on, if Lewis barks, if the door suddenly opens, leave me and run."

"Leave you?!"

"Yes. Don't even hesitate. I'll be toast anyway but at least you and Calvin and everyone won't get caught too."

"Sounds like you've done this before," said Abby, a little hurt.

"It does," said Ryan.

"It's news to me," said Calvin.

"And me," said Saint Mark.

"We can talk about the past in the future," Kitty told them. She took her pulse and fanned herself. "Whew, it's been hours but alcohol really makes your blood race! Okay, love, take the keys out so the door chime won't go off."

"You thought of everything," said the lad, complying with her order. "I love you, mon cerise. What's 'good luck' in—"

"'Bonne chance.'"

Everyone said, "Bonne chance."

The girls got out. Kitty knelt to pop her knees. Jill followed suit. They paired up and disappeared into the dark.

FOUL

Jill climbed in the passenger seat and shut the door, sweaty and wide-eyed. She saw her Vikings coat swaddled over Calvin's skirted legs and grabbed that shit back. "Oh my God, that was so exciting!"

Calvin blinked back to wakefulness and crossed himself to thank the Lord for not letting him pass out with his noodle on the horn. He checked the others. Ryan and Abby huddled quietly by the window, gazing at the stars. Saint Mark had climbed up to Jill's old seat.

Probably because in the hatchback area, Val was—

Jill grabbed Calvin's arm, hissing, "Is she *blowing* him? *Ewww!*"

Calvin looked at Mark's agitated eyes. "If you actually do got a quote on fellatio, mate, I'll let you speak."

The Saint ground his teeth.

"Seatbelts!" The lad fired up the Volvo and cranked the heat. The clock said 5:08. He took the winding route of Rocky Road; Rte. 666 was more direct back to town but it'd be just Calvin's luck to pass Sheriff Steve Schultz doing morning rounds and the cop would totally recognize Ma's Volvo and the lad's dumb team haircut.

"Spazz and Val first, by the church," said Calvin to himself. "Then down Walnut Street to Abby's."

"I'll get out there too," said Ryan.

"Then we go home," Calvin told Jill.

"Thanks," she said.

"I live on Barley Lane," said Mark. "At the bottom of Suicide Slide, turn left. We'll go right past my house."

Jill turned to snarl at him. "Drop this jerk off right here, Connor. Don't even slow down."

Ryan said, "At the bottom of Suicide Slide, turn *right*. Let's take him to Hagan Hill and leave him there."

"Ooh the haunted part of town!" said Spazz from the back. "Hope ya brought yer holy water, Saint Narc!"

"Calvin," pleaded Mark, "you're the driver so that means, legally, you're responsible for my safety."

"I certainly am," said the lad.

After a harrowing sail down the steep finish of Rocky Road, the section called Suicide Slide, Calvin went left on Barley Lane. "There," Mark pointed. "That driveway with the wagon wheel."

The Volvo slowed down at an old farmhouse and Mark propelled himself out like he'd pulled the ejection seat cord.

Calvin rolled along to Roaring Spring Pike and turned right.

"No shed in Corgan's back yard," he told Jill, "just like you said. Can't believe Art made it all up."

"You can't?" she snarked. "Coming from the same guy who bleached your hair and tried to blackmail Rayche last week?"

The Ape's jaw dropped. "Oh no. Grades for boobs?"

"Never mind, I don't wanna talk about it."

"What'd Rayche get a D in?"

"She *didn't* get a D. She got a B." Jill looked ever so proud. "I took care of it myself."

"Ha! You busted out a mechanical pencil of your own?"

"Goddamn right I did."

The Ape dropped everyone off by turns. When it was just him and Jill in the car, she asked, "How'd Kitty know how much I weigh?"

"I didn't say anything."

"I *know* that—you woulda told her my thighs are super-thick."

"So are hers. Thick thighs are not a bad thing!" Calvin turned onto Maple. "Did she touch your arm? She did with me and 'extrapolated' what my size was. That was the day I met her. The day of the orange."

Jill was done talking. He parked next to Da's Caddy. Rose's Beetle and Robbie's pickup weren't there. He checked the dash clock before killing the engine: 5:22.

Without a "Yep," or "Thanks," or even "Bye," Jill got out and sprinted barefoot across the yard to her house next door.

Calvin fetched her heels from the back and got the front door key ready. *Ma'll be right at the glass block wall, hands on hips, foot tapping.*

The only detail he missed was the woman's dressing gown. "What in Jaysus's good name?" she said, pinching the words through her teeth. "What's happened to your face? And you've a fucking skirt on—*her* skirt! Where's your bloody trousers? And your bloody sister? Why was Jill with you? And you drove *my* car without being bloody licensed?!"

Calvin held up Ma's keyring by the leathern fob.

She snatched the keys and motioned him to start talking.

"My 'bloody sister' left Corgan's party with someone else. I dropped Kitty off first. She's safe. I saw to her needs. A lot of shite happened at the party. I don't remember the details myself—"

"The drink played a part there."

"Smell my breath, I'm as sober as the Pope's farts."

Ma went to slap him, then touched his cheek. "Have you hit your head again?"

"I'm fine. But I'm pretty sure someone took advantage of Jill."

The concerned hand on her son's cheek became a horrified grasp of his shoulder. "Took advantage? Raped?!"

"I dunno. Her dress got torn off. Her boyfriend vanished too." Overcome by it all, the memory gaps and the horror, Calvin's eyes got damp. "I think they killed Jenny too. Like literally killed her. There was *blood* on some of them."

"Christ our Lord!"

"Maybe they were playing at being vampires. Ryan's weird. And did I mention Kitty and Val locked themselves in a bathroom to keep Saint Mark away? He's such a creep." He looked down at Ma's brown eyes. "The important thing was to get the girls the hell outta there. Even if it meant wearing Kitty's skirt cuz my jeans died."

He ran out of words and started sobbing.

"Laddy," his mother said, "you did good. Go get some sleep. I'll put a wallopin' on your arse later."

⚾ **CLUBHOUSE** ⚾

Twelve hours later, Mr. Maguire's blue Ford Bronco came by arrangement to 30 Maple Street and collected Ryan. Calvin hustled down the road to join them. It only took Art a few minutes to get the Bronco across town to Cemetery Lane. The Watson house—"my pappy's crappy habitappy"—was right behind the graveyard. Spazz, spying the rest of the Suicide Kings outside, ran to join them.

Art wanted to call their little clique the Dead Man's Hands, an awesome name killed by nerdy syntactic pedantism. "Shouldn't it be Dead *Men's* Hands? Or Dead *Mens'* Hands? What do we call each of us: a Hand? A Finger From the Hand? A card from the actual Dead Man's Hand? If so, who're the aces and who're the eights?"

"I ain't gonna be no dog balls or double-barrel butthole," Spazz had said, forever changing the way Calvin saw the number 8.

Nitpicky issues sunk *every* potential group name. Calvin had put forth the One-Eyed Jacks ("too cliché"). Spazz pitched the Royal Flushers or Acey-Deuceys based on their toilet wordplay (precisely why they got vetoed). Ryan liked the Inside Straights (but Art was all, "That one's tryin' way too hard *not* to be gay!").

Spazz tried out the Four Aces and assigned the suits. "Obviously *yer* the spade," he told Art, and got a fist in the face. When Calvin said the white kids could form a sub-group called the Three of a Kinds, a four-way brawl broke out.

The Suicide Kings was Ryan's idea. No one loved it. No one hated it. Wasn't great. Didn't totally suck though. Talk about cliché! But it was also risqué.

It won by default.

Rather like how these four sophomores ended up friends in the first place. They didn't have a decade of history like Kitty Howe's Cable-Knit Cardigan girls or Sean Corgan's Scoundrels. Calvin, Ryan, Art, and Spazz had all been in Troop 666, yes, but so had Gus, Crowe, Zedz, Chicken, and others. Our heroes had no unified cultural focus, like the Burn-Out Buds, the Breast Strokers, the Vo. Techies (Found-On-Road-Dead Division), or the Gelatinous Cubes. All four were townies, not from subdivisions, but they didn't live on the same block or anything. Spazz didn't even start hanging out with the other three until his sidekick, Denny Sandmiller, moved away.

Really, the four fell in together just cuz.

This morning, Art tried to hold the usual Saturday morning poker session but the others were no call/no shows. He finally heard from Ryan about lunchtime when the guy stopped by the Maguire house, still in his suit from the dance, presumably on his way home.

Ryan suggested they all meet here and Art made the arrangements.

The four boys stood in a phalanx before a Celtic cross headstone, engraved BARBARA L. PHILLIPS, JAN. 4, 1952–OCT. 13, 1978.

No one spoke. Not even Art was dumb enough to yap before Ryan finished paying respects.

A couple minutes later, Ryan gave a nod like *I'm done here.*

"Finally time to dig 'er up?" said Spazz. "I'll get the shovel."

The guys had a laugh. Ryan said, "Kinda weird that I stepped onto church property and didn't immediately get turned to a pile of cinders."

Another laugh.

"God clearly preserves you for important work later," said Calvin.

"Your good pal 'God,' yeah."

"What happened to your face, Irish?" asked Art.

"What happened to yours, African?" Calvin shot back.

Art had a line ready for that: "You should see the other guy."

No one got it. They lapsed into quiet.

"Did I pull a Con-norrhea, all dain bramage," said Spazz, "and *miss* the part when he splained how his face sprouted a manure patch?"

"What about the part where you passed out in Amy Corgan's closet?" said Calvin.

"Pretty sure I fucked one of her Pumas. Let's change the subject!"

"I don't wanna talk about last night either," said Ryan.

"We can talk about the past in the future," said Calvin.

Art, feeling left out, took off his glasses to clean them with his shirt tail. "Me? I stayed home and made a half dozen M.S.S.M.s. Don't worry, I'll issue minefield maps to y'all once I install them."

"You are *sooo* gonna assassinate the President," said Ryan.

The boys took in the crooked rows of weathered gravestones. The crumbly edges glowed coral in the rays of the pink sunset.

Spazz put a hand to his temple. "I can behold the future, and it's got 'us talking about last night anyway' written all over it."

Calvin checked his Swatch. "It *is* the future."

"Why ya got the old one on?" said Art.

"Nothing gets by you, does it." Calvin was sporting his classic Jelly Fish with its translucent band and face. "My good one never left my wrist but somehow it got totally water-logged."

"You fell in the ice-cube lake that Apple Core-gan made in his kitchen," said Spazz. "I busted a barstool over Davey's Neon Noodle."

Calvin turned to Art. "I busted my face on the Sips-for-Pips table. My jeans died defending Kitty."

Art pointed a few rows down at some open grass. "That plot's open. We'll bury the dead jeans there."

"Those jeans deserve a hero's funeral," said Ryan.

The boys pocketed cold hands, rocked back and forth on their feet. Spazz took out his Reds. "Mind if I smoke?"

Ryan waved at his mom's grave. "She won't mind."

Spazz gave Calvin one, then Ryan too when he held out a hand.

Art was positively horrified. "Am I the only Suicide King left who ain't committing actual suicide?"

Spazz held his Zippo for Ryan, who took in a large inhale. "Gotta drown my misery somehow."

"No comfort from that?" said Calvin. He pointed at Ryan's puffy black coat, indicating something pocketed within.

"The Book won't help here. Sergeant Slaughter's giving me shit about Abby. He let it go last night at the dance cuz he didn't wanna make a scene but he laid down the law when I got home today." Ryan scrubbed a hand through his blond hair. "He's all, 'you're around too much sausage.' Meanin' you guys. And the football and baseball teams and wrestling and back when I was in Troop 666."

He waved at the headstone before them. "My mom obviously ain't been around but neither are my brothers' moms. Trevor's is dead too, and Steve and Charlton's mom won't come anywhere near my dad. If the only company I got is Sergeant Sausage, that's his fault."

Ryan took another drag and looked at the Marlboro appreciatively. "I finally hang out with a girl, and he's all, 'Gotta improve your game. Ain't no son of mine'll be a chubby-chaser.'" He gazed into the middle distance. "Just what I need, another voice telling me what to do."

Art laid a hand on Ryan's shoulder. "Like my dad says, 'Always *somethin'* holdin' a man back.'"

Spazz laid a hand on Art's shoulder. "Your dad rocks! Heartless-Artless here killed me with a paintball gun and Mr. Maguire still lets 'im use it! *All and all that's just a / 'nother thumb's up for Paul!* My old man woulda plunked the barrel up my butt like a full-auto suppository."

Calvin kept his hands to himself. "I've been through this too. Ma's wanted me to dump every girl I dated 'til Kitty. She still calls Jenny 'the MacDonald wench.' She was real cross when I came home with Jill last night." Despite Art's concern, or because of it, the lad let that thread dangle. "That, and the fact that I had Kitty's skirt on."

Art gave a snotty laugh. "What?"

Calvin ignored him. "My ma can say whatever but I'll be friends with who I wanna be friends with. Ryan—tell your da to get fucked."

"That'd make me a Suicide King for real," said Ryan. "Dad's fully prepared to add to his kill count. I ain't *that* eager to meet the Devil."

Spazz agreed. "Skip ain't no one you say 'no' to, less'n the question is, 'you want *another* sock in the chops?'"

Ryan shrugged. "Maybe he's right and I'm too good for Abby."

"Plenty chicks in the sea, Ruby Red Phil-lipstick. Fat ones, thin ones, undead ones. I keep sayin', you can do my sister's corpse for a buck." Spazz pointed his cigarette at a headstone a couple rows over.

"Wait up, you actually have a dead sister?" gawked Art.

"As she lives and breathes! Or, well, the opposite. Sheryl was kid number 2, died a million years ago. Yer good pal Liam here's lucky number 7."

"Catholics pump out them puppies," smirked Ryan.

"Sheryl's pro'bly pretty dry by now," said Spazz. "You'd hafta hose her down before ya roll 'er in flour and aim for the wet spot!"

"Must be nice to *have* a girl to roll up in flour," Art whined.

"You got your precious standards," said Calvin.

And you got a fat crippled girlfriend, Art's narrow eyes came back.

"I'd need the whole bag of flour for Abby," said Ryan.

"Maybe not the whole bag," said Calvin. "Val would only need a teaspoon. A little dab'll do her."

"Keep yer little dab away from my squeeze, Cal-culator the Masturbator!" said Spazz. "I *behold* the way she looks at ya! It's the way I'm gonna start lookin' at yo moms—AAUGH!"

The Suicide Kings jumped as one; Perry Phillips stood right behind them. "Now you know why I survived Korea, and why lots of slant-eyes didn't," the old man said, rounding on his son. "You got no situational awareness."

Ryan expressed his annoyance by stamping out his cigarette. "I heard ya comin'. What was I supposed to do, make a run for it?"

"You're desecrating your mother's grave, son."

"She won't mind."

Calvin likely saved his friend's life by butting in and saying, "I think

Davey raped Jill last night."

The other kids bucked. Skip remained standing at attention.

Calvin went on: "Corgan wasn't in control of the situation. We had a huge brawl. Look at my face!"

Skip's eyes menaced Art. "You weren't there, isn't that right?"

"No, I stayed home."

"You're a crappy excuse, Maguire. Everyone else went to the party and got fucked and/or got fucked-up. Can't even pin a crappy accessory charge on you. You're a crappy hitter, a crappy fielder, and the only black kid I ever seen who can't run for crap."

"In my defense," said Art, "my craps ain't crappy. I can crap for crap. Ask my momma. Clogged my fair share of toilets."

The wicked noise of Skip's laugh bounced around the graveyard. "Get in your dad's Bronco and drive around the block, Richard Pryor. Say nothing to no one about what your Irish friend here just brought up. ¿Comprende?"

"Uh, sí. Gotta get to Video Onslaught for my shift anyway. See you guys at Mass tomorrow."

⚾ MANAGER'S OFFICE ⚾

The second the mulatto kid was gone, Skip got to ranting. "Connor, if you'd said Artie there took advantage of a girl, I'd believe it in a second. He's got ill-intent eyes. Weak fielding, worse hitting. He sticks to you like a booger on a gold-digger's finger. Some boys are star systems, pulling planets into their orbit. Seanie's a star. You're a star, Calvin. Art's a moon, at best." Pointing at Ryan and Spazz: "You're comets, going wherever, trailing ice. The rest are dumb asteroids floating away."

Other dads had seen action in Vietnam, like Art's and Davey's and Reggie's; and Sheriff Steve had gunned down two criminals in his seventeen years on the job; but only Perry "Sergeant Slaughter" Phillips relished in his reputation as a killer. He loved making kids nervous.

The Suicide Kings' anxiety was unfounded. Skip had but one killing ahead of him.

"Your stats are amazing," he told the fat mick. "Seven innings, one run, two hits allowed, sixteen K's, no walks, and an ERA of 1.00. You are slaying them all … except Davey. Them 2 hits? Both his. He's pretty much the only one to *foul off* any of your pitches."

"I'm *not* making shite up about him to get revenge," said Connor.

"Didn't say you were. Got a phone call today from Davey's asshole dad Ralph. Don't like that sumbitch even a little bit. He treats his only son like a redheaded stepchild. I had a hard time believing what he said to me—that you tried to shoot poor Brion while he was taking a leak."

Connor's physical reaction said it all—*that's not what happened.* "Bollocks! Where would I get a gun?"

"Seen Seanie's pop at Gruber Gun Shop," said Skip. "I told Ralph to put his son on the phone. Brion started spewin' this psychotic non-sense about how he's the victim of a vast conspiracy. You and Jill and Sean contrived to keep him away from Kitty. He's been eye-fucking her for years and now that you're ballin' her, *someone* needed to fill that gap and keep Davey's dong from danglin'. That'd be Jill."

"It's always about pussy."

Skip turned aside dismissively. "Maybe you found one of Tony Corgan's irons in his garage. Then you walked in on Davey pumpin' the purple girl's pooper and she was embarrassed at getting caught and told you it was rape. Maybe *you* pumped her pooper and Davey caught you and this is a way to save your thing with the blind girl. Maybe Davey had a few too many Rolling Rocks and *did* take advantage of Jill. Maybe Davey tried to pump *you.* Or vice versa. I don't know. I wasn't there. And I don't much care, either.

"What I do care about is getting us all back in the sunshine so's we can hold hands and sing 'Kumbaya' and get to States."

The old man expected Big Boy to react poorly, then get violent.

He did not expect Big Boy to skip directly to violent. He took a clean blow to the chin from the younger, larger lad turbo-charged by anger. Phillips staggered back, grasping a gravestone to keep his feet.

Spazz and Ryan tried to restrain their solar center but the mick tossed them aside. He stood tall, thinking he'd made his point. So confident, righteous, in charge. No wonder kids followed Connor. No wonder Seanie polishes his balls. No wonder Davey hates him.

"Jill is my friend, dare I say it," the kid said, "but you don't give a fuck about what happened to her. All you care about is the team."

"From your lips to God's ass, yes, that's all that matters." Skip wiped his mouth and blinked to see a light smear of blood on his liver-spotted hand. "Bit of a cheap shot, son."

"'Maybe Davey pumped *you.*' Not cheap at all."

"*Deserved* is the word I'd use," said Ryan.

The old man had to give his son credit: Ryan wrote the book on not giving a fuck. While other teens pretended not to care how the rest of high school perceived them, Ryan lived it. There was pure defiance in his blue eyes. The boy faced Dad's music every day for sixteen years. He knew he'd lose this matchup like he lost all the others.

He did not care.

Trevor was in jail, Charlton was out in L.A. handing out cult leaflets, and Steve was coke-heading his way outta Cal U ... Perry wasn't about to let his youngest boy follow them to the dumpster. Not over some chubby chick, not over the chubby Irish friend, no sir.

"You'll be dealt with later," he told his son.

"Yeah, threaten me some more. Never mind the witnesses or that we're on 'holy' ground. That's all S.O.P. for Sergeant Slaughter."

Skip's thousand-yard stare penetrated Ryan's very soul. His right fist penetrated Ryan's septum. The kid swooned back into his mother's headstone. The crossbar on the Celtic cross thudded right in the crook of his neck, below his ear. The *squik!* noise was sickly.

Connor dove at Skip to tackle him. Skip fired out a jab and caught the mick on the left clavicle. Big Boy's Reeboks slipped on the flagstone path and he landed on the grave plot of someone called Barnaby.

The kid got back upright and made fists of his own.

"We're even, dipshit," said Skip.

Spazz took a knee and checked Ryan. He was still alive, breathing, semi-conscious, chuffing laughter that spread the blood from his nose onto the grass of his mother's grave. "You raise 'em tough, Skip," said Spazz, "but you ain't no better than Davey's asshole daddy!" This wild-child stood, making serious fists but ruining it with his silly catchphrase: "Yer makin' my dick itch, and when *that* happens—"

"Watson, close your trap! You're only on the team cuz you're left-handed and get the ball to the plate without it bouncing. I'll happily drown you in a toilet bowl for another chance at States."

Spazz massaged his throat like Darth Vader had Force-choked him.

"I hate everything about this," said Connor. "Y'know what? I quit, Skip! If this is baseball, I want nothin' to do with it."

Skip sneered. "Go ahead—quit."

"I'm not bluffing, Mr. Phillips."

"Good, cuz I'm raising the stakes. How're you getting a job without a college education? You'll never graduate with the F's you're putting up in math. And that deal Lucky was gonna make with you for some wheels? Fuck that, your fat ass can walk."

The old man got back in Calvin's space again.

"And once you quit the Axes," he said, "all the protection you've gotten from Sergeant Slaughter here goes away. Davey and Chicken and anyone else can stomp your gonads until the cows come home, and I won't lift a finger. Hell, I'll have a pizza party for them."

Connor's sweaty face got pale. "Well. Lemme think it over."

"Smart. Tell your 'friend' Jill to be smart too and pick her company better. Then this crap won't happen ... if it even did."

The man turned and left. Didn't offer his son a ride home.

⚾ CLUBHOUSE ⚾

The three boys sat with backs propped on tombstones and smoked Spazz's Marlboros until the adrenaline faded.

"Take one bovine," said the wild-child, "and one pile o' feces. Put it together, and you gots all that bullshit comin' out Skip's mouth."

The Ape said nothing. All the ill emotions moshed in his brain. He turned sixteen tomorrow. A young man, scared and confused.

The Satanist couldn't hold back his emotions. The other boys got up and let him weep at his mother's grave alone.

Spazz offered Calvin a ride but the lad pulled tight his despicable scarf of many colors and walked. He took Main Street so he could stop at Video Onslaught and rent a tape. He told Art nothing about what happened, no matter how much the guy cajoled. Calvin got *Hollywood Vice Squad,* hoping Princess Leia got naked in it.

Chapter 24

POLE POSITION AT THE PIZZA PARTY.
CALVIN'S BIRTHDAY.

✶ FAMILY SECTION ✶

EILEEN ELBOWED HIM TO stand for the hymn. From her sniper's nest—the last row of pews in the nave—she'd watched plenty of mothers nudge sleepy, bored, or hungover teens to wakeful positions. She done the like herself with Robbie and Rose (and, truth to tell, Calvin the Second) but never with reverent Calvin the Third until recently.

"Just tired," the lad hissed after the congregation was done singing "Lord, who throughout these forty days."

"Wouldn't be if not for those bloody Corgans," said Eileen. She had a few things to bring up with Tony and Helena about their wicked son Sean turning the Corgan home into a regular den of iniquity. Eileen scanned the room once more but the 9 a.m. service was certifiably Corgan-free. *Well. We'll be at the Pizza Putt after Mass for his birthday lunch, and I'll lay out my grievances then, so I will!*

She felt her son's forehead; he was warm and drained, and pulled away in case she touched his eye bruise. The boy's tie and jacket hung askew in defiance of all straightening attempts.

Father Sean's sermon about perseverance included a cheeky warning against calling the I-99 roadwork delays "a malediction."

"Rejoice in hope, endure in affliction, persevere in prayer," the priest said. "Romans 12:12. Here, Paul cautions his people to be patient ... the Romans also built lots of highways, but not in one day!"

He got a nice chuckle.

When Mass ended, the Connors and Howes had a huddle. Eileen was most curious at Eric Howe's desire to talk to Mark Duffy. "Saint" Mark was present before Mass, then vanished into the sacristy when the Howes arrived.

Father Sean came by to wish Calvin a happy birthday. The lad said thanks and asked for a quick confessional. "I said a few dirty words doing my Algebra homework," he told the grown-ups. The jest only made June Howe more suspicious of what he might need to confess to.

"Well," said Eileen, checking her little watch. "We'll see you at Pizza Putt at 11:30?"

"I don't know," said Eric Howe. "I might have trouble keeping my temper if I see that Sean there."

"Oh my God," said Kitty, turning red.

"We will be there," said her mother, firmly. That was Gudrun Schultz, the crop-destroying caterpillar, speaking; not June Howe, the harmless married butterfly. She, too, wanted a word with Mr. Corgan!

FOUL

After a regroup back at the Maple Street Usonian, the Connors headed out for Pizza Putt. Calvin the Second drove Ma in the Caddy and Rose drove Calvin the Third in her VW Beetle.

The Ape ran a hand over the Bug's upholstery. "Surprised it dried so fast. They had to fish it out of the Axsubewa Crick, right?"

"Ha-fuckin'-ha." Rose made an immediate wrong turn, going straight on Maple instead of left onto Third. "I ran outta gas on the way to the mall. One of Pete's friends saw us and gave us a ride back."

"Where you stole Ma's Volvo. Surprised she didn't call Axsubeen Vice and report it as grand theft auto."

"Ma was downstairs 'watching telly' and never even suspected."

"You went to Corgan's in the Volvo but left with ... who?"

"Your mom."

"You can't make a ma joke with me, Sis—she's your ma too!"

"As if! We sure as hell ain't related." The girl pulled the Bug into Schoenberger's Pharmacy on Main Street and dug into her *bag of holding* for two singles. "Get me a pack of Kools. Ask for matches. Keep the change, birthday boy."

Calvin took the cash and, in the same move, plucked her keys from the steering column. It'd be just like Rose to "jokingly" drive off and make her li'l brother walk the six blocks to his own birthday party.

The lad prowled the aisles for the innocent item. Boys talk a brave game about buying a *Playboy* or box of rubbers at the drug store without being anxious, but that's bollocks. As Kitty says, "You can't trust boys." He needed something moral to bring to the counter so he could then, offhandedly, ask for the immoral thing.

He jerked to a stop at the home pregnancy tests shelf, his dress shoes squeaking on the linoleum. *Now the girl buys a stick at Schoenberger's and pees on it.* He checked the box. Da was right—that's how they worked, like *Next Generation* technology in the real world!

He swept along, making jokes to himself in Star Trek voices.

As Picard: "Dr. Crusher! Send some urine sticks to the bridge."

As Worf: "We Klingons kill a rabbit to find out. And eat the flesh!"

Mrs. Adkisson gave him the stink-eye from the aspirin aisle. Calvin's fucked-up face didn't help matters. No one outside his peer group believed his tale of accidentally tumbling into the Corgan dining room table. He'd omitted the taking-off-his-Wranglers part except with Father Sean. He never edited his sins in the confessional.

"Sounds like you had quite the crazy weekend," the priest told him. "You've left the drinking and girls scene, but your sobriety did not stop a black eye. Was it God's will? Who can say.

"Apologizing to me or yourself for misdeeds does nothing. Apologize to God. He will know your sincerity. After all, He knows your heart. He'd rather you look forward than behind.

"I read about your baseball prowess in the paper. Athletics are good tests of our ability to handle change and failure."

"About that," Calvin had said. "I'm thinking of quitting. I don't like the other players or the coach, or these situations I end up in."

"But you excel at the game. This is a chance to bring the community together, to demonstrate your strength of character, to give schoolmates something to rally around. Plus pitchers can make quite a bit of money. Think of the good that can do."

Always comes back to that, Calvin had thought. *Even priests say it.*

"I know you're fond of Kitty, and she is a sweet girl," Father Sean went on. "And you take your faith seriously. Put your mind towards school and church, give your heart to Jesus and Miss Howe, and choose baseball over booze and debauchery."

"Pack of Kools," he said over his gulp. He set down his innocuous spearmint Binaca and orange Tic Tacs. His sweaty fist strangled Rose's two beans and the tenner Ma had given him for his birthday.

The lady at the front register was cold and quiet. As ever. When Calvin was ten and counting fiddling pennies to buy Wrigley's Spearmint, this lady said nothing. He'd never once heard her voice.

She could've been twins with Jill Pedersen's mom, Kimmy McSween: both wore foundation and eye-shadow and whore-red lipstick; both had peroxide-blonde hair with Charlie's Angels feathering stuck in the '70s; both glued brightly hued plastic to their fingernails; and both used a cocked-hips resting position that stressed their T&A.

All in service of looking twenty-five long after that age. Jill's ma was thirty-five, but this lady was older. *Way* older. Like forty.

The other difference was attire. Ma McSween looked sloppy in her maroon Pizza Putt T-shirt and grease-spotted apron. The silent register lady at Schoenberger's wore a traditional white pharmacist's coat over a pale blue dress. The costume made her come off slutty, like a porno actress playing a nurse.

The register lady fetched his cigarettes though she knew him to be underage.* As she stretched up to pluck the pack from the overhead rack, Calvin noticed the nametag dangling from her mammoth left titty.

KITTY

His shillelagh expanded and his brain contracted. His finger suddenly pointed behind the lady to the spank rack. Blockers hid the magazine covers except the very top inch so you could pick out the titles. He first aimed at Kathy Ireland's eyes—the Swimsuit Issue had been out for weeks and he finally had the scratch to buy it—then panned to Ginger Miller. "That *Penthouse,* please. I like the letters."

He declined the paper bag and strolled across the parking lot with his wares open, like a true lad.

The Howes' sapphire blue Chevy Celebrity station wagon rolled down Main Street, giving him a honk. He waved back with the hand holding the *Penthouse* and menthol smokes, then felt a total arse.

---

* America of the '80s didn't take smoking laws seriously (cf. the ashtray footnote in Volume 1, Chapter 2), unless some bureaucrat had a pinecone up his butt.

Rose laughed through her bubble gum. "Couldn't of fucked that up any worse 'cept if ya still had Kitty's skirt on!"

FOUL

Originally, Pizza Putt was a meager take-out joint called Corgan's Pizzeria.* In 1982, Tony Corgan acquired a neighboring building, had it demolished, and added a dining room with neon light piping, classic '50s-car memorabilia, nonstop oldies, a wacky mini-golf course, a water ice counter, and an arcade room.

Pizza Putt was an actual destination, a reason to go to Axsubeen and endure the sticky eye-drool of toothless local yokels. Weekends were killer business, even in the winter when the mini-golf was closed. Church folks, birthday parties, lunch before/after a trip to Logan Valley Mall. The lot was jammed; Rose had to park next door at O'Sullivan's Wallpaper & Paint.

She raced ahead of Calvin to open the door and trigger the frame sensor. A tinny speaker spat out a loud swirling quasi-fart, equal parts funeral dirge and middle finger: Pac-Man's death dirge.

"You're such a child, Sis," said the lad.

"See?" said Rose. "Your voice sounds *just* like that noise!"

They found their brother Robbie chatting with Eddie and Kitty Howe in the vestibule. The grown-ups were inside at the cash register, having urgent conversation with employees Kimmy McSween, the Other Waitress (an older one who wasn't memorably mammoried), and Justin, a balding fat guy who ran the joint when Mr. C wasn't around.

"Mr. C isn't around," said Justin. "He and Mrs. C always take

---

* Tony Corgan had wanted to call it "Tony's Pizza" but feared customers might confuse his place with Tony's Pizza in East Freedom, Tony's Italian Restaurant in Martinsburg, Tony Baloney's in Coupon, Tony Jabroni's in Foot of Ten, Tony and Vince's in New Enterprise, Vince & Tony's in Newry, Tony & Toni + Toné's! in Broad Top City, or one of the seventeen otherwise unaffiliated eateries named Tony's Pizza to be found in Altoona's Mill Run, Rosehill, Calvert Hills, Red Hill, Logan Hills, Gospel Hill, Beverly Hills, Dutch Hill, Park Hills, Highland Park, Columbia Park, Mansion Park, Knickerbockers, Logantown, Juniata Gap, Llyswen, and Toy Town neighborhoods.

Valentine's weekend off."

"Then we'd like to speak to his son," said Ma Howe.

"Oh honey, he never works the weekends after one of his parties," said Ma McSween. "Too busy cleaning up the house before his folks get home!"

"Well. That's the point, so it is," said Ma Connor. "Sean wouldn't *have* to clean the house up if his parents kept it clean to begin with, if you take my meaning."

"Sean won't get away with it this time," said Da Howe. "The kids won't tattle but I will!"

"His parents already know," said the Other Waitress.

"We make two dozen pies for those parties," said Justin.

The grown-ups exchanged a four-way look of frustration. "No point fighting City Hall," said Da Connor.

"I used to think that Sean was such a nice boy," said Ma Howe. "This is what's become of our town once we started letting all these non-Germans in."

"Excuse me?" said Eileen Connor, born Eadaoin Ní Dubhthaigh.

"I meant *Italians,*" said Gudrun Schultz hurriedly. "They aren't *really* named Corgan, right? It's Corleone or something."

"Sean and his dad have red hair," said Da Howe.

"That means nothing, Eric! Calvin's mulatto friend has blue eyes. I've seen *actual* colored people with red hair!"

"The birthday boy sees lots of food," said Calvin the Third. With teenage tartness: "Can we sit finally?"

Ma McSween led them into the dining room. She had a table for nine all set up and reserved.

Calvin said to Kitty, "We come here every Saturday after poker and I've never seen the little wanker working."

"Excuse me," said his mother, "the little what?"

"No one."

"Exactly," said Kitty, giving Calvin's shoulder a squeeze. "We don't need to talk about Sean right now."

Kimmy McSween passed out the menus. She was Axsubeen High's 1972 Prom Queen. After graduation, she married a Schultz's Lumber driver named Buck Pedersen and had her daughter Jill. After years of delicious rumors—two-timing, spouse-swapping, swinging—Kimmy ejected Buck's ass and returned to using her maiden name.

The coy sparkle of those Prom Queen years never left the flirty woman's eye. Big-tittied Kimmy McSween's big titties contributed in no small part to Pizza Putt's revenue stream.

Again, a destination.

Kitty told Calvin, "Tu n'as pas porté d'eau de Drakkar!"

Calvin said, "Tu as dit que ton père *détestait* l'eau de Drakkar!"

"Exactement! Merci!"

"Vous êtes les bienvenus."

"*Tu* es le bienvenu! We're not in vous-land, remember?"

"What're ya babblin' about, Kate?" said Eddie.

"Sounds like ye're talkin' about Drakkar Noir," said Robbie.

"Not *Drakkar,*" said Kitty. "*J'accord.* It means, *I agree.*"

"Très bien," smirked Calvin.

"I hate Drakkar," said Da Howe. "The smell makes me sick."

On a day with many likely sweat-causing moments, Calvin had to avoid using Drakkar cuz Kitty's da hated it. The Ape's Right Guard was on its own!

Lunch went nicely. The families welcomed each other. Robbie and Rose didn't bicker. Eddie was in Rose's close proximity and managed not to masturbate once. The mothers gossiped over Kimmy McSween's lurid history. The fathers discussed baseball.

After bringing out the pitchers of soda, Ma McSween wished her "kiddie kindred soul" Calvin a happy birthday and thanked him for rescuing her daughter Friday night.

She patted the lad's shoulder. Ma Connor looked ready to chew up Kimmy's hand and spit the Lee Press-On Nails back in her face.

"What do you mean, 'rescuing' Jill?" demanded Ma Howe.

Kimmy belted a big laugh that sent breast flesh undulating in waves under her maroon Pizza Putt T-shirt. "You know teenagers and their parties! Jillian looked great and probably loved the attention she got for it. I bet she had a few too many wine coolers. We've all been there!"

Eric Howe and Eileen Connor said, "I've no idea what you mean."

"I've seen you with the Dew," Calvin told his ma.

"I've seen *you* with the Jack," Eddie told his dad.

Kimmy's eyes did the backstroke through her thick band of blue eye shadow. As she walked off: "Thanks again, Calvin!"

The birthday party turned into a press conference, everyone peppering the lad with questions. "It won't happen again," Calvin told them all. "We both wanted to go to the party, of course—"

"Me especially," said Kitty. "It was my first ever party."

"—but the second we got there, I realized I didn't want to be around that insanity anymore. So I got the car keys—"

His words hydroplaned across the sweat in his pits. He nearly admitted to Kitty's folks that he'd driven her home.

"You did the right thing," said Ma Connor. "You got the girls together and got them out of there."

Thanks a million, Ma. You try to rescue me by confessing for me.

"Thank you," said Ma Howe. She didn't mean it. But, she said it.

"I'll be honest, the whole thing still bothers me," the lad went on. "I don't wanna be around Sean and baseball and any of it now. I wanna quit the team. Actually, I wanna *move* and never see this town again."

"There's the door!" said Rose, and Ma gave her a *thwap!* for it.

"Don't quit," said Kitty's da.

Calvin sat up at that. "What?"

"He's right," said Ma Connor. "Base ball is a good opportunity for you. Remember Perry Phillips saying you'll get a scholarship?"

Kimmy McSween and the Other Waitress swooped in with the pizzas, and not a minute too soon. Calvin was one hungry hungry hippo.

They devoured all of the two pies except a few rinds of crust. Pizza Putt sold frozen ice-cream cakes but Eileen Connor had brought her own; she got the bakers at Merk's Super-Merket to make a cheesecake (remembering that Kitty liked them) in the shape of a shamrock.

"Surprised you didn't order it shaped like a bottle of Tullamore," said Robbie. He bucked as his shin fielded a sharp kick.

Everyone sang the still-copyrighted song that the chronicler need not transfer to alliterative allusion and Calvin blew the candles out.

He told Kitty, "The cheesecake is sans cerise."

She gave her spritely tinkle of enchanted mirth.

Calvin got some gifts. Kitty's hands jittered as she handed over hers: *Made in the U.S.A.,* the Beach Boys' greatest hits on cassette.

Remembering he had something for her, he handed over the orange Tic Tacs. She was tickled pink.

Kitty revealed she'd gift-wrapped the cassette tape herself.

"Wasn't that nice," said Calvin the Second.

Calvin the Third was floored. Da's usual routine was to sit like a man asleep with his eyes open, but he was positively *chatty* today. He even ordered a glass of Iron City.

You never really know what people are thinking, what goes on in their lives, Da once said.

When he's not busy, he thinks he'll turn idle, like his birth father, Aul' Ossified Olly, Ma always said.

Be happy he's with you today. Your father does love his family, Ma said after this feast.

Calvin smiled. He was happy and not just cuz it was his birthday. This was the first time that the two complete families sat as one.

It was also the last.

FOUL

Once everyone fell into food coma, Calvin took Kitty into Pizza Putt's arcade room. The *Pole Position II* machine was a sit-down model with side-by-side car seats for versus play. Perfect for a private chat.

"This is pretty clever," said Kitty as they wiggled into the seats. "I've been dying to talk to you!"

"Same here," he said. "Gimme your hand."

"Not yet."

He knew what that meant—Kitty's da was nearby. How did her "Daddy Radar" work? There were too many beeps and boops in this room to hear footsteps. Perhaps she smelt the pepperoni and light beer sailing through his walrus mustache.

The man knelt to peer in the arcade game's bucket seats. "Hey Calvin, I just wanted to say thanks for being my daughter's scout crow and getting her home safe."

"Well. Of course! You're welcome. Anytime!"

"We'll be out here, Smiley." Da Howe left them alone.

"'Anytime,' ha ha!" said Kitty.

"He knows I drove you home?"

"Even if your mom didn't give it away, I already told him."

"What?! Why?"

"Well. The sneaking with Jill worked—Lewis didn't bark until I put my key in the door. But Daddy wasn't home. He drove around Overlook until he saw Abby's car. He checked it out and saw her battery was dead and said he woulda used jump cables but her thing wouldn't open. The hood. So he parked down the street to wait for us."

"Was that after we left? I woulda recognized his station wagon. Especially with that totally maimeó-blue paint job!"

"He saw your mom's station wagon so it was before we left. He said he fell asleep. He woke up after sunrise and Abby's car was still there but your mom's Volvo was gone. He figured we must've left in that so he came home and woke me up to give me a hug. I told him you got me home cuz Abby's battery died." She found his hand, pulled him close. "And *that's* the only thing he knows."

"What if Saint Mark talks to him? He saw us making out in the yard—saw me with your skirt on!"

"Mark won't say nothing," said Kitty. "Did you see him at Mass?"

"For, like, a second. He took off in the back so fast!"

"Good. Forget him. I'm gonna need a new tutor."

"I only get A's in Sex. Ed., love."

Her lips, sweetened by an orange Tic Tac, got close.

He leaned over to receive her kiss—

"You gonna actually *play* that game?"

The teens pulled apart. Some twerp almost jumped in Calvin's seat. The kid was about ten and could've used five across the face.

"I'm talkin' to you! Whaddaya, deaf?" The little bastard ran over to Kitty's compartment and made an annoyed whine that she was there.

"We're busy," Calvin told him. "Whaddaya, *blind?*"

Kitty's pink glasses bounced off her jolly laughing cheeks.

"Holy crap, nice face!" the twerp told the Ape. "You get run over by a Mack truck? And how come ya talk like yer gay?"

"Please go away," said Kitty, no longer amused. She did the Arms of Frustration gesture and slammed the twerp's shoulder.

"Ow! I'm tellin' Mr. C yer hoggin' the game without playin' it!"

Calvin dug out two quarters and jammed them in. "There. We're playing it, you cunt. Piss off!"

The twerp snarled like *I'm gonna get you!* and left.

"Wow," said Kitty, all excited, "are we actually gonna play it?"

She gripped her steering wheel. The screens gave a choice of race-tracks. When she stepped on her gas pedal, she inadvertently picked the hardest one.

Pizza Putt was the Spinal Tap sort of arcade: they kept all their games silent in attract mode, but twisted the goddamn volume to 11 once you paid your 25¢. *Pole Position II's* tooting fanfare tooted so loud that Kitty's russet hair blew back.

A sampled female screamed, "PREPARE TO QUALIFY!"

Kitty went, "Yippee!"

She had so much fun. He stopped playing his own side and gave her pointers on when to brake and which way (and how hard) to steer. He wanted her to finish a lap, and with his help, she did. She fake-pouted when time was up and asked to play again.

He was out of quarters. He'd blown all his cash at Schoenberger's Pharmacy on smokes, breath-fresheners, and porno.

And anyway, they were out of time.

Chapter 25
LEAVE ROOM FOR THE WRATH.
PRESIDENTS' DAY.

FOUL ⚾

"TWO FOR EAST JABIP."

Kitty, hanging on Calvin's arm, poked him like, *Behave!*

The old gaunt gent at the ticket window, one Johann Gruber, said, "Har-de-har." His vocal cords were badly out of order.

"I meant Altoona," said Calvin. "The Penn State station."

"One way?"

"Round trip."

"Shame." Two tickets ground through the printer. Gruber tossed them over the counter. Calvin had to bend to fetch them.

"You give him that shiner, young lady?" said the gent. "I hear this one gets fresh a lot. On other people's lawns."

"Yes, Mr. Gruber," snapped Kitty, "I did it."

"Careful, aul' fella, or you're next," Calvin told Gruber.

The kids waited out on the platform, on a bench with Joe Camel pasted over it. The valley hosted a sharp wind today, one that gleefully slipped between their many layers. The murder pecking about the bracken on the far side of the tracks shivered their feathery arses off.

"Can you spot him?" she asked.

This was the first time Calvin would be taking her out with no chaperone so he checked over his shoulder for the sapphire blue Celebrity wagon. He realized what she meant and looked up. "Ah! He's perched at the top of the station, on the roof." The Ape gave the crow scout a wave.

"*Rrwrk,*" the crow said back.

"That old man's always been nice to me," said Kitty. "This time he was a jerk. Even brought up that one time on Corgan's lawn! You really are the Devil."

"Must be why Ryan follows me around."

"... Ryan doesn't *really* worship Satan, does he?"

"If it's all an act, it's the best one ever."

"He's having an effect on Abby. She always had independence, all 'I don't conform' and stuff, but Ryan is really changing her."

"Well." He touched her chin to aim her face up at his own. His glove's finger traced the lipstick she had on, a subtle red. He wondered how difficult it was to put on. "Ryan and Abby had blood on their lips at the party."

"*Ewww.* From the big fight when Jenny showed up?"

"This was hours later. And it wasn't a lot of blood. I'm sure they didn't sacrifice a baby and eat it or anything."

"That's not funny."

He let go of her chin. "We can talk about the past in the future."

"Or never. I'm fine with that. Like I said, Abby's changing."

She played with the jingle bell safety-pinned to the end of his putrid scarf of many colors. She had Excalibur today to help in public restrooms. "It's cold, Calvin. So cold that I can see your breath."

He laughed. "I guess you hear everyone saying that. We'll be warm on the train. Today, of course, it's late."

"So's my period. It was supposed to come last week."

The crow scout went, *"Caw."*

Slowly, Calvin said, "We covered periods in Falcone's Health class. There's blood, and P.M.S. (which stands for something), and foam things you stick up there ... and then it stops for a month."

"A+, love. You left out one thing: not having one is a sign that a girl's pregnant."

The wind kicked hard. Calvin barely felt it.

Kitty swept her free hand up to keep the dark glasses from flying off. "It's not a *definite* sign. The month after my very first period, I didn't get one. My mom took me to Dr. Jacoby and he goes, 'When girls are young, sometimes the train misses the station.'"

Calvin groaned. "He did not say that!"

"Yes he did! That's exactly what he said!"

"Doesn't that just 'punch my ticket.'"

Kitty didn't ride the train enough to get it. "He told me to drink plenty of fluids. I got my period the next month and I was fine."

"Dr. Jacoby's answer for everything is 'drink plenty of fluids.' No wonder Gus is so huge!"

"It's good to be hydrated! Plus it gives the doctor something to tell the patient that's easy for them to do. And if you use orange juice as that fluid, then it's also good for you."

He gave her a proud squeeze. "You got the whole routine down, Kitty! You should be a nurse when you grow up."

"Or a doctor. Girls can be doctors, y'know."

"Naturellement. Then you can look for a cure for blindness."

"Oh, can I 'look' for that, Mr. Man?"

Calvin's face straightened a tie it wasn't wearing. "All I meant was, you could help people like you."

Kitty slid away from him. "Not everything about me has to do with blindness. I can be a doctor for people like *you,* and do Tommy John surgeries and study cerebral contusions. Or I can be a pediatrician or a gynecologist or an oncologist or whatever."

Calvin had no idea what those words meant. The world spoke in code a lot lately. "Sorry. I'm being biased again."

She snuggled back up to him cuz it was so cold. "I got a little mad there. You and Abby are the only ones I'm comfy talking to. I like that we can discuss things and that we listen to each other."

"Except certain things in the past, that we'll discuss later."

"Yes. And just to clear this up about the party—I had a great time. And everything you did was fine. I'm glad you never stopped being friends with Jill, cuz she ended up helping me."

"Did she tell you what happened? To her? At the party?"

"I'm not gonna tell my mom about missing my period. She'll think it's because we're doing it. And this'll all end, and we'll never meet up again and Eddie'll kick your ass and I'll be back at the doctor's drinking more fluids. Besides, I can't be pregnant anyway."

"It'd be a sin if you were!"

"Right."

"I love you, y'know," he said.

"Do you?" she said.

"I do."

"Good."

The crow scout sounded the alarm and took off, followed by his murder. A shrill horn cut the cold air soon after. Calvin marveled when the train's pantographs drew sparks from the frozen wires overhead. "This is us, love." He helped her up and fixed her jacket for her.

FOUL

They sat curled on a lumpy vinyl seat, tickets in the courtesy clip atop the seat-back in front of them. On the weekends and holidays—it was Presidents' Day—the conductor was a lazier sort of gentleman. With her head on his shoulder, his hand on her thigh, and the ka-chunk of steel wheels underneath them, he felt good.

Which was great since the view sucked.

The run up the western ridge of the Axsubewa Valley was always a slow adventure, with great plunges visible beyond the trackbed's ballast stone; railway lines didn't bother with guard rails. As the ride turned north, it settled to smooth curves around endless ugly shite. Gray roadways at East Freedom/Brooks Mill. Bulimic trees at Newry. Gravelly snow piles at Duncansville. Calvin couldn't remember when he'd last seen a fresh field of green grass.

The first Altoona stop was Logan Valley Mall. The one after was Lakemont Park, closed for the winter. The Skyliner and Toboggan rides skulked, lonely. No waving hands, no distant squeals. The centerpiece attraction, Leaps-the-Dips, was condemned, a real eye-sore.

Calvin hated Altoona. And Pennsylvania in general. Wide stretches of blah. Tight clumps of rusted metal and cracked concrete. County Kildare felt more alive, so much to see and do, people to meet, aul' fellas to annoy and run away from, shops to walk to, parks with rolling hills and trees, football pitches, Dublin right down the road.

Altoona was a relic of the train industry—itself a relic of the United States—with a show-offy curve of tracks and the Mallo Cup factory.

Whoop-de-bollocksy-do. He had classmates who aspired to move here after graduation! Calvin saw no life scenario where he'd make such a choice. Even one of the city's biggest faces, Lucky Cheeseboro, lived outside Altoona in some cushy enclave.

When me and Kitty get married, I'll convince her to split. Connors have picked up and started roots elsewhere for over a century now. He pictured it: in Miami, with his Lambo, Kitty at his side. She loved him, he loved her, for real and forever.

He finally got why people liked Phil Collins.

The train bounced on a dodgy section of overpass. Kitty gripped him tight. His hand slid up her thigh another inch.

His Bugle Boys' crotch rose another inch. This particular pair of jeans also saw duty at scrimmages and would be relieved once the team's baseball pants came. Paddy Millar's mother Lottie, the Team Mom—a role last held by Snatch Mueller's mother Charlotte—was in charge of the uniforms. Real baseball pants put him that much closer to being a real baseball player. Skip talked college scholarships, Lucky talked getting drafted by the majors. Calvin now had a snappy answer to "Whaddaya wanna be when ya grow up?"

He was the Next Big Thing.

What if, when he finally took the mound in a real game, he sucked?

Would the hype, which was not his creation, become his prison?

He saw how the grown-ups reacted when he threatened to quit playing. Skip wanted to kick his ass. His ma wanted that scholarship so they wouldn't get a big tuition bill. Kitty's da wanted to see his future son-in-law on the Pittsburgh Pirates. Their behavior was disgusting. None of them cared about how he felt, what he was going through.

But … they had a point. *What else am I gonna do?*

The practices had made him better. He was learning to embrace short bouts of patience; they helped on the mound. You can't get more in-the-moment than an at-bat. It was awesome striking out his teammates and seeing them slog back to the dugout, eyes down.

For years he ignored all the talk of baseball, about the Yankees and Dodgers and the 15-day DL and left-handed middle relievers and Astroturf sucking. Now that Calvin *listened,* one thing tickled his ear over and over: baseball players made a million dollars a year.

I can buy that Beach Boys/Miami Vice life that America promised me!
But …

What if he never became a player for, say, the Seattle Mariners? What if his dreams drowned? What if his ability to pay for that Lambo-life dried up? What if he regretted reading the *Sports Illustrated* Swimsuit Issue instead of his homework: *The Old Man and the Sea* and *The Rime of the Ancient Mariner?*

"What's with all the water imagery?" he said, his guffaws jiggling Kitty's noodle.

She didn't hear him. His hand, and hers, were occupying her.

He hadn't needed to thread up the Bellend Howl in a while. He was a walking letter to *Penthouse* now, getting looks and offers. That was dirty and he felt guilty, but he wasn't the same Calvin who jumped at those chances. Kitty was his everything. Not one short clip in a series, or a trophy for his shelf, but a friend. A partner. *Dare I say it?* A hero.

Kitty did training and practice too, used short bursts of patience all the time. She met the challenges God set before her every day.

Lucky Cheeseboro told him everyone faced challenges, everyone had self-doubt and shyness. Everyone. Even the President.

"What's the secret?" the lad asked.

"Confidence," said Lucky.

"Okay. What if I don't have that?"

"Just fake it. How the fuck are they gonna know?"

As true as any ten words in the Bible.

It's like that spy novel he read once where the hero walked right into the enemy base. It wasn't cuz he had the villains' uniform on, it was cuz he acted like a fellow coworker who belonged there.

Confidence changed everything.

He saw it with Kitty. The lass wore wispy skirts pulled up past her waist and the kinds of cardis his maimeó adored, yet the way she carried herself and overcame challenges made her way sexier than Cynthia Brimhall, Calvin's favorite playmate (Miss October 1985).

Her thighs squeezed together on his hand. The shudder along her body let him know that he'd hit the right spot.

This insider's knowledge of female biophysics and coital rapture elevated him above his classmates; children really, little boys whose spare time was consumed by banal crap like Nintendo and *Star Wars*. Take Art Maguire. Instead of asking girls out, he'd hide in his lair for months working on stupid shite like landmines made from shotgun-shells, utilities with no clear purpose.

Art was decidedly not "in-the-moment." That kid needed a good blowjob. Even a shitty blowjob would do!

Things will only change when you do.

Fartin' Martin had a point.

"I've never watched *The Wonder Years,*" said Calvin.

"Don't," said Kitty. "It sucks."

FOUL

The kids entered the Polar Cinema's screening room. "There's no one here!" Calvin guffawed. "It's *never* this empty."

"We must be early," said Kitty.

"Or the movie sucks. I wanted to go to the King & Queen and see *Bill & Ted* but you insisted on this one."

Lady Em was beside herself. "Well! If *that's* your attitude, perhaps I shall pick a new consort!" As Kitty: "Or is it courtesan?"

They got some good seats in the middle and settled in. Kitty took a sip from the unwieldy cup of Diet Coke while Calvin noshed a Mallo Cup. Easy listening purred from the speakers. Slides projected on the screen advertised local eateries and asked trivia questions.

"Kenny Baker," he said.

"Who?" she said.

"The question was, 'Name the actor in R2-D2's costume.'" After a few slides, the answer came. "Score one for me."

"No fair! Read me the questions so I have a chance too."

Shrill giggling bounced high off the Styrofoam ceiling tile. A fanfare—*here cometh a daft teenager.*

"Please God, don't let them sit near us," prayed Kitty.

"Here's the next one—'In *Terms of Endearment,* Jack Nicholson's character is a former blank.' I've no idea."

"Astronaut."

"Really? Thought that was some soap opera flick."

"Yeah, it is. Mom taped it off cable. She loves that movie."

Rustling came from the row directly behind them. "You gotta sit in the center," giggled a girl, "not on the sides!"

At that voice, Kitty sat up straight.

"But if we sit in the corner, we can make out in private."

At that voice, Calvin sighed the sigh of bad luck.

The girl was Shelley Quince. She had a crow's beak nose, a turkey's tailfeather arse, a chicken's legs, and the biggest chest since Foghorn Leghorn. She literally dragged her date by the hand; he wore a brimmed cap pulled low and shades over his eyes; he'd thrown high the collar of his white Members Only jacket and tucked his ginger Davey-Dangle tail tuft inside.

"I *thought* that was you, Shelley!" said Kitty.

"Oh my God! Kitty!" said Shelley. "You're on a date too?"

"*We* ain't," said Sean, plucking his hand from her grip.

"I haven't talked to you in like, forever!" said Kitty. She shifted to a comfortable position to "face" the Breast Stroker girl, and that meant no more handholding with Calvin.

"We were both at the table the other night during Sips-for-Pips," said Shelley, "but it was *sooo* noisy!" With a proud liar's wink in her voice: "I'm with Sean Corgan, but *shhh!* We're just friends."

"Where's Kare at?" said Kitty.

"In Pittsburgh with her grand-pop," said the little wanker. He plucked off his Ray-Bans to wink one green eye at her like, *Keep it under your hat.*

"He took off his super-expensive shades and winked at you, love," supplied Calvin.

"Hello, Sean," said Kitty. "Long time no see."

Sean wasn't sure if she was being sarcastic or using a mere turn of phrase. His default reaction was "nonchalant" so he went with that.

Calvin answered for him: "'Hi Kitty, nice to see you too.'"

Shelley's eagle eyes went wide. "Calvin, your eye looks *sooo* bad!"

The lad stole Art's line: "You should see the other guy."

Sean actually laughed.

"Let's move up and sit with them," said Shelley.

"I still say, let's sit in the corner," said Sean.

Kitty told Shelley, in a pouting-baby voice: "Your date and my date don't get along."

"Awww," the girls said together, laughing at the end.

"It's not a date," said Sean.

"So what's your beef with him?" Shelley asked.

Asked *Calvin.* "It all started my first day at Axsubeen. Fifth grade. We both brought *Star Wars* toys out at recess—"

Sean's poker face folded. "Holy shit, I did *not* steal your goddamn Squid Head! It's been like, five years … give it up."

"I didn't say you stole it."

"Yeah you did."

"No he didn't," Kitty and Shelley both said.

"He was *thinkin'* it." Sean sat back with a dismissive wave. "Ever since, this guy looks at me like I'm Darth Vader."

"That's exactly how I behold him," nodded Calvin. "Like Darth Vader … when he was burning up on the funeral pyre."

"Aren't boys silly?" said Shelley.

"Indeed they surely are," replied Lady Em.

"You still do that Lady Marjorie voice? Ha ha! I haven't watched *Upstairs, Downstairs* since I was a kid!"

"We came to watch a movie, rem'ber?" said Sean, standing up.

Shelley snared his hand. "Yeah, and we're gonna move up and watch it with them."

Sean let himself be dragged to the aisle.

In the brief moment they had alone, Kitty apologized to Calvin. "I haven't talked to Shelley in forever. I'm sorry."

"Me and Shite-Stain there talk every day."

"Maybe you're turning into friends, like with Jill."

"Wouldn't lift a finger to save the little wanker's life." Calvin folded his considerable arms. "I'd give the *middle* one to end it."

"God gave us this challenge, love. We'll beat it."

"Wish he'd beat it."

"Would you stop?" she said, out of patience with his cracks.

The teens sat four abreast, boys on either end, girls chatting up a storm in between. Kitty and Shelley talked about elementary school and *21 Jump Street* and laughed over some distant memory of a Catholic summer camp when they were younger, where they met the mythical Li'l Joey. Shelley started reading Kitty the trivia questions off the screen slides and Calvin felt useless. "I'm off to the loo, love."

"Loo!" whooped Shelley.

"I'll join ya, chief," said Sean.

That halted the whooping. "Behave, you two."

FOUL

The Polar Cinema's lobby was empty, despite the holiday matinee show starting in mere minutes. The Ape didn't hold the men's room door for the little wanker. Sean's low-brim Pirates cap and Ray-Bans conveyed no irritation. An overhead speaker played the same easy listening as in the screening room: *the Honeydrippers commemorating the choice occasion when a couple first converged.*

Calvin drew out a couple of Kools he'd swiped from Rose's pack. The boys stood at a stall and smoked the crumpled cigarettes, flicking their ashes in the direction of the toilet bowl.

Sean said, "My dining room table really kicked your face's ass."

Calvin said, "I heard you broke *your* arse on the kitchen floor."

"My glutes are so toned that I bounced right to my feet."

"My parents are ready to kill you. Kitty's too."

"Pro'bly cuz you two were flapping your lips instead of shutting them. Speaking of—do I even hafta tell ya, 'Talk and you're dead?'"

"Miss McGillicutty won't hear about this from me."

Sean pulled off his Ray-Bans and tucked them in his collar. "This was all her idea. Shelley, I mean. The Breast Strokers are the next table over at lunch and she's been eyeing me up for weeks. One day she slipped me a note. I mean, I woulda boned her at the party but too many people were around."

So chilled out. Just one dude talking to another.

Calvin called the bluff. "All I hear is a bloke saying, 'my girlfriend's not putting out—time to cheat.'"

"Shelley wanted to go to the rink," the little wanker went on. "We get there and she's all, 'It's too cold out here!' What a whiner! I'm like, 'Let's go park, the IROC's heater rocks.' But *nooo,* Shelley's all, 'We gotta do something first.' And here we are."

Calvin smirked. "At a Corey Feldman movie."

"*That's* what would piss off Kare the most. 'Cheating on me with the big titty girl is fine, but going to a fucking Corey Feldman movie?!'" Sean took a puff off his Kool. "Speakin' of, I never noticed Kitty's rack before. Now I get Davey's boner."

"You get Davey's boner every night."

"That's a good one."

The easy listening song on the overhead speaker ended. The men's room went chilly in the silence.

Calvin found himself asking, "How do you do that?"

"Do what? Look this handsome? Rule the world?"

"Shut the world out like that. I insult you and you're all, *whatever.*"

"You do it too." Sean puffed again. He was only pretending to smoke. "I brought up Kitty's big titties and you didn't flinch."

"Well. I ain't giving you the satisfaction."

"Same here. We all got powers and abilities, chief. Like how a fat mick prick lures in all the hot chicks. Amazing. What's your secret?"

"Character," Calvin said. Quipped. Scolded.

"... okay," Sean said. Just said.

Christopher Cross began a libretto about a bastard lawbreaker bustling his buns to Baja California.

"*I* rope 'em in with my emerald eyes and ten-inch cock," said Sean.

"Your cock is never ten inches."

"Sorry, eleven. 'Twenty-eight centimeters,' as you foreigners say." The little wanker spread his hands. "You let shit get to you when you oughta be cool, but then you act cool when you oughta get mad. Me lyin' about my dick got you mad. Why? What the fuck are *you* insecure about? *You're* the one with the laser sword wang. I saw you sticking it in Jenny MacDonald out on my front lawn."

"Davey's always calling me a faggot, you're going on about my shillelagh ... this is why I wanna quit baseball."

"Yeah, Skip told me. We had a powwow with Lucky. He did the conference call thing from his office at the dealership."

"About me?!"

"About your wang. It's all we talk about. Rumor has it you put it inside Kitty in my back yard."

"That never happened."

"Good to know. Davey never took advantage of Jill, either."

"Bollocks, I saw it!"

"Oh yeah? What did you see? You were concussed, chief."

"Why would you stick up for a rapist? A criminal?!"

"Cuz he's not those things, plus he's my friend. Davey's scared shitless of you now. He thinks you might actually kill him."

Two-thirds of a guffaw left Calvin's gob.

Sean lowered a brow. "You two need to settle this. I need you *and* Davey out there or we never get to States."

"It's all about this 'States.' Skip said the same thing."

"Skip wants to stay in Axsubeen and keep spankin' boys after practice. Not me, chief, I wanna *split*. I asked my dad to get me in Larsen Academy but they rejected me. 'You have the money but Pizza Putt is the wrong kind of rich.' What a crock! They let Jon Oldroyd go there and his dad's biz is heating oil. It sucks. Larsen woulda been my ticket to a big college. Now I gotta get a scholarship like the rest of you losers."

"What're you talking about? Your da can pay for college!"

"If he's paying, I'll be forced to do business management so's he can make me take over the family biz. Fuck pizzas. Fuck mini-golf. Fuck *Pac-Man*. If I got a scholarship, I can get my MBA and go to Wall Street. I'll own the bank that cashes your checks, chief."

Calvin took a satisfying drag. "We play poker at Art's and there's this saying: 'Don't tip your hand.' You did it just now. You showed your cards to me. If I quit baseball, I don't have to deal with you anymore *and* your future is ruined."

That gambit didn't even give Sean pause. "Back to that powwow with Skip and Lucky—none of us want you to quit. We all got reasons. I told 'em you don't got the balls to do it, but they think you do. So guess what? That discount Lucky's gonna give ya on a ride won't be the 50% off he gave my dad for my IROC. For you, it'll be 100%." He tugged the cuff of his Members Only jacket. "You're Baseball Jesus, chief."

Calvin's mouth hung open.

"Bullshit," he said.

"Bullshit, bollocks, and shite," he said.

"No, it's true," said Sean. "Gotta agree to a few things, though."

"Of course I do. Like, don't quit the team."

"That's one. Another is, no more taking one of my dad's guns and blasting a hole in the bathroom wall."

"Everyone's saying that. It didn't happen!"

"Perfect. Say it *just* like that. Now say, 'Davey didn't do nothing to any girl.' Say, 'I'll never quit Axsubeen Axes baseball.'"

The burners in the Ape's brain were stuck on high. He wiped his forehead. "Makin' me sweat with all this crap. I'm on a date here."

"Me too."

"Thought you were 'just friends.'"

"Nah, you had it right—Kare don't put out. She's like Jenny. Guess all rich girls are that way. They don't hafta use sex to keep us around. That's what trashcan chicks like Jill and Valerie do."

"Don't talk about my friends like that!"

"Jill's your friend now?"

"My friend, sure. Dare I say it? *Love thy neighbor.*"

"I hear Val *loves thy neighbor* for cash. Who would buy that shit?"

Calvin's oven door opened a crack, turning the light on inside. "I just figured out why you keep striking out with chicks, Corgan."

"This'll be good. Shoot."

"In Bible Study I found the meaning of life. It's a question, see, and how we answer it determines our fate."

Sean smirked through an uninhaled exhale. "Can't wait to hear it."

"The question is, *Who, then, are you to judge?*"

The little wanker's poker face stood up to this.

"Your answer—the wrong answer—is, *I'm me, chief.*"

The emerald green eyes showed growing fissures of red.

"You're good at lots of shite even without the silver platter—looking suave and playing ball. But you suck with girls. You know who would 'buy that shit?' Desperate blokes like *you*. The kind who can't turn on a girl for real, who can't talk their way into their knickers, but who got the bucks to buy their way in." Calvin took a sweet drag off his Kool. "If money's tight, I hear Lorey Adkisson don't charge a dime."

The little wanker said nothing. He pitched his half-smoked butt in the toilet and sashayed to the sink.

"Try this—pay attention to *eeeeverything* the pussy says," Calvin told Sean's back. "Girls are psychotic, so you gotta use psychology back. You don't pay attention to them at all! Kare's probably like, 'Sean don't care about me. Only himself.' She looks at *me* and says, 'How come he's got more pussy than days of the week? I gotta find out!'"

Sean flicked on the sink. "I stole your fuckin' Squid Head."

Calvin's Kool clung for dear life on his stunned face. "You did?"

"What'd I just say, chief?" The little wanker used the sink mirror to eyeball the Ape as he washed up. "I stole Sigourney McKee from you way back when, too. You were mackin' on her and I saw you scratching your head. I told her you had lice and it was contagious."

"You cunt!" said Calvin, so loudly that he momentarily blotted out the Christopher Cross. "I *loved* her! Why would you do that?"

Sean killed the tap and flicked his damp hands at the tile. "Cuz you let me get away with it."

"Go and shite, that's no reason!"

Sean pushed the hand drier button and raised his voice. "You're so afraid I'll tell everyone how you cried in the Office that one time. Davey said you got pissed when Fartin' Martin brought it up."

The drier died and Christopher Cross took the background again.

Calvin wanted to die himself. He *had* wept in the Office. With Sean right there. It was his first major punishment and it was all so avoidable.

The school had banned Binaca when some kid pumped a whole can down his throat and passed out. That made it cool. Sean made it cooler: slouching on the recess wall, he'd flip his jacket lapel, turn his head, and take a secret squirt. He sold his spare cans like a drug dealer. Stupid Li'l Calvin, who'd spent Friday nights for years watching Crockett and Tubbs chase down dealers, went and did business with a dealer ... when all he had to do was walk to Schoenberger's Pharmacy and buy a can.

Sean popped his fancy Ray-Bans on. "I *do* pay attention to what the pussy says, chief." He drew a tampon-size white and green tin can from his pocket. "The pussy says, 'I hate smoker breath.' Want a hit?"

The Ape cleared the distance between them in one step. His right hand slapped the Binaca away. His left, now a fist, drove directly into Sean's right eye. The Ray-Bans snapped against the little wanker's face. A sliver of black plastic with a sharp point drove into Calvin's third finger, above the knuckle. It was worth it if only to see that smug look on Sean's face become a raw O of shock.

The heels of Sean's Pumas slipped on the tile that he'd just wetted down and his coccyx broke for the second time that weekend as it struck the sink ledge. Calvin's momentum carried the two atop the counter. The Ape's left shoulder made the mirror shriek in protest. Sean's right leg struck the sink's tap so hard the handle snapped off; the ball end did a real number in bruising Sean's calf, while the exposed fixture underneath shore a hole in his stonewashed 501 Blues.

A jet of water sprang up … or would have in some Corey Feldman movie. This being real life, this being a dumpy former burlesque theater in dumpy ol' Altoona (the left testicle in Pennsylvania's crotch), the water pressure sucked majorly. A mild trickle splattered the boys' feet.

The little wanker raked his fingers desperately and caught the end of Calvin's repugnant scarf of many colors. The Ape pulled away. The woolen thing went taut and propelled Sean across the bathroom.

The impact with the far wall knocked the wind out of him. He lay on the bathroom tile, clawing at his throat, gasping. The Irish Raging Ape stood over the little wanker and spat. The luger missed, hitting the wall; the mucus was pink with blood.

Calvin checked himself in the mirror. The fracas had bent it into a funhouse mirror and an unholy psychedelic bend went down his face.

Sean started to breathe, slow, deep drafts.

"When Shelley beholds your fucked-up face," said Calvin, "she might feel sorry for you. She might pork you to make it feel better."

"Sounds familiar, thanks, chief." Sean got to his feet. "I'll scream your name out during 'in·SEMM'·eh·NAY·shin.'"

Calvin kicked the broken shades over. "Don't forget these."

"They're trash now. Don't panic, I keep a spare pair in the Z. I buy Ray-Bans in six-packs."

The Christopher Cross song ended, followed by the *Coming Attractions!* fanfare. The lad bent to fetch the Binaca can and took two hits. The alcohol-infused minty mist burned his bloodied lips.

Pain never hurt so good.

FOUL

The 'Burbs sucked, and it had little to do with Corey Feldman.

As the kids made for the exit, Calvin told Kitty she was lucky not to be able to see it. "All that swooping camera shite. Thought I'd puke!"

Sean joked he could make a better movie with his butt. "And Princess Leia never got in a gold bikini. What a gyp."

"She don't do nude scenes," said Calvin, basing that on *Hollywood Vice Squad*. Carrie Fisher was barely in it and wholly clothed when she was. *Gotta get that tape back to Video Onslaught so I don't get a late fee!*

Shelley was quite distressed. "How could Corey be so cool in *The Lost Boys* and be so dorky in this?" She pointed at the lobby poster for *Dream a Little Dream*. "Well, that's out soon. Ooh it's got Corey Haim too. We should double-date for that!"

"You're just friends," Calvin reminded her.

Shelley pointed at his face. "You didn't have a fat lip earlier." She looked at Sean for answers and went "Oh my God!" at his bruised right eye and dry flakes of blood on his nose.

"What happened back there?" said Kitty.

"We're just friends," said Sean.

Calvin's guffaw filled the lobby.

After some goodbyes on the cold sidewalk, the couples went their separate ways.

FOUL

Kitty's parents made her promise to call twice: when they got to Altoona and before they left. They used a payphone outside the Burger King down the street from the Polar Cinema. A mass transit bus rolled up, squealed its brakes, honked at some asshole in a Ford pickup, and rumbled off, forcing Kitty to shout through the whole call.

"Calvin's got a timetable," she yelled. "We're taking the 3:50 train back so you can pick us up at 4:10. Okay. Bye bye!"

"We coulda taken that bus and gone to the mall," said Calvin.

"No," said Kitty. "No malls. Malls have Mall Chicks."

"I have never beheld a chick singing in a mall. Have you? Those videos show it, Debbie Gibson and whoever, but that's not real life."

"Is the rink near here?"

"Got me. I can ask." He laughed. "I'm no good on skates."

"Me neither. That's why we should go! It'll be great."

Some lady at Burger King said there were two rinks and directed them to the indoor one. It was closer. Her eyes never left Excalibur.

The kids walked the eight blocks in the freezing wind to discover the indoor rink was packed. They waited in a queue that started outside. "Definitely worse than the lunchline," said Kitty, teeth chattering.

Calvin had just enough cash to cover their entry and skate rental. "Good thing we bought round-trip tickets!"

They spent twenty minutes skating, sidled against the hockey boards or toppled over each other on the ice. People learned fast to make wide arcs away from them. It was the longest continuous stretch of bodily contact they'd shared. Neither the frozen water below nor the billion staring eyes kept the kid's shillelagh from its rigid salute.

On the train ride back, they sat holding hands and smiling like fools. "Thank you," she said.

"What for?"

"A new environment. I'm never allowed to be alone in new places. It's so nice to be somewhere strange for a change!"

"You're a poet and don't even know it," he said. "I hate that Sean and Shelley showed up and kinda ruined our day together."

"Didn't ruin it for me." She sighed like, *they did kinda ruin it.* "I feel sorry for Kare."

"Do you now? I don't."

"Why not? I know she's stuck-up but that don't mean she deserves to get cheated on by her boyfriend. That's terrible."

"Sean's a wanker. Serves Kare right for dating him in the fir—"

"No! *Who, then, are you to judge?* Kare's okay with who Sean is or she wouldn't be with him."

"That's my point—Kare doesn't *know* who he is. Sean took Shelly out to public places. He's so casual about it but he had a goal."

"You reduce everyone's actions to schemes and stuff. That's how boys interpret life."

"True. Spend a month as Art Maguire's friend and you'll question what his schemes are. And now the guy's making munitions!"

The lass sighed again, this time like, *I am Art's friend too and I know what you mean.* "We girls have a whole different interpretation of things, love. I guarantee you, Kare knows what Sean's like."

I know what you're like, Ape, and I am with you. That's what Kitty was saying. He hugged her tight.

"If you can feel sorry for Kare, I can feel sorry for Jill," he said. "I honestly don't think she knew what Davey was like."

"Back to school tomorrow," said Kitty, nakedly changing subjects. "I won't have tutoring until I find a new tutor. Want to meet up?"

"I got my driving test and an Algebra quiz to study for."

"In all labor there is profit, my mom likes to say."

"School is labor, all right. What is that, Psalms?"

"Proverbs. Know what else is labor? When a woman gives birth."

"Cuz she got lay-bored first. Get it? Lay? Laid?"

"Assez, mon gâteau au fromage!"

FOUL

Calvin needed thirteen minutes to find Kare's number. He combed every sheet of the two forests' worth of paper on his desk and finally found where he'd scribbled it after seeing it in Art's calculator—on that page of Biology notes that was in his Trapper Keeper but wasn't his.

Armed with the digits, he double-checked that Rose's Bug wasn't in the driveway before grabbing the kitchen phone.

"Hello?" said some guy. He sounded like Starscream.

"Uh, is Karen there?"

"Hold on."

Kare got on the line. "I got it, Dad." There was a hang-up click, then she said, "Calvin?"

"Lucky guess!"

"No, I knew."

"Well. One benefit of a foreign accent—parents never ask me, 'Who shall I say is calling.' Your da's got a distinct brogue himself!"

"Yes," the Mall Chick said, all acid and bile, like she was *sooo* done hearing about her dad's weird voice.

"I know it's odd, me calling, but ... something happened today."

"Your girlfriend already called to tell me about it."

He burped a little. "Me and her talked it over on the train back."

"I'm sure you did," said Kare. "People love to talk."

"Not like that! We were concerned now."

"Kitty wasn't concerned, she was *upset*. It was sweet of her to call me." He heard a bed squeaking. "You don't seem upset, Mr. Ape."

"Neither do you, Ms. Mall Chick."

"Don't know why I should be. It's exactly the kind of thing an asshole would do. Y'know. Cheating on their significant other."

"I ... agree."

"*You* would never do that to your girlfriend, right?"

Kare's tone startled him. *She's teasing me. She wants me to flirt, to unfasten her bra again. Why did I call her?*

"So, like, it's done," she said. "Whatever. Why should I be upset over anything my ex-boyfriend did?"

"Your ex-boyfriend?"

"Is there an echo? Kitty's blind, you're deaf. The perfect couple!"

"When did you dump him?"

"Just now.

"Does *he* know?"

"He'll find out." The sound on her end got louder. *She's in the loo.* "I'm too good for him, don't you think, Calvin?" He pictured her looking at herself in the mirror as she said this. "I should cheat too."

"That's the obvious thing," he said. "Revenge."

Do not look for revenge but—

—leave room for the wrath?

"Thing is, Kare ... if you already dumped him, it's not cheating."

"True, yeah. Then I'd just be an available gal, off doin' her thing!"

She wants me to riff on that. He melted his buttery baritone: "Oh you're available? Like, tonight?"

"*Mayyy*-be. But you're not. You were just on a date!"

You should hang up. Now. "When you say 'doin' your thing,' does it have to be *your* thing?"

"I could be doin' *someone else's* thing, yeah baby," said Kare with a laugh. "Oh, Connor ... you're trouble!"

The front door slammed open, making the glass block wall wobble. Rose roared into the kitchen with a smile wide enough to snare whales. "Get off the phone, fat-ass! I got real news to spread!" She put her gum out in the trash. "Your pal Corgan banged Shelley up in the 'Toona today! Right in a Burger King parking lot in his Camaro. Matty saw it and almost shit. Cunty Kare's gonna end up with Shelley's gonorrhea!"

Rose stomped off to her room.

Calvin started to apologize into the phone but Kare had hung up. So did he.

As Rose got on her clamshell phone, the Ape grabbed his own clamshell: the black hardcase which Video Onslaught used for its tapes.

FOUL

The video store was a five-block walk. Shorter if you cut through people's yards, which Calvin did after some jerk in a speeding black 5.0 nearly flattened his arse on Maple Street. Art was working (good), solo (better, he'd be able to rent a nasty).

Art opened the clamshell to check if *Hollywood Vice Squad* was rewound. It wasn't. Art used the rewinder. "That'll be fifty cents, sir."

"Bollocks, I want a refund!"

Some Mueller housewife came in and made for the romance aisle. Calvin busied himself at the new releases shelf. "There's a *Poltergeist II?* And a *Caddyshack II?* What's next, *She's Having a Baby II?*"

"Everything's a sequel anymore," said the housewife. She came up to the counter and set down the box for *Terms of Endearment.*

"Jack Nicholson plays an astronaut in that," Calvin said to her.

Art was talking, maybe to himself: "The *Rocky* series has consistent titles, all Roman numerals, but the *Friday the 13th* flicks do not. It goes *Part 2* with a number then *Part III* with Roman numerals, which was dumb cuz that's the one in 3-D and you don't spell '3-D' with Roman numerals, and the next one's *The Final Chapter,* no '*Part IV*' in the title, but even then the title's wrong cuz it wasn't the *final* chapter—there's a *Part V*—'cept *that's* messed-up too cuz the poster and tapes and stuff all say '*Part V*' but the movie itself, like the title screen, just says *Friday the 13th* [colon] *A New Begi—*"

"Tapes are due back in two days, right?" the housewife snapped. "I don't wanna waste one of them days waitin' to pay you, boy."

Art rang her up with steamed glasses. She left. He said, "Bitch."

"She had a point, African. Blah blah blah."

"Not that. She called me 'boy.'"

Calvin took a goose-step towards the saloon doors in the back.

"Mrs. Fanucci'll be back soon," said Art. "Be quick."

The Ape hustled into the porno closet.

A hot rod parked in front of the store. The driver revved the engine twice before shutting it off. "It's Oldroyd in his new ride," Art called.

"Bollocks." Calvin put back the copy of *Miami Spice* starring Amber Lynn and rejoined Christian society.

"You can split out the back if you want," said Art, too late.

Jon Oldroyd burst in Video Onslaught's front door, smiling right at Calvin. "Yo, there ya are!"

Calvin had not seen Jon in some time and jolted at the change. His face still had zits (and acne scarring) but was less brat-like. His blond hair had gone sandy brown. No hateful sneer, a reaction to his parents' divorce. He was taller. And so buff! "Steroid Oldroyd," said Calvin.

"What're you, Spazz? He used to call me Hemorr-Oldroyd." Laughing, Jon offered a hand. Calvin went ahead and shook it. Jon nearly picked the Irish Raging Ape up and slammed him through the hardwood floor à la Bamm-Bamm Rubble.

"You been pumpin' dudes in your dorm at Larsen?" said Art.

"Is that how ya talk to customers?" said Jon, laughing again. "Which are you better at, Maguire, pitchin' or catchin'?"

"Very funny, Oldroyd."

"I was talkin' about baseball! Probably still on the J.V."

Art thumbed out the window. "That's *your* Mustang? Guess the heating oil business is good."

"Good enough to be the *right* kinda rich for Larsen," said Calvin.

"Yeah man, my dad's an oil baron," laughed Jon. "So Connor, I hear yer big shit on the mound."

"There's a lot of hype now," said the lad.

"You bet there is! Cheeseboro's coachin' ya one-on-one." Jon saw Calvin's gray eyes checking out his biceps so he zipped off his Adidas sweatshirt. "Dig the guns? We got an awesome gym at Larsen! Trainers, a cardio room, diet plans with whey protein."

"Way protein?"

Jon slapped Calvin's gut. "You know that Right Guard commercial with the Boz?"

Calvin was at sea. "That's the deodorant I use, but ... "

Art, of course, was portmaster here. "I seen it. Brian Bosworth's teaching a class in etiquette."

"That's the one." Jon pointed at himself. "I was in it."

"What?" the lads said.

"It was shot in Pittsburgh near my mom's. They looked for guys like me who got Boz's build and hair. I got to keep the shades too."

"Awesome," said Art, half-awe and half-envy. "Were you Boz's fluffer too?"

"Same old Maguire! We gotta get him laid, Calvin."

The lad swirled a hand, as if to say, *After you*.

"Ha! Got yer license, Irish? I'll let ya take my ride for a spin."

Calvin was already spinning, like a record. His instinct was to run, to fight, to drive Jon's Mustang off a cliff—

"A Mustang? Was that you who almost ran me over, Oldroyd?"

"Sure was. Ya move quick for a fat fuck! Believe it or not, I was headin' over to yer house—"

"How do you know where I live? I never had you over."

Jon surged on. "—we saw ya but ya went cross-country. I saw the tape in yer hand and figured where ya was headed." He held up his keys.

Well. His *key*. The only other thing on the ring was a slick acrylic Ford oval. "Can ya drive stick?"

"I can now," said Calvin, snatching the key.

Jon ushered him out the door. "I wanted the convertible at first but the hardtop's got a five-liter V8 with 225 horses."

Calvin nodded. "I'll take that over the breeze in my hair any day."

Engrossed in hot rod talk, the lad neglected to say "Bye now" to Art.

FOUL

It was a 1988 Mustang LX 5.0 in jet black. Calvin got in and found the driver's seat already adjusted all the way back. He found a girl in the passenger seat, too. Jon knelt down to chat in through the girl's window.

It was already rolled down, despite the chill air. As if in preparation for this very moment. "Meet Tiffany," said Jon. "Tiff, this is Calvin."

She had a regal blonde crown of hairsprayed curls, long lime green fingernails, pink bubblegum popping between lips surfing in whore-red lipstick, a zebra-pattern skirt over fuchsia Coloralls, a puffy coat zipped down to show a white mesh shirt … but Calvin's eyes had parallel-parked neatly between the girl's fleshy mounds.

"A pleasure," he said, shaking mitts.

"Likewise, I'm sure," she said, quaking tits.

A shrill trill of beeps nearly popped the lad's weasel.

"Just the phone, bro," said Jon, showing Tiffany an open hand. The girl fetched a black handset thing bolted near the stick shift, pulled the curly-cue cable out so it didn't *thwap!* her face, and handed it to Jon.

The guy hit a button and went, "Yo!" He stood up to get some privacy, giving Calvin and Tiff that very same thing.

The Ape was afraid to ogle her again. Was she Jon's girlfriend? She seemed past high school age, but not much past. He adjusted the rear-view to give himself something to do.

Tiffany grabbed the mirror away and tilted it until she saw his eyes in it. "View's better over here," she told those eyes.

He looked over.

She looked hot to trot.

"Taking care of it now, Mr. Bone," said Jon, hanging up with a button press and squatting down again. He handed the phone back and laughed when Tiffany couldn't get it back in place. "No, you gotta put the thing in the hole, Tiff!"

"I know how to put a thing in the hole," she said. To Calvin. Delivering the line as if in a porno.

"All right, Connor," said Jon, "fire it up!"

Calvin started the engine. That gravelly purr sounded like love.

"You know that house up on Mine Road Run?" said Tiffany.

"Mine Run Road, so you mean the geodesic dome."

"Yep. Down the street from Make Out Point."

He put his hand on the gear shift.

She moved that hand down to a long lever, angled up. "You gotta release this first, Calvin."

Chapter 26
THE COST OF "BELOW COST."
TUESDAY, FEBRUARY 21, 1989.

FOUL

CALVIN STOWED HIS KELLY green down jacket and fugly scarf of many colors, swapped books for the early classes, and shut his locker.

"AAUGH!" he wailed. Sean Corgan was leaning on the next locker over, hiding in plain sight. The little wanker's face was fucked-up from their fight but not nearly as awful as Calvin's.

Sean waved the vapor of Calvin's wail away. "Nice rot, chief. There's this company, Binaca, who make a thing for that."

"I make a thing that keeps your ma company."

"But if you keep your trap shut, no one'll smell your bad breath either." Sean looked away, all cool. "Y'know that thing we talked about? Psychotic girls and listenin' to what the pussy says? It worked."

"I heard. At the Burger King, in the back seat of the IROC."

Sean's poker face burst into a dozen different Halloween masks: monsters, killers, shocked ghosts, sad clowns.

"Took Oldroyd's Mustang for a spin last night," said Calvin. "The back seat in that thing's barely big enough for a bag of groceries. The Camaro's back seat must be bigger."

The little wanker's mug cycled back to the original placid poker face. "Don't know what you're talkin' about, chief."

"Then you're the only one who doesn't." He flicked Sean's chest to scooch him out of the way of homeroom.

FOUL

Ma critiqued Calvin's driving the whole way to Altoona. He got to the

PennDOT test center at maximum sweat level; Right Guard's back was against the wall, shield cloven, gladius notched. The building was full of nervous teens, nervous parents, nervous immigrants, nervous former drunk-drivers, and impatient folks who'd just moved from Ohio and needed a PA license. Calvin did Algebra homework to kill time.

"34!" That was the number on the lad's ticket. He got up.

The examiner was gray-haired, soul-free, and clipboard-wielding. Gray Man gave no reaction to Calvin's bruised face. No clicked teeth. No sharp pencil scratch on the form.

Outside, the Irish Sweating Ape beheld the test course. A fat white stripe near the doorway was the start point. Gray Man told Calvin to pull the car up. The lad went to fetch the Volvo from the parking lot. When Gray Man didn't follow, he thought he'd fucked up right away.

Wrong, he realized. *Gray Man's a dick.*

"I've only my permit, sir," said the lad. "I can't drive without a licensed driver in the passenger's—"

Gray Man clicked his teeth, made a check on the form, lowered a brow at Calvin's Lone-Ranger-Mask bruise, and followed him to the lot.

The course wasn't hard at all. Calvin used the indicator on every turn, made complete stops at every line, and nailed the parallel park without molesting any orange cones. For this bit, Gray Man needed to exit the Volvo and judge from afar, promising it wasn't a trick.

It wasn't. Calvin Connor III passed.

His photo ID ensconced forever the lad's black eye and insanely dumb Davey Dangle. Calvin had no idea how many people would see this photo, and how long of a cultural shelf-life it'd have.

"Thanks a million for letting me use your car and stuff," he said.

"'And stuff,' you're ever so welcome." Ma took back her keyring by the leathern fob. "Which way is the dealership?"

⚾ TRANSPO OFFICE ⚾

Every area resident with a TV or radio had the address memorized: right off I-99 at the Golden Mile of Cars, in bun·YOO'·tee·full al·TOO'·nah!!

Calvin pointed out Lucky's Callaway twin-turbo Corvette, jauntily parked by the showroom's front doors. The lobby was glass-lined and erotically lit with neon. The man himself, Richard Louis Cheeseboro, chatted with the blonde booby gal he kept as his concierge.

Lucky tipped his navy ballcap (today's featured a white lowercase cursive *a* for Atlanta) to Eileen and greeted Calvin with a handshake and a backslap, like an old friend. "What's with the shiner? You two homos beating each other up again?"

"It gets rough with two blokes in one bed."

Lucky demanded to see the license right away. "Sharp pic!"

Ma scoffed. "Disgraceful the way the kids groom themselves."

Lucky showed off some '89 stock (GMC's Jimmy and Sierra K1500, a Geo Metro, a Pontiac Grand Prix, and Chevy's Cavalier, Celebrity, and S-10) before taking them back to his office. The walls were lined with newspaper clippings of baseball foibles, Topps baseball cards, and glossy photos of Lucky on the mound. One pic showed him, aged fourteen, holding up his uniform at an Axsubeen High pep rally. The shirt was brown polyester with 1 3 ironed on the back in white.

"See anything ya like out there?" said the salesman, settling his leathery ass behind his desk. "Sorry—did ya 'behold' anything?"

"I 'beheld' sticker prices that far exceed our budget," said Ma.

Lucky gave Calvin a look like, *You were s'posta warm her up for this!* He settled into a cold pitch. "All righty then—tell me yer budget and we can go from there. I got something for everyone."

"Like snake oil?" Ma went on. "I was under the impression this wasn't to be a normal auto sale."

"I'm not giving him a free car. If he told you that—"

"Hang on," said Calvin. "I got wind that the discount went up."

Lucky picked an odd time to glance at his fancy desk phone with its conference call functionality. "Is that a fact?"

"What *is* this deal?" said Ma. "We get a special price if my son becomes your mascot? I'd like it spelled out, so I would."

Lucky laughed, and not a rehearsed one, either. "The deal is, he gets a nice, safe, *quiet* certified pre-owned vehicle. I get a nice, *quiet* endorsement package that helps me sell more cars."

"This deal isn't on the books," translated Calvin, "and I keep my trap shut about certain details."

Ma didn't like that. "In those adverts with Ed McMahon it says 'celebrity endorsement.' You want that, but without those words."

"When you see that in a commercial, that's a legal thing," said Lucky. "Ya gotta let the viewer know if someone's gettin' paid to pitch the product. But like I told your son, he *ain't* gettin' on TV with me, or on the billboards or print ads in the *Distorter*. Leaving out child labor laws and such, doing endorsements removes his status as an amateur."

To the lad: "College players can't make money from sports in any way. If ya don't get drafted in the Bigs and ya try to play college ball, you'll have the NCAA up yer ass."

"That means *I* have to sign the paperwork," said Ma.

Lucky gave an easy smile. "All this talk of paperwork and legalities … that's not what makes a relationship. I'm being a friend here. Let's back up to the first part—putting Calvin into a nice car.

"How this business works is, my dealership has a contract with GMAC. I buy the cars from them wholesale and resell them to John Q. Public at what we call 'sticker price.' I also acquire used cars in trade-ins or other means, and mark them up for resale.

"So, if I sell a car to a family member—I love my Aunt Dottie and I want her in a reliable ride—I'll do it at the wholesale price, what we call 'at cost.' I don't make nothin' … but I don't lose nothin', either."

Calvin went for broke: "What if you just gave them the car?"

"If I sell it for anything less than wholesale—we call it 'below cost'—I lose money on the deal, and I *never* do that."

"In return for a car, you always get something," said Calvin.

"Exactly. When I hand over the keys, I'm gettin' back *something*. Payments are the usual and most preferred thing to get in return, but in Calvin's case, I'll get something better."

Ma's tolerance had ebbed. "We get a car. In return for …?"

"In return, Calvin'll point to the big Lucky Cheeseboro dealership sticker on his bumper every time he shows it off to a friend or teammate or his uncle or folks at church. He'll say lots of really nice things about the upholstery, the handling, how sexy the color is, how it came with free tire chains and a first aid kit, how he got a great deal from that loony bastard wearing the Roman centurion costume on TV.

"Also in return, Calvin conveniently shows up here on high-traffic days, like the big Presidents' Day sale we just had. He'll come in for regular service, oil change and tire rotation. Normally my guys'd have him outta here in under an hour but his service will take four or five so the Next Big Thing can schmooze with all the prospective buyers. If they ain't heard that he's Roger Clemens Jr., I'll drop that nugget." Lucky gave that easy car salesman grin. "But I ain't gonna need to. Once he starts strikin' out a dozen kids a game, everyone'll know 'im."

The Connors soaked that in. Lucky gave Calvin a look like, *Plus a couple more stipulations that we'll talk about in private.*

"Nothing formal at all, then," said Ma.

"The transaction will *all* be formal," said Lucky. "You can't simply *give* a car to someone. We'll have a bill of sale and transfer the title. Yes, Eileen, you'll have to sign cuz he's a minor."

"This deal makes no sense," said Calvin.

Ma gave him a *fwip!* on the shoulder to keep quiet.

Lucky put up a hand, like *No, let's hear him out.* "What don't ya like about it, King Kong?"

Calvin grabbed a pen with the car/burger/boob logo from a dealership mug full of them. The car salesman automatically slid over his branded pad of paper—*ad hoc* algebra was common in this office.

"I can't figure out how you'll get your money back," said Calvin. "Let's say the car I get is $10,000. The sticker price. You woulda paid like half that to Chevy to get that car here."

An amused look hung on Lucky's mug. "Sure, go with that."

"You need $5,000 back to break even, but c'mon. You tried to *sell* us a car when we first got here, when Sean told me I'd get it 100% off. That means you don't want five grand back, you want at least twice that. So we're back to you getting ten grand in return. How the hell can I get that much to you by schmoozing?

"The tryout day, the little wanker said I can make four bucks an hour at Pizza Putt. I'm gonna say I'm worth eight bucks an hour for your schmoozing." He scribbled figures and did long division. "I'd have to do 1,250 hours to pay you back. That's a lot of holiday sales!"

"Well," said Ma. "Every feckin' week he's on News Radio 1240 AM having a 'Going Out of Business' sale."

"I don't have fifty-two sales per year," said Lucky. He was less amused now. "One a month. When there's no holiday, we 'go out of business.' And we almost do—a lot. The car business is tough, Eileen."

"If I came up here every month and spend five hours schmoozing," said Calvin, scribbling, "I'm looking at almost twenty-one years."

Ma said, "Show me a car, even a new one, that lasts so long!"

"That's my point, Ma. I don't get this deal at all. And he knows I'm outta here in twenty-eight months—June of 1991, when I graduate. So the most times I can schmooze up here is twenty-eight. Five hours each, eight bucks an hour, that's still only $1,120."

"What about when you talk up the car to friends and family?" said Lucky. "Add that in, too. Let's say it takes ten minutes each time."

"Times six for an hour, each hour is eight dollars ... I'd need to do it 6,660 times to get to ten grand total. The Devil's number." He set down the pen. "Lucky, I've lived in two countries, I've gone to four different schools, two different churches, summer camps, vacations, but I'll bet my left bollock that I haven't even met three thousand people *in my whole life,* much less sixty-six hundred!"

Ma gulped. "Does this mean the deal's off?"

Lucky smiled. "What deal? We're just three people talking. But I gotta hand it to yer son! For all the bitching about his math grades, he got every answer right."

Ma was incredulous. "You can do math like that in your head?"

"I'm in sales. I can do math like—" Lucky snapped his fingers.

Ma *fwip!*ed her son again. "You've been feckin' about in maths class all this time, boyo?"

"Doing problems out of a book is boring," said Calvin. "Doing it here, like, applies to me." He pointed at the scribbled figures. "These answers apply to me. If they're right, then what am I missing?"

Lucky took the sheet of computations and crumpled it up. "For one thing, yer seriously undervaluin' yerself, tater tot. Pound these numbers with your schmoozing at twenty bucks an hour. Or fifty.

"But the *real* thing yer missin' is that car sales ain't wage work. Car sales ain't 'eight bucks an hour, five hours per shift.' Car sales is about gettin' that goddamn Suburban off my lot and gettin' payment checks flyin' into my safe." His eyes went wide, smoothing out the leathery skin around them. "If some asshole who otherwise ain't buyin' shit actually buys that Suburban based on *you*—yer schmoozin', yer hype—then I break even. Gimme three or four sales, brother. That's it. Even if it takes all twenty-eight months, I'm winning."

He got to his feet. "But *you'll* be winning the second you drive off my lot. I'm thinking pickup truck. Something big for the big boy."

FOUL

"I don't understand it," said Ma.

"I do understand it," said Calvin, "and it still feels like a scam."

"Not that. *Them.*"

Mother and son were eating inside the Hollidaysburg McDonald's cuz food was never permitted in Eileen's Volvo 240 Estate. Across the dining room, two young men were also having dinner. One had a definite Boy George air with his billowing shirt and made-up face. The other had the Rob Halford thing going on, all black leather.

"Two guys, Ma. So what?"

"Two poofs you mean. An abomination in the eyes of the Lord."

"I guess."

"I'd expect that filth up in Altoona but we're halfway home." Ma sipped her vanilla shake. "That isn't revolting to you?"

"As long as I don't hafta watch 'em kiss or blow each other—"

Her thin hand slapped the thin fry right outta his mouth. "How can you say such things? At the supper table no less!"

"It's the '80s, Ma. We aren't stuck up like your g-g-generation."

"Men aren't born that way in *any* decade. It's all this MTV! Those Yank preachers have a point—Satan infects this place!"

"Lemme tell you what Kitty and I talked about on our train ride home." Calvin wiped his face with a napkin. "She made me aware of my, like, physical presence in the world. For her, that's an imaginary concept. She's got no true idea how good she looks, or how the stars shine at night, or how shadows change a room to make it creepy, or what colors are. White people, black people, those are just words to her.

"*But,* without ever seeing purple in her entire life, Kitty told me with absolute wisdom why Jill wears it all the time."

"The poor lass is colorblind," Ma joked.

"Wrong. Purple is Jill's costume. What we see, the part of Jill that faces the world, is her disguise—the purple Mall Chick. The *real* Jill hides inside that cuz she's unable to face life as herself."

Ma urgently set down her shake and said, "Just like the Phantom!"

"Who?"

"*Of the Opera.* He wears a mask to hide his horrible face."

"Ooh, there's a movie of that coming out with the Freddy Krueger bloke in it. That'll be awesome." He saw her withering eye and returned to his story: "Way back when, I went out with Jill. And, dare I say it, I'm still her friend. I know all about how Jill is afraid of judgment. She hates that others don't accept who she is, she hates her body, she hates her 'momma' the tramp, and it really hurts her that her da's gone.

"The purple Mall Chick, however, rules the world!"

Ma's brown eyes drifted from his face to consider that. "How did Kitty figure that out?"

"Y'know how her hearing is sharper than ours cuz she relies on it? She's *hearing* everything we say, our tone of voice or whatever, little clues in our words, while we're busy *looking at the disguise.*

"That opened doors in my head, Ma. Like those guys over there. Your entire judgment of them is based on what you see."

She held up a finger. "But *that's* the disguise they show the world!"

"True. We have no idea who they are underneath it. Take Ryan Phillips and his all-black, Satanist, quiet-bloke thing. That's what *he* shows the world. I'm kinda uneasy about staying friends with him cuz I have no idea what he's hiding under that disguise!"

Ma nibbled a dry fry. As an Irishwoman, she regarded ketchup as poison. "I'm going to bring up the MacDonald wench, right here at McDonald's. There's a *monster* under that disguise. I've always said."

"Oh absolutely. Jenny despises everyone. Including herself."

"Her future's got divorce and drug addiction and abortion written all over it. I hear she came to the party with that black kid."

"Just to piss everyone off. She paid for it!" Calvin sipped his Classic Coke. "Sean has his too-cool-for-school act and Kare has her too-rich-for-you 'tude. They got it all, but they kinda lust over me."

That rocked Ma out of her seat. "The Corgan boy is a poof?"

"I never said that! Sit down!"

Calvin saw Boy George and Rob Halford were frowning at them. "Sorry—she's so excited. We don't have the special sauce in Ireland."

Ma rapped the table with a knuckle. "You sympathize?!"

"They're being themselves. If they burn for it, that's on them."

"Decent society crumbling is our problem. When you're my age, lad, you'll look around and not understand the world. You'll see the youths wearing 'disguises' that are … obscene to you."

"If you say so, Methuselah."

"And now you say the Corgan boy is one too?"

"Will you stop? Sean don't wanna jump my bones, but he wants to keep me on the mound so college scouts'll come and see *him*, too."

The lad wiped his face again to get all serious. "Him, Lucky, and Sergeant Slaughter had a conference call about making sure I stay on the team. The *original* plan was for Lucky to sell us a car 'at cost.' Suddenly he's fine with *giving* me a car."

"For schmoozing," said Ma. "Bloody silly word."

"He didn't say it out loud, but one of the 'in returns' is that I hafta keep quiet about witnessing Davey taking advantage of Jill."

She grabbed his hand. "You saw it?"

"I think." Moisture doused the steel in his gray eyes. "I stopped him and he jumped out the window. Later, Jill was naked and crying." He grabbed a fresh napkin for his face. "I don't know, I don't remember, I was head-injured. I've asked Jill but she won't talk about it."

"It's a terrible thing to go through. She'll be scared and confused."

Calvin watched Ma fumble for her shake. *Jaysus, did she ever get—* He couldn't bring himself to think the phrase all the way through.

"You can't take the deal," his mother said. "They'll be buying your silence. It's immoral."

"Kitty says I'm the rare one who doesn't wear a disguise. What you behold is what you get. If I take the car, I'll be hiding the truth inside and pretending it's fine outside. Now you know why I want to quit."

"Well. Maybe there's another way. Did you 'behold' the Larsen campus when we went past it?"

"I did. It's cool I guess. What about it?"

"We got a call today from a Mr. Bown."

"Mister Bone?"

"B-O-W-N. He's Larsen Academy's athletic director. He read about your base ball tryout and went to a couple of your practices."

"It's called scouting, and I know exactly who you're talking about. Lucky pointed him out. He even said he was probably from Larsen."

"Mr. Bown was very impressed. Impressed enough to discuss your transfer." Her rock-hard face was ever so proud.

"Go and shite, Ma."

"It's an elite academy. Like those Brit places. Eton. The student body's small so each boy gets closer attention. That leads to better learning and college opportunities."

"Did you memorize the pamphlet? Here's what your Mister Bone left out: I'd hafta live there in a dorm, wear a bollocksy shirt and tie … and it costs like five grand a year."

"Tuition is $17,000 per year."

The lad choked on his Big Mac.

"They have a church on campus too," said Ma. "It's a non-denominational chapel, but still."

"I've been invited into something Brit-like *and* Protestant? Why are we even having this conversation? I'm not switching religions!"

"You wouldn't need to. Students must be Christian but Mr. Bown says they like to have a few Catholics for balance."

"So I'd be a freak outsider. You want me to be Worf!"

"I won't let you be a bum like Robbie, pestering everyone for handouts. I want you to be like Da and get a good education."

"So I can be 'happy' like him? All Larsen wants is for me to take them to States. Just like Skip. No different than the deal at Lucky's."

"The deal at Lucky's is the Devil's work. They want you to cover for crimes. He's going to shed some old clunker on you and write off the loss on his taxes. He won't even talk about the paperwork!"

"Did you see his clothes? The guy's shabby. Shabby and shady."

"That dealership is in trouble. 'We almost go out of business every month' were the only true words to leave his lips, so they were."

"The inside of his Corvette is filthy. He's a bum, Ma."

"Bums don't last long in business. Look at your father. Everything with him is organized. Everywhere he's worked has gotten returns."

"Wait, is your Mister Bone gonna pick up the tab?"

"Larsen won't do full scholarships. For athletics, they'd cover 60%. Wanna work that out for me, Einstein?"

"Shut up. 20% is easier: seventeen times two is thirty-four, add two zeros, $3,400. Times two, that's $6,800."

"That's not 60%."

"That's the 40% we gotta pay. If I pick Larsen, I don't get a car."

"You'll live there and not need some shitty Chevy. You'll graduate with a certificate from the Larsen Academy for Affluent Boys."

"Another nail in the coffin, Ma: it's all boys."

She did a fingers-folded-and-eyes-squinty thing, Ma's equivalent to an SS officer shining a light in your face. "You have a girlfriend."

Calvin drew the final crumpled Kool from his coat pocket and worked his greasy fat fingers on some matches. This would be the first time he'd smoke in front of his mother but after this conversation, he felt she could handle it. He was sixteen, licensed to drive, and a known bumper of uglies.

Ma had smoked as a youth, famously giving it up forever when she learned of her first child's incubation. "Just like Robert and Rosaleen," she sighed at him. "And your father."

"You want me to be like Da." He chucked the spent match in the tiny aluminum ashtray and exhaled smoke through a shite-eating grin.

"Mr. Bown isn't the only one who's called of late," his mother went on. "I've taken other calls at the house."

"Seniors drooling for Rose. They're a different 'Mister Bone.'"

"*Girls,* lad. They hang up when I ask for a name. This 'Kare' or the like, wanting to rope in the Next Big Thing. Girls *will* try."

Calvin wanted to deny that and hope it was true.

"Got a light?" Boy George called from across the room. His voice was more Neil Diamond than Neil Tennant.

Rob Halford held up a hand to make the catch.

"All yours," said Calvin, chucking the matchbook. A precision throw, right on target.

"Thanks," smiled Boy George.

"Enough fraternizing with the fairies," hissed Ma. "Let's get back. You've an Algebra quiz to study for."

Chapter 27
Deals sealed by hand.
Thursday, February 23, 1989, through
Saturday, February 25, 1989.

⚾ I. FLEECEM, ATT'Y AT LAW ⚾

CALVIN GOT OFF THE early-late bus with Spazz Watson at Main near Saint Brigid. "To what do I owe this honor, Calvin the Connor-vore?"

"Got some business to attend to, Liam."

"Pick me up an eighth!" Spazz boogeyed on down Cemetery Lane.

Calvin had no idea what that meant. He slogged a block west on Rte. 666 (Main Street) to a red brick storefront. Built in 1890, it had hosted a tailor, a whorehouse, a cobbler who specialized in whores, and a work-shoe shop. It presently held a little man in a single big room.

Calvin entered the Law Firm of Bachner, Esq. The place smelt less of justice than of bourbon. "Can I help you?" a little voice called.

The lad found a little man hidden behind his Compaq Deskpro 386, IBM Selectric II, amber glass ashtray the size of a Buick Skylark's hubcap, and green-shaded porno-set desk lamp.

And stacks of briefs, law books, legal pads ... some a yard high.

Calvin stuck to the script. "You don't know me, but Gail and I—"

"Of course. Hello, Calvin," the little man said. Everyone in town knew the Irish Satan who murdered Troop 666, threw a baseball like lightning, and fucked a rich girl on someone's lawn.

Opening this talk by mentioning Mr. Bachner's teenage daughter was a mistake. The last half of the lad's sentence was gonna be, "—both go to Axsubeen High," but from the terrified wind-swept look on his face, the little man feared Calvin was about to say, "—are going to make you a grandfather."

Calvin approached the desk. "I saw Gail between classes and asked if you do contracts. She said yes and I could just stop in."

"Contracts, yes." A mix of relief and puzzlement. Gail Bachner was a righteous girl and Vince Bachner was glad to know she'd stay that way. But what contract would a high schooler need? "If you mean baseball contracts, an agent would be better versed. You want someone on your side who knows all the ins and outs of collective bargaining."

"This is about endorsements."

"Agreements to endorse products or services are covered by many types of contracts. The basic one is a personal services contract."

"Cool. What is that, exactly?"

"A piece of paper that says Party A will do certain tasks for Party B in exchange for compensation. Usually cash."

Calvin mulled that. "Suppose Party B doesn't want Party A to sign a contract? He says the reason is that Party A is too young."

"Sounds fishy. I take it Party A is you? Or a minor, at least?"

"Let's go with that," said Calvin, using Lucky's phrase.

"A minor *can* sign a contract which *can* bind him to obligations. In many cases, it would require an adult to co-sign."

"Party A's Ma, for example."

"Of course, but not necessarily a parent or guardian."

Calvin mulled that.

"Why is Party B desirous of keeping Party A's name off the contract?" asked the little man.

"Party B doesn't want *any* names on the contract. Or any contract, period. Just a bill of sale and a title transfer."

"You're giving Party B a car?"

"Party B is giving one to Party A."

The little man mulled it over. "That's dubious. What Party B seems to want is a 'handshake agreement,' which is another form of contract. Two people hash out the terms verbally and never sign anything. Perfectly fine among friends for small favors. If one party comes up short, a handshake agreement would be difficult to make actionable; that is, taken to court for resolution. One party might even count on that; such as, if the deal involves illegality. Written contracts are invalid if they obligate either party to break the law."

"I don't know if any of it is illegal," said Calvin. "Isn't that what lawyers are for?"

The little man sparked up a Merit Ultra Light. "Speaking broadly here—this is not legal advice, mind you, nor applicable solely to the hypothetical example we're discussing—it would be unwise, at best, for Party A—minor or not—to enter any handshake agreement. Especially in return for goods like automobiles. What sort of endorsement could a minor provide to cover such an onerous expense?"

Calvin spread his hands. "I agree. My question is, can Party A take advantage of that by *forcing* Party B to write it down?"

The little man considered the large Ape standing before his desk. "Why don't you take a seat, Mr. Connor."

FOUL

His hand jerked the crank to let some winter air splatter on his face. He wasn't rollin' in a Countach or cruisin' in Oldroyd's Pony. He was truckin' in a silver Silverado.

He'd always been indifferent to pickups. Robbie had a beet-red beater Toyota truck and it sucked. He'd driven Mr. Maguire's Bronco once and it handled like an upside-down boogie-board in the riptide. And, most important, none of Lucky's C-this and K-that came in green.

The '86 Silverado's silver finish was a neutral color. The slate gray vinyl interior matched his eyes. He could always put something green in it, as an accent color ... like one of those smelly pine tree placards.

He liked the high view and roomy cab. It was the least used of any vehicle Lucky offered him. On Saturday, he went back to the Golden Mile of Cars to test drive it again.

"Shame you didn't bring your mother," said Lucky. "You coulda rolled home in it tonight."

"My brother gave me a lift. 'Sides, I brought something better." The lad proffered a manilla folder.

Thirty minutes later he drove the pickup off the lot.

He tooled around 'til dark, headed south on Rte. 666 (Hollidaysburg Pike), put in a tape *(Phil Collins augured an event was adjacent by appraising eventide's atmosphere),* and drummed on the steering wheel.

Chapter 28

EARLY DISMISSAL.
MONDAY, FEBRUARY 27, 1989.

FOUL

POPPING IN THE MAGUIRE house back door, he beheld Paul and Annie's breakfast was yellowy scrambled eggs and grape juice.*

"Congratulations on your new truck!" Ma Maguire said, though her pale skin quaked at the idea of Calvin driving her only child around.

The lad made sure to plug the dealership to Mr. Maguire.

"I wouldn't buy a Chevy even if the salesman was Bill Cosby," the man said. "It's a stick, right? Better gas mileage. A good skill to have too. You never know when you'll be somewhere and need to drive one."

"Like at a party," said his wife, "when the boy you rode with gets too drunk to bring you home."

"Arthur's way too responsible to go to parties, Ma Maguire." Calvin took his leave and went in the garage.

"—it's a Manic Monday on Wacky 103 and *snow is a-coming!*" said the boom box. "Get to the store before all the milk's gone! Yer listenin' to Hyperspace Eddie Pace with my sidekick, Lightspeed Lisa—"

"Bollocks, it's gonna snow?!"

Art got to his feet. "Ten inches! Just like my schlong-a-dong—"

"When? Tonight?"

Art refused to say, all passive aggressive. *Interrupt my joke, will ya?*

"Be that way," said the Ape. "Have fun walkin' to school now."

Art apologized and followed him out to the driveway. "Wow, you got the exact same truck as Dick'll," said Art, laughing at the Silverado. "Hope yours don't have 'gasket trouble' too!"

---

* Took a while but we got there.

"Heh?" said Calvin.

"Chevy Silverado C-10, right? Of course, Oldroyd's was green."

Calvin liked his pickup 2% less than a second ago. "I swear to the Lord I'll never grow a mulchie mustache or wear a cowboy hat." They climbed in. "Seatbelts! You're my first passenger, Art!"

"You got Armor All on the windshield there," Art pointed out. "Why's the seat sticky? You gotta clean vinyl after banging girls on it!"

"You're my *first* passenger. Wanna be my first back seat bang too?"

"Pickups don't have back seats."

"We'll improvise." The lad backed the Chevy out of the Maguire's driveway without clipping the Bronco or the mailbox. The price for such success was stalling out—much to the bemusement of the kids waiting at the corner of Cherry and Third for Bus No. 10.

Calvin rolled down the window and yelled at them, "I'm never taking the bus again!" He cleared his throat and said to Art, "Why would I, when I can roll in a 262-cubic-inch V6? The 4.3-liter engine's got electronic fuel injection. Y'know, for performance. Self-adjusting front-disc brakes. Silver iridescent metallic paint, molded urethane steering wheel with grip stitches, see here? AM/FM radio with ETR™ (Electronically Tuned Receiver). A coat-hook up here, pretty neat. Glovebox has a lock but I trust you. Open it up! Check out the complimentary Lucky Cheeseboro GM Chevrolet first aid kit!"

Art could not stop laughing. "Did ya memorize that shit?"

Calvin guffawed back. "Don't even know what half of it means!"

"It's used, right? It don't have that new car smell."

"It's an '86. And don't call it 'used,' it's 'certified pre-owned.'"

"Jesus Christ. Like 'sanitation engineer.'" Art turned away to stare out the window at Main Street. "Yeah, bro, this is cool. Real nice."

"Envy comes out your mouth when you let the Devil cum in it."

Art bucked. "What the—didja just make that up?"

"I'm the Irish Shakespearean Ape, so I am."

Calvin got in line to turn left from Main onto Bald Eagle Pike and follow Rte. 666 up the Big Hill. No matter which way you approached this T-junction, your light would be red and take forever to change.

His passenger was quiet. Too quiet. "What's eating you, boyo?"

"Don't wanna be jealous, Calvin, but the sun shines out your ass."

"Well. You know what they say about the Luck of the Irish."

"I fall into a pit of shit and stink for days. You fall into a pit of shit and come out wearing a brown suit."

Calvin bucked. "What the—did *you* just make that up?"

"Example: I let go of the dishroom door. It smacks you in the face. You go to the sink to stop the bleeding ... and get to Cindy before me. If *I* get to her first, yer still a virgin."

Gee. Zuss.

Fuh. King.

CHRIST!

Calvin crossed himself twice.

Art ranted on: "A tree falls on you—while yer fucking her!—and you need Tommy John surgery and *instantly* yer Roger Clemens. Even with that Bugs Bunny pitching action, you throw smoke!

"Me? I'm the one who crashes into your gross dishwasher chick in the rain and fucks up his shoulder so bad I end up on the J.V. for life. Shit's not fair, bro! I played little league for years, went to the batting cages, I watch baseball all the time ... I got a lifetime head-start and I still suck donkey dick! Guess that's the Luck of the African."

"Luck works both ways," said Calvin. "I also got a wicked brain bruise on that summer camp. I forget things, conversations, whole days. But I don't mope about it. I get out there and try." Three cars managed a left turn before the light went red again. "Bollocks! This intersection really needs one of those arrow thingies."

"Now ya got Larsen recruiting you too," said Art. "Jon Oldroyd *just so happens* to catch ya at my work with his hot rod and a hooker."

"His girlfriend. She goes to Altoona High. Nothing happened."

"You were in Video Onslaught for one minute and he shows up. That was a sting operation. Asshole barely noticed I was there."

"Quit crying in my Silverado, Art, the interior isn't waterproof."

The kid sighed, at Calvin, at himself. "I'm sorry. I appreciate the ride. Now I don't gotta be on the bus with Jill growlin' at me."

"I noticed that lately. What's the deal?"

"None of your business."

"Very much my business. Don't wanna get killed in any crossfire."

"It's only crossfire if two people are shooting."

Calvin saw his chance and turned in front of a Schultz's Lumber truck. The back end of the Silverado fished out a bit but they squeaked through unscathed. Art's gangly hands gripped the dash for dear life.

As they climbed the Big Hill, Art's gangly hands formed fists. "There I was in the hallway, mindin' my own business, when Jill goes past and she's all, 'Yer a loser and a liar!' I grabbed her and go, 'You better explain yourself, woman!' But she only cried until I let go of her. I *thought* about deckin' her … but I got standards. I don't hit girls, talk crap, or take advantage."

"You fix grades for girls in exchange for beholding their tits!" said Calvin. "I'd call that 'taking advantage!'"

"Where'd you hear that?!"

"You told me."

"I didn't mention 'tits.' Who'd you hear that part from?"

"I hear all kinds of stuff, African. I'm asking what's true here."

"And *I'm* asking who you heard it from, Irish!"

"I'm not at liberty to say. Friend of a friend."

"Ha! Then it's Jill. You always tip your hand—Rayche agreed to my deal, then backed out, so the friend of a friend is Jill."

"I plead the fifth. *You* just confessed to the crime."

"Yo, what crime? I tell them I'll fix their grade if I get some tits. If they agree to the terms, they owe me boobage!"

"A 'handshake agreement' is the legal term."

"Shaking hands with girls is weird."

"And a contract isn't binding if the parties need to break the law."

"Yo, what *law?* It's not like statutory rape or anything!"

"Art, name another instance when it's legal to bargain for tits."

"What is this, *L.A. Law?* And I notice *you* ain't asked about my services lately. I guess Falcone got Mr. Hussing off your back."

"I don't need those services anymore. And if I did, Jill offered to do it for free. She did Rayche's—said it's easy."

Art gasped. "You told Jill how my surgery works?"

"She already knew. Only thing I told her was to make sure to change this semester's grades on all future report car—"

"That's a fuckin' trade secret, man! Jill'll tell everyone and take over my action!" The kid gnashed his teeth. "No more 'good friend discount' for you. From now on, everything's 'bad friend credit terms.' What *happened* to you?! You used to be loyal and shit."

"What happened to *you?* You used to not blackmail chicks or make homemade landmines."

"Guess I changed, Calvin."

"Nothing will change until *you* do. Looks like you did."

Art pulled a classic teenager move here: he muttered a comment designed to provoke interest. "Shoulda knocked her out at Corgan's."

It worked. "You were at Corgan's party?" said Calvin.

"I mean back in the day. Here's my Pit of Shit Theory again: *you* go to Corgan's party and get to fuck the hottest chick in school on the front yard. *I* go and sneak a babe out back to hide behind the tool shed, and *still* get interrupted by Zedz and his ralphing."

The Ape drew a breath. *No going back now.* "What shed?"

Art's cinereous skin went red. "The one in Corgan's back yard!"

"It doesn't exist. Me and Kitty couldn't find it."

"Kitty couldn't find her ass if—" Art stopped himself. "Sorry. And I meant the neighbor's shed. Next door. It woulda been dark when you went lookin', right? So you missed it."

"Last week I was still taking the bus to school. But one day, I sat in the window seat for a change. Remember?"

"I *knew* that was weird! You were scoping back yards in Overlook Estates ... double-checkin' my in·FOH·may·SHUN. Goddamnit!"

"I asked Zedz too. He remembers puking but he did it on the patio. Slid open the glass door and leaned right out and yakked."

"There's more to the story."

Calvin rolled up his window. "Better not be more shite."

"It's not. Me and Jill *did* talk at that party. Gave her the Calrissian smile, never fails to make 'em wet." Usually Art demonstrated. Not today. "We went out for a smoke—"

"You hate smoking. Jill too. If 'Momma' does it, Jill does not!"

"We went out to get *away* from the smoke—the same reason you and Jenny left early, remember? I'm tryin' to confess here!"

No one did *noble-and-victim-simultaneously* quite like Arthur Aganju Maguire. "Sorry. Go on now."

"Never got to kissin' or tits," said Art. "I made that up. Me an Jill just talked. I told her my dad's black and she rubbed my arm, like 'There's black under here?' No one believes me 'til they actually *see* my dad. I got a line for it now: 'I'm two drops of coffee in the milk.' The reverse of how dark brothers go, 'I'm two drops of milk in the coffee.'"

Calvin had two drops of acid tingling his butthole.

"Suddenly Jill backed off, all *ewww*. I thought it was my breath and busted out the Binaca. Nope. It was racism. She even went, 'Don't tell anyone, okay? Keep it a secret.' Meaning she didn't want the other Mall Chicks to know she was friendly with a negro, I guess."

The lad nodded with empathy. "I believe it. Jill's never exactly been, uh, welcoming of other color people."

"You mean 'colored people.'"

"I mean, 'people who are another color.'"

"Besides the default color? Yo, see how biased y'all are?"

"I *see* it, mate. And Jill's the biased one! Just the other day I put in a good word for you. She goes, 'No way, I'm no nigger-lover.'"

Art's icy eyes fired little frozen crystals. *"Now* you say it."

Calvin pushed the turn signal down and waited for a chance to turn left into the school's pot-holey student lot. His big hands were damp on the wheel, his boxers stuck to his puckered arse, his pits dripped under his wool sweater. "I was quoting her! You said it's fine if friends say it!"

"Oh, we're still friends?"

"You'll know it if we're not! I let people be themselves. If they bother me, I stop hanging out with them."

"A *real* friend would've killed Jill after she said that about me."

"Why should I, Art? It's your battle."

"My battle with *your* friend, 'dare I say it.'"

"It's just words. Vocabulary. 'Sticks and stones' and all that. What you do to girls is *real,* mate. It's a sin!" Calvin parked and killed the engine. "Art, you have *no* idea what else has happened recently."

"I'm startin' to piece together the story, bro. The Ape got some purple lipstick on his dick?"

The boys sat in the C-10's rapidly cooling cab. Other kids in the student lot joked with pals, walked with arms around boy/girlfriends, crossed Bald Eagle Pike to get the school day started.

"You know what the payments for this truck are?" said Calvin.

"Zero dollars a month?" said Art.

"My conscience. That's what I paid for it."

"Sweet deal. Just fuckin' die already." Art leapt out and slammed the door. As he hustled away, he pulled off his glasses to wipe his eyes.

Don't go, I didn't mean it like that, stop being a baby ... these came to Calvin's mind but no words left his mouth. He had his own battles and there was no time for Art's histrionic, hurt, the-world-hates-me exit, for the kid acting out a John Hughes Movie Moment in real life.

FOUL

Art never answered Calvin's question ("When's the snow start?") but it's fine since Wacky 103's forecast (10″ starting at 2 p.m.) was wrong. News Radio 1240 AM got it right, as usual: 12–14″, starting at 9 a.m.

After a quick confab with the Axsubeen School Board and the Transportation Chief, Fartin' Martin got on the P.A. to announce early dismissal, effective immediately. This was ten minutes after homeroom ended. Calvin joined the jocular herd racing to lockers to grab shit and split, then went against the flow, looking for Kitty. She heard the jingle of the bell on his loathsome scarf of many colors and called his name.

They went single-file out the building and down the long cement pathway to the crosswalk for the student lot. Some kids crossed Rte. 666 (Bald Eagle Pike) without looking, all *Cars gotta stop, it's the law.*

Calvin, possessing this thing called a brain, waited for a suitable gap. Hard to feel legally righteous after a half-ton flattens your arse.

The snow started, fast and furious, enough to show footprints and tire tracks by the time they got to Calvin's Chevy. "There's no step," he said, waiting for verbal permission to give her physical help up.

"I do hope this contraption goes well in the snow," said Lady Em.

Calvin got giddy. "I'll put the complimentary Lucky Cheeseboro GM Chevrolet chains on!"

Kitty enjoyed the crisp interior heat while Calvin used the complimentary Lucky Cheeseboro GM Chevrolet full-size jack to hoist his baby up. A good inch of snow was down by the time he finished lashing on the tire chains ...

... to the front wheels. Yep.

"Really coming down," he said, getting in and sweeping tendrils of exhaust with him. Kitty coughed and wrinkled her nose. He put the truck in first and they skidded forward.

"Wow, that is *sooo* noisy!" she said.

"Chains might be a little loose." He turned right on Rte. 666 and kept below 30 m.p.h. "Broken chains love to hump the axles," Robbie once said. It was less than a mile to Kitty's house anyway.

They turned left onto Washington Way. The Silverado slid down the incline, flailing this way and that in the virgin snow. He went right on Liberty Road and parked in front of the Howes' mailbox. Neither the maroon Chevy Celebrity sedan nor the sapphire blue Chevy Celebrity wagon were in the drive. Da Howe would be at Schultz's Lumber; Ma Howe may have dashed up to Merk's Super-Merket in East Freedom for bread and milk.

Kitty dashed out and ran to her front lawn.

"Steady on!" he said, fetching her school bag and Excalibur.

She didn't listen. She was busy swooping.

There was no other word for it.

The girl spread her arms and jogged about the front yard in looping circles. Her wide cheeks aimed up at the sky, collecting flakes. She made no noises like a child would, a zooming car or diving plane. She simply swooped. She knew this plot of earth by heart and was never in danger of colliding with a tree or box shrub.

Calvin realized this is what she wanted to do in Corgan's yard— she'd heard it was flurrying and wanted to swoop.

He had no desire to swoop; it was cold and snowy and it sucked out here. "I'll be at the door when you're ready, mon cerise!"

The girl stopped her swooping and followed his voice. The front door yielded to her key. The Howe House rule was *deadbolt always on* when anyone was home; logic indicated that the place was vacant.

Since Eddie was a tubby goof who'd forget the deadbolt, the kids called his name a few times. Lewis, the fluffy mini-bear guide dog, greeted them with his big white face, hot breath, and a single *woof*.

"Lewis, go get Eddie," said Kitty.

Lewis twirled his head *No*, making tags jingle in a signature tune.

"We're safe," she told Calvin.

The lad barred the door and set Excalibur against the wall. All their ephemera fell carelessly to the entranceway tile, coats and shoes and her pom-pom hat and his vile scarf of many colors. Calvin plucked his girl-friend up and she clutched arms 'round his neck, legs 'round his hips, the same fireman's carry (well, Peter-North-as-a-fireman's-carry) they used on the toad in the hole night.

Her shin *doink!*ed Lewis on the snout, ending his tail-wagging.

Calvin threw Kitty on the living room's comfy sofa. Her long russet hair and deep voice splayed out. "Tunes!" she said. He flicked on the hi-fi. Wacky 103 was at commercial; afternoon D.J. Meester Miami Salami read copy for Pizza Putt over stock rock beats.

"We need Phil Collins."

"You hate Phil Collins!"

"I'm getting soft."

"You're getting hard."

"Why, so I am," he said, the butter in his baritone boiling.

She pushed him back and made her jolting Arms of Frustration.

"What's the matter, mon cerise?"

She fanned her hot neck. "I …," she said.

"I can't believe I'm saying this," she said, a tinkle of tense mirth.

"First, I love you," she said.

He felt sweat coming on. "I love you too. I won't lie to you, I'm frightened at where this is going." "

"All you gotta do is listen. I'm the one who's gotta admit it." She wiped her lips. "Rem'ber we talked about how people wear disguises?"

"Vividly." He went cold. "Did you cheat on me?"

"Please let me talk. All will become clear."

He settled back on the far side of the sofa. Lewis sat nearby, looking back and forth, unsure what all the anxiety scent was about.

"The Jill Pedersens of the world choose to wear a disguise," she said at length. "I'm *trapped* in mine. I don't mean my clothes or my style but my dark glasses, my guide dog, and Excalibur. They're my prison. They're a blessing cuz they help me get around. Without them I'm *completely* lost. That's a curse. It's only happened one time in my whole life. I had none of my tools, no family or friends around, no idea where I was. It was the most frightening experience …

"Do you know the word 'trauma,' Calvin?"

"I think it was on the vocab list once."

"So you don't. Okay. Trauma means a major injury that leaves lasting damage. Like your cerebral contusion."

"Wait, it sounds familiar now."

"Trauma can be damage to anything, your body, your mind, your soul. People think mental problems equals crazy but it's not like that. Ask anyone who's been in a war. They're normal as long as they don't think about what they saw. Or what they *did.*"

Calvin thought about the veterans he knew: Art's da, Ryan's da. Desmond Kelleher, his neighbor in Leixlip, who'd fought in the Second World War (for the Crown, if you can believe it). Aul' Fella Kelleher never told war stories and Ma warned her children never to ask him about it. *He doesn't want to remember.*

"That kind of trauma follows you forever," she said. "I will always have to deal with it."

"Christ our Lord, you killed someone?!" he said.

"Calvin, don't talk. Just listen."

"I'm sorry, Kitty."

"Before you ask 'What happened?', I *don't* want to talk about it."

"It's about Schultz Park, right? Dr. Jacoby mentioned it, then got all quiet like he screwed up by telling me. He said going to Schultz Park would be trauma to you."

"It would be 'traumatic.' That's the adjective form."

"How j'say it in French?"

"Traumatique."

"Naturellement."

"You never get over trauma, Calvin. You just get used to it. I talk with Sean a lot, Father Sean I mean, and he's like, 'God sets no challenges before you that you cannot overcome.' I *hate* that! I know it's the truth but sometimes I wanna tell God, 'C'mon, stop it! I already *know* I can overcome trials … I don't need constant reminders!'"

She collected herself. "I'm like, 'We can talk about the past in the future,' and you're like, 'Cool.' I expected you to be the Irish Raging Ape, demanding answers. You don't, though. I love that!"

"You'll tell me when you're ready, Kitty."

"Will I? What if I'm *never* ready?"

"That's … cool too. What I don't know can't hurt me, right?"

"Oh Calvin, *no*. NO! That is *sooo* not true! Gimme your hand."

He did so. Her hand—hot, sweaty, shaking—squeezed his.

"I'm grateful for all you've done for me. You let me out of my prison. Got me to new places, away from Excalibur and my guide dog and this house. Showed me states of mind I never knew existed. Passion and fear and wine coolers … and life!"

Her voice swooped through a snowstorm, happy, free.

"For the first time ever, I didn't feel like a blind person but *just a person*. That means so much, love."

Calvin was overwhelmed. He'd never had such an impact on anyone before. He started to weep.

"You also made me realize, for the first time ever, that I am *waaay* not ready to be set free in this world."

Kitty's voice was lead, scraping the cobblestone of his heart. He'd never gotten news with such impact before. He kept on weeping.

Jaysus, she's breaking up with me.

"I'm sixteen, I'll be in college soon, I'll be an adult," she said. "Out there, my own place, my own life. Yes. That will happen. But I am NOT ready for it. The world is scary enough for people in general, much less handicapped people. I'm not ready to be alone, to be away from my family. To be with only one person, like as a lover."

A tear fell from behind her dark glasses, making a sweeping circuit down her wide cheek.

"If this is about Davey," rasped Calvin, "I'll kill him."

"It's not about anyone. *Do not look for revenge.*"

"Then it's me. I'm to blame."

"No one is to blame. Quit being a boy and reducing it to a scheme! Listen to my feelings here. This is … how it is."

"We can take things slower."

"How will that help? Exciting things are happening to you! I get the feeling you won't recognize your own life in a year. Or a month."

"You have no idea what your life will be like tomorrow."

"Yes. Exactly. I would only pull you down."

"Then pull me down—I don't wanna go *up* without you!"

"You're gonna go up or down without me, regardless."

"Bollocks. I can wait for you."

"No you can't. Think about how not-true that is. Baseball season is coming up. You'll be awesome and the future will carry you away."

"I'll quit, or I'll won't play until next year when we're juniors. Whatever it takes! I *will* wait for you, mon cerise!"

"No you won't."

He made his own Arms of Frustration. "Stop telling me that! I have free will—I'll decide what I can and can't do! I have challenges put before me too. The Devil tapped me on the shoulder and tempted me, and I went *nyah-nyah!* and waved my balls in his face!"

The light and delight in her laughter had to pass through her tears to reach him. "You're saying you've been a good little boy, eh?"

"I swear on a stack of bibles!"

"I have no way of knowing if you're telling the truth, but it doesn't matter. That's not why I'm doing this. And the second you leave, you'll be with someone else. I've heard the rumors."

"You're listening to rumors? YOU, of all people?!"

"I hope you'll be happy with whoever you end up with."

"How can I be happy without you, Kitty?"

"Weren't you happy without me before we met?"

"Not really. And now that I've seen—fuck, now that I've *beheld*—wait, now that I've *experienced* the joy that is you ..."

"It's so sweet how we say 'beheld.' I'll miss it. I could keep using it but it wouldn't be the same." She used her cardi sleeve to clean her face. "This is hard for me, Calvin, cuz I love you. I thought about waiting to tell you, but the longer we go, the harder it'll be."

"Please don't make this so final. Let me help you face this trial!"

"No. You can't. I hafta face it alone."

Calvin was out of angles. Schemes. Her calm defiance tipped her hand and he saw she was holding a flush, queen-high.

All he had was the king of hearts.

"I might never be happy again," he told her.

"Me too. We won't get over it. We'll just get used to it."

He hung his head, then looked up and closed in for a hug. A kiss. A goodbye kiss.

"Calvin, don't," she said, stern. The timbre of her voice got Lewis involved. The dog jumped on the sofa to put himself between them.

The lad stood to go. Only now did he hear the radio. Their breakup had had a soundtrack. How awful would it have been for this moment to be scored by Guns N' Roses, Information Society, or, ironically, Phil Collins ... but what Wacky 103 actually broadcasted was far worse.

"Get'cher buns down to Lucky Cheeseboro GM Chevrolet, in bun·YOO'·tee·full al·TOO'·nah!!"

FOUL

Tingling from hurt and loss, Calvin cleaned his windshield with a Lucky Cheeseboro GM Chevrolet ice scraper. Three inches on the ground now. He sat in the cab, staring into nothing, until he came to himself and stared into nothing. Literally; the windshield was covered again.

His Swatch had both hands straight up.

The Silverado slid crazily on Liberty Road. The chains weren't doin' dick. He knew better than to try Rocky Road with its Suicide Slide, so he made his way to Rte. 666 (Bald Eagle Pike). The incline at Washington Way's terminus defeated him. He was in sight of Bald Eagle Pike but kept stalling and sliding back and spinning the wheels.

The rear wheels. The drive wheels.

A Dodge Ram pulled over, ejaculating an aul' fella in a green John Deere cap and camo-and-orange jacket. "I see the problem," he said, and helped the lad jack up and re-chain the Silverado proper. The aul' fella didn't comment on Calvin's weepy face.

Rte. 666 was jammed. Everyone had fled work and the plows were late to the party. No one got anywhere. Five inches on the lawns now. The lad spent ages stuck right in front of Toby Stewart's decrepit house with the eerie green light in the second story window. His steel gray eyes barely saw it. His mind saw a constant parade of classmates and grownups asking him why he and Kitty weren't together anymore.

She dumped me, didn't say why, ha, that's girls for ya.

He had no clue what *she* would tell people.

Woulda helped if she gave a legit reason. "I'm not ready to go into the world." That's no reason! "I cheated on you. You cheated on me. I'm moving to Delaware. I'm so sick of your B.O." Now *those* are reasons!

Honking horns brought him back to Earth. He flipped the bird and moved forward the whopping twenty feet that traffic had advanced.

There's two kinds of chicks, psychotic and boring.

Took fucking ages to get to the Big Hill. The road surface was a hellish combination of thick snow and solid ice. At the bottom there was a T-junction: left (Roaring Spring Pike), right (Rte. 666 [Main Street]), or straight (into the CITGO to die in a fiery explosion).

The stoplight changed without a single car moving. Calvin stalled. *Does Lamborghini make automatics?* Stick shifts were so different! The gearbox on Robbie's '80 Toyota was mayonnaise. Jon Oldroyd's '88 Mustang was baklava. The '86 Silverado was silky cheesecake, with a dry graham cracker crust underneath and squishy cherries on top—

Sans cerise, pour toujours.

He had no time to weep at that. The truck found ice and drifted down the hill towards the Subaru in front of him, the world's slowest drift, glacial, minutes of screaming and panic. Three feet later, the tire chains found macadam and the truck jerked to a stop. And stalled.

His dashboard had no clock, but his Swatch read half one when he pulled into his driveway. Ma's Volvo was there. Da would have his own adventure getting home in the Caddy. And Rose's Beetle? Who knew where that was today. Correction—who cares.

The lad stood in the vestibule, shoulders weighed by snow and worry and loss. Ma came to greet and scold. She hated that he'd taken the deal for the truck. She loved that he finagled the deal to gain the upper hand. She hated the stress of him out driving in the snow. She loved that he was home safe.

She drew up short at the sight of him.

Calvin's sweaty hand used the glass block wall to steady himself. "It's over," he said, grabbing her for a hug.

The Connors were only passively touchy-feely, and Ma was but half the Ape's size. "Laddy," she urged into his chest, "you're getting snow in my permanent."

Chapter 29
I'm not that kind of guy.
Tuesday, February 28, 1989, through
Thursday, March 9, 1989.

FOUL

THE BLIZZARD PETERED OUT around 3 p.m. after seven inches. After the usual half-hour pause—the quietest the Axsubewa Valley ever got—people went out to shovel and sled. All and sundry heard the Adkissons ruining the silence with their fucking four-wheelers.

At 4 p.m. the blizzard went *Psyche!* and shat another six inches.

Everyone gave the sky the finger and went back inside, even the goddamn Adkissons.

The sun came out Tuesday morning, distant and stuffy, like a Brit going, "Nasty business, that." Calvins the Second and Third got to shoveling. Ma helped by clearing off the cars and bringing out hot coffee. "If only Rose had come home and covered this bit," she said, pointing out the one open quadrant of driveway and its 13″ of snow.

The real bitch was digging out the curbside mailbox. Soaked through and exhausted, Calvin the Second went inside for air. Calvin the Third didn't want to go inside for any reason. Then Ma'd say, "Surely you did *something* to cause her to walk away!"

Ma had issued four variations of this question already.

The lad wanted to be far from here. In the sun. On the beach. Pumping iron. Dancing at the club. In a cigarette boat with Tubbs, chasing a drug dealer played by some rock star.

Phil Collins had been on *Miami Vice* once.

He stabbed his shovel into the snow bank and took off down the street. Running. Getting away from it. Going over all of it.

We met on January 27th. She dumped me on February 27th.

She'll dump you a month from now, dude.

He ran south. Maple Street wasn't so much plowed as steamrolled, the path exactly two car-widths. He had to swerve back and forth to avoid a couple stepsides out on business.

At the T with Mueller Way, he went right. He took off his obnoxious scarf of many colors, tore the jingle bell off said scarf, stowed said scarf, and pitched said bell into the street.

He passed the Mueller farm. The joint was fugly. The henhouse was in extreme disrepair. The barn was half burnt from a devastating fire years ago, near collapse. Plaster and paint peeled away from the homestead. Weed patches and brambles stood where, over at the Millar farm, there were neat rows of pruned ornamental bushes. The pond was a stagnant bog, punks and stalks poking through the snow-top. No one knocked on Old Man Mueller's door to ask to fish there.

Yet every Mueller alive, all the Hanses and Friedrichs and Heikes and Gretas, berated the Millar family as "lazy Irish half-breeds."

This was Axsubeen. Calvin's hometown.

He crossed over Railroad Street and thought of his old hometown, Leixlip. Of people he never saw anymore, like his Maimeó and Daideó, Aul' Fella Kelleher next door, Father Ernan at Our Lady's Nativity. He thought of Gerald "Fookin' Gerry" Coughlin, his boyhood best friend with the bent teeth, and their crew: Billy, Declan, and Shite-Shower (poor Mal Higgins). He missed Birdy—Bridget McAmis, his first crush. Calvin loved Birdy's red hair and wicked "larf."

You'll be with someone else. I hope you'll be happy.

He turned onto Willow Street. On the left was Schultz Park with its old coal mine hills and ridgeline backdrop. Kitty never came here.

His friendships in Ireland were over. None of them sprang for a long-distance call. None of them wrote. He looked them up when he went back with Robbie and Ma last summer. Birdy had moved. Billy was away on holiday (ironic). Declan and Shite-Shower didn't seem interested beyond saying "Hi." And Fookin' Gerry became a fookin' hooligan, talking bollocks to grown-ups and knocking over a candy stand in the cornershop. Calvin made an excuse and never saw him again.

Right on Fourth then left on Railroad. The sidewalks in front of the businesses were still snowed under. Seeing Pizza Putt got him thirsty.

Soda pop and pepperoni and arcade games. This place represented his time in America. So many quarters spent playing *Rampage,* crushing buildings as King Kong and carrying the woman in a red dress.

I expected you to be the Irish Raging Ape.

So many hours hanging with Anthony "Sandy" Sandmiller and Art Maguire. More friendships that were over.

You never get over trauma, Calvin. You just get used to it.

East on Third. His lungs burned. His tits hurt, all that fat swinging up and down. *Is Art gonna sit with me at lunch Wednesday? I'm not moving to the Rejects Table with Mia Pintcure and Leggers!*

Everyone will talk.

Last week he soaked in all the glorious schadenfreude of watching Sean Corgan and Brion Davey squirm over the news of their breakups.

2UP. Your turn, laddy.

He got back on Maple and slowed to a walk. The cool-down, Coach Falcone called it. He passed the Phillips house, the Schaefer house. At his house, someone (Ma probably) had put away his shovel, as if anyone was gonna pinch it.

Next door, Kimmy McSween's pickup had been there when he took off running, but was gone now.

BLEACHERS

"Oi! It's your friend, dare I say it. The Ape."

No reply.

"The door was open. You decent, Pedersen?"

Silence. He went to the bedrooms. A Madonna poster was on Jill's door. Calvin put his fat hand on the Material Girl's face and pushed.

The Mall Chick lay on her bed, surrounded by purple pillows and college-ruled paper and photocopied articles about amphibians. Her legs were buried in billowy gray sweatpants, making those puffy thighs look like hippos. She had a loose yellow top on with no bra. The room felt gloomy, like it was steeped in sad shadows, despite the drawn curtains and bright light from all the sun and snow outside.

Calvin was drenched, panting. His B.O. surfed on the tendrils of cold air sliding off his kelly green coat. Beholding that Jill was in sleepwear, he turned around. "Sorry. I yelled to get decent."

"It's okay," she said. She tried to pull up a blanket but there was too much shit on the bed. She used a pillow for cover instead.

He turned back 'round and let his gray eyes tilt down to her. Jill looked quite different with her auburn hair yanked back into a scrunchy and no makeup. She wore makeup all the time, even softball practice.

"Kids are sledding and you're doing homework, Pedersen?"

Her eyes begged him to stop calling her that.

"'Jillian,' I meant."

"'Kathryn' won't appreciate you being in my bedroom."

"'Kathryn' won't care. She dumped me yesterday."

A hand went to Jill's gob. "Oh my God. What'd you do?"

"You're the same as my fucking ma. Why's it automatically gotta be something *I* did?"

"She loved you, man. The Ape hadda do *something.*"

"Well. You dumped Davey—what did *he* do?"

"Holy shit." She turned away. On the verge of tears.

"I'm sorry, I'm such an arse." He came over and sat next to her.

"I don't want to be touched," she warned.

"I won't. Just need to catch my wind. I was running."

"Okay."

Neither of them spoke. Calvin wished her boom box was on.

"Broke up with Art too," he said. "I confronted him about the shed story. He admitted it was bullshit, then said some awful shite about you and Rayche and me. I wasn't having it. He got cross and stormed off." He frowned at her. "Art never did anything to you, did he?"

"*Art?* No!"

"So, lemme ask you … Sean says I shot a gun at the party. I don't remember that. I seem to recall *you* with a gun."

She refused to speak.

"*Thou shall not kill* and all that, but Davey deserves a bullet."

She looked away again.

He needed to stop, to lighten the mood. He scanned her Biology project notes and saw the headings were written first in blue ink and then retraced in red. "Ah! I ended up with a page of your Biology notes in my Trapper. Mystery solved."

"Burn it," she said. "Got stuck with Chris Schoenberger the Burn-Out Bud on this project and I'm totally done with the whole thing. And life in general." She wiped her face and aimed her brown eyes at him, daring him to fuck up this conversation once more.

He got nervous and fished for a new topic. Jill's room was as messy as his, only purpler. "Your Chucks," he pointed. "Lavender of course. Always looked good on you. Do they come in green?"

"I hate them anymore." She blinked a few times, a burst transmission: *That was lame but thanks for trying.*

He nodded: *No problem.*

"Yes, they come in green," she said.

"What's up with the shirt? Never beheld you in yellow before."

"You can say 'see' with me." Jill tugged at her shirt. "My dad got me it for Christmas. He's such a failure. It's *waaay* too big. And what kinda dad can't remember his daughter's favorite color?"

He thrust out his lower lip. "Gotta say, yellow suits you."

"You think so?" A brightness entered her face. "I been thinkin'—don't tell anyone this, okay?—but when I got home from the party and saw myself in the mirror there with Amy's clothes on, the red top and blue sweats, I said to myself, 'Self, you don't look half-bad!'"

"You called yourself 'Self?' I'm calling you 'Self' from now on!"

"Shut up. My point is, I wanna work in some fresh shades. You really think yellow could work for me? I gotta get new jeans then. *Blue* ones. Or black ones!" She gave him a hopeful grin. "Take me to the mall in your new truck. Let's go shopping!"

"I hafta bathe first."

"Yes, you stink! B.O. to the max."

"Conserve water—shower with a friend."

"As if." Her mouth scrunched up. "Maguire woulda offered me a sleazy trade—'I'll take ya to the mall if ya shower with me.'"

"That *does* sound like the kinda shite he'd do."

"And the kinda 'shite' Momma would agree to. The guys she gets with are all skeevy. She's so embarrassing. I'm not like her, you know that. I mean, if I wanted to take a shower with you, I'd just do it."

He wiped his face. "I'm not that kind of guy."

She popped a paw to her puss but it didn't hold back the laughter.

"Thanks," she said. "I needed that."

"What are friends for?"

"Dare I say it! I wasn't kidding about going shopping though."

"I'll think about it, Jill. The roads'll be shite 'til later."

"Everyone in your house has a car now! Like, one car for every day of the week. How can you guys afford all that?"

"I got a deal on mine from Lucky Cheeseboro."

"*Pfft.* Must be nice to get a free car."

"It wasn't free. I gotta do appearances at Lucky's dealership now. And he'll be my coach for life, even if I transfer schools." His voice grew small and hollow. "Worse, I had to sell my soul to the Devil."

"Whatever."

"I'm serious. One of the terms is killing me inside—I need to keep my mouth shut about some things."

"Like what?"

"Like, things that'd get other ballplayers in trouble." He wiped his forehead sweat into his Davey Dangle. "I helped write the deal but ... Jaysus, Jill, it's wrong. Immoral. You'll hate me."

"Why?"

"I only have that truck because of what happened to you."

Her eyes looked to one side, then bugged up at him. "Wait up, what do you *think* happened to me?"

"I have no idea. I was head-injured, and you won't tell me. But I did see *something,* that I can't talk about anymore or the deal's off."

Jill Pedersen did the last thing in the world that Calvin Connor ever would've expected ...

... she laughed.

"When we go shopping later," she said, "I'll tell you *exactly* what happened on the way."

GROUPIE SECTION

It's amazing how many hiding spots a teenage girl could come up with in a single-wide trailer. But Valerie Crenshaw's Granny had found them all. Including, Val sighed, under the baby shark.

It was a genuine baby shark, sealed in a pint-size jar and preserved in formaldehyde. It'd been a gift from some uncle of Val's who'd gone to Brigantine on the Jersey Shore. Granny hated the thing, just like she hated mounted deer heads and antlers on Harley handlebars. Tucking folded banknotes under the jar had hitherto guaranteed their safety. It was the *last* place Granny would look.

And, it was—Granny stopped looking once she found Val's money.

The girl sighed. She pulled on her natty hooded sweatshirt and went to rummage in the Yugo. This, likewise, was a gift from an uncle.

Well. Not so much an uncle as some older dude. And not so much a gift as an arrangement.

Gravel crunched and the ice over potholes popped. She extricated her tiny self out of the tiny Yugo, still shy the five bucks she needed, and beheld Calvin's silver truck rolling up.

The big dude cranked down his window. "Jaysus, this place is a bloody maze!" he said, crossing himself. "There's trailers for miles! Didn't think it was so big."

"Is that what she said?" said Val.

Irish laughed. He loved her slow sticky way of talking, so she put that drawl to use: "You got cash, Calvin? I wanna buy smokes off Old Man O'Reilly and he won't sell me nonc 'til I pay my tab."

"Who's that?"

"The super. He runs the trailer park. I owe him five bucks."

"Just hit the CITGO when Spazz is working, he'll take care—"

"Nah we can't no more. He got busted selling to minors."

"What? Someone actually enforced that law?"

"It's crazy, right? Some bureaucrat had a pinecone up his butt and wrote citations everywhere in the area. Both Liam *and* the CITGO got one. Old Man Adkisson didn't fire him but he's gotta work like five shifts for free to pay the fine."

"That sucks. I still love that you're calling Spazz 'Liam' now."

"Wish he was here, I'd just swipe *his* 'Bros. I'm jonesin', man."

Calvin patted the passenger seat.

GROUPIE SECTION 🎾🎾

"This, then, is the reason Lincoln signed the Morrill Act of 1862. The

President wanted colleges in every state teaching agriculture, engi-neering, and military science. That's how Penn State was founded. They still teach agriculture and have a farm with livestock and dairy. Next time you go, visit the Creamery. Best ice cream on the planet."

A dork office aide knocked and gave a note to Mr. Chudoff. "Miss Palfrey," said the teacher, passing back the note, "you're excused."

Everyone looked at Tiffany. She collected her books and left with the office aide. She could feel the dork's drooling sophomore eyes all over her. She swiped the note from his greasy hand and read it. "Gotta hit my locker for my jacket," she said, mystified.

At the Office, Mrs. Koltz signed her out. "That's your uncle out there?" asked the old bitch. A silver pickup was parked out front.

"Yep," said Tiff, rolling with it. She headed out, making her walk casual. Mrs. Koltz would watch, suspicious. Tiffany Palfrey had had a record number of doctor appointments, house fires, and relatives in the hospital (or grave) during the '88-89 school year.

The driver of the pickup turned out to be the guy from Axsubeen High. The pitcher from Ireland. Tiff got in. "Hi, Uncle Calvin!"

"Howdy, darlin'," said the lad in the worst cowboy accent ever.

"Told Jon to stop doing this. They're gonna catch on eventually."

Calvin backed the Silverado out. "Jon's got nothing to do with it. You mentioned how many times you got early passes outta Altoona High during our little joy ride."

"Our little joy ride with no joy?" she sniped, unzipping her jacket. The cabin was warm. She fixed the front of her cable-knit sweater. It wasn't a boring cardigan like the heavy girls wore but cut low and cropped up. It always gave the illusion of falling off her shoulder.

"You wear *that* to school, Tiffany?"

"I'm not in school anymore, Uncle Calvin. But I'll take it off if it offends you."

GROUPIE SECTION

Kare's phone was super-spiffy, with a transparent plastic case showing off the circuitry innards. Neon yellow piping flashed when someone called. The phone needed to be plugged into a power socket—*that's* how awesome it was.

At the flickering light, the Mall Chick Queen turned down her stereo and *Madonna belted up about her being becoming so ablaze, burgeoning to such brilliance, that it was disabling.*

"Hello? Hey, didn't expect you to call. Yes I got plans Friday night, I'm no loser. Cancel them?! To go do what? ... no way, I *hate* Corey Feldman! Why would I go to the theater to see something *he's* in?"

Kare's eyes grew wide at the answer.

GROUPIE SECTION

The Monday after the blizzard was unseasonably warm. The snow had melted nicely. After practice, Calvin went east down Rte. 666 (Bald Eagle Pike) to a coin-op car wash owned by one of the Schultzes. He was dying to rinse the salt off his baby.

There were four stalls and only the last one was open. Some folks liked to roll down the elephant door and lather up in private. The Ape never understood why. Who needs privacy to clean a Continental?

A navy blue Honda Civic hatchback pulled up to his stall, getting in line for when he vacated it. Rayche Schultz climbed out that Honda. She strode over to Calvin's truck with a blackmailer's smirk. "You took Kare to the movies on Friday, didn't you?"

"I plead the Fifth!" The clock was ticking and Calvin's coin supply was limited so he kept working the soaper brush over his tailgate.

Rayche fetched the hose gun off the opposite wall. *"Someone* took her to the theater, Connor. Kare wouldn't give details 'cept that she really, *really* enjoyed getting dirty in the back row."

"That's so unlike her."

"She said she was getting revenge."

"On Sean?"

"On Corey Feldman."

"Well." The lad shrugged. "No one deserves happiness more than our poor Miss McGillicutty."

Rayche smirked. "Jill, then Jenny, then Kare ... I mean, is it your goal to date *all* of us Mall Chicks?"

"Just the hot ones."

She playfully aimed the hose gun at him.

"That won't work until I switch this off," the lad said, brandishing the soaper brush back. With much gurgling and grunting, a dribbly white ooze slurped out of the bristles.

"Yeah I know, dickhead," said Rayche. "My dad owns this place."

Calvin slithered over to the stall's elephant door and rolled it down.

FOUL

On many occasions he reached out to Kitty Howe.

Called. Ma Howe answered, and told him not to call again.

Called again. Eddie answered but used only Spanish. "No Kate, señor. ¡La gatita no está aquí!"

Tried to talk to her at school. Lady Em said, "The ruffian will remove himself from my person."

Wrote her a note but threw it out. Abby Malone would have to read it to her. Ryan gave updates, presumably through Abby but who knows how the guy got his information. The updates were basically *Kitty's fine and thinks she made the right move.*

One more conversation was all Calvin wanted. To answer the questions. Ease his pain.

Art had switched lunch tables after all, joining the Gelatinous Cubes. He made several attempts to patch up his friendship with Calvin but the lad was cool to them all. "Saturday poker's still going on," said Art, and Calvin told him he was busy on weekends. Which was true: Mr. Bachner had filing work that needed doing. He paid $4.25 an hour, above the table. Gail, the little lawyer's daughter, showed Calvin the ropes. Gail was a nice girl. No arse, but nice. She was one of the Proverbs Patrol so the Ape was never getting that arse. The kids did spend their breaks together discussing Bible Study.

The law office was quiet. No Phil Collins on Wacky 103.

Called Kitty a week later. No answer. Left a message.

Called the Lyons house long-distance. If anyone would understand the Ape's pain, it's "Cindy." The man with the deepest voice in the world told him Wren was grounded and not allowed to come to the phone.

"Up to her old tricks again, eh?" said Calvin.

"Try again after the 15th," said Satan, hanging up.

Calvin would indeed call again on March 15th ... to talk about something far more serious.

FOUL

Thursday was an outdoor scrimmage on a damp Axe Field, the first since the blizzard a week and a half ago. One week from Opening Day. Skip put Calvin on the mound for some simulated game action.

He slaughtered them all.

Sixteen at-bats; every Varsity hitter except catcher Sean Corgan got up twice. Brion Davey—who, since the party, had avoided all contact with the Irish Raging Ape—got the only hit, a line shot up third. The toothless goon also flied out to right.

The other fourteen batters struck out. Irish was a machine. Cold as ice. Lucky Cheeseboro practically creamed his pants.

Josh Adams—a Varsity pitcher, a senior, last year's Opening Day starter—feared he'd be riding the pine next week.

Chapter 30

THERE IS NO 'TRY.'
THE IDES OF MARCH.

FOUL

THE LAD SAT AT the kitchen table, staring out the slab window at the first glimmers of dawn. A crow croaked like *Christ, morning already?*

Calvin was up at 5:30 every day now. He'd taken Coach Falcone's diet and exercise plan seriously. Weight loss wasn't the goal, nor was muscle gain; pitchers derived their power from stamina, strong legs, tough backs. The lad alternated morning routines: push-ups/sit-ups down in the telly room where his grunts and sweat didn't wake anyone, or long jogs. Today, he'd have black coffee, an orange (peel and all), then go for a run.

"Morning," said Calvin the Third, obligatorily.

"Morning," said Calvin the Second, just as phoned-in. The man shuffled in and reset the Mr. Coffee to make rude noises. Da sat at his throne at the kitchen table and went through the paper. This was *his* morning routine. Once Ma got up, the kitchen would be full of racket, meal-making and child-berating and News Radio 1240 AM.

A small story on page 1 of the *Altoona Mirror* covered the start of the West Penn Conference's Varsity baseball season. Calvin the Second passed that section over to his son.

Calvin the Third turned to the continuation on page 7. Altoona Area High played at Bishop Guilfoyle today; Axsubeen High was at Larsen Academy tomorrow. A photo showed young Calvin discussing strategy on the mound at Axe Field with Sean Corgan, likely taken by one of the growing crowd of non-parent weirdos at their practices. In the pic, Calvin's mitt was close to, but not wholly covering, his face. Luckily, the doo-doo brown cap covered his Davey Dangle 'do.

"Got my picture in the paper again, Da."

Calvin the Second sparked his morning Merit Light. "Really," he said, not looking up from the Business section.

Calvin the Third set the paper aside. Ma would want to clip the article for her scrapbook (which even she called his "jacket" now).

Son stood. "Opening Day's tomorrow. Coming?"

Father said, "I'll try."

Da said "Yes" and "No" a thousand times a day at work; he was the big boss at Schultz's Lumber. It was his job to give firm answers. At home, Da made no commitments. "I'll try" was all ya got.

And "I'll try" always meant *No*.

And "I'll try" were the last words Calvin Ciaran Connor II spoke.

FOUL

The lad didn't own a Walkman to occupy his mind but kept the jogs fun by playing little games. Spot one car from every color of the rainbow. Glance into windows as he passed, hoping for a boob. Sometimes he'd run the Bellend Howl and pretend-screw swimsuit models. Since sweatpants didn't hide shit, he'd then have to think of nuns.

Today, he noticed something interesting: hubcaps were a clear indicator of economic standing. A car in the driveway with all its hubcaps? That family's doing okay. Car missing one or two? Not so well. A junker, missing them all? Food stamps.

Hubcap propped on the mailbox pole? Good Samaritan.

Hubcaps mounted on the garage siding? Fuckin' weirdo.

He circled back to Maple, slowing to his cool-off walk. Rose's Bug was gone. *She's off early,* he thought, checking his Jelly Fish Swatch. It was 6:30. *Real early.*

He jerked to a stop at his front door. It was open. Perry Phillips stood in the doorframe. "Son," the old man said. "Your mother asked me to wait for you."

"What's going on, Skip?"

"Your dad collapsed. Ambulance left a few minutes ago. I saw it pull up so I came over to lend a hand."

The boy's Reeboks dragged over the front stoop. He was parched from the run. Words clawed at his chalky throat. "Where?"

"I guess Altoona Hospital. It's the closest one. Your mom and your sister took off after the ambulance."

"I ... need water." He pushed inside to get some.

The kitchen was a mess. The table had been pushed back against the counter to make room. Two of the chairs were overturned. The linoleum was littered with ash, broken mug shards, and sections of the *Mirror*. One page, soaked brown with coffee, had his picture on it.

Chapter 31
KEEPING THE ASTROTURF TIDY.
OPENING DAY.

⚾ PRESS BOX ⚾

SCHOLASTIC BASEBALL HAD FALLEN to third behind football and basketball by the '80s but Axsubeen High School treated Opening Day like it was the '50s with a pep rally. The softball girls were honored too. At 1:30 p.m., the proud student-athletes waved their passes, left their classes, and got their asses to the gym to prep for the crowd.

A dais was set up, a few dozen chairs got hauled in from the caf for visiting dignitaries, all the bleachers were pulled out. Boys wore church-fine shirts, slacks, shoes, and pus orange or doo-doo brown ties. Girls wore nice dresses. Parents and grandparents took pics, pinched cheeks.

Through the wire-shot windows in the gymnasium's doors, faces bobbed up and down: students passing by, trying to catch glimpses.

Art, Ryan, and Spazz were joined by Gus Jacoby, a poor substitute for Calvin but not a boring one. The blob had gotten the Davey Dangle; it seemed crooked, like a cap slightly askew. Senior Josh Adams initiated freshman Gus by planting a slice of bologna on the spiked portion atop his dome. It took five whole minutes before Gus figured out what every-one—*everyone!*—was laughing so hard at.

The room's bright chatter got shadowy with the arrival of Calvin Connor. He wore his full church suit. His hair was newly shorn, a buzz-cut. His steel gray eyes had had their souls crushed underfoot.

After a chat with Skip and Coach Falcone, he shook both men's hands and joined his friends.

"Gus, how come you smell like a sandwich?" he asked.

They all laughed, and it wasn't a phony laugh to cheer up a friend.

"At least I don't look like the principal," Gus joked back.

Spazz gamely slapped the mookish boob's back. "You *really* sunk low if Jabroni-Jacoby's givin' ya fashion advice, Cal-eidoscope!"

Calvin slipped off the sportcoat. "I thought 'tie' meant 'suit.' I popped down to Steeler's Shears and told Mr. Mueller, 'gimme a man's haircut.' I was sick of looking in the mirror and not liking what I saw."

"Just in time," said Ryan. "They're shaving the numbers in now."

Calvin was mortified to behold blocky numerals etched into the Scoundrels' temples. They'd used a beard trimmer. The **4 4** on the left side of Reggie's skull was crooked. Sean Corgan saw Calvin's gawk and sauntered over. The others slowly followed.

"How's he doin'?" the little wanker asked.

"What do you care?" said Calvin.

"I fuckin' asked, didn't I?"

"He's at death's door." The lad was not looking forward to giving this answer a million times. "It was a stroke."

"What's that?" asked Gus. Chicken nodded like *I don't know either.*

A young man with a cocksure coiffure appeared at the Ape's left. "Bill Radcliffe, *Axsubeen Reporter,*" he said, producing a pad and pencil. "How's it feel to be the center of all this hype, Calvin?"

The lad looked Radcliffe up and down. He'd never met the man, but knew his work well. "Feels way better than when you put my picture on the front page for buying Binaca."

"Yesss," Radcliffe purred, feeding the kid with: "But you must be excited at the idea of using your lightning arm to strike out the batters from Larsen Academy. Is that fair to say?"

"As fair as when my ma read that I was, and I quote, 'another hopeless teenage addict for alcohol-based breath-fresh—'"

"This guy's all right, chief," Sean told Calvin. "Calls me for quotes all the time. Don't piss off the press!"

Radcliffe saluted him with the pencil.

"Bollocks," Calvin told Sean. "He blasted you in that same article. Ma cut it out and saved it." To the reporter: "She curses the name 'William C. Radcliffe' anytime she sees it."

"I give the community news that it can use," said Radcliffe. "Got dozens of letters thanking me for exposing the rampant drug use here."

Spazz jumped in: "Ain't rampant enough for me!"

"Says the young man recently cited for selling Camels to kids."

"Whatever, I carded that ten-year-old—his fake ID was flawless!"

An older man with two cameras and zero ambition appeared at Radcliffe's side. "Can I borrow you for some pics, Calvin? Throwing to your catcher here would work."

All these strange men know my name. Calvin looked at Sean.

Sean looked back, like *Maybe he ain't all right. Let's fuck with him.*

Calvin nodded. He fetched a ball from a farm pail full of them (can't have a baseball event without baseballs handy). The photographer set the boys up about ten feet apart and snapped away. Sean and Calvin did a throw and catch, then shot the camera the bird.

"That's for the *Distorter!*" said Sean.

"Print *that* on the front page!" Calvin yelled to Radcliffe.

The photographer had frames sans le majeur and left. Radcliffe stalked over with some steam. "How's about I run a full profile on the Connor family? Your sister's escapades'll make delicious copy."

"That'll look great on you," said Calvin, "with my da in a coma."

Radcliffe scoffed, like *Sure kid, tell me another one.*

Sean jammed a finger at Radcliffe's tie. "Who the hell are you to talk to us like that?"

Us. Sean was team captain. Calvin was officially part of the team.

The Scoundrels, following their leader, got in Radcliffe's face too, even Davey. It was the closest Calvin had been to him since the party. Ryan waved for the rest of the team to get over here.

"When we lost 17–3 to Hollidaysburg last year," Paddy Millar told Radcliffe, "you used a picture of me pickin' my schnozz! The headline was, 'Axes Dig For Gold, Come Up Empty.'"

The reporter for the *Distorter* calmly smiled at the twenty boys making angry noises. "Over the years, I've had more than a few Millars send in postcards threatening to hogtie me."

"So that's how you get revenge?" said Sean.

"That's the power of the press, kiddies—be nice to us, we're nice to you. Be a jerk to us …" The man made a show of looking around. "Ain't no one from the *Mirror* here. Or the *Post-Gazette.* Yinzers and people from the 'Toona don't care about Axsubeen. I do. I work here. I'm all you got."

He pointed a finger at Calvin. "Stop calling us the *Distorter,* start answering my cupcake questions with standard answers, and I'll make you look like a hero, Connor."

Calvin pointed at Paddy. "Leave him alone too."

"Everyone," Sean corrected, "the whole team."

"Done." Radcliffe held up his pen and paper. "So?"

"I'm excited to be an Axsubeen Axe," said Calvin dutifully.

The young reporter made a note of it.

FOUL

The A.V. Club's Peter McLlwayne hooked the phonograph to the P.A. and spun *Hit Explosion,* a 1983 K-Tel compilation with *Joe Jackson's jolly ditty of two kooky cookies treading steady through glowing gloaming.*

The student body filed in. Many folks Calvin didn't know asked for news of his da's condition; he gave the same answer to them all: "He had a stroke. He's in a coma and it doesn't look good."

"You shoulda stayed home," said Ryan.

"I sure as hell wouldn't be here," said Spazz. He mugged for some yearbook committee squirt taking candids with a Minolta.

The Honorable Wilhelm Josef Schultz V, mayor of Axsubeen Borough took the dais. Mr. Falcone slit his throat with a finger; Peter McLlwayne picked the needle off the record.

"Welcome to the 1989 Axsubeen Axes baseball and softball teams," Big Billy trilled. "I'm a former player myself. The only Axe to throw a perfect game and one of just three to make it to the Bigs. They retired my number 5 at Axe Park, but they'll never retire me from Axsubeen. I've never missed a game!"*

Click click! went the cameras, "Yaaay!" went the crowd.

Big Billy made the traditional public bet: a bushel of Schultz's

---

* A politician telling half-truths to a crowd? Who'da thunk it:

    1) Big Billy played in four whole games for the Orioles in September 1972.

    2) He wore 1 5 in 1965 when he threw that perfect game. He didn't get 5 on his back until his cousin Stefan Schultz V—now Sheriff Steve—graduated.

    3) Big Billy missed *plenty* of Axes games during his six years of minor league action ... and the odd one in recent years when facing mayoral duties (hangovers).

Family Farm corn against a case of Mallo Cups from Altoona's Mayor Alain Petrowicz (an alumnus of Larsen Academy). Big Billy thanked everyone from Principal Roger Martin down to Groundskeeper Señor Pássaro Urban Yustinus, a.k.a. "Spuy."

Next up to the dais was another ex-Axe/ex-MLBer: Richard Louis Cheeseboro. Lucky was nice enough to point out the seventh- and eighth-grade baseball/softball teams, sitting up in the bleachers, who otherwise got no public regard. He thanked "Team Mom" Lottie Millar for her fund-raising work—everyone clapped except the deposed former Team Mom, Charlotte Mueller. Most of the parents in attendance were moms, but a few fathers had gotten away from work (like Art's da, a plumber). Eileen Connor would certainly have attended were she not at Da's side in the ICU. She would've sat in the very back row.

Lucky made an "accidental" plug for Lucky Cheeseboro GM Chevrolet, on Pleasant Valley Blvd. (a.k.a. Altoona's Golden Mile of Autos); just take the Frankstown Road exit off I-99. The crowd chuckled politely. He yielded the mic to Varsity softball coach Susan Geoffries, who made a brief speech on girl power and the dedication of the team. The girls' season started Saturday with a home match against their traditional rivals, Bellwood-Antis.

Skip's turn was brief. He noted the discipline sports gives a young man and promised they'd trounce Larsen Academy for Affluent Boys in their own stupid stadium an hour from now!

The players waggled fists and woofed.*

"But we can't take the field," said Skip, "without uniforms."

With pomp and applause, the teens were brought forward one by one to put their V-neck polyester pullovers atop their shirt and tie or dress. The photographer captured each kid's moment in the sun. For publication purposes he'd only submit shots of Calvin, but he'd make prints on commission—like the one he took ages ago of gawky fourteen-year-old Lucky that hung prominently at the dealership.

Some kids got big cheers (Sean Corgan, Detta Roberts, Paddy Millar, and Jennifer Murray, who, as captain of the Varsity softball

---

* Woofing got big in January 1989 with the debut of *The Arsenio Hall Show*. By that summer any kids still woofing got beaten up, even those woofing ironically.

team, had the honor to wear 9 9). There were gasps at seeing Ryan Phillips's 6 6 shirt was white—Skip had put his son on the J.V. squad. William/Bill/Liam "Spazz" Watson was lovingly booed by the Axes; he blew them a kiss (with tongue) and head-banged away from the dais.

Art ran a hand over the doo-doo brown silk-screened Axes on the front of his white shirt. "I'm geysering in my pants!" he told Calvin, and added, with playful spite, "*You* know what that feels like."

The Ape was brought up last. "Finally our diamond in the rough," said Skip, "Junior Varsity pitcher Calvin Connor III."

The loudest applause so far ... for an unathletic stooge who'd only started playing baseball a month ago! Calvin was embarrassed for the crowd. These same folks had burnt him at the stake as the betrayer of Troop 666 and as a shameless seducer of a poor little rich girl.

Calvin reached the dais and unfurled his fresh laundry. The 2XL top was loose around his chest and shoulders, the way pitchers like it. He turned his back on the crowd to show them the glossy black eight-inch block numeral 4. Big cheers.

He was facing Skip now. "I wish your dad could've been here to see it," said the old man.

"It's actually more fitting that he's missing it," said Calvin.

FOUL

After the mysterious disappearance of some precious monogrammed velour bathrobes during a football game in '83, no Axsubeen athlete had been permitted to enter a locker room at Larsen Academy. The Axes got into baseball regalia in their own locker room and got on a waiting bus. Skip assigned seats to surround the lad with his coach and catchers: Sean (window), Calvin (aisle), Lucky (aisle), and Gus (window).

The bus driver, yet another Schultz (Paul IV), turned left onto Rte. 666 (Bald Eagle Pike). They passed the student lot, stuffed with parents and alumni. Horns honked, hands waved, a sweater got pulled up.

Gus blinked. "Did I just see—"

"Titties!" hollered Spazz.

"WHERE?!" asked a dozen teenagers.

Bus No. 4 curved 'round a bend. Only a lucky few saw them titties.

Everyone was afraid to speak to Calvin. He broke the ice himself. "Coulda stayed at the hospital but I hadda get away. What if I suck?"

"You won't," said Lucky. "We did all them drills to get ya ready."

Sean reviewed the pitch signals with Calvin: one finger for a fastball, two fingers horns-style for a change-up, three for a knuckle-curve, and the trick signal (no fingers) that the pitcher shakes off.

The lad hardly heard him. He wondered why the little wanker never confronted him about the rumors that the Ape took his ex-girlfriend Kare to a Corey Feldman movie.

Sean had Shelley Quince to bang now. Maybe that's why.

Teenage politics made his head hurt when his heart already pained him so. He picked at his uniform, nervous energy.

"Relax," said Sean. "You're on the J.V., man. You'll only play if we're up big or down big. Skip knows you're goin' through heavy shit." The guy mulled that. "Or, he might put you in for that exact reason."

"All right, Seanie," said Lucky, "snap that trap. You been doin' an awful lot of yappin' lately and we're payin' for it!"

The man gave Calvin a sorrowful look. It came off comical and corny, like an overdone pout in one of his TV ads. "I'm sorry about your dad. If there's anything I can do, let me know."

Calvin had already heard words to this effect many times but they didn't help. Words couldn't help. *Except if Kitty said them.*

Blind kids stuck out in crowds and he hadn't seen her at the pep rally. But it *was* Thursday, when she took classes at the Blair County Institute for the Blind up in Altoona.

"Saw Eddie Howe pointing at you," said Sean.

"Probably wants to kill me," said Calvin.

"All he's gotta do is sit on ya," said Gus.

Calvin, Sean, and Lucky turned to give the roly-poly pudgeball a laugh. Sean said, "One fatty calling out another!"

"That's how the world works," said Lucky. "Only queers get to call each other 'faggots.' Only blacks are allowed to call each other 'nigger.' Then again, only niggers *would* call each other 'nigger' and be fine with it!" Lucky gave them a grin like, *Am I right?!*

Calvin's poker face had never been through such a test.

FOUL

The Axes arrived at 2 p.m. This was Calvin's first trip inside Larsen Academy's wrought iron gates. Tasteful streetlights lined the entryway pavement. Winter-dormant cherry blossoms ran down the median. The front lawn was a full acre. The Ape expected a crowd of alums in shiny silver Larsen sportcoats, waving pearl-handled canes disgustedly at the farmboys. There wasn't a soul present.

Larsen's chapel and dormhouse were Colonial American; its main building, Gothic Revival; its gardens, French; its attitude, English. The parking lot teemed with imports: BMW, Volvo, Jaguar, Audi, Porsche. Not a single Celebrity wagon or C-10 with a car/burger/titty Lucky Cheeseboro logo on the back bumper.

The campus roadway rounded a corner, revealing a graveyard that crept everyone the fuck out. "They only bury ya here if ya get shot climbing over The Wall!" said Spazz.

A parking lot adjoined the sports fields. Balfour Diamond at Larsen Park, for that was the baseball field's absurd name, was on the far side. "Lots of lights," said Gus, pointing at the Musco poles.

"Lots of turf," said Lucky, fingering the playing surface.

"What's the deal with AstroTurf?" Calvin asked.

"It sucks," said everyone, even the bus driver.

A couple dozen Larsen students milled near the path to Balfour Diamond. At their head was a mounted policeman.

Then came the first egg. "Windows up!" Skip ordered.

The second egg splattered on Spazz's window. The wild-child put his tongue on the glass and pretended to lick the slurpy yolk.

Someone in the crowd flashed the opposite of sweet titties. "Get outta my face with that hairy honky ass!" yelled Reggie Roberts.

The bus parked. Calvin saw why the mounted policeman didn't stop the Larsenites' hooliganism: he was one of them, not a cop but another rich kid in fancy security regalia (and atop a palfrey). He moved the horse by the bus door to shield the visitors from detritus.

"On your feet, ladies!" said Skip. "Grab the gear!"

The team crunched up in the aisle. Calvin felt warm bodies in front and behind. He stumbled down the bus steps into the cool March air and beheld a horse's fat dun arse.

Sean Corgan shoved him from behind. "Move it, rookie!"

Calvin followed the path, shielding himself from the insults and foreign objects. Passing a shiny chain-link gate, his baseball cleats hit the AstroTurf. It was like walking on inlaid brick; none of the spongy give of real ground. A quick jog brought him into the visitors dugout along the third base line. He picked a melting M&M from his ear.

Spazz crashed into him and nearly lost his armful of bats. "That was intense, eh, High Cal-iber?"

"Too right. What'll it be like when we leave?"

"A million times worse, babe, 'specially if we win!"

The dugouts at Balfour Diamond at Larsen Park were luxurious. A safety fence kept foul balls from bonking the backups. The bench had padding for buttocks and back. Trash cans with Hefty bags. A fridge and a shelf for propping spouted water jugs like the ubiquitous Gatorade barrel. A toilet in a closet. Bat racks and helmet cubbies.

And a television! *Totally awesome!*

Someone scratched FUCK YOU LARSEN on the Lexan screen-shield; someone else obliterated the first word and wrote LOVE above it.

"They put the games on TV here?" said Calvin.

"They have their own TV *station,*" said Art.

"It's closed-circuit," said Ryan. "Security cameras too."

"The only people watchin' the game are rich kids back at the dorms," said Zedz. "Too busy havin' circle jerks to come."

"Ain't that the point of circle jerks?" said Spazz. "To cum?"

"Well," said Calvin. "In Matthew it says, *You shall love your neighbor as yourself.*"

Zedz's reply was a word balloon filled, *Mad* magazine-style, with funny typewriter characters, fish skeletons, and small explosions.

Calvin told him, *"I did not come to save the righteous but the sinners."*

"I sure as shit ain't here to save no sinners!" said Paddy Millar.

"Instead of attacking them, *educate* them," Calvin persisted.

"Oh we can do that!" said Reggie. He fetched a random bat and held it like a rifle. "Bow down, buttholes!"

Calvin grabbed a bat and held it like a katana. *"Alas, sword of the LORD! How long 'til you find rest?"*

Skip said, "In Psalms it says, *Shut your holes and form up!*"

The players bunched together in the dugout and knelt down. Skip stood at the top step to address them.

"I've talked to God. In Korea I talked to Him plenty times. He said America was on the side of right. And so's Axsubeen, damnit!"

The players cheered. Ryan declined to join them. Calvin the Irish Catholic wanted to raise a finger (or two) (or just the middle one).

"This is my thirtieth season, boys. I won the conference title back in '73, the year Ryan and Seanie and y'all were born. We had a first round exit in States, a tough 1–0 loss in extras. We fought tooth and nail until the bitter end and didn't go out like a bitch!"

"We won't either," muttered some of the players.

"Guys, I hate Larsen. Buncha millionaire cherry-pickin' dicks— they tried recruitin' Seanie but he told 'em to kiss his ass!"

"Damn right!" said the little wanker.

What a "crock of shite," thought the Irish Raging Ape.

"Their pitcher's name is Dolly Smythe," said Skip. "You kiddin' me? And you'll know who he is cuz his name'll be on his back. The only name on *our* uniforms is this one!" Skip slapped the Axes across his tits and started a cheer. The veterans joined in:

> *Fight, fight, with all our might!*
> *Swing, score, runs galore!*
> *Tag, throw, get out the foe!*
> *Axes, Axes, kicking asses!*

Skip thundered onto the field with a "CHARGE!"

The boys came in his wake, hollering, pumping fists, and woofing.

They heard boos. Skip pulled Calvin aside and waved a hand at the bleachers: pupils in silver blazers and dads in silver alumni cardigans. "These assholes'll do more than boo at us. Don't be surprised if you hear taunts about your dad. And your sister."

"My reputation proceeds me." Calvin tipped his cap for the crowd.

Skip laughed. "You got balls, 4."

The lad took in the scene. Balfour Diamond at Larsen Park's AstroTurf was shiny and green. A man in silvery gray overalls sprayed a hose over the infield dirt, which seemed to be all dirt and not 50%

pebbles like at Axe Park. Thirty-foot foul poles shone bright yellow. Bleachers ran in a semi-circle from one dugout to the other, like an aluminum Pac-Man gobbling the field.

The outfield wall was an actual wall, covered in pads, not ads. It was 320 at the left pole (normal), 350 at straightaway center (West Penn minimum), and 300 at right (shortest in the conference). Lefty pull hitters like Brion Davey loved that short corner in right. The design was no accident; this was a hitters' park. Rich kids are born and bred to dig big numbers next to their names.

Above the wall in left stood a ten-foot Fan-O-Vision "screen," rows of yellow bulbs inside a mesh grate. The Fan-O-Vision did animated graphics and low-resolution monochrome television feed conversions. The dot-matrixy text reminded Calvin of report card surgery, a cheat he no longer needed: baseball had soldered a loose wire in his brain.

Plus, he got a tutor. *Not* Saint Mark Duffy. One of the softball girls volunteered: Steph Millar, the fourth Mall Chick. The stacked one. Almost Shelley Quince levels of top-heavy. Calvin and Steph worked hard on polynomials and inequalities in the library. His quizzes stopped coming with a D on top, but he didn't.

Larsen Academy had tutors on hand for every subject. Jon Oldroyd and Mr. Bown had pitched that hard. "Most of my classes are like ten dudes," said Jon. "The smallest is four. All I gotta do is snap my fingers and I get a tutor, and it won't be some senior being nice but an expert in the real world. That's what Larsen's all about: resource management. Like how Lucky Cheeseboro's your personal coach. He knows his shit cuz he's been there. We'd love to get him working with our ball team."

Over by the home dugout, Larsen had a snack stand with a charcoal grill. A man in those silvery gray overalls was making hot dogs.

In their second meeting (when they drafted the personal services contract), Vince Bachner, Esq., had brought up the free hot dogs Lucky Cheeseboro gave away at his dealership. "That's how he gets away with saying 'getcher buns down at Lucky's' on radio and TV," said the lawyer. "The F.C.C. might consider it a vulgarity otherwise."

"They're free, too. Is that like 'no purchase necessary?'"

"Precisely. Everything in the car sales business is *juuust* this side of legal. But if Lucky's as desperate as you say, he'll jump at our deal."

Spazz grabbed the lad's shoulder. "Holy shit, we're famous!"

The Fan-O-Vision showed all four Suicide Kings as they stood chatting. The picture was super-crappy after being down-converted to light bulb dots yet it was definitely their back numerals: 6 9, 4, 6 6, and 2 4. Ryan dashed to reposition himself at Spazz's left and made the first three numbers all sixes. "Like some shit written on the boys room wall," said Spazz. "'For a good time, call 666-9424!'"

J.V. Coach Falcone got the Axes paired up along the base line for pre-game stretches. The Ghosts took up the field and threw some balls around. Larsen had Major League-quality uniforms, cotton button-down shirts (silvery gray for the Varsity, white for the J.V.). The silver caps bore a fat-bottomed ghost with an O-face, reminiscent of a certain movie's logo if you ditched the red slashed-circle. **GHOSTS** stretched nipple to nipple; the players' last names arched over the back numerals.

The Axes unis, by contrast, looked like a flea market item. The doo-doo brown of their caps and pus orange of their shirts looked like colostomy-bag filler.*

Art the Pedant pointed out that the Axes' numbers were the usual boring block font with an embarrassing gap between the digits—e.g., 1 9—while the Larsen numbers were fat, curvy, tightly packed, and altogether sexier: **19**.

Spazz bucked like Art had shown him a beefcake poster. "This ain't a fuckin' fashion show here, Humping-Art Bogart!"

"*You're* the one in pink shoes, mate." Calvin pointed at Spazz's cleats, whose red color had been delicately bleached by Val.

"Pink is heavy metal, Con-Artist!" said Spazz. "Whoa, that one's got *both* of y'all's names!"

FOUL

---

* This description of today's uniform colors is brought to you by O'Sullivan's Wallpaper & Paint. Want to decorate your rec room in official team colors? O'Sullivan's carries blends of Ghost Silver and pus orange in semi-gloss *and* satin, plus a wide range of doo-doo brown wood stains and varnishes. Mention this ad and get 10% off your order! Stop on by O'Sullivan's Wallpaper & Paint, right next door to Pizza Putt on Railroad Street in historic downtown Axsubeen.

A call from the umpire signaled the end of warm-ups. A yell from the bleachers signaled the end of Calvin's carefree teenage life.

"Hey Calvin! Over here!"

"No autographs!" Spazz shouted back.

Steel gray eyes followed the sound and widened to see Abby Malone. The big girl stood in the first row of bleachers behind the visitor dugout. Abby had put a knee on the dugout's concrete roof so she could lean out and wave both arms. Her royal blue winter coat stood out from all the silver gray.

Calvin jogged over and leaned on the dugout's nuts-high fence-screen directly across from her. They were eye-level with each other. Five feet of open air, the depth of the dugout, separated them.

Abby's slanted face was blank, ashen even. *Da's dead,* thought Calvin. *The news got out and she heard and came to tell me.*

One slabby hand held out a note.

He stretched but couldn't reach. She put both knees on the dugout roof to lean further out. He took the note and unfolded it:

I'M PREGNANT

"You're pregnant?!" he hissed at her, going ashen himself.

"No, you idiot," she said back. Tears started to fall from her eyes.

He was an idiot. His mind played dumb on purpose. It was obviously Kitty's handwriting. She didn't write much and it was always crooked and roller-coastery—

—I'M PREGNANT

He heard the words in his head like they came out a megaphone. He staggered back from the dugout's fence rail as if shot. "What?" he said. "When? How?" He looked up at Abby's face for answers.

He found Eddie Howe's wide-cheeked, breathless-red face in its place. "'How?' How do you think, jerk-off?!" the guy shrieked.

The Ape's legs gave out and his arse tumbled to the AstroTurf.

Larsen fans chanted, "Ax-su-been sucks! Ax-su-been sucks!"

Nearby teammates raced over. The ones in the dugout perceived that Calvin had been shoved backwards by whoever it was on the roof and they dashed out too. The boys got Calvin to his feet.

This mass of pus orange and doo-doo brown caps got the silver blazers and gray cardigans chanting louder, which caught the attention of the Ghosts on the field. When those boys started to drift over, the Larsen reserves rose from the home dugout to see what was up.

"AX-SU-BEEN SUCKS! AX-SU-BEEN SUCKS!"

An arse started the violence.

Not a person, an arse. A middle-school arse. Some Larsen twerp in a shirt-and-tie, silver blazer, and short trousers scrambled on the dugout roof and showed his pasty butt to the Axes.

Eddie Howe gave this kid a shove, nearly casting him down to the field. Adults in the bleachers ran down to stop this nonsense, while the Ghosts on field-level scampered over to get vengeance.

A second Larsen kid grabbed Eddie but looked unsure how to deal with him—the pudgy prick wasn't adorned in Ghost Silver and had attacked someone in that costume, *but* he'd also made threats towards Axsubeen's famous blue chip.

A shower of popcorn hit Eddie and the second Larsen pupil, and also Calvin & Co. on the field. Team goons Brion Davey and Felon Adkisson had had enough: they pointed fingers up in the stands and directed curses. They were doused in soda next. The goons laid hands on the dugout's roof to climb it and vault into the stands. Lucky Cheeseboro and Coach Falcone intercepted them. The Ghosts pulled the Axes away from their own dugout; kids in pus orange (or white) shirts felt surrounded and shoved away the kids in silver (or white) shirts.

The action went live up on the Fan-O-Vision, drawing boos.

Skip issued his piercing whistle. "AXES—RETREAT! INTO THE DUGOUT!"

The Axes got under cover quickly. Ryan Phillips grabbed Calvin and pulled him down the stairs. "What was that all about?" he asked.

Though unharmed, Calvin seemed concussed. "Eddie's my biggest fan."

Cracker Jacks and Pepsi dribbled off the lip of the dugout roof to smack on the floor. Davey wiped sticky soda off his polyester uniform and wiped his hands over his hair; a kernel of popcorn stuck in the 8 9 he'd shaved into the right side of his noodle.

Skip counted heads and knew everyone was safe. "Trying to get yourself killed, 4 ?" he said, slapping Calvin on the back. The team celebrated the brave, stupid rookie already causing Larsen grief. Calvin had won over a few seniors with this stunt.

Though he'd done nothing.

Well. He'd done *something*.

I'm PREgNaNT

"Pardon me," said a man, stepping into the dugout. He wore a tan woolen peacoat and a gray flat cap. "I'm Algernon Bown, Athletic Director of Larsen Academy."

Mister Bone, thought Calvin. *Does he want me to switch teams right now?!*

"I'm issuing your school a warning," said Mr. Bown.

Sean Corgan zipped in front of Skip to respond to him. "Oh yeah? Let's hear it. Are we the 'wrong kind of poor' for ol' Larsen?"

The man looked over the top of the diminutive wanker's ginger head to address Perry Phillips. "If there's another disruptive episode with the attendees, I shall petition the umpire for a forfeit."

"They started it!" said Felon.

"They hit him and threw shit at us!" said Sean, waving at Calvin.

Again, Mr. Bown ignored Sean. He'd dismissed the little wanker from his mind last year when advising the board to reject his application. Instead, he gave Calvin a neutral look, then Skip a haughty one. "This scenario is in the West Penn rulebook, and there *is* precedent."

"If one team were to *unexpectedly* lose the game before it even starts," said Skip, "I know a few burly men who won't be happy."

Mr. Bown got it. "Any man who speculates on scholastic sports is a degenerate, Mr. Phillips." He turned and left the dugout.

A stentorian blast came from the Balfour Diamond at Larsen Park public address: "THE LARSEN ACADEMY APPRECIATES YOUR HELP IN KEEPING THE ASTROTURF TIDY ... GIVE A HOOT, DON'T POLLUTE."

The Axes loosed a raucous cheer. Spazz tried to shove Calvin out for a curtain call, but Skip stopped that shit.

FOUL

The Axes stood on the third base line with caps over hearts as *the Larsen Choir, those beautiful bastards, belted out the battle-cry of the body politic's banner in boyish soprano and bullshit bass.*

The performance did not crack the lad's poker face.

His father lay dying in a hospital half a mile from here.

The lad's poker face was solid.

Kitty's pregnant!

It was news worth repeating: *Kitty's pregnant!*

Calvin was a rock.

The game started. He sat in the dugout, eyes focusing on a random point in the safety fencing. Players struck out, hit fly balls, stole bases. Teammates sat next to him to see if he was okay.

"I'm gonna puke," he said a few times.

Finally he did, scrambling to the closet loo. It was occupied. He got to one of the trash cans in the nick of time.

"Bloooyack!" went Spazz, engendering laughter from the others.

"Peee-yoo!" gagged Gus. "Wha'ja eat for lunch, a used diaper?"

At that image, Calvin turned green and ralphed again.

"Get it out now, sailor," said Lucky. "Opening day jitters happens to the best of us. Even me. Shit, this one time, I was with Boston …"

The young lads listened to how the Red Sox played a day game and Lucky was hungover from the night before and threw up during the eighth inning. They'd never look at the mound at Fenway the same again!

Lord, save me, thought Calvin …

> *Do not fear nor be dismayed, for the LORD, your God, is with you wherever you go.*

> *Well. If the Lord was with me, I just upchucked His arse into the bin.*

Chapter 32
WHO EMPOWERS ME?

FOUL

J.V. Manager Falcone and Varsity Manager Skip Phillips wore full baseball gear, including pants and cleats, and spent the whole game at the top of the dugout or manning the base coach boxes. That left Lucky Cheeseboro and Steve Schultz V to supervise the dugout. Both men had pulled a game shirt overtop their regular clothes to comply with West Penn rules ("all players and staff on the field-of-play must wear a uniform"). It was wild to see Sheriff Steve in a childish pus orange shirt, number 5 on the back, with his gun belt and cop trousers under it.

The bench coaches kept the J.V./backups involved, cheering on their teammates and busting opponents' balls. Larsen's starter, Dolly Smythe, worked pretty hard, loading the bases in the first and second but getting out of the jam each time. The Axes' Josh Adams did better, not letting a Ghost reach base until the third when Snatch Mueller bobbled a routine grounder.

"So much for that nickname, kid," said Lucky.

"Actually," said Art Maguire, pedantic finger in the air, "we call him 'Snatch' cuz this one time—"

Reggie Roberts elbowed him, "Chill out with that, nigga! You tryna tell a grown-up about his mama's cooch?"

Art bristled at being chastised but kinda loved that Reggie considered him black enough to call him *nigga*.

Backup catcher Gus Jacoby curled up on the padded bench and took a nap. With Sean ahead of him on the depth chart, Gus's only action would be catching warm-ups in the bullpen.

Calvin picked his butt. Baseball pants and undergarments were not conducive to slouching. He put on his concentration helmet to shut out the creeping dread. When that failed, he picked his butt some more.

"Got ants in yer pants?" said Pete Hennessey, pointing, laughing.

"Back off," said Brion Davey. He flopped down next to Calvin.

The proximity felt awkward and menacing to the lad. He had enough on his mind!

Davey was sweating. Nervous. "For what it's worth, I'm jealous of ya," the goon said.

The Ape wasn't ready for that. "I'll bite—why?"

"My dad's a major league prick, Connor. You got no idea what he's like. He beats me up constantly, yells about everything I do or don't do. If I could wave a magic wand and put my dad in your dad's place, I'd do it like—" Davey snapped his fingers.

If I could wave a magic wand, I'd bring my crow scout back.

"You've been avoiding me for weeks," said Calvin, "and when you finally say something to me, it's that."

"You're not the first person to shoot a gun at me," hissed Davey.

"So I keep hearing."

The goon torqued his gap-toothed snarl at Calvin. "Who told you that my dad shot at me? I never mentioned it to anyone!"

"Uh … I meant, 'I keep hearing' about me shooting at you but I don't remember it. I was concussed, mate. You saw me hit the table."

This was a semi-bluff. Calvin had no true idea what happened but Jill *did,* and she'd told the Ape all the gory details on the way to the mall.

Davey called the bluff: "Don't bullshit me, faggot. No more conspiracies. No more fuckin' lies. You don't fire a shot at someone and just forget it! You don't see another guy naked and just forget it!"

Calvin saw Davey's bet and raised big: "I'm not gonna feel sorry for you about your asshole da or anything else. The things you did are unforgivable. You tortured Kitty for years. You took advantage of my friend, dare I say it—or you *tried* to. What God gave ya to work with is kinda pathetic for a bloke your size. But you did the Devil's work with it, so you *deserve* getting shot at."

The fire in Davey's eyes filled his mind with smoke. In lieu of a comeback, he coughed lamely.

"Sheee-it," drawled Calvin, "yer lucky to still be alive, pardner."

It was another bluff. For all his chips. Calvin didn't care about

Davey enough to menace him, to *dominate* him as Fartin' Martin kept putting it, but he figured, *Say something mean and he'll fuck off.*

Davey fucked off.

Art Maguire immediately took his place. "What was that about?"

"Nothing." Calvin stood up. Seeing Spazz, he mimed smoking.

Spazz tugged Lucky's sleeve, "Yo, Coach Co-Cheese—we're goin' to the bullpen to smoke a doob."

Lucky waved them off. If the man had any concern for Calvin's nerves or stomach, or for Larsen's smoking policy, he didn't show it.

"Lemme come too," said Art. Ryan was in the on-deck circle and Art didn't want to be the only Suicide King in the dugout.

The three slithered up foul territory.

"Quit diggin' up the Hershey Highway," said Art.

Calvin didn't realize he was still picking his butt and stopped.

"They got TV cameras," said Art. "Lucky's all, 'cameras put you in a fishbowl—every nut-adjustment is embarrassing public record.'"

The bullpens at Balfour Diamond at Larsen Park were enclosed cages with a mound, a dirt patch for the catcher, and a short wooden bench. Calvin chose the mound as his seat and wanted to die when Art told him, "Now yer butt'll have dirt stains on it, Irish."

"The pants are already doo-doo brown, African. Go away."

In the game, Paddy was stranded on second by three weak efforts at the plate, including a strikeout by Davey. Calvin was stranded in his mind. His ex was expecting. Calvin Junior.

Calvin the Fourth, that is. Li'l Eye-Vee.

How? he thought. *How'd it happen?*

"Pot's better for your belly than Pepto-Bismol, Conn-isseur!" Spazz pulled the batting gloves out of his ass-pocket and futzed with them, creating enough cover for lighting up.

Art, mortified of getting caught, went back to the dugout, which helped cover the joint's transfer to Calvin. Spazz showed him how to cup his hand while dragging to help cover it and how to let out the smoke while moving around to help cover its dispersal.

Calvin couldn't do any of that and coughed for a full minute after his drag. He threw up again, which helped cover it.

Life slowed down once the weed kicked in. He got sucked into the

Fan-O-Vision, its yellow bulbs and jittery frame-rate. The broadcast was far from network quality: no close-ups, instant replay, commentary, chyrons, wipes, fadeouts, or commercial breaks.*

Looking at the crowd was a direct violation of Skip's policy but he wanted to know where Eddie Howe was. *Probably in a sniper's nest with a bolt-action Carcano.* He wanted to find Abby. Maybe Kitty was with her. The Blind Institute was close and school would be over now.

He saw Jon Oldroyd's cunt da with that mulchie cowboy hat. In a different row he saw Jon Oldroyd's ma. When he saw Jon Oldroyd's smokin' hot girlfriend, the straps of his athletic cup started wheezing.

He stirred at the crowd noise. Jason "Doggy-Door" Pearse hit a line drive to right that Jon Oldroyd caught with a sprawling dive. Ryan Phillips, on third, ignored his father's "stay" sign and broke for home. Oldroyd's throw was a laser beam and Skipson was out by two steps. Inning over. Still scoreless after three and a half.

Making the last out at home plate was a sin. Ignoring a direct order from the manager was a mortal sin. Telling one's da to "go suck cocks in Hell!" was the kinda sin that led to wars. Skip pulled Ryan from the game and stuck Reggie Roberts in his spot. Reggie was on the Varsity so this move put a pus orange shirt at every fielding position, but Roberts was a far weaker fielder and hitter.

The wheels came off one pitch into the bottom of the fourth.

Leading off for Larsen was Peter Bown, the cleanup hitter; he had to be the son of "Mister Bone." The kid had an angular face, the sturdy walk of a full wallet, and a big-cock-confidence smirk.

On the mound, Josh Adams shook off Sean's trick signal twice. The baseball gods didn't go for such chicanery and punished the Axes. Bown pulled the first pitch down the line. First baseman Felon Adkisson blocked it with a wrist-twisting mitt by his chin, more self-defense than plain defense; the ball caromed into foul territory near the Larsen dugout.

The Axes defense was swift: both second baseman Snatch Mueller and pitcher Adams raced to cover first while Felon and Sean thundered into foul ground for the ball. Bown was a smart runner; seeing no one

---

* Not a bad thing, really.

was covering second, he turned at first and put on the jets.

Sean knew he'd get to the ball first *and* be facing the infield, so he yelled, "Get down, Adkisson!" to clear the way. Felon threw himself to the turf and gave Sean a clear view of Josh and Snatch crashing into each other at first base; both had turned to run back and cover second.

"Shit," said Sean, bare-handing the ball. Seeing that shortstop Chicken finally got his beak out his ass and covered second, Sean fired.

Chicken parked his right foot on the bag and gloved the ball. He gave a triangular grin at the runner, a grin which said, "I'm about to fuck you up the ass, ése!"

Bown screeched to a halt and turned back. Two Axes fielders lay face-down in the dirt by first base; a third was pulling himself up from foul ground; while the catcher desperately charged over to cover the bag. When Sean held up his mitt to catch the ball, the runner switched directions and started the rundown. Bown's feet were adroit and he twisted his shoulders at opposite angles to create confusion. His only hope was that the hillbillies would fuck it up.

Which, naturally, they did. Sean sent the ball back to Chicken, who immediately lobbed it back, goose-tailed and wonky, practically a knuckleball. By now, Snatch pulled himself from under Josh Adams and onto his knees. Josh, dazed and unaware, jerked to his feet.

They were both in Sean's path and he had a ball to catch, so he climbed Snatch like a staircase and vaulted over Josh.

One of Sean's cleats kicked the 4 2 ironed on Josh's back, right in the wide gap between the two digits. The catcher sprawled forward arse-over-tits and landed mitt-first, then face atop mitt, then torso atop face. The cleat on his other foot kicked up and popped Josh's chin. The pitcher bit into his tongue, nearly chopping the tip off.

The ball sailed by them and bonked Snatch on his cap's crown—right on the button there, the spot that hurt the most—and rolled into unmanned foul ground. Bown turned back to second and rounded for third. It was unguarded—the third baseman, Doggy-Door, had gone to second for the rundown.

Right fielder Reggie Roberts was charging towards the ball. Bown saw no one to cover home and broke for it. Center fielder Paddy Millar booked—Lord, did he book—perhaps no one had ever run so fast in a game at Balfour Diamond at Larsen Park—and got to home plate before Bown did.

Reggie's throw was a mile wide, however.

Bown stepped on the plate and did a triumphant serpentine dance back to the dugout, dodging all the obstacles: his teammate Doughy Heatherington in the on-deck circle, various Axes fielders with heads hung or bits bleeding, and Larsen's manager/first base coach, Sallowaid Astor, who offered Peter Bown not one high-five but two.

The crowd's cheers woke Gus Jacoby in the dugout. The blob wiped stagnant drool off his chest protector's shoulder pauldron. His tea-saucer eyes bulged when Lucky told him to limber up.

Out on the field, Skip, Falcone, Sheriff Steve, and the two umpires checked on the downed Axes. Pitcher Josh Adams's tongue was meat-loaf. Sean Corgan's mouth made soft "I'm fine, chief" noises, but his left wrist made loud cracking ones that bent his emerald eyes. The rest of them were unhurt beyond their shame. Sheriff Steve, who'd come to the game in his patrol car, took Sean and Josh to the hospital.

Skip eyeballed Heatherington—a left-handed hitter—and pulled the lineup card from his ass-pocket. "Makin' a double-sub," he told the home plate ump. "Gus Jacoby's replacing Sean Corgan at catcher, and Spazz Watson's coming in for Josh Adams as pitcher."

Sallowaid Astor, a bearded blusterfuss who marked his lineup card with a Mont Blanc, sniffed. "This 'Spazz' will hit in the 2-spot, then?"

"It's a double-sub, not a double-switch," snapped Skip. "Try to keep up." He turned to the ump. "It's an injury substitution for the pitcher, so Spazz gets a full warm-up out here."

The Ghosts manager wasn't happy about that—every second that passed would drain the crowd's enthusiasm and his team's momentum.

Spazz had to walk a mile to reach the mound plus he was stoned so his warm-up took an hour. Just as the ump yelled "Play ball!", he threw up both hands for time-out and pointed at Gus's loose shin-guard.

Gus fixed it, then immediately asked for time to go to the mound and review the pitch signals. "I forgot 'em," he said.

"My boys have class in the morning," said Astor, making a show of checking his Cartier Pasha. "We only have sixteen hours to wrap this up, Phillips!"

Spazz's pipe-cleaner left arm flailed fastballs more-or-less accurately. His blond locks swayed over the top edge of his 6 9. He gave up a hit, got a double play grounder, then struck out the final batter with a record-tying three pitches. Spazz gave the Larsen dugout a devil-horn hand gesture as he sashayed off the mound.

Lucky kept the bench noisy. Spazz entered the dugout chanting his favorite Iron Maiden song, *a cantankerous cacophony of cataclysm where the clock closes in on the cows coming home, carrying the killing of all, even kids yet to come out their momma's cooches.* Calvin, back on the bench with his blood doing the marijuana macarena, felt an orgasmic rush at all the racket.

The Axes fed on Spazz's heroics in the top of the fifth. Paddy Millar led off with a walk. Gus and Reggie struck out but no matter, Brion Davey drove Dolly Smythe's next pitch over the short fence at the right foul pole. The inning ended with Axsubeen up, 2–1.

Then Spazz fell back to Earth. Walking a guy after nine pitches was embarrassing enough; walking the other team's pitcher on nine pitches was worse; Spazz topped it by letting Dolly Smythe steal second.

Skip sent Sammy Dzedzy to the bullpen to warm up. Lucky donned Corgan's mask and mitt to catch. Spazz did his best against Larsen's leadoff man, Reese Decker, but gave up another walk.

Fetching his lineup card again, Skip headed to the mound and this time did a double-switch: he sat Reggie, moved Spazz to right field, and put Zedz in as pitcher, batting 3rd. Zedz's thunderthigh diarrhetic ass threw nothing but miserable left-handed lawn-dart slop. Sanford Biercester, the next hitter, swung his bat like a man swatting at a wasp with a rolled-up newspaper and struck out swinging.

Jon Oldroyd was next and nubbed a knuckleball twenty feet forward. Zedz and Gus broke for it. The pitcher knew better than to get in the way of a rhino in catcher's armor and turned aside. As he did, Zedz's black cleat snared into the 'Turf and turned his ankle.

"Throw to third!" yelled Skip.

Gus heard that and made the play of his life, bare-handing the ball and whipping it to Doggy-Door. Dolly Smythe was forced out.

The umpire called time and once again adults jogged out to kneel by an injured kid. When Falcone lightly prodded the white stirrup sock over Zedz's ankle, the kid bucked like barbed wire had gone up his ass.

Skip called to the dugout, "1 4 ! 2 1 ! 4 ! 2 4 !"

Tony Fanucci, Pete Hennessey, and Art Maguire came out and carried Zedz off. Skip pulled Calvin Connor aside and told the ump, "He's comin' in."

The Ghosts manager hit the roof. *"Another* full warm-up on the mound? You got a kid at first who's warm already!"

"Your ears work, Sallowaid? I said, *this* kid's comin' in."

The ump said, "The quicker you get back in your dugout, Mr. Astor, the quicker he'll be warmed up."

"Captain Bush League here, dragging this out," said Astor. "Watch him do a mound visit after the first pitch!"

FOUL

Calvin got on the mound and realized his glove was back in the dugout. Some of the Axes had a laugh, like *Dumb rookie!,* before remembering he was their last pitcher and only hope.

Lucky dashed out the dugout with the mitt. "If you talk to the ump, remember to mention where ya got yer Silverado."

Calvin had never been so high in his life. His warm-up took three minutes. The mound was a little springy under his cleats, not like the rockpile at Axe Park. He nodded at the ump, who called, "Play ball!"

I have the strength for everything through him who empowers me, Calvin thought. *Kitty taught me that one. It's from Filipinos 4:13.*

The P.A. boomed and he nearly popped the rosin bag. "LADIES AND GENTLEMEN! CHANGE OF PITCHERS FOR AXSUBEEN ... NUMBER FOUR, CALVIN CONNOR THE THIRD ... NEXT UP FOR LARSEN ... NUMBER NINETY-NINE, PETER BOWN."

Maybe Pete liked Wayne Gretzky, or driving on nearby I-99. It didn't matter. Anyone ballsy enough to wear **99** on their back should be taken seriously.

Calvin squared his shoulders, donned his poker face, and faced the world, ready to beat its arse 'til it was red.

Gus put one finger down and Calvin grasped to recall the signals.

He nodded and stood erect. He remembered to keep a foot on the rubber. He wound up to deliver his first pitch—

"Time! Time!"

Calvin shit himself.

The Larsen manager, standing in the first base coach's box, waved the umpire over and pointed at Spazz in right field. "That player's foot-wear does not meet conference standards."

"What the flamin'—flyin'—" said Skip. He cleared the distance from the visitor's dugout steps to first base in three strides.

"Those cleats are clearly pink," said Sallowaid Astor. "Axsubeen's colors are orange and brown, and the team must maintain a uniform presence."

"You call *me* Captain Bush League?" roared Skip. "Nice of you to wait until the moment my blue chip's about to make his first pitch—"

The ump got between them. "Relax or I start ejecting!" He turned to Perry Phillips. "Mr. Astor has a valid claim. Players must maintain a uniform look. Only black, white, orange, or brown shoes."

"My boys only got one pair each—we ain't Imelda Marcos here! And I ain't lettin' no one play barefoot!"

"Then find a bench player with the same size cleats!"

"11½," squeaked Spazz.

Skip nearly wrung the headbanger's neck. His eyes darted to and fro, checking all the Ghosts' shoes. "How comes I see some *gray* shoes, Astor? Ain't Larsen's colors white and *silver?*"

"'Ghost Silver,' yes," said Astor, "but finding a sufficient quantity of baseball cleats in silver is onerous. We have special dispensation from the West Penn conf—"

"You have Special Ed.!" Skip stomped towards his dugout.

"Don't talk to your pitcher, Perry, or it's an official mound visit!"

Calvin shut his eyes. He couldn't believe this childish bullshit. "Excuse me, Mr. Umpire?" he called. "Can I talk with the catcher?"

The ump waved him on, like *Fine.* The bearded butthole Larsen manager glared at the Ape, like he was getting away with murder.

Calvin pulled Gus close. "We gotta uncross our signals, mate."

"Ooh! Ooh!" said Gus. He put his big mitt over his face. "You too!"

Calvin did the same. "Thanks a million. Fastball is one finger, change-up is two, knuckle curve three. And the no fingers. Use that."

"When? I don't pick the pitches like Corgan does, I just make the signal Skip sends to me."

"What?"

"All that crap he does, touchin' his hat and pulling his ear. That's where I get my signals from. And lookit, your curve is three fingers? Spazz's curve was two! Can't we just use that?"

"Jaysus Fookin' Christ with double cheese, never mind."

"We *gotta* mind. I gotta know what yer throwin' so I can catch it!"

I have the strength for everything, Calvin thought, *even for having Lenny from* Of Mice and Men *as my catcher.*

"I'll pick the pitches," he told Gus. "It'll always be a fastball. If I pick my arse, that means a change-up or curveball's coming. And I'll shake you off sometimes, too. Got it?"

"'Kay. And when Skip signals me, I'll pretend I got it and nod."

Spazz finished tying on Pete Hennessey's size 12 Nikes (in white) and the ump signaled game on.

Calvin's heart played bongos while his pits got slick. A ghastly look crept over his face. Determination. He glowered at Peter Bown. The batter backed up a step, despite being sixty feet away.

This was the debut of Calvin's mask. Not his concentration helmet, not his poker face, but a welding helmet's blast shield, only with the white-hot smolder of arc-fire on the *inside.* He would wear this mask during games until he could pitch no longer.

The ball blew out of his hand. Like most folks facing the Next Big Thing for the first time, Bown was taking all the way. He wanted to see (and mentally time) how hyped-up Connor was.

"Low," the ump called.

Calvin didn't think the ball was low, and realized he was leaking that through his slouch. He snapped upright and put the mask back on.

"4! The runners might go, watch 'em!" called Skip.

Hitherto, Skip had ordered him to ignore all runners. Calvin didn't know how to pitch from the stretch, or even what that was.

He glanced over his right shoulder at the lead runner. Decker had a hell of a lead off second base so Calvin fired the ball that way. Blink and you'd miss it. Decker was caught completely off guard and panicked for a sec. The pickoff throw got to shortstop Chicken Ysderrhi so fast that the skeevy prick had no hope of actually catching it; he had to bat it down with his bare hand, going "Ow!" at the pain.

Decker dove back to the bag. "Safe!" said the second base ump.

"Pitchers strangle the ball when they're tense," Lucky had said. "Ya gotta be tender, like yer fondlin' a gal's right titty."

The Ape put the ball in his glove and fondled Kitty's titty. Kitty's not so itty bitty right titty.

The next pitch was greased lightning.

The third was a Japanese bullet train.

The fourth was the Enterprise-D going Warp 9.

Bown swung past all three, falling over during his follow-through on the last one. The Axe fielders cheered as they headed off. It took Calvin a moment to realize the inning was over.

He got to the dugout shivering, high, parched. He wanted a belt of whiskey. He hacked up a little bile into the trash can and flopped down by Zedz. The grumpy prick had a towel full of ice on his ankle.

Sheriff Steve made his way back into the dugout between innings and told everyone the bad news: Sean's distal radius was broken. "Clean snap too," he said, pointing at the spot on the top of his own wrist. "The doc was amazed the back part didn't burst through his skin."

"He's done," said Skip.

And so is our chance at States, he didn't say.

"And so is his scholarship," smiled Calvin.

Zedz looked over at him like he was nuts.

Spazz was due up but not much of a hitter, so Skip put in Pete Hennessey. The time-out for cleat-swapping peeled Sallowaid Astor's pickle. Hennessey was a fellow lefty which meant he could stay in to play first base. He got a clean single off Dolly Smythe.

When Chicken Ysderrhi walked, Larsen Manager Astor yanked Smythe for a kid whose uniform back said "Yulle."

"All these rich cunts have weird names," said Calvin.

Paddy Millar welcomed Yulle to the game with a rope to left. Skip held the slow-footed Hennessey at third.

Bases loaded, no outs for Gus, with Calvin on deck. "This is less than ideal," said Skip. The lad had never taken batting practice, or stood in the batter's box, or worn batting gloves or a helmet. He didn't even own a bat! "Tie his hands," Skip told Lucky.

Lucky determined Calvin was a right-handed hitter and found a helmet with a left ear-guard. "Don't do nothin' but stand there, slim. You'll strike out but that's fine. Davey's up after ya. Let him have a chance with the bases loaded."

The big Ape stood in the on-deck circle with a bat propped on his shoulder, watching Gus Jacoby's turn at the plate.

Young Yulle, a righty, was gangly and unorthodox. The ball fluttered from his fingers with dizzying spin or none at all. Gus was like a deer in the headlights and struck out on four pitches.

Calvin got in the batter's box, the wrong one at first. He looked out at the field and saw it was bases loaded. The scenario kids dream about. It was totally foreign to the Irish kid. *How did I end up here? Well. I had no idea what my life would be like—*

Yulle's first pitch was a fastball inside. Calvin yelped and backed away. "Only thing missin' is you holdin' the bat with your pinky out," teased the Larsen catcher.

Calvin stared at the pitcher Yulle and tried to ignore his teammates, the cheers from his dugout, the yelling from the stands—

"Get a hit!"

Kitty?

The next pitch wasn't so inside and got called a strike.

"Hit the ball, mon gâteau au fromage!"

It's her!

On the next pitch, Calvin put everything into a swing and made contact, catching the barest edge of the ball and nubbing it to the dirt. He spun around in the follow-through and landed next to home plate.

The Larsen catcher calmly stepped around him, fetched the ball, put one cleat on home plate, then tagged the Ape's fanny.

Double play, inning over.

A lot of things were screamed across Balfour Diamond right then, but the loudest was Art Maguire's "JESUS H. CHRIST!"

Calvin went back to the dugout for his cap and glove. He and Davey left the dugout at the same time. "You did that on purpose, faggot," said the goon. "Took away my chance to hit a grand slam."

The Ape stalked after him. "Get your arse where it belongs!" he said, pointing to left field.

"We gotta warm up!" said Gus from the plate. "Hurry up!"

Calvin threw the practice pitches and peeped the stands. He found her: five rows back on the first base side. Kitty and Abby huddled as one, their big winter coats not keeping out the chill. The backdrop behind them was Larsen's chapel. The green copper dome roof and steeple rose up behind Kitty's pink pom-pom knit cap. A late-winter sun gave the steeple's cross a nice halo.

A crow sat atop the cross.

This felt as clear a sign of God talking to Calvin as when Ryan claimed he heard the Voice of the Other.

Calvin heard a voice, too. A faint one. High and needy.

"Da!"

He threw what they call an immaculate inning, striking out Heatherington, Wilkey, and Morton on nine pitches. All fastballs.

Calvin and Gus sat with Lucky in the dugout, quiet and focused. The TV had no sound, or else it'd been turned down before being ensconced in the dugout wall, but Art Maguire's endless chatter accented the action plenty.

Top of the seventh, and final, inning. Still 2–1 Axsubeen. Brion Davey walked on four pitches. So much for Yulle! The Ghosts brought in Warburton, a new pitcher in a bright white J.V. uniform.

Lucky said, "Usually there's ushers chasin' down any coon who sets foot on this field."

"Oh man, that ain't right!" said Reggie, who laughed anyway.

"Yeah," said Art, not laughing, "that ain't right, Lucky!"

Calvin barely heard them. His mask was on.

Warburton was like Calvin in many ways: hefty, sweaty, throwing smoke. His skin tone and handedness set him apart. The black lefty got Felon to foul out before fanning Snatch and Doggy-Door.

Bottom of the seventh. "This is it!" said Gus, shepherding his hero out to the mound. "You'll get 'em, Calvin!" he said. "After that shit in Troop 666, I think you're invincible."

Calvin sighed at such naked friendliness. He almost preferred it when teammates called him a cumstain.

"Ever gotten a blowjob, Gus?"

Gus sputtered a laugh, leaving spittle on the tines of his catcher's mask. "Only from your mom," he said. "She 'sucked' at it, too."

Calvin gave a genuine guffaw. "If we pull this off, I'll get you one."

"Ewww, not from you!"

"Play ball!" the ump called. The crowd cheered. Somewhere an idiot was blowing a moose horn.

I have the strength for everything.

MOOO-WOMP!

"LADIES AND GENTLEMEN ... PINCH-HITTING FOR LARSEN ... NUMBER FOUR, CALVIN CAMERON."

"Not worthy of the name, mate," Calvin Connor said from the mound. "Or the number!"

Calvin Cameron barely made eye contact, as if the Ape was not worthy of a response. He pushed his sparkly silver helmet back. He hit left-handed, which Calvin Connor heard was dangerous.

The pitcher peered in for the sign.

The catcher didn't move.

The pitcher shook him off and picked pant fabric out of his butt.

The catcher didn't move. Gus forgot the butt-pick was a sign. He realized and said, "Oh right," and got set.

Calvin Cameron replanted his front foot, an act of nerves maybe?

Calvin Connor wound up and delivered a focused change-up. The ball painted the far corner of the plate at a measly eighty miles per—

Calvin Cameron hit that shit out of the park.

All the fuck the way out of the park.

Brion Davey raced back, checked his speed at the warning track, and stopped dead at the wall. The ball flared past the sun on its way up and cleared the Fan-O-Vision on the way down. The big screen's yellow bulbs lit up Davey's red face, beaming HOMERUN!!!

The home crowd roared lustily as young Calvin Cameron trotted the bases. The game was tied 2–2.

Sallowaid Astor sent a second fresh face to the plate: Robert Biddle-Bosko, number **88**. Calvin struck him out on three fastballs but Gus bollocksed up catching the last one and Biddle-Bosko ran to first.

Calvin had no idea that was a thing and argued the call.

Skip, and Doggy-Door and Chicken and Snatch et al., told him it was legal and shaddap will ya.

"No outs," Gus reminded him as Reese Decker came up to bat.

Calvin wiped his sweaty forehead. He was drenched. The rosin felt like frozen crystals on his hand. He shook off Gus's lack-of-signal and picked his butt. Someone in the crowd laughed. He delivered another change-up. Decker was sitting on it but only caught the bottom edge, blooping it to shallow center.

Paddy Millar charged in, called off second baseman Snatch, and dove headfirst on the 'Turf. The ball bounced in and out of his glove.

Biddle-Bosko booked it, rounding second. Decker had to stop at first cuz Paddy threw the ball back to the infield quickly.

To no one. Shortstop Chicken, for whatever reason, hadn't moved to cover second. Paddy's throw bounced off the bag and up towards the mound. Any real ballplayer would've made the catch with his eyes shut but Calvin made a soccer goalkeeper's body block.

"Pick up the ball, culo!" yelled a blushing Chicken.

Calvin hurriedly did so. The play was over. The Larsen crowd were on their feet. Tie game, no one out, first and third. A single ended this.

The Ape made fists to stave off the adrenaline/pot tingle in his fingertips. Crisp air tickled his hot neck. *Titties,* he thought.

Calvin heaved a heater to Sanford Biercester and got a strike.

He picked his butt. Someone in the crowd laughed. The next pitch was a change-up outside. Biercester laid off it.

He picked his butt. Someone in the crowd laughed. The next pitch was a change-up outside. Biercester laid off it.

He picked his butt. Someone in the crowd laughed. The next pitch was a change-up outside. Biercester laid off it.

Annoyed, Calvin didn't pick his butt and ripped his fastest pitch to date … a mile wide. Biercester took his base. Bags full. No outs.

I have the strength for everyth—

Bollocks, mate, who're you kiddin'?

The noise, aggression, fear, joy, schadenfreude, anxiety … it broke the lad. He no longer wanted to play, to win, to lose. This didn't matter! The rosin-splattered hand holding the ball went to his face to push back the tears. Everyone present was staring at him. Pointing. Look at the little boy out there, ha ha, go cry to Mommy! Look at the small child, that shrimpy seven-year-old, all of four stone soaking wet, on the verge of tears cuz he lost his grip on his balloon's ribbon, all alone in a world of older kids picking on him, whose da was never around and was dying nearby, but Calvin was never four stone except maybe when he was four, these were not memories but visions, of the future, no Lambo and *Club MTV,* not his future but the child's, on the verge of tears cuz he lost his balloon, looking for a da who was never around—

Kitty's pregnant! What the fuck am I doing, playing ball?

Everyone present, every motherfucking person here, was staring at him … except her, cuz she couldn't.

Gus's catcher pads clacked as the blob raced up. Seeing blood, he called, "We need a towel!"

Calvin lowered the hand from his face. There was blood on the ball.

Gus was right there, catcher's mask down, cheeks all splotchy red like his dad the doctor, tea-saucer eyes moist from the cool wind, his forehead greasy from too much pizza and cheeseburgers. Gus had seen movies. He knew this was the time for lighthearted banter and confidence building. "Ya ever had the pistachio ice cream at Schultz's Farm Market?" he said. "I mean, it's no blowjob but it's good!"

"Kitty's favorite," blurted Calvin, or that's what he meant to say.

"Kitty's pregnant," blurted Calvin, instantly wanting to die.

Instantly wanting to blow up Altoona for saying it to Gus Jacoby, of all people. His glove went up to cover his entire face.

"Holy shit!" Gus drew back in shock. "Uh, don't worry. I got your back, Calvin." The kid looked around. "Where's that damn towel?!"

Calvin's hands were yanked away. The umpire supervised the toweling off of bloody fingers. He inspected the incriminating lip (the lad had bitten into it) and the red drops down his white uniform front. The bloodied ball was excused from further service.

Larsen's manager came over and turned an injury visit into a cock-measuring competition. "Now the *kid's* doing bush league stuff?"

Calvin knew "bush" *(n.)* hedge or shrub, "Bush" *(pp. n.)* 41st [and current] President, "bushed" *(adj.)* tired. He said, "Your ma's bush."

"What was that?!"

Skip said, "Beat it, Sallowaid, this is an injury visit."

"The only injury is all the walks he's giving out! Blue, this is their one mound visit, and I won't hear otherwise."

"I agree," said the ump.

"Then scram!" said Skip. "Mound visits happen in private!"

The umpire pulled Mr. Astor away. Skip and Gus huddled with Calvin. "You look like the canary who volunteered for coal mine duty, son," said the old man. "Is it time for the Sermon on the Mound?"

"Opening day jitters," said Gus. He poked his manager in the gut with his mitt, a friendly move. "Ain't Maalox time yet, ha ha."

Skip took the joke but kept his eyes on Calvin.

"He's all right," said Gus firmly. "He can do anything."

"So I keep hearin'. What's your take on it, Irish? Gonna get through this and prove I was right about you?"

"Don't have to prove nothing to you," said Calvin. He hocked up some bloody snot and spat it on the 'Turf.

"Wanna bet?" said Skip.

The man turned around and left. No thumbs up. No "Good luck."

Gus ran back to the plate. Four steps in, his left cleat caught on the right shin guard's straps and the blundering buffoon collapsed in a heap.

"Play ball!" the home plate ump yelled.

I have the strength for everything through him who empowers me.
Who empowers me?

"NEXT BATTER ... NUMBER ONE, JON OLDROYD."

Of course this prick wears **1**. Jon would wear a portrait of himself on his back if the rules allowed it.

"Picture yerself makin' a good throw," Lucky had said many times. "Yer mechanics should be robotic, the same each time, bang-bang-bang, strike, strike, strike. That's why we practice, amigo, why we do drills, so when it's time to strike sumbitches out, you know *how* to do it and you know you *can* do it. Now ... go do it!"

Calvin Connor's first pitch to Jon Oldroyd hit him.

⚾ __CLUBHOUSE__ ⚾

It was a fastball headed right at the black slab of **GHOSTS** on Jon's silvery shirt. The kid saw it coming and turtled his upper body, bracing for impact. The ball hit his left shoulder with a sharp thud.

Of the approximately one hundred fifty people at Balfour Diamond at Larsen Park, two were instantly happy. Jon Oldroyd was one of those two, obviously—he'd just won the game. It even counted as an RBI.

The guy trotted up the first base line with a laugh and a smile. The other runners advanced a bag and when Bobby Biddle-Bosko stepped on home plate, the game was over.

The one hundred forty-eight non-instantly-happy people picked from a grab-bag of emotions: shock, booing, confusion, realization, joy, celebration, "We won!", disbelief, heartbreak, awareness, anger, "What was that?!"

Perry Phillips screamed, "Fuck!"

Calvin would've added a suffix of -ed, for that's what the Axes were. He, of course, was the other instantly happy fellow. Happy cuz it was over. It really didn't matter to him how the game itself ended, just that it did.

He'd shown he was capable of greatness on the mound. On *this* mound. The ball might've slipped from his sweaty hand, or he might've beaned Oldroyd on purpose.

Calvin didn't say. He put his mask on and headed for the dugout.

He never saw Brion Davey's fist.

The Irish Raging Ape lay unconscious on the AstroTurf as the fight played out. The Larsenites didn't throw popcorn this time. They sat back and watched the losing side beat the shit out of each other.

Chapter 33

YELLOW LIGHT.
SAINT PATRICK'S DAY.

FOUL

YULLE?

    Oh.

FOUL

Yell ...

    ... O ...

        ... yeah!

FOUL

Yellow.

    Yellow.

        Y   L   O   .

                "Yellow?"

"Hmmm."

                "Hellow?"

"Hello?"

The yellow sea parted. Whitecaps of virulent violet dots crashed from the center to the sides. He could see again.

Well. See-ish.

Behold.

He beheld well enough to know Kitty was there.

Her dark glasses. Excalibur. "Hello?" she seemed to say to him.

"Hello ... love," he said. His mouth was so coppery.

She stumbled forward into his bed. His hospital bed. It was night, or dark out the window. There were voices in the hall, parents, sobs.

Her free hand fought the blindness to find him, finally located one of his hands, and squeezed down onto the IV's injection needle. "Oh sorry," she said, pulling her hand back. Excalibur got stuck in the bed's railing. She swatted the safety loop off and let the cane clatter to the tile.

He reached up for her, hugging her, picking up hot moist points where her tears fell on him. "I'm so happy you're okay," she said.

"Never had a bad day in my life."

His voice couldn't produce all that. The words were far from true.

"We followed you here, me and Abby," said Kitty. "Sheriff Steve put you in his car. There were all these people at the emergency room. I called my parents on the payphone and they came up."

"I'm fine," he said, though he felt anything but.

"They went to the regular entrance and asked where Calvin Connor was." Tears choked her words. "And the woman there said he passed away, and my mom fainted. It was so awful."

Oh no. "Passed away?"

"Oh no!" She shut her mouth, afraid to say more.

He closed his eyes. The yellow light remained.

"I didn't mean for you to find out like that!"

"It's ... " He wanted to say *okay,* but it wasn't okay.

They held each other for a long minute.

"Ready now?" he said.

"Ready? For what?"

"Face ... the world," he said. "Be in it."

"Come on, that's not fair, Calvin. And I guess it doesn't matter anymore if I feel ready to be in this world or not. I *have* to be now. But I won't be alone."

"Not alone ... with me."

"Yes," she said. "That's true. That's sweet. My parents are right out there with your mom and Rob and Rose. I had to beg them all to leave so I could get a moment alone with you. They're so mad, confused. My parents, I mean. Your mom ... she's, like, shell-shocked. When my mom told your mom that I'm pregnant, your mom had nothing to say. She's not even crying anymore.

"But she hugged me and told me she loved me."

"My ma?"

"Yeah." She snorted up some snot.

"Never ... tells me," he said. "Or hugs me."

"She loves you. Even if she doesn't say it. Parents are dumb but they love their kids. I am *always* going to tell my child I love her. I will always hug her."

"... or him."

"Yes. Or him. My parents   oh my God. They want to murder you right now, but because of your dad ... "

"Acting nice."

"Acting nasty. They know if they kill you, my child loses her dad."

"Ireland ... we say ... da."

They held each other for a long minute.

He reached up. "Can't ... behold you." He pushed the hair from her face. "Feels ... like you." He held her wide cheek in his hand.

Her hand went to his face, too. It didn't like contending with his oxygen tube but she managed.

"You have a brain bruise," she told him. "They said you'll be able to see and walk and all that in time. You'll be fine."

"How?"

"How'd it happen? Well. We can talk about the past in the future."

His skull nearly sprung a leak as he let out a single weak guffaw.

"You're lucky," she said. "Your trauma lets you forget things. Mine never goes away."

"Trade you."

They held each other for a long minute.

"So scared," he said.

"Me too," she said.

"... me," he said.

"You?" she said.

"Gonna be ... a da," he stated. "Me."

Chapter 34

Rabbits being massacred.
Monday, May 1, 1989.

⚾ **TRAINER'S TABLE** ⚾

CLAUDIUS JACOBY SAT IN his office with Heidi Maier, previewing the day's appointments. "Almost all ladies today," the doc said.

"Lots of labwork results," said the nurse. "Lots of Z32's."

"Well sure. People get cooped up in the winter."

"You ever read *Watership Down,* Claude?"

"No. It was a cartoon too, right? Watched it with Gus. It's about bunnies. Five-O and Bigwig."

"It starts with a warren of rabbits being massacred."

"They don't make children's entertainment like that anymore."

"If we still did rabbit tests, we'd be guilty of the same slaughter."

"Only if they're positives, Heidi. I feel bad about Kitty."

"Teen pregnancy is bad enough, but when it's a handica—"

"They're *all* teens." Dr. Jacoby waved the schedule. Every Z32 encounter code was for a patient still in high school. All six of them. "Axsubeen High's gonna need a maternity ward!"

"Kids are dumb," said Nurse Maier, "they never think. And boys, I mean, there's only *one* thing on the boys' minds."

"Yep." The good doctor jingled a key and opened a special cabinet in his office, the one with the red glass and an emergency placard. He pulled out the Dewar's and added medicinal doses to their coffee.

… read Kitty Howe's side of things in *Fair Territory* …

… the Chronicle of Calvin Connor continues in *Base on Balls* …

} "Applied Narcotics" ·

ROBBIE'S JOKE ON PAGE 141 was not pinched from Monty Python per se, but from *The Rutles: All You Need is Cash*. The chronicler once used the joke on Twitter and sourced it by @'ing its author, Eric Idle.

Mr. Idle did not, initially, recognize his own joke.

The body text employs the typefaces Equity A (and EQUITY A CAPS) with flourishes in **CONCOURSE**, ADVOCATE, and `Triplicate`. These lovely fonts were designed by and licensed from Matthew Butterick. Visit https://mbtype.com.

The chronicler wishes to express grateful acknowledgement to editor Diane Fulmer.

To Nèdra Bretagne, "Encore une fois, je vous remercie pour l'édition et les conseils!"*

Much love to my mother Diane for support and soup.

A click of the espresso martini glass to Goldie, the Mysterious Stranger, for hating that Jill had thick thighs.

And thanks to the reader. Some authors shoot for the stars, desiring adulation and fat checks from licensing rights. I'm much happier knowing one person—i.e., you—actually read my book.

This work is dedicated to my father.

At age 50, Dale had a stroke and was hospitalized in a coma. I printed out a very early draft of this story and sat at his bedside, holding

---

* Nèdra and I are still in vous-land.

his hand and reading it aloud. His fingers twitched in mine at the "trainee of treble" joke on page 224.

He passed away a week later. On Father's Day.

Dale was both like Calvin the Second—he smoked cigarettes and enjoyed beer and pretzels while sitting in the basement watching his booby shows—and quite unlike him. If my dad said "I'll try," he would. He came to his sons' Scout camp-outs and social events.

Another vital difference is, my brother and I are both his sons.

Christopher Morlock
February 4, 2024

About the Author

photo © 2024 CHRISTOPHER MORLOCK.

You could only dream to have a résumé as awesome as **CHRISTOPHER MORLOCK**'s. In addition to writing novels, he's run fast food joints, delivered mail, humped cable on film sets, reviewed music, sold baseball cards, edited websites, acted on television, written articles, and won poker tournaments. And at any point when he *wasn't* doing one of the above, he could be found fucking your mom.

Kindly visit www.christophermorlock.com.

www.ingramcontent.com/pod-product-compliance
Lightning Source LLC
Chambersburg PA
CBHW071154250626
47159CB00001B/90